Praise for
Isaiah's Legacy

"I am in awe of Andrews's ability to consistently bring Scripture alive with such depth and richness of character. Written with elegance and incredible insight, *Isaiah's Legacy* is a vivid and relevant look at a lesser-known chapter of Old Testament history—masterfully brought to life."

　　—Tosca Lee, *New York Times* best-selling author of *Iscariot*

"With her signature depth and deft touch, Mesu Andrews delivers another breathtaking story that breathes life into a seldom-studied time in the Old Testament."

　　—Roseanna M. White, best-selling author

"I picked up *Isaiah's Legacy* by Mesu Andrews with trepidation. Not because I feared the writing, which is excellent, or her storytelling, which paints the Bible characters with vibrancy, but because I knew the story of Manasseh's horrifying fall from grace, found in 2 Kings. I knew what I'd have to read to find redemption at the end. What I didn't know was how beautifully Mesu Andrews would weave that devastating fall or the desperate need I would have to see the splendor of God's restoration of the broken and defeated Manasseh. *Isaiah's Legacy* is a soul-gripping look at the possibilities of sin's corruption and God's powerful sovereignty above all— even the stories we think we're writing of our own lives. What a beautiful reminder that the light of God's love and the strength of His hand can reach into the darkest hearts to transform lives for His glory and the ultimate fulfillment of His story."

　　—Pepper Basham, author of *My Heart Belongs in the Blue Ridge* and the Mitchell's Crossroads series

ISAIAH'S LEGACY

A NOVEL *of* PROPHETS & KINGS

MESU ANDREWS

AUTHOR OF *ISAIAH'S DAUGHTER*

WATERBROOK

ISAIAH'S LEGACY

This book is a work of historical fiction based closely on real people and real events. Details that cannot be historically verified are purely products of the author's imagination.

Trade Paperback ISBN 978-0-7352-9188-1
eBook ISBN 978-0-7352-9189-8

Copyright © 2020 by Mesu Andrews

Cover design and photography by Kristopher K. Orr
Interior map created by Stanford Campbell

Published in the United States by WaterBrook, an imprint of Random House, a division of Penguin Random House LLC.

WATERBROOK® and its deer colophon are registered trademarks of Penguin Random House LLC.

Library of Congress Cataloging-in-Publication Data
Names: Andrews, Mesu, 1963– author.
Title: Isaiah's legacy : a novel of prophets and kings / Mesu Andrews.
Description: First edition. | [Colorado Springs, CO] : WaterBrook, 2020.
Identifiers: LCCN 2019047757 | ISBN 9780735291881 (trade paperback) | ISBN 9780735291898 (ebook)
Subjects: GSAFD: Bible fiction. | Christian fiction.
Classification: LCC PS3601.N55274 I85 2020 | DDC 813/.6—dc23
LC record available at https://lccn.loc.gov/2019047757

Printed in the United States of America
2020—First Edition

To my PapaPat,
who left this earth while I wrote this story,
who worships now at the throne—and whom
I'll see again someday.

CHARACTER LIST

Adaiah	*Manasseh's royal treasurer*
Adnah	*various characters: Shulle's mother, a cat, and Shulle's maid*
(King) Ahaz	*Hezekiah's father (abba)*
(King) Ashurbanipal*	*King of Assyria (668–627 BC)**
Assoros	*Manasseh's prison guard*
Aya	*Isaiah's wife*
Azariah	*High priest*
(King) Baal*	*King of Tyre**
Baka	*Manasseh's personal guard*
Bekira	*Manasseh's first-born child, a daughter, with Shulle*
Belit	*Babylonian sorceress*
Eliakim	*Hezekiah's best friend; Nasseh's tutor*
(King) Esarhaddon*	*King of Assyria (680–669 BC)**
Gemeti	*Manasseh's Babylonian wife*
Haruz	*Shulle's abba, Shebna's brother*
(King) Hezekiah*	*King of Judah*; Manasseh's father (abba)*
Isaiah	*God's prophet; Queen Zibah's father (abba)**

Jashub (Shear-Jashub)	*Isaiah's firstborn; Zibah's brother*; Kenaz's father (abba)*
Jericho	*Shulle's rescued maid*
Kenaz	*Jashub & Yaira's son; Manasseh's cousin*
(King) Manasseh *(Nasseh)*	*King of Judah*; Hezekiah's son*
Manno	*Ashurbanipal's commander*
(Prince) Mattaniah (Matti)	*Hezekiah's brother*
Meshullemeth *(Shulle)*	*Shebna's niece; Manasseh's wife*
Nahum	*Yahweh's prophet*
Onan	*Zibah's personal guard*
Panya	*Manasseh's Egyptian concubine*
Penina	*Shulle's rescued maid*
Queen Abijah	*Hezekiah's mother (ima)*
Queen Naqia*	*Sennacherib's wife*; Esarhaddon's mother**
(King) Sennacherib*	*King of Assyria (705–681 BC)**
(King) Shamash-Shumukin*	*Assyrian King of Babylon (667–648 BC)*; Ashurbanipal's brother**
Shebna	*Manasseh's tutor; Shulle's uncle*
(King) Tiglath-Pileser*	*King of Assyrian (747–727 BC)**
(Pharaoh) **Tirhakah***	*King of Egypt (690–664 BC)**
Yaira	*Zibah's friend; Kenaz's ima; Jashub's wife*

(**Bold** indicates biblical character; * indicates historical character)

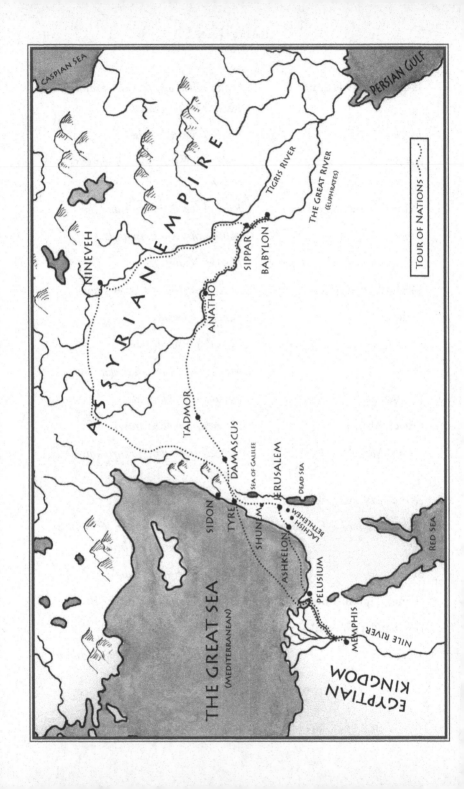

CASPIAN SEA

PERSIAN GULF

A S S Y R I A N   E M P I R E

NINEVEH

TIGRIS RIVER

THE GREAT RIVER
(EUPHRATES)

SIPPAR
BABYLON

ANATHO

TADMOR

DAMASCUS
SEA OF GALILEE

JERUSALEM
DEAD SEA

SIDON

TYRE

SHUNEM

LACHISH
BETHLEHEM

ASHKELON

PELUSIUM

THE GREAT SEA
(MEDITERRANEAN)

RED SEA

EGYPTIAN
KINGDOM

MEMPHIS

NILE RIVER

TOUR OF NATIONS ·········

NOTE TO READER

King Hezekiah was Judah's most righteous king and restored the nation to Yahweh-worship after his depraved father's idolatry nearly destroyed it. Hezekiah's only son, Manasseh, became Judah's wickedest king and destroyed everything his father rebuilt. Queen Hephzibah—Hezekiah's wife and Manasseh's mother—was the woman who loved them both.

Why would I write this tragic tale? Perhaps a better question: *Why would you read it?* Because after all the research, prayer, and study, I'm convinced Hephzibah's son is the greatest prodigal journey in Scripture.

You're about to walk with me into Manasseh's dark world. It may feel overwhelming at times, but if you remain focused on God's promises—as Queen Zibah does—you'll reach the indescribable Light of truth. The God who allowed Manasseh to reject Him also pursued the wayward king and guided him home. That God did the same for me. He can do it for you—and all the Manassehs in your life.

> The people walking in darkness
>   have seen a great light;
> on those living in the land of deep darkness
>   a light has dawned.
>
> ISAIAH 9:2

PART 1

In those days Hezekiah became ill and was at the point of death. The prophet Isaiah son of Amoz went to him and said, "This is what the LORD says: Put your house in order, because you are going to die; you will not recover."

Hezekiah turned his face to the wall and prayed to the LORD, "Remember, LORD, how I have walked before you faithfully and with wholehearted devotion and have done what is good in your eyes." And Hezekiah wept bitterly.

Then the word of the LORD came to Isaiah: "Go and tell Hezekiah, 'This is what the LORD, the God of your father David, says: I have heard your prayer and seen your tears; I will add fifteen years to your life. And I will deliver you and this city from the hand of the king of Assyria. I will defend this city.'"

෨ ISAIAH 38:1–6 ෬

PROLOGUE

I am Shebna. Small in stature, weak in body, strong of mind. A Levite. At sixteen, I was too weak to serve in Yahweh's temple, so *Abba* begged the prophet Isaiah to teach me alongside the royal princes of Judah. Isaiah agreed though I was smaller than many, older than all, and smarter than most.

When King Ahaz persecuted the prophets, I replaced Isaiah as royal tutor. I taught royalty all day, and I endured Abba's abuse at night. But my brother, Haruz, suffered worse. He was big as an ox; timid as a mouse. Odd. Distant. Ima tried to protect him, but she died when he was five. My protection came from the love of my chambermaid, Adnah. But Abba sent her away with my dim-witted brother when Abba discovered Adnah and I planned to secretly wed.

I was powerless to stop him.

When King Ahaz died, my childhood classmate Hezekiah took the throne and made his abba-in-law, Isaiah, foreign minister.

I became his palace administrator—and powerless no longer.

Months later, news arrived that Adnah was pregnant. I bought Haruz a farm in northern Israel. Abba died a few months later, and I buried him in the pauper's grave he deserved. In less than a week, Adnah's child died as well.

Had Yahweh judged my vengeance?

Hoping to atone, I sent a maid for Adnah's care and a farmhand for Haruz. Maybe I could appease the god who let wicked Levites live too long and innocent children die too soon.

My treasury grew fat with no wife or child to spoil, so when King Hezekiah sent me as ambassador to Egypt, I spent my wealth on their gods. I worshipped Seth and Anubis, gods of chaos and death. The gods showed me favor with a coalition between Egypt and Judah to withstand the power-mongering Assyrians.

Isaiah, jealous of my diplomatic success, prophesied Yahweh's wrath and turned Hezekiah against me. The king demoted me to a royal secretary and made his best friend, Eliakim, palace administrator in my place. I was forced out of my luxurious palace chamber to a hovel in Jerusalem's Upper City. Bitterness bloomed into hatred when I could no longer pay Adnah's maid or Haruz's farmhand.

Years passed and the Yahwists grew in power and arrogance. They condemned any god but their own and tolerance became a sin. But when Assyria's threats increased, King Hezekiah's trust in Isaiah waned, and he sent me on secret diplomatic journeys. This time, however, my efforts were in vain. Assyria's army descended like locusts—at the same time King Hezekiah fell deathly ill. Had all the gods failed us?

One morning at dawn, Jerusalem woke to find 185,000 dead Assyrians outside the city gates and Hezekiah's health suddenly improved. Isaiah convinced Queen Zibah that Yahweh had worked both miracles and regained royal favor.

Gossiping traders took news of the supposed miracles to Merodach-Baladan, Babylon's dethroned king. He came bearing gifts to honor the only nation to defy the indomitable Assyrians. Since I'd met him in my travels, Hezekiah chose me to greet the displaced king and his envoys. They arrived with Babylon's chief sorceress—expert in dark arts.

Belit, a stunning woman, was tall and muscular with black eyes that looked through me.

"You, little man, are to be my master," she said in Merodach's hearing.

The Babylonian royal studied me before speaking. "I've learned never to argue with Belit," he said. "I'll give her to you—if you'll use her skills to destroy the Assyrians."

I saw something spark in Belit's piercing eyes. She would not be easily *used* by anyone. Three days later Babylon's chief sorceress became my house slave and delivered a scroll from Haruz that my beloved Adnah had died giving birth to a daughter. The baby lived, but I had no desire to see a child that should have been mine. I sent money for a wet nurse and every year provided seed for crops. That much I must do for Adnah's daughter and a brother I no longer knew.

When visits from foreign dignitaries ebbed, I was relegated again to royal secretary. But now I had a partner who hated Yahweh as much as I hated Isaiah and Eliakim. Belit brought me great pleasure as a priestess of Babylon's starry hosts. Though Belit and I never married and she never taught me her dark arts, we began carefully including a group of disgruntled noblemen into our worship at a secluded grove outside the city wall. We introduced Babylon's gods to Judah's highest officials—and my power subtly returned.

When Isaiah prophesied his daughter would bear Hezekiah's heir in her old age, I asked Belit to induce another miscarriage for the queen. Imagine my disappointment when Zibah delivered a healthy boy, Manasseh.

"Be patient," she insisted and then proved her skill on another Yahwist. Since Isaiah was my prime target, Belit's first victim was his wife, Aya. I delivered a drop of potion in a cup of mint tea under the guise of a friendly visit. Aya fell ill later that day, and Belit's midnight curse stole her breath by dawn.

My patience was rewarded when Queen Zibah's only son still hadn't spoken a word by his third Passover. Belit's magic had worked. The boy was sensitive to noise, recoiled at physical touch, and ignored everyone and everything except his favorite toy—the exact childhood oddities that had plagued my brother Haruz. Prince Manasseh's birth may have been a miracle, but Belit's dark arts had gutted Yahweh's promise of a worthy heir.

Today when I arrived at the palace, the chief secretary announced our day's writing task: invitations to foreign dignitaries for Manasseh's coronation as Judah's co-ruler, two months hence. Pondering the royal humiliation that would come with the prince's first public event, I was buoyed through the day's tedium.

But on my way home, merchants' gossip darkened my hopes for disaster. King Hezekiah had chosen not me but Isaiah and Eliakim to teach his son.

"When will the king and queen realize that I'm just as good—no, *better,* than Isaiah and Eliakim . . ." I began ranting the moment I saw Belit, but she silenced me with one finger against my lips.

"You will join Manasseh's teachers," she said, "and the daughter of your beloved Adnah will help you destroy the Yahwists." Drawing my chin upward, she stared down at me; flecks of yellow appearing in her eyes— pulsating, mesmerizing. "Your brother's daughter is key, Shebna. Promise Queen Zibah that only you and the girl can prepare her son to rule."

I couldn't look away, lured into the darkness she used to woo me. Her plan was brilliant, and I willingly agreed. Gripping the back of her neck, I pulled her into an impassioned kiss. We would set the plan in motion— after I took pleasure in Belit, my greatest weapon against the Yahwists.

I

Meshullemeth daughter of Haruz . . .
was from Jotbah.

2 KINGS 21:19

Jotbah, Judah
693 BC, Seven Years Before Hezekiah's Prophesied Death

I hated weeding the garden alone, but I'd rather Abba copy his scrolls inside than bear our neighbor's cutting remarks. Why did others ridicule what they couldn't understand? Abba couldn't tolerate wool against his skin, and linen cost too much for him to own more than one robe. Garden work would ruin it, so one day he worked bare chested—and earned the wrath of the village elders. They had treated him with suspicion ever since. Though it happened three years ago when I was only five, I still remembered the shame on Abba's face. We held each other that afternoon and wept, prisoners in our own home.

Fury strengthened my grip on a wayward green sprout. "Ouch!" Dropping the thistle, I sucked on my finger and removed the barb with my teeth.

"Are you all right, Meshullemeth?" Our neighbor's singsong voice rubbed at my raw mood. I spit on the ground and returned to my work. Of course I was all right. It was just a thistle.

"Haruz works that poor little girl like a mule," the neighbor woman said to her maid. "I don't know why the elders don't take her away from him. She should be with a *real* family."

I pretended not to hear and kept my back bent, head down. Abba and

I were a real family. What did she know about our lives? How many eight-year-old girls could write? I could. How many could read the Torah? Perhaps I should write a complaint to the elders about *her*. I sighed. Abba would never allow it. He would quote King Solomon, *Anxiety weighs down the heart, but a kind word cheers it up.*

Abba was too nice.

The ground under my feet began to tremble, and I looked at the neighbor woman to see if she noticed. She was too busy talking. By the time she looked to the southeast, I knew it was the pounding of many horses.

"Shulle, get in the house!" Abba shouted from the threshold of our little house. Tucking my robe into my belt, I ran fast as a deer. Maybe someday Abba and I would follow one of those pretty creatures into the forest. Live alone. Away from the wagging tongues of Jotbah. He always made me hide when travelers passed by. I once asked why, and he said because I was his only treasure.

I dashed through our curtained doorway and closed it behind me. Abba knelt beside it, gathering me in his arms so we could peek outside together as the caravan passed. A line of chariots and horses led a golden coach over the rise, followed by a cloud of dust that made our neighbor woman cough. She was too nosy to go inside and escape.

Surprisingly, the first chariot stopped in front of her house, and a little man dismounted and approached her. His driver remained in the chariot, while the little man talked with our neighbor. In a moment both began pointing our direction.

"What are they saying, Abba?" He was tugging absently on his beard, so I captured his hand between mine. "Fear, surprise, excitement, or joy?" It was our game to decide why he tugged at his beard. Abba couldn't always tell me how he felt.

He kissed my hands and explained. "That man with the soldiers is my older brother, your *dohd* Shebna. I haven't seen him since your *ima* and I left Jerusalem many years ago. I don't know why he's come."

The little man bowed to our neighbor, and two soldiers followed him as he walked toward our house. That's when I noticed his face looked just like Abba's. Smaller, but the same hooked nose and close-set black eyes.

Abba nudged me toward the ladder in our one-room home. "Hide in the loft."

I hurried and hid under my tattered blanket. It was warmer than the bread oven, but I thought my father was afraid, so I obeyed.

I peeked from beneath my blanket to see Abba grab his linen robe from the wall peg. Forgoing his sandals, he stood barefoot beside my ladder, tugging harder at his beard. "Done nothing wrong," he whispered. "Done nothing wrong. Done nothing wrong. Done nothing wrong . . ."

A bony hand drew back our curtain. Dohd Shebna and two soldiers stepped across the threshold without an invitation. The little man's lips curved into a smile, but his eyes squinted, studying every object in our home—and then landed on Abba.

"You're even bigger than you were when you left Jerusalem."

Abba studied the packed-dirt floor. "I was a boy, Shebna. Eighteen years old."

"You were old enough to marry my Adnah."

"The Torah says honor your parents." Abba shifted from one foot to the other now, pulling hairs from his beard. "I obeyed our abba." I didn't like the effect this little man had on him. It was our home, not his, and Abba's beard had just grown back after the elders accused him of stealing the neighbor's cow. They found the cow two days later in the forest. Why did people think they could accuse and belittle a good man just because he was different?

I threw off my blanket. "We'll offer you bread and wine, as the laws of hospitality command, but you are not welcome here if you disrespect my abba." The startled looks on all four men's faces lasted only a moment before Shebna and his soldiers began their mocking.

"You have the fire of your ima, little one." Dohd Shebna laughed. "What is your name?"

"Her name is Meshullemeth," Abba blocked Dohd's advance toward the ladder. "She isn't a part of the conversation."

"On the contrary." Dohd Shebna fixed his gaze on me. "Meshulle-meth is the very reason I've come to Jotbah. She must return to Jerusalem with me and help the king and queen teach Prince Manasseh how to communicate—"

"Get out!" Abba shoved him into his two guards. "You can't take her from me. Leave!"

The guards drew their swords, and I rushed down the ladder. "No!"

Shebna stepped between his men and Abba. "Put away the swords." He fixed his eyes on me. "You look just like Adnah." Mouth gaping, his arrogant smirk was gone.

"You knew my ima?"

He nodded. "She was my dearest"—pausing, he looked at Abba before finishing—"my dearest friend."

Abba lifted me into his arms, and I circled one arm over his shoulder. "Dohd Shebna came a long way," I said softly. "Perhaps we should listen to what he came to say."

Abba pecked my cheek with a kiss and whispered, "We must not let him separate us, Shulle." He set my feet on the floor and nudged me behind him as if he were afraid Dohd would snatch me away. Then he reached for our circular leather mat and laid it on the floor, while I chose our three best cushions. "Sit down," he said to our guests, handing them the worn pillows I'd chosen. I brought out the loaves of bread I'd saved after breaking our fast this morning. It was all we had for the rest of this day, but it was unthinkable to let visitors leave without feeding them.

"Did you bake these?" Dohd asked me as Abba offered the loaves to the men and joined them around the leather mat. Abba nodded permission for me to answer as he filled four cups with watered wine.

"Yes. I baked the bread this morning, my lord." I called him *lord* because of his fancy purple robe.

"You're quite grown up for an eight-year-old." He picked up his cup and looked at Abba over the rim. After a long drink, he added, "You've trained her well, Haruz. I'm impressed."

Abba stared at the bread on his plate, but I saw a faint smile. "I've trained her to read the Torah and write Hebrew and Aramaic, but it's Shulle who trained me to entertain a guest."

Dohd took a quick sip and set aside his cup. "Which is why she must come with me to Jerusalem. Prince Manasseh is soon to be made co-regent and shows many of the same signs you did at age five."

"Why can't you teach him?" Abba reached for his beard again.

"I plan to, but children learn best from other children who understand them." Dohd waved me over to join them. Abba's open arms were my safe invitation. Once I settled on Abba's lap, Dohd spoke to us both. "When King Hezekiah was a small boy, he witnessed his older brother being sacrificed in a pagan altar fire. Hezekiah was so traumatized he lost the ability to speak until a little girl named Ishma—who had also been traumatized by captivity and slavery—helped restore his speech. That little girl became his best friend and was given permission to learn alongside him and the other royal boys of Judah."

I turned a disbelieving stare on Abba. "How have you never told me of Ishma?"

He chuckled, rubbing his thumb over my hand. "I have. Ishma was taken into Isaiah's household, adopted as his daughter, and given a new name, Hephzibah. You know her as Queen Zibah."

"The queen was a slave?" I couldn't imagine it. "She was the little girl who helped King Hezekiah?"

Abba nodded, and Dohd touched my arm as gently as if he were stroking a dove. "I'd like you to be that little girl for Prince Manasseh, Shulle. He hasn't been traumatized like his abba was, but he has some of the same issues your abba dealt with at his age. I believe having the prince learn alongside a friend who loves and understands him—like little Hezi and Zibah did—will be of more benefit than the best tutors in the world."

"What's in it for you, brother?" Abba's hand rested over mine, and his breathing quickened. Was he nervous or angry?

I braved a glance at Dohd. His small black eyes were piercing—but had little effect on Abba since he seldom looked up. "I'm offering Shulle a better life in Jerusalem, Haruz, where she'll be treated like royalty. She'll be a companion to our future king."

"He'll make her a concubine."

"No!" Dohd leaned forward, putting his pleading expression in Abba's line of sight. "Do you think I'd let Adnah's daughter become a concubine?"

Abba looked away. "I think you'd do anything to prove your power is bigger than your stature."

"You're too much like Abba." Dohd slammed his cup on the mat. "I've been nothing but kind since entering your home, and you've done nothing but accuse and insult me. Would you rather keep your daughter here in this hovel all her life? What can you give her? Who would marry her without a dowry? Without an abba who can make the match?"

Abba's hand grew tighter around mine, and I nearly cried out—as much from despair at my future as the moment of pain. Who could I marry in this awful little village?

"We'll go with you." Abba's voice was reedy and weak.

"What?" I whispered as his hand released mine.

Before he could answer, Dohd Shebna said, "I didn't invite you, Haruz."

Abba looked directly into his brother's eyes. "If she goes, I go." I'd never before seen him stare boldly into another human face. The courage my abba showed in that moment was like that of a warrior in battle. I'd always known I was his treasure, but now I realized he was giving up his life for me—willingly leaving everything familiar so I could embrace the unknown.

"I won't go, Abba." I wrapped my arms around his neck. "I don't need a husband. I love you, and I don't ever want to—"

"All right, Haruz," Dohd said, sighing. "You may come to Jerusalem as well."

My sorrow turned to joy as Abba's arms slid around me like a shield. He buried his whispers against my ear, "We must never forget, Shulle,

'Hear, O Israel: The LORD our God, the LORD is one. Love the LORD your God with all your heart and with all your soul and with all your strength. These commandments that I give you today are to be on your hearts.' Jerusalem will try to steal your heart, but we must not let it."

He kissed the top of my head and released me. I turned to thank Dohd Shebna who waited with a bright smile and a small folded bundle in his hand. He unwrapped it, revealing something brown and sticky. Candied dates! My stomach rumbled so loud both of his soldiers laughed. "Take one," Dohd said, "before the monster in your stomach attacks us all."

I shoved a whole date in my mouth and lolled it to the side so I could talk. "You must be important to require so many of the king's guards."

His smile disappeared as he wiped dripping syrup from my chin. "I was important—until two arrogant men took away everything I'd worked for." His breath smelled like spices, and those piercing black eyes drilled into mine. "I'll be important again someday, Shulle, and you will be too. I'll make sure you have candied dates every day of your life."

2

Hezekiah had very great wealth and honor. . . .
He also made buildings to store the harvest of
grain, new wine and olive oil. . . . He built villages
and acquired great numbers of flocks and herds,
for God had given him very great riches.

2 CHRONICLES 32:27–29

Jerusalem, Judah
Two Months Later

Queen Hephzibah's five-year-old son sat on a miniature version
of Judah's throne, ignoring the gold scepter in his lap to play
with his favorite wooden toy. If her husband would look at
their son instead of the audience, he'd see the irony. She studied the broad
shoulders and muscled back of King Hezekiah while he addressed the
gathering. Why couldn't he give their boy more time to be a child? *Because
you are a king first and abba second,* she answered silently. And her husband must prepare Judah for his death—prophesied to come in seven
years.

Zibah closed her eyes, trying to block out life's worries and the effects
of the chaotic courtroom. How much more would the noise affect her five-
year-old son? Inhaling a sustaining breath, she peeked at Manasseh, who
sat quietly on his throne beside her stool. The pieces of cloth she'd stuffed
in his ears dulled the noise and kept him calm—at least for the moment.

"He's fine." Hezi's whisper startled her. "You worried for nothing. He's
perfectly peaceful in front of all these people." He kissed her head and re-

turned to the front of the dais, instructing those still streaming into the crowded courtroom to move all the way to the side walls. Even the balconies were filled to capacity, the day Judah would name their son co-heir and king.

But why must the council rush Manasseh into a public coronation, when he spoke only two words to his parents in private? Ma and Ba, his attempt at Ima and Abba. Yet he was brilliant when given blocks to build with or when asked to add and subtract with those same blocks. He was currently enamored with the simple spinning wheel on top of a stick, but how would Hezi respond when his son wasn't the model of peace and decorum? Was her husband really oblivious to the weight he was placing on Nasseh's shoulders today? Or was he in denial—simply because they couldn't change Abba Isaiah's prophecy?

Nasseh's ridiculous jeweled crown pressed his little brow into a frown. Actually, she'd seldom seen him smile. He spent hours intently slapping that wooden wheel to watch it twirl. Sighing, she had to admit that even if she snatched him away to his chamber, he'd likely be spinning and frowning in his own little world. Would he ever become a part of theirs?

She'd tried preparing him for his coronation years ago, whispering while he nursed at her breast, "You'll be king someday, my son. King like your abba." She hadn't thought he was listening. But when this morning's schedule was disrupted, his nurse sent for Zibah to calm him. "You must wear a purple robe and crown today, love, so you can be like Abba."

He looked at his mother with wide brown eyes, so innocent and clear. "I king today."

Why couldn't his first sentence have been something simple about a cow or a goat?

The noisy throne room hushed, drawing Zibah's attention to her regal husband. "Today, Queen Hephzibah and I introduce our son and my heir, Prince Manasseh, on whom I confer all the rights and privileges of Judah's co-regent." He stepped aside, sweeping his hand toward their beloved boy.

Nasseh twirled his toy, blissfully unaware that he was the center of attention.

Eliakim, the palace administrator and king's best friend, stood on the other side of his small throne and whispered. "Would you like to look up and greet your guests, my king?" Nasseh turned away, sending the scepter rolling off his lap. The crowd gasped, but Eliakim lunged and caught the priceless heirloom.

Zibah pressed a hand against her racing heart while Hezi calmed the audience. "A five-year-old co-regent will require a bit more training than I needed as co-regent at twenty." A flutter of laughter eased the tension.

Like an ivory comb, Hezi's wit had smoothed many tangles in Judah's politics. She'd loved Hezekiah ben Ahaz from their first touch, when she was five and Hezi, eight. Her voice had vanished after witnessing her parents' murder, his mind lost after watching his brother sacrificed in the fire. They were two broken children, brought together by sheer chance—or more aptly Yahweh's design—and restored by each other's touch. Infuriating as her husband could be, he would always be the life in her veins.

As if knowing her thoughts, he turned and winked, nodding his invitation to escort their son forward. Wavering between indignation and trepidation, she leaned over to speak softly to their boy. "Nasseh, it's time for you to be king now. Will you follow Ima to where Abba is standing? He'd like to hold your hand."

Nothing.

How did Hezi expect him to spend one day a week in court listening to foreign emissaries and domestic disputes when he couldn't even follow simple instructions?

She placed her hand beside his toy. An offering only, not daring to touch the toy or take it away. "Perhaps you could hold Ima's hand and help me walk to Abba so I don't get lost?" He took her hand and scooted off the small throne. A victory. He usually complied if he believed he was helping her.

Wearing a lopsided grin, Hezi watched them approach, utterly at ease with the packed courtroom. "My friends, many of you have traveled from far and wide to witness my son's historic ascension to Judah's throne. Manasseh will be educated by the finest minds in our nation. Eliakim ben

Hilkiah, the brilliant engineer of our city's water tunnel, will be our son's hands-on instructor in Solomon's writings about wisdom, animals, building, science, and the stars." Hezi pointed to our childhood friend, who, at the moment, held our son's scepter. Eliakim's cheeks flushed to match his hair.

"Isaiah ben Amoz," Hezi called. "Will you join us on the dais please?" As the prophet rose from the royal advisors' gallery, Hezi recounted his credentials for the audience. "Of King David's lineage, Lord Isaiah has faithfully served every king of Judah since my great-grand-*saba* Uzziah. Most importantly, however, he serves as Yahweh's prophet to this generation."

Zibah watched as Eliakim helped the elderly prophet up the dais stairs. Abba Isaiah and his wife, Aya, had adopted Zibah after her parents were killed and she'd been rescued from captivity. He'd been a loving abba to Hezi when King Ahaz abandoned faith in Yahweh.

Abba embraced Eliakim and Hezi, their fondness for each other evident, even though his prophecies had been a thorn in their sides. Perhaps eight years of prosperity had healed the wounds. Still, Zibah hesitated when Hezi suggested Eliakim and Abba teach their only son. What if they didn't understand Manasseh's unique challenges? Nasseh was bright and could learn anything, but could these two well-intentioned men provide the patient guidance he needed?

"Lord Isaiah will instruct King Manasseh in the law of Moses and prophetic interpretation," Hezi was saying, "and will add foreign policy as the boy grows older."

Abba bowed to uproarious applause.

The sudden commotion startled the five-year-old, hurtling him toward Zibah and sending his toy to the floor. Trying to climb her as if she were a tree, he clutched at her neck, eyes bulging with terror. He snatched glances at the onlookers as if noticing them for the first time.

"Shh, my love," Zibah soothed. "It's just a little noise."

"He's unaccustomed to large gatherings," Hezi said to the crowd. He stepped in front of his wife and child to block the source of Nasseh's fear.

Eliakim picked up the toy, held it close to the prince's face, and spun the wheel to distract him.

The familiar object settled him long enough for Zibah to glance around her husband at the crowd. She wished she hadn't. Some sneered. Some shook their heads as if her son's distress disqualified him to rule. They didn't know the power of her love. Zibah absently combed Nasseh's dark curls and watched him disappear again into his world with the spinning toy. When her nephew Kenaz was five, he ran and played with other children in the garden, chattering like a hoopoe bird.

She kissed Nasseh's forehead and tried to press down her rising panic. "When Yahweh takes your abba to paradise," she whispered, "you'll be a mighty king, but for now, you are Nasseh, Ma's precious boy."

His lips curved into a slight smile, proving he'd heard her.

She ruffled his hair and placed him between her and Hezekiah. Nasseh continued spinning the wheel, and Hezi looked at her as if expecting her to remove the toy from his hands. If he'd spent any time alone with their son, he'd know what a poor decision that would be. "Make your announcement," she whispered to her husband.

After a disapproving sigh, King Hezekiah turned to the coronation gathered. "Visiting emissaries and citizens of Judah, I present to you my son and co-ruler, King Manasseh, the fourteenth heir of David to sit on Judah's throne. Praise be to Yahweh!"

"Praise be to Yahweh!" the crowd responded, and though Hezi modeled modest applause, the sudden noise startled Nasseh again. This time his fear turned into tears.

Zibah gripped her son's hand as if it were a sword, then marched off the dais and out of the court like a soldier to battle. Blinded by her own tears and spurred by men's judgment, she hurried their pace through the crowded halls. *If we can just get to his chamber, he'll be calmer. We'll both be calmer.*

"My queen!" someone called from behind. "My queen, wait!"

She kept going, dragging her son through the overcrowded palace on a day that should have been a celebration. A hand grabbed her arm and whirled her around.

"Shebna?"

He seemed as shocked as she by his lack of decorum. "Forgive me, my queen." He bowed. A young girl stood beside him. She knelt before Nasseh, bowing her head as she extended her hand. Timid at first, Nasseh touched her hand with one finger. The girl giggled, and Nasseh glanced up at Zibah with a tentative smile. Before she could reprimand Shebna or his little companion, the girl turned up her palm, and Nasseh placed one finger in the center. The little girl didn't move or try to hold his hand, but within moments he gripped her hand in his and offered her a toothy grin.

"I'm Shulle, my king," the girl said. "It's nice to meet you."

Zibah shoved the girl away. "Shebna, what sort of trickery are you playing at?" Nasseh hid his face against her.

The girl stepped back, clinging to a man standing behind Shebna—a man covering his ears with both hands. "Come, Abba. Come with me." She gently guided him to a quiet corner near the harem stairway.

"Forgive me, my queen," Shebna said. "That was my niece, Meshullemeth, and if you'll follow me to the stairs, I believe she and my brother, Haruz, can help King Manasseh."

"I don't trust your help, Shebna." Zibah placed Nasseh behind her, shielding him from the self-seeking man she'd known since childhood. Early in Hezi's reign, Shebna's arrogance and deceit had earned a personal censure from Yahweh through Abba Isaiah. According to all reports, he hadn't changed.

Shebna nodded to Nasseh's treasured toy. "Haruz liked to twirl the tassels on our abba's robe when he was a toddler. Abba thought it cute until he tried to break the habit." He sniffed and nodded toward the giant of a man who now faced the wall and tugged at his patchy beard, obviously struggling with the noise and chaos of the crowded main hall. "When the 'habit' couldn't be broken, our abba broke Haruz instead. As you can see, he's struggling now because it's out of his routine, but he can learn to be content in any *familiar* environment. King Manasseh can learn to cope with anything if we teach him, my queen." Without waiting for her answer, he rejoined his brother and niece, leaving Zibah drowning in turmoil—around her and inside her.

Pulling Nasseh closer, she joined Shebna's family. The girl looked to be a few years older than Nasseh, perhaps closer in age to Kenaz. Zibah stepped behind a stone pillar and large planter full of ivy to provide a sufficient barrier for them to speak without shouting.

"I'm sorry I was rude," Zibah said to the girl before Shebna began spewing lies or blaming Abba and Eliakim for all his troubles—as he was known to do.

She bowed respectfully. "I'm sorry I approached the king without asking your permission, my queen." Nasseh had released Zibah's waist when he heard the girl's voice. "May I offer him my hand again?"

"You may offer," Zibah cautioned, "but he seldom even allows his cousin Kenaz to hold his hand."

The girl knelt before Nasseh again, head bowed. "Do you remember my name, my king?" She offered her hand, palm up, once more.

"Shua," he said, placing one finger in her palm again.

Zibah covered a gasp, restraining both joy and wonder.

"That's *almost* right. My name is Shu-*lle*. Can you pronounce the *l*'s?"

"Shu-lllll," he said with a silly grin, squeezing her hand in his.

She laughed with him and then pressed his hand to her forehead with a bow. "It's my deepest honor to meet you, King Manasseh. I'm sure you'll be a wonderful king."

Tears flowed freely down Zibah's cheeks while the children continued their interchange. Glancing up at Shulle's abba, she guessed him to be twice the size of Shebna. He'd grown calmer in the quieter space, now combing his beard with his fingers rather than tugging violently at it. Still averting his eyes, however, he seemed far more interested in the stone pillar than in Judah's queen.

Shebna leaned close and whispered, "Our abba sent Haruz away with a young wife to Jotbah, considering him too much of an embarrassment.

Haruz's wife died in childbirth, so he raised Shulle alone. I believe he's done a fine job—though he shares many of King Manasseh's unique challenges."

Curiosity loosened Zibah's tongue. "What brings you to Jerusalem, Haruz ben Joseph?"

"My brother believes his teaching methods and my daughter's influence can help King Manasseh in the classroom as you helped King Hezekiah when you were children."

Zibah choked out a derisive laugh. "Your brother presumes too much, Haruz ben Joseph." She glared at Shebna. "My son will learn all he needs to know from Abba and Eliakim. Neither Hezi nor I would trust you to teach our son, Shebna, when you've repeatedly placed personal gain above Judah's best interest."

"It's your son's interest I'm thinking of now," Shebna said with his familiar rancor. "Haruz and I lived with a Levite abba who didn't understand my brother's needs. Isaiah's rigid demands and Eliakim's mousy methods will discourage your son from learning. I am a skilled teacher, and I don't need to prove Shulle's ability to connect with your son, my queen." Shebna closed his eyes and exhaled before speaking more calmly. "I'm asking you to speak with King Hezekiah on your son's behalf. Shulle and I can help Nasseh absorb whatever Isaiah and Eliakim teach him." He held her gaze and waited.

Shebna seemed sincere. Zibah remembered the years he'd replaced Abba as royal tutor. He had been both passionate and proficient in the role. "How will you help Nasseh *absorb* his lessons better?"

"May I demonstrate?"

Zibah didn't stop him, so he knelt beside Nasseh and Shulle. They were taking turns twirling the wooden wheel on the stick. "Greetings, my king, I'm Shulle's dohd Shebna, and I'd like to ask you a question or two. Is that all right?"

Nasseh ignored him, continuing his fascination with the spinning toy.

"I like to sing," Shebna went on. "Shulle taught me a silly song about a fish and a frog. Would you like to hear it?"

A smile curved the young king's lips, but he offered no reply.

"Hmm. That's too bad. I can't sing it for you unless you say, 'Yes, please.'"

"Shebna, he can't—" Zibah's protest was cut off by her son's voice.

"Yef, peez."

Too stunned to even blink, the boy's ima gaped while Shulle and Shebna began singing the silliest lyrics Zibah had ever heard. Haruz joined them with his deep bass voice. Once again moved to tears, Zibah quickly picked up the simple words and sang along. Nasseh mouthed unintelligible words and brightened the hall with a brilliant smile.

Yahweh, thank You for this breakthrough. Thank You for creating a path when all I saw for my son were stone walls and unscalable mountains.

For the first time, Zibah believed her son could be truly happy in life and rule Judah with the strength of his abba's character. As they belted out the third chorus of the fish song, guards and palace visitors began to point and laugh. Zibah didn't mind. But the Shebna of old would have cared very much. She marveled at the man singing beside his giant brother and precious niece. Perhaps bringing his family to Jerusalem had truly changed him.

Yahweh, can I trust Shebna to teach my son? Zibah closed her eyes and listened but heard nothing but singing. She'd learned not to expect a burning bush like the one Moses saw, but sometimes she at least felt a sense of divine direction. Not this time. This time, she must decide to walk a path Yahweh let her choose.

Zibah interrupted Shebna's song. "Bring Shulle to our schoolroom tomorrow. I'll speak with Hezi about the matter, but I can't promise—"

"We'll be there, my queen. Just after dawn."

Nasseh let go of Shulle's hand only after Zibah promised he'd see her tomorrow.

Then Shebna bowed to her son. "You will be a mighty king, and I would be honored to be among those who might shape your mind and heart."

3

Keep on, then, with your magic spells
 and with your many sorceries,
 which you have labored at since childhood.
Perhaps you will succeed,
 perhaps you will cause terror.

ISAIAH 47:12

Evening, Same Day

Moving to Jerusalem's Upper City two months ago was hard for Abba, a man who needed space and quiet. Dohd's five-room house was more spacious, but his maid, Belit, was as friendly as a mountain lion with a thorn in its paw. The walled courtyard was the size of our small garden, and houses surrounded us on all sides. Dogs barked. Couples argued. Children squealed. And the smell of our street's drainage trench grew rancid in summer's heat. Abba retreated to his private chamber when we returned from the palace this morning and hadn't emerged. Dohd said to let him rest.

"Belit, Shulle must wear her blue linen robe tomorrow." Dohd Shebna's voice sounded high-pitched, a sign he was tense.

"It's stained." Belit slopped gruel into bowls and placed them on a round leather mat in the center of the gathering room.

I'd grown more nervous as the day wore on. "Perhaps I shouldn't go, Dohd. I don't want to embarrass you."

He wagged his head. "You could never embarrass me. You'll wear your cream-colored robe and red belt." He kissed the tip of his finger and placed it on my nose. "This evening you begin special lessons with Belit."

"So I can help Nasseh better?"

Belit clanked a wooden spoon on a copper pot. "Not exactly."

Dohd shot her an angry look. "What Belit meant was that she'll teach you how to save Nasseh from terrible, terrible danger."

Belit placed spoons beside our bowls and set a pitcher of fresh goat's milk on the table. Then she added a basket of warm bread. She still hadn't looked at me.

"Everything smells wonderful, Belit."

"Here." She shoved a bowl of raisins and pistachios at me so I could add them to my gruel.

I sprinkled a handful of the mixture into my bowl and passed it to Dohd. My tummy hadn't growled the whole time we'd lived in Jerusalem. "What danger could threaten King Nasseh? Doesn't he have guards to protect him?"

"He does, yes, but this kind of danger is different." Dohd swallowed his first bite of gruel and set aside his spoon. "Belit," he whispered, "make sure Haruz's door is closed." While she checked, he continued in a whisper. "The same danger threatens you I'm afraid, little Shulle. I've been cautiously planning your rescue since the day I met you in Jotbah."

Belit returned and nodded at Dohd, and they looked at me like hungry hawks watching a field mouse. I wished Abba would come out of his chamber. "What I'm about to say will be hard to believe at first," Dohd explained, "but I need you to trust me, Shulle. Simply do what I ask for tonight, and by tomorrow Belit and I will have proved what we say is true. Can you do that, little one? Can you trust us tonight and obey Belit?"

His smile looked different somehow. Forced. Like a growl without noise. A trickle of sweat ran down my back, and my tummy felt funny. I turned to Belit, and she raised her eyebrows.

"Can I ask Abba if it's all right?"

"No, dear." Dohd picked up his spoon and resumed his evening meal. "You see, Haruz and the other Yahwists *are* the danger. They've been deceiving Judah with their lies, and you must learn the truth so we can help King Manasseh realize the dangers of Yahweh."

I couldn't believe what he was saying. It was blasphemy! "Yahweh is the only true God, Dohd. He—"

"Tonight," he interrupted, "Belit will demonstrate a special skill in dark arts. Then in the morning, if you're still convinced Yahweh is the only god, you may tell your abba and the king and queen—anyone you like—about our activities. But if you realize that the Yahwists have deceived Judah with their strict laws and command to worship only one god, then I'll ask you to train with Belit and help us make King Nasseh the greatest king in Judah's history."

"No. No!" I couldn't believe the son of a Levite would suggest—

"Is your faith in Yahweh so fragile that it can't stand a single night's test?" Belit's eyes narrowed in challenge, her voice like the purr of a cat.

"Your abba is sleeping," Dohd coaxed. "He won't even know it happened."

My faith was unshakable. I'd known of Yahweh from my earliest memory. I could recite much of the Torah and most of Solomon's proverbs. Nothing they could say or do could change my beliefs. I lifted my spoon. "Fine. One night. But you'll never convince me any other god exists." I scooped a bit of gruel into my mouth.

Dohd removed the familiar sticky bundle from his pocket and placed my daily treat on the table beside me. "You may have as many dates as you like tonight, Shulle."

Ignoring him, I left the dates untouched. I wouldn't betray Yahweh for a few candied dates.

~

My teeth chattered in the spring night air, and I could barely keep my eyes open. The sky was inky black as Belit dug up her last turmeric root. On this horrible night of lessons, I'd watched her kill and skin a snake, catch frogs and drain their blood, mix potions and fashion charms. She'd removed a wad of hair from her waist pouch, mixed it with the blood and wrapped it in the snake's skin, and then waved it at the sky while chanting and dancing. With each forbidden practice, my stomach twisted into tighter knots until, finally, we came to a task I could do without guilt. I helped her harvest a basket of herbs. But even that she ruined by saying harvesting under the light of moon and stars strengthened the plants' magical powers.

If Abba knew what I was doing, he'd have used his strap on me. He'd only punished me with it once before, when I refused to apologize for shouting at Jotbah's elders. They'd falsely accused him of immoral behavior with a woman in town. I wasn't sure what *immoral behavior* meant, but I'd been sick on the night of the crime, and he'd been home tending my fever. "He couldn't have done it," I explained to the elders—in Hebrew and Aramaic, since they seemed too thick to understand. Still, they whipped Abba publicly, and I shouted my indignation until the beating was over.

Abba demanded I apologize for my disrespect. I refused, and he reached for his strap. "'Rebellion is like the sin of divination, and arrogance like the evil of idolatry.'"

Belit had committed all four sins tonight. Was I guilty for watching?

"Over here, Shulle." Belit waved me toward the terrifying caves near the city's Corner Gate, where paupers buried their dead. I moaned inwardly. We'd passed them on our way out of the city, but I'd given them wide berth.

"Stand here beside me," she said, pulling me close and looking to the sky. "The month of the bull has nearly passed, but Enki smiles on you tonight. See his horns?" She directed my attention to the stars and drew the bull's horns with an imaginary stylus in her hand, then she drew his front legs charging forward.

"I see it!" Like a candle's glow, the starlight connected, and I saw an image of a bull in the sky. Fear quickly replaced excitement at the enormity of the moment. Had I just beheld the power of another god? Or had I imagined it, tired from a night without sleep?

"Stand by us, O gods of the night." Belit lifted her hands. "Heed my words, O gods of destinies. Prove yourselves in daylight with the power you've displayed in tonight's darkness. May the power of your light follow Shulle into this day and shine on her with your favor."

I didn't want the power of any gods shining on me, but when Belit turned to me, her dark eyes shone with a yellow glow. "I was a gift to Shebna," she said, "in the year King Hezekiah fell sick, the same year he was healed, the same year my Babylonian masters visited Jerusalem. It was three years before King Manasseh was born, Shulle. The same year you were born."

My whole body began to shake. "I want to go home."

She smiled, and her eyes glowed brighter. "Your birth and my arrival in Jerusalem—our destinies intertwined. The gods have shown me, Shulle, you and I will determine the future of nations. It is written in the stars."

I jerked free of her grasp, stumbled, and fell to the ground. I couldn't breathe. Too terrified to scream. Too horrified to run. What had I done? Belit was more than Dohd's maid. She was a real sorceress, and tonight I'd been her aide. If anyone discovered it, I could be executed.

I tried to crawl away, but the giant witch hoisted me over her left shoulder like a sack of grain. "It's time you realize there's more than one god, little Shulle." She grabbed the herb basket and supplies and marched back to Dohd's house.

As we entered the courtyard, she set me on my feet, and I inhaled the sweet scent of myrtle blossoms—like waking from a nightmare to the safety of dawn. "I need to sleep," I said.

"Of course, you must sleep," Belit said, nudging me toward the chamber we shared. "And when you wake, your whole life will feel new." She set aside the basket and supplies while I fell onto my mat, exhausted. A blanket fluttered over me, and Belit tucked it all around to ease my shaking. I closed my eyes, willing sleep to claim me, but saw only the dreadful glow of a horned bull in the night sky.

"Shulle, wake up." Dohd Shebna shook my shoulder. "Wake up, my girl."

I startled from a deep sleep and sat up, pulling the blanket up to my neck.

Dohd stood over me, a single clay lamp casting haunting shadows on his face in the dim light of dawn. "Do you remember the curse Belit spoke last night under the sign of the bull?"

Still foggy from sleep, I nodded. How could I forget anything from last night?

"Do you remember the hair from her pouch?" Again, I nodded. Dohd smiled and offered his hand. "Come with me, little Shulle, and you will see proof of Belit's skill and the power of her gods."

I refused his hand but followed him out of my chamber. We walked a few steps down the hallway and stopped in front of Abba's room. Dohd entered without knocking, and I heard Belit's rhythmic chanting inside.

I stood on the threshold unable to comprehend the sight. Abba's beard had been shaved clean, and he lay in a loin cloth on his mat—covered in festering sores. My whole body began to tremble, and I covered my mouth to silence the scream building inside. *Yahweh, please no!*

Dohd returned to kneel beside me, and in a whisper he changed my life. "It was your abba's beard Belit used in her incantation last night. I don't know how she did it because she won't teach me her dark arts, but you, Shulle—*you*—she's willing to show you the secrets to this marvelous power over men and gods."

"Marvelous?" I cried, anger and despair coming out on a sob. I shoved him away. "How is this anything but cruel?"

Dohd's eyes narrowed. "Just as Belit called on the gods to send sores, she can also restore Haruz. You need only recognize the starry hosts' power and begin your training as Belit's apprentice—secretly."

My stomach rolled, and I groaned, thinking I might retch.

"When we return from our meeting with Queen Zibah and King Nasseh, you'll see how much better your abba is, and you'll understand why we've gone to such great lengths to show you the power of other gods. When Yahweh wished to prove his power at the burning bush, didn't he make Moses's hand leprous? Yahweh was once a powerful god, Shulle, but no longer. Now, it's the starry hosts that are proving their power to you—to *you*, Shulle. Think of it."

I couldn't think of it, not with Abba lying ten paces away in such pain. "I want to talk to Abba before we go."

"Of course," Dohd squeezed my shoulder. "Though he's delirious with fever, you should still be cautious with your words. If you keep silent about the curse, Haruz will be restored by the time we return this afternoon. If you betray us . . ." Eyes cold, he led me to the mat, where Belit knelt beside Abba with a bowl of broth and a spoon. "As you can see," he said in a normal tone, "Belit shaved your abba's beard to help it grow more evenly. Now, she's feeding him bone broth so he can regain his strength. The sores came on suddenly last night, but Belit's knowledge of herbs will help him recover quickly."

Abba weakly raised his hand to me, but I could see that even the slight movement made him wince.

"Don't move, Abba. I'll come home soon to check on you."

Belit looked at me over her shoulder. "The bone broth works miracles." Her eyes met mine. They weren't glowing yellow or pulsing this time, but a shiver still ran through me.

Dohd hurried me from the room, and I wiped my tears. "Good, good," he said. "Pinch your cheeks for a little color and put on that cream-colored robe with the red belt. The sun is rising, and I promised the queen we'd be in the classroom by dawn."

I obeyed and twisted my hair into a loose braid. After grabbing a piece of bread and a handful of raisins, I walked through the gathering room and met Dohd at the courtyard gate. Jerusalem in dawn's light was magical, giving me hope that Belit could heal Abba as promised. But what if she did? Had Yahweh lost His power as Dohd said? *Yahweh, if You hear me, show me Your power so I don't have to serve other gods.*

I didn't know if Yahweh would listen to a little girl. The Torah said I had to bring an offering, but Dohd would never allow it. Lavender hues glowed around Solomon's temple, reminding me that I'd never be allowed to set foot in its sacred courts. Only the priests spoke directly to Yahweh. Had the Almighty ever heard my prayers?

We walked past the temple to the palace beside it. My legs ached by the time we traversed the city's hills and steps, but my aches were soon forgotten in the splendor of this new world. Though ancient, Solomon's palace was even grander than the temple. Gigantic blocks of stone fit perfectly together, creating an enormous structure. But it was the details that made it truly spectacular. Mosaic tiles. Ebony and ivory inlays. Cedar walls and doors. Everywhere I looked, my eyes guzzled the beauty like a beggar led to a banquet.

Judah's royal guards in their shiny armor left sharp weapons sheathed while Dohd and I marched past. Our sandals echoed in a maze of quiet hallways, but we weren't the first to arrive at the schoolroom.

"Good morning, Lord Shebna." The old man introduced as Lord Isaiah at the coronation walked toward us, his gnarled hand extended.

Dohd's grip on mine tensed, and his funny smile appeared—the growl with no sound—as he grasped the man's wrist in greeting. "Good morning to you, Lord Isaiah." Dohd nudged me forward. "May I present my niece, Meshullemeth."

I bowed, as Belit taught me. "Shalom, Lord Isaiah. I'm honored to meet you."

Lord Isaiah chuckled, a happy sound like water babbling in a stream. "As I'm honored to meet the girl who so quickly captured my grandson's favor. My daughter, Queen Zibah, told me you cast quite a spell over him."

Had Yahweh already told the old prophet I'd been out with Belit last night? "I assure you, my lord, I know nothing of casting spells!"

"You see, Nasseh? There they are." The queen's voice from the doorway stole our attention. "I promised we'd see Shulle and Lord Shebna this morning." Light shone behind her, making every jewel in her plaited brown hair sparkle, but dark shadows bruised the delicate skin beneath her eyes. Her night must have been as distressing as mine. A second woman with a boy followed the queen into the classroom, and behind them—

"King Hezekiah and Lord Jashub," Dohd said, tugging me to my knees and prostrating himself on the stone floor. "It's an honor to be in your presence."

4

Whom did the LORD consult to enlighten him,
and who taught him the right way?
Who was it that taught him knowledge,
or showed him the path of understanding?

ISAIAH 40:14

Zibah had spent most of the previous afternoon and evening trying to assure Nasseh he'd see Shulle again and most of the night
trying to convince Hezi to at least meet Shebna's niece and witness her connection with their son. She was exhausted by the time she arrived in class with her two kings.

Hezi pecked her on the cheek as he led Nasseh toward Shebna and the
little girl. "Rise, Shebna," he said, walking past him and kneeling in front
of the man's niece. "Queen Zibah tells me your name is Shulle."

She bowed properly. "Yes, my king." Before she raised her head,
Nasseh reached for the girl's hand.

"Shullll, Ba." He looked at Hezi, beaming. Zibah thought her heart
might melt.

Judah's king gasped as if he'd just been showered with gold coins and
glanced at the adults in the room. "Did you see how boldly our new king
took his friend's hand?" Hezi grasped Shulle's other hand, completing
their circle. "So, you're an angel sent from Yahweh to draw my son out of
his lonely world."

"I, uh . . . I . . ." Shulle looked at her dohd, and Shebna coaxed her with
a proud wink.

Hezi squeezed her hand and drew her attention back to him. "Do you promise, little Shulle, to help my son learn everything Lord Isaiah, Lord Eliakim, and Lord Shebna will teach him so when Yahweh takes me away, he'll become the best king Judah has ever known?"

She nodded so vehemently her spiral curls danced like willow fronds in the wind. "I promise, but—" Glancing at the adults, she seemed utterly overwhelmed.

"Go ahead," Hezi coaxed. "You may say anything you wish."

"You said Yahweh will take you away. Where is He taking you?"

Her question sucked the air from Zibah's lungs and joy from the moment. Hezi worked to keep his features pleasant, but Zibah bowed her head to hide tears.

"A few years ago," he said, "I became very sick. Yahweh healed me and gave fifteen more years of life."

The little girl's silence drew Zibah's attention to the quizzical pout that prefaced Shulle's next words. "If Yahweh had power to heal you, why won't He let you grow old?"

From her lips, it was a question. In Zibah's heart, it had been an accusation for eight long years.

"Your quick mind reminds me of Queen Zibah when she was a little girl." Hezi began his explanation with a genuine smile. "I don't know why Yahweh gave me only fifteen more years. But I do know this. Though we don't always understand God's plan, we can trust His goodness for a future we can't yet see."

Nasseh jerked his hand away from Shulle's, his brow wrinkled in consternation. He stood like a stone before his abba. What was he thinking? Would he speak? His hands fisted wildly; his chest heaved with every breath. Eyelashes fluttered against his cheeks as his eyes scanned the floor, then left and right. Without warning, he flung his arms around Hezi's neck in a ferocious hug.

Never having received such affection from his son, Hezi responded as any parent would—not realizing Nasseh's aversion to confinement. Zibah lunged to stop him, but Hezi enveloped Nasseh in his strong arms. The warmth and strength of his abba's love seemed to overwhelm Nasseh. He cried out, recoiled, and shoved his abba away. Hezi sat back on his heels, red splotches creeping up his neck.

Weary of her role as arbitrator, Zibah fell silent in the awkwardness. Everyone stared at the floor.

Everyone, that is, except Shulle.

"Nasseh loves you," she said, tugging Hezi's hand and pulling him back up on his knees. "He can't bear to be closed in, so you must start by offering your hand, my king."

Hezi obeyed the eight-year-old girl as if he were the child and she the teacher. When Nasseh grasped his hand willingly, Shulle continued. "Nasseh, your abba doesn't understand how to hug you nicely. You must show him." She nodded, coaxing, "Go ahead."

Nasseh took two steps forward and reached around his abba with one arm to gently pat his back. Zibah covered a grin and felt someone lean over her shoulder.

"It would appear your husband isn't too old to learn," Eliakim whispered.

"When did you get here?" she asked the latecomer.

"Just in time for the hug lesson."

Her brother, Jashub, and his wife, Yaira, huddled next to Eliakim with their son, Kenaz, also impressed by today's young teacher.

Reaching his limit of hug time with his abba, Nasseh abruptly released him and wrapped Shulle's neck with the same affection. Her cheeks instantly pinked, but to her credit she applied the same principles Nasseh had given Hezi, gently patting his back with one hand.

"Well, Shebna," Hezi said, "it appears your niece has secured your place among my son's instructors. You will join Isaiah and Eliakim, teaching Kenaz and Nasseh all they need to know to effectively rule Judah someday."

Nasseh finally released Shulle from his exuberant hug but still held her hand while seeming to engage with what Hezi was saying.

"Kenaz, I expect you to learn as well. You'll become one of Nasseh's chief counselors someday."

"I would be honored, Dohd Hez—" He looked at his abba, who corrected him with lifted eyebrows. "I mean, I would be honored, my king."
His abba, Jashub, was Zibah's brother and had married her dearest friend,
Yaira, during the Assyrian crisis. Kenaz was a miracle boy, given to the
couple in their later years.

Yahweh, both of these boys are Yours. Use them for Your glory. Zibah's
heart felt full and blessed. Yesterday's coronation and last night's struggle
had been difficult, but this morning's victories had instilled a new hope for
what each day might bring.

Glancing at the sweet girl who had made it all possible, she found
Shulle standing alone, tears glistening on her cheeks. When Zibah hurried
over, the girl wiped her tears and donned a forced smile. "Are you all
right?" Zibah knelt in front of her.

But Shulle stepped back, her cheeks pale, her focus on someone behind them. Zibah turned to find Shebna approaching.

"My queen," he said, slipping his arm around Shulle's shoulder, "I
hope you'll allow us to begin our lessons with King Manasseh today." The
girl furtively wiped fresh tears with a trembling hand.

"Tell me, Shebna," Zibah stood, towering over the little man. "Why
would Shulle be frightened of you?"

His smile dimmed but not entirely. "I'm sure I have no idea." He bent
only slightly to meet Shulle eye to eye. "Dear niece, why would the queen
think you're afraid?"

She clasped her hands behind her and looked at the floor. "Perhaps she
misinterpreted my tears. I'm concerned for Abba. He wasn't feeling well
when we left this morning, and when King Hezekiah said Yahweh would
take him away in seven years, it made me afraid that Yahweh would take
away my abba too." She wiped more tears, affirming her genuine distress.

Nasseh crossed the room to join them, grabbed his toy from Zibah's
pocket and tugged at Shulle's hand, coaxing her to play. Shulle was too
polite to refuse, but Zibah nudged him aside. "Nasseh, Shulle is sad. She
doesn't want to play."

Relentless, Nasseh pushed his way back to Shulle. With a sigh, Zibah prepared for the clash of wills that happened whenever she forced her son from his chosen path.

"I believe it's time for our first lesson," Shebna said, retrieving two folded parchments from the pocket of his robe and then showing them to Nasseh. Each bore a simple circle drawing—one with a smile and one with a frown. "Shulle is feeling *sad,* my king. Would you take a quick peek at her face and then point to the parchment that matches her *frown*?"

Nasseh glanced away from his toy to see Shulle's face for no longer than a blink and tapped the parchment with the frown.

"Excellent, my king," Shebna said. "You are very smart. Now, if you'll look once more at Shulle's face, you'll see her eyes are red because she's been crying. She's been wiping her nose, and she's got that dreary *frown.* Point to the *sad* drawing." Again, he emphasized the words *sad* and *frown*, but this time Nasseh refused to look. He kept twirling the wheel on his wooden stick, his more usual response to the world around him.

Zibah felt the familiar sting of embarrassment. "I'm sorry, Shebna."

"Please don't apologize, my queen," he said. "King Manasseh has accomplished much in our short introductory session. He deserves a little playtime." His enthusiasm seemed genuine, exposing Zibah's expectations as perhaps too high.

"You're right," she said, combing Nasseh's dark curls with her fingers. "He has accomplished good things this morning." In one morning, he'd taught Hezi to hug properly and recognized what *sad* looked like. Looking at Shebna once more, Zibah decided it was time to admit she'd been wrong. "Forgive me for mistrusting you, Shebna. You've shown true kindness and expertise in your dealings with our son. Hezi and I are grateful for the guidance you and Shulle will provide for Judah's new king and the far-reaching impact it will have on our nation."

Shebna pulled Shulle to his side, and they bowed as one. "It is our honor," Shebna said, "to play a part in shaping the heart and mind of our new king."

Shulle rose from the bow but avoided looking at Zibah, her cheeks wet with tears again. Was her abba so desperately ill? Or was there more to the girl's sad frown? "Perhaps you should return home so Shulle can check on her abba."

The girl looked hopeful. She turned to her dohd, waiting for his decision. "Perhaps we'll leave after the midday meal," Shebna said. "My maid is with him and would send word if there was any real concern."

Shulle nodded and donned a smile that seemed less than wholehearted. "All right, Dohd. It will be as you say." She turned her attention to Kenaz, who had helped entertain Nasseh with his twirling wheel. "Would you introduce me to the other student, my queen?"

Zibah wondered if it was maturity or something else that made this girl so compliant.

5

With whom, then, will you compare God?
To what image will you liken him?

ISAIAH 40:18

My first day in class went so slowly that I was sure Belit had somehow caused the sun to stand still. King Hezekiah and Lord Jashub left the classroom to begin their day in court. I expected the queen and Kenaz's ima to leave as well—to do whatever royal ladies do. But they were as involved in teaching their sons as the three tutors. Perhaps more so.

In the morning, we took turns identifying happy and sad faces with the parchments. Nasseh seemed to enjoy the game, especially when everyone—even the adults—began making silly faces beyond a typical smile and frown to test him.

Abba had once told me that his ima had taught him to read faces before she died. It was the only memory he had of her, but it was obviously quite vivid, and he described it to me often.

"Ima's hair was black and always in a long braid down her back. She didn't smile much, so the smile parchment was crisp and new, but the frown had to be replaced every new moon because I pointed to it so much," he said. "Ima's face was round, and all her teeth showed when she smiled. I wish I could see her smile again." Abba never spoke of missing her, but I knew he did. Like I knew he missed my ima, Adnah.

"Yes, Shulle is sad again," Dohd Shebna said overly loud to regain my attention. "But she's going to show us her happy face now." I saw the threat in his eyes and tucked away my sadness for later.

After our midday meal, Lord Isaiah stood and recited his first vision while the rest of us sat on comfortable cushions. Nasseh tried to lay his head in the queen's lap, but she coaxed him to sit up the way Kenaz and I were sitting. My eyes drooped as the aged prophet droned on until I was startled by Dohd Shebna's snoring. I elbowed him awake but noted Lord Eliakim was also studying the inside of his eyelids.

With a single *clap!* Lord Isaiah finished his recitation. "Now it's your turn, children." He looked at Kenaz first. "How much of my vision can you repeat from memory, Grandson? It must be word for word." As son of Lord Isaiah's firstborn, Kenaz had surely been reciting this vision since he'd said his first words.

"Um." Kenaz looked at his ima and back at Lord Isaiah. "In the year King Uzziah died, I saw the Lord . . ." He gulped loudly. "Um."

"High and exalted," Lord Isaiah coaxed.

"High and exalted, and the train . . ."

"No, no," Lord Isaiah corrected. "High and exalted, seated on a throne, and the train of his robe . . ."

Kenaz sighed, shoulders slumped. "I can't remember it, Saba."

"What about you, little Shulle?" the prophet asked. "Can you recite any of the vision?"

I nodded and began, "In the year that King Uzziah died, I saw the Lord, high and exalted, seated on a throne; and the train of His robe filled the temple. Above Him were seraphim, each with six wings: With two wings they covered their faces, with two they covered their feet, and with two they were flying. And they were calling to one another: 'Holy, holy, holy is the Lord Almighty; the whole earth is full'"—I hesitated slightly—"'of his glory.'" I stopped reciting when I saw Lord Isaiah's bushy gray eyebrows pinch together. "Did I do it wrong, my lord?"

First he looked at Eliakim and then at Dohd. "Shebna, have you taught her the prophetic writings?"

Fear shot through me. If I'd done something wrong, would Belit let Abba die? "No, Lord Isaiah! Dohd didn't teach me, and I only remember up to the part where Dohd started snoring."

Queen Zibah and Yaira laughed, and the others joined in, relieving some of my fears. Lord Isaiah wiped happy tears from the wrinkles around his eyes. "Well, I suspect you'll have no problem learning the Torah."

"Abba already taught me much of the Torah." Without thinking I began reciting, "'In the beginning God created the heavens and the earth . . .'"

When I got to the sixth day, Nasseh said, "No!" He laughed like the others had done. "No, no, no," he said.

I laughed with him. "Are you tired of me reciting?"

He stopped laughing and grew serious. "No."

"Did you hear her mistake, Nasseh?" Lord Isaiah asked. "Is that why you stopped her?"

"I made a mistake?"

Nasseh kept spinning his toy while Lord Isaiah explained, "At the end of the sixth day, Shulle, when God assessed all He'd made, He said it was *very* good. I believe you left out the word *very*. Was that her mistake, Nasseh?" The boy king met his saba's question with a nod and satisfied grin.

Queen Zibah kissed the top of his head and said, "If he caught her mistake, Abba, it means he knows every word."

Lord Isaiah turned to Dohd, a look of wonder in his eyes. "Is it possible the boy knows all we've tried to teach him but simply hasn't communicated what he knows?"

"It's not only possible, Isaiah. I'd say he's proven it to be true." Dohd's chest puffed out a little when he answered, and I remembered what he told me in Jotbah. *"I'll be important again someday."* "Perhaps we should all thank Shulle for her error in recitation." He began the applause, and everyone joined him. My cheeks warmed, but I couldn't stop a smile. I'd never been so pleased about an error in recitation. Abba certainly wouldn't be clapping about it. *Abba.*

I leaned over and asked Dohd, "Can we go home now and see if Abba is better?"

"Yes, my girl," he whispered. "You've done well." At Dohd's suggestion, class ended for the day, and we began our walk home.

The moment we entered the courtyard, I ran toward the house. "Abba!" I shouted, so focused on reaching his chamber that I nearly stumbled over him and Belit seated on cushions in the gathering room. "Abba?" I reached out to touch the scabs on his face, but he brushed my hand away.

"Don't touch. Belit says it could spread." He slurped another spoonful of bone broth. "How was your first day?"

I opened my mouth, but nothing came out. Who cared about class? When I left this morning, Abba could barely move. I had prayed Yahweh would show me His power. Was it Yahweh who healed Abba or Belit's starry hosts and spells?

"I need help cleaning your abba's chamber." Belit's stare burned me with anticipation. "We should do it now so he can rest after he finishes his meal." She stood and started down the hall without looking back. She knew I'd follow.

We entered Abba's chamber, and Belit closed the door behind us. The room smelled like infirmity. I covered my nose. "Did you do it?" I asked.

Her lips slowly curved into a smile, and she stepped closer. "I can teach you every herb to put in bone broth and every healing word to speak over the sick. What does Yahweh offer but false promises and harsh rules?"

It was true. Yahweh seemed to care only about rules and sacrifices. Perhaps he no longer had much power and *couldn't* give King Hezekiah longer than fifteen years.

Belit folded Abba's soiled mat and sheets. I helped gather the putrid bandages and dirty cloths. When the room held no trace of Abba's infirmity, the woman paused with her hand on the latch. "Your abba will be completely free of disease when we return to the kitchen. I've asked the starry hosts to give you proof." She hurried down the hall, and I followed the sound of Abba's laughter.

Belit walked through the gathering room, but I stopped and stared at Abba's fresh, pink skin that had been covered with scabs only moments ago.

I ran to her in the courtyard, then placed the soiled items near the wash barrels. "Teach me your skills," I said through dry lips. "I want to know everything about your gods."

She held my chin, but there was no tenderness. "I'll teach you, but you must win the young king's heart and make him rely on you more than breath. Only then can we both gain power and position when he alone rules Judah."

"I'll do as you say." I didn't care about power or position, but I knew I must learn her skills—if only to protect those I loved.

6

They conceive trouble and give birth to evil;
their womb fashions deceit.

JOB 15:35

689 BC, Three Years Before Hezekiah's Prophesied Death

Zibah hurried to keep pace with her nine-year-old on their way to this morning's class. She wasn't sure which of them was more embarrassed after he'd walked into her and Hezi's chamber moments ago and caught his parents in a rather impassioned kiss.

"Why must you do that?" he'd shouted and rushed out the door.

Hezi had laughed, assuring her their son needed to learn about these things sometime. But Zibah had charged down the hall after him. "Nasseh, wait!" she'd shouted in a hoarse whisper. "It's how a man and woman show love for each other."

He'd burst through the hallway doors and entered the main palace corridor, continuing to spin his leather flail and walking faster. The new toy Shulle's abba had fashioned for him a few days ago fascinated him, but now he rolled it between his hands frantically, sending the attached strings into flight. Perhaps this wasn't the best time for a discussion about the awkward encounter. Palace guards and servants watched them march past at breakneck speed.

When they arrived in class, Shulle and Shebna were already there. Abba Isaiah chose a scroll to begin the day's lesson. Nasseh placed his favorite crimson cushion beside Shulle and plopped down on it, still whirling the flail.

"Good morning, Nasseh," Shulle said. He ignored her, focus locked on the toy. She turned to Zibah. "He's upset. What happened?" The girl read him like Abba read his scrolls.

Unnerved, Zibah didn't appreciate her tone. "It's a private matter." She'd sounded sharper than intended, and Shulle's instant tears tore at her heart. "Forgive me, love. I didn't mean to be so harsh." Zibah reached for her hand, but the girl pulled away.

Zibah noticed that Shulle had been moodier recently—to be expected when a girl began changing into a woman. Zibah and Yaira had talked with her about the changes her body would soon undergo. The poor girl had only Shebna's foreign maid to help her, so—loving her like their own—Zibah and Yaira had invited her into their chamber during their monthly uncleanness to teach her the beauty and sorrow of womanhood. At first she'd been embarrassed, as all young girls are, but by the second day, Shulle had learned the rhythms of rest and service that marked the seclusion of women. Zibah and Yaira sent her home with full confidence that she could teach Shebna's maid the mercies of Yahweh's laws for women when Shulle's courses began.

"No need to apologize." She turned away and swiped at tears.

"Shulle, I—" Zibah wanted to explain, but Yaira and Kenaz arrived with Eliakim, and Abba was anxious to begin the lesson.

"'Woe to those who plan iniquity,'" Abba began reading, "'to those who plot evil on their beds! At morning's light they carry it out because it is in their power to do it.'"

Shulle whispered something to Nasseh, causing him to squeal.

Abba looked up. "Settle down, Manasseh." He squinted at his scroll, found his place, and resumed. "'Therefore, the LORD says: "I am planning disaster against this people . . ."'"

Reaching into her shoulder bag, Shulle retrieved a cup and gave it to Nasseh. She removed another for Kenaz, into which she emptied a small bag of dirt. She motioned for Kenaz to pour the dirt from his cup to Nasseh's. He did, and Nasseh watched with fascination. She whispered, "Now, Nasseh, pour the dirt back into Kenaz's cup."

"Excuse me, young woman—," Abba said.

"No! I'm keeping it." Nasseh pulled his cup tightly to his chest, spilling much of the dirt.

"Nasseh," Zibah said, reaching for his cup, "a good king is never greedy and is always grateful."

But he pushed her away. "It's mine." He grabbed Kenaz's cup too and turned his back to them all. "Shulle brought the cups for me."

A heavy silence descended on the room with the mantle of discouragement on Zibah's shoulders. "Nasseh, we talked yesterday about the difference between *greedy* and *grateful*."

"Excuse me, my queen," Shulle said. "I did bring both cups for Nasseh. And the dirt. I have more gifts in my bag if he'll let me offer them."

Zibah felt all eyes on her—Abba, Shebna, Eliakim, Yaira, Kenaz. She looked at her son, clutching the cups, huddled over them with his head bowed. She'd commandeered something Shulle was trying to teach and tried to bully Nasseh into her own agenda. Would she ever learn to reach him? "Forgive me, Shulle. Speak to Nasseh as if you two are the only ones in the room."

The girl brushed Zibah's hand with a gentle reassurance before inviting Nasseh to a path only they shared. "My king, would you be willing to help me tidy up by putting the dirt into one of your cups?"

Nasseh glanced over his shoulder, measuring the girl—and finally turned. He and Shulle placed the dirt into one cup, and he gave the other back to Kenaz so he could help pick up the dirt too. Nasseh's frustration began to rise when his fingers weren't as agile to pick up the smaller pieces of dirt. He slammed the cup on the floor.

"May I show you how my abba sweeps up spilled sand?" Shulle calmly retrieved more tools from her bag. A tiny brush—a few dried sprigs of broom tree tethered with a leather string—and a hand-sized wood shovel, whittled parchment-thin on its edge. "We simply brush the remaining dirt into the shovel and dump it into your cup."

She demonstrated, and Nasseh's face lit with a smile. But when he looked at Kenaz's near-empty cup and Shulle's empty hands, he sobered.

"Why didn't you bring three cups, Shulle?"

Zibah felt the moment like a cool splash on a summer day. Her son had just looked beyond his own desire and noticed the need of others.

"I did, Nasseh." Shulle retrieved a third cup from her bag, and Nasseh's whole countenance changed.

A slight smile curved his lips, and a tinge of pink colored his cheeks before he poured the dirt into her cup. She poured the dirt into Kenaz's cup, and around their circle it went, while Abba resumed his lesson on Micah's writings. All day, the leather flail lay untouched at Nasseh's side while he engaged in pouring dirt with his classmates and answering questions from his instructors. Shulle had demonstrated that as long as Nasseh's hands were busy and he remained alert to others, his superior mind could conquer a number of things at once.

By midday, even the adults were weary of learning. "Tomorrow, we'll tour the Gihon spring," Eliakim promised, "and keep our minds alert while we learn by doing." He nodded in Zibah's direction, affirming that he understood the milestone Shulle taught them today. Shebna and Abba had already begun packing their bags, and Yaira leaned over to offer her encouragement.

"Our little Shulle seems to know—"

"Nasseh, stop!" Kenaz's shrill voice drew Zibah's attention.

Her son held Shulle's head as he pressed his mouth firmly against hers, moving his head awkwardly in attempted passion. The poor girl stood with her hands at her sides, eyes as big as gourds.

"Manasseh ben Hezekiah!" Zibah jumped to her feet and dislodged the girl from her son's grasp. "You will apologize to Shulle immediately for treating her so shamefully."

His brow furrowed. "I love Shulle," he said, rocking frantically. "You said this morning this was how a man and woman show love."

"But you and Shulle aren't married, Nasseh."

"You didn't say husband and wife, Ima. Shulle is twelve—old enough to be betrothed—and I am king. Which makes me a man."

Zibah looked to Yaira for help, but her friend was rushing Kenaz out the door behind Eliakim and Abba. Only Shebna and Shulle remained, neither of whom seemed overly upset. Shadows of pink still lingered on the girl's cheeks, but Shebna had the same smirk Hezi had worn this morning.

"It's normal for a boy Nasseh's age to begin thinking of girls in this way," he said. "And Shulle understands that we're here to teach our young king more than is written in scrolls."

He nudged his niece toward Zibah, and she looked up with a shy smile. "Nasseh's kiss wasn't shameful, my queen. I believe for him it was purely educational. I was surprised but not offended." She reached for Nasseh's hand and began rocking with him as she spoke. "Someday, you'll love a woman enough to marry her and experience a real kiss—like you saw between your abba and ima."

His rocking slowed, and he faced her, eyes still averted. "I will marry you, Shulle."

The girl glanced at Zibah and then ducked her head. "I'll see you tomorrow, Nasseh. No more kisses."

He stood as still as a stone until Shebna and Shulle left the classroom and then turned to Zibah. "Is it your responsibility or Abba's to teach me how to love a woman?"

7

Some sat in darkness . . .
because they rebelled against God's commands
and despised the plans of the Most High.

PSALM 107:10–11

Same Night

"Wake up, girl."

I bolted upright in my bed, met by strange squeaking noises and Belit's shadowy features. My nightmares came so often that I reached out to make sure she was real.

She slapped my hand away. "Hurry up." Yes, it was Belit. She wrapped my cloak around my shoulders and shoved a small clay pot into my hands. "We have much to accomplish tonight: two cures, a curse, two charms . . . and Shebna says you're ready to advance in your training."

Too sleepy to care about what advanced training involved, I opened the clay pot to smell what was in it— "Aagh! What's this?"

"A carrier solution of juniper oil, beer, and powdered minerals. We'll add the bat's blood under the stars." She hefted a jiggling, squeaking bag over my shoulder.

"Oh no!" I shrugged it off and nearly dropped the clay pot.

One bat flew out of the bag before Belit stepped on the opening and beat the sack with her walking stick until the squeaking noises stopped. Then she draped the pack over my shoulder. "Now, hurry—before all the blood drains into the roughspun."

A soft flutter against my back made me shiver, but I hurried after Belit into the darkness—as I'd done every moonlit night for the past four years. When the moon reached its zenith, Belit awakened me from a dead sleep and traipsed me out the Corner Gate, past the burial caves, and into the hillsides and valleys to harvest herbs, mix potions, and learn from the greatest sorceress who ever left Babylon—or so she called herself. After witnessing the power of her curses and the seduction of her charms, I was inclined to agree. She never applied her skills to Abba again, so we'd lived together in relative peace, my dear abba oblivious to my dark instruction.

The spring night air was chilly. Belit stopped near one of the caves and set aside her own bag. "Get the bat blood ready to mix."

I placed the stinky solution on a rock ledge, skinned the bats I removed from my bag, and mixed their blood into the pot. The mingling smells caused my stomach to sour, but adding the sweet-smelling herbs would reverse the effect.

Belit had grown quite a reputation among pagan worshipers in Judah and beyond. Merchants spread the word of a gifted *ašipūtu* in Jerusalem, so the cost of Belit's services had more than doubled. I, of course, hadn't seen a shekel of the profits and had been sworn to silence. Dohd Shebna had no idea how wealthy his maid was becoming.

I finished tonight's orders and realized Belit was standing over me with an odd expression, holding her precious two-edged sword. Her eyes were black. No yellow flecks or pulsing. A good sign. "What is it?"

"Tonight, you will harvest a mandrake, Meshullemeth, and your training will move to a higher level. Do you understand the significance of the mandrake harvest?"

A mixture of excitement and dread raised the hair on my arms. I knew only that the root held power and its harvest marked the passage into womanhood. "I'm twelve years old, Belit. I understand the power of a mandrake." I grabbed at her sword, but she pulled it out of reach.

"Be careful, little Shulle. Both edges are sharp as an obsidian blade."

More gently now, I clasped the hilt with both hands. It was heavier than I'd imagined.

She led me to the base of a nearby hill and motioned to the open pasture. "Find your mandrake."

They were easy to spot this time of year with their deep-green curly leaves and round orange fruit. I stood beside an especially large plant, its leaves spreading over the soil a measure equal to the length of my knee to the ground.

"Draw three circles around the plant with the tip of my sword," Belit said. "We shall rob its roots and fruit this night, but we must ask permission first."

I did as instructed and looked up to find her removing a blue cloth from her bag.

"Do you remember how the ceremony goes?"

I set aside the sword and nodded, proceeding to Belit's bag. I'd read her scrolls about harvesting of mandrakes—though I didn't recall reading anything about the next level of training she'd mentioned. Reaching into her bag, I found a small pouch of grain, removed it, and pressed a few kernels deep into the soil beside the roots. I took the scarf from Belit's hands and placed it over the sprawling green leaves and delicate orange fruit, making sure not a single leaf was exposed to call on the gods for protection. I looked to the moon and stars and began the prayer I'd memorized from Belit's scroll. "I have paid a fair price for the sacrifice. Now, grant me the plant of life."

When I reached for the sword to harvest the root, Belit gripped my hand on the hilt. "Not yet, little Shulle. This morning's kiss revealed King Manasseh's manhood has sparked, and you must be ready to quench his fire." The yellow flecks appeared in her eyes, and my stomach clenched like a fist. "Tonight, your real training begins. We harvest your mandrake after."

Like watchmen blowing shofars on the wall, warnings blared inside me. "I want to go home."

"It's too late," she said, eyes glowing brighter. "What would your abba say if he discovered you'd been deceiving him all these years? Serving and worshiping the very gods he despises? You've gone too far to ever go back."

"I've done it to protect him from *you*!"

"And so you have, dear Shulle." She smiled. "Your abba is safe and well and will remain so—for as long as you continue to woo the young king. With the skills I teach you in the Grove, you can bend the will of any man to your own."

I didn't want to bend a man's will, and I knew enough about the Grove celebrations from Dohd Shebna and Belit's familiarity when they returned. Stolen glances and sly touches hadn't escaped my notice. "I'll tell Dohd if you take me to the Grove. He would never—"

"Shebna has chosen your instructors." She grabbed my arm, fingers digging in like spikes. "Your abba will be sent back to Jotbah within the week to ensure your activities remain hidden. What a shame if he were to discover the truth and need to be silenced." She released me, and I stumbled back, suddenly dizzy. "Sit down," she said, shoving me to the ground. "I've brought something to ease tonight's training."

I buried my face in my hands. *Am I to lose Abba* and *my freedom?*

She offered me a cup. "Drink all of it. Quickly."

Again, I obeyed. "Uhh, that's awful."

"It's mandrake root."

Fear shot through me like a dagger. "You poisoned me."

"No. It's called compassion. I mixed mandrake powder with juniper tea so you'll be more, shall we say, *relaxed* for your first night of training as a priestess." She offered her hand. "I wish someone had done as much for me."

The ground felt as if it shifted; the trees around us seemed to be swaying. Belit's mighty arms came around my waist to steady me. "What's happening to me?"

She was close, yet her voice sounded far away. "Try to imagine a face you love. It will be over soon."

The night was darker when Belit wrapped my cloak around me and led me out of the Grove. The sounds duller. I felt numb yet trembled from head to foot as horrifying memories of the priests' *lessons* replayed in my mind.

Their awful chants haunted me. Their rough treatment turned into pain-ful rituals. Belit promised the mother goddess would carry me into ecstasy. But the mandrake tea had made it all a distorted nightmare, and Asherah carried me only to humiliation.

So I chose Ishtar to be my patron—the goddess of love *and* war—and was designated as her priestess. I received "love" offerings from two noble-men in a white tent and secretly declared war on them both.

Belit escorted me back to the mandrake. "Please, Belit. I just want to go home."

"Lift the sword," she said, devoid of emotion.

Aching and exhausted, I shrugged off my cloak.

Belit lifted one corner of the blue scarf, showing me where to place the tip of her sword. "Angle it slightly and then press your body atop the hilt. Let your weight drive the blade into the soil but be careful not to damage the main root."

I did as she instructed. One slice into the earth. Then another. All around the base of the plant, and then I let the sword drop to the ground. I dropped with it.

"You must pull out the root, Shulle."

"I can't." Tears finally came. "You do it, Belit."

She gripped my arms—her fingers cold, palms hot—staring at me with eyes yellow as the sun. "You must harvest the root, Meshullemeth. You have one task to fulfill in your lifetime, and you'll need the power of this moment to complete it. You must marry Manasseh ben Hezekiah and teach him to follow the dark ones. Succeed, and the gods will reward you. Fail, and you will wander as a restless *etemmu* in the great netherworld beyond." She lifted me to my feet and shoved me toward the waiting plant. "Harvest the root and seize your destiny, *Queen* Shulle."

Was she mad—or was I? Still muddled from the night's horrors, I slipped my fingers around the base of the leaves, wiggled the plant gently, and pulled. The tap root dislodged from the earth's grip, and I stumbled back, shaking the excess soil from the root.

Belit clapped triumphantly and joined me, wiping the dirt away.

"Let's see the gods' plan for you." The clouds cleared as we worked, the moonlight revealing a fat, long central root with a small upper shoot on each side and two lower shoots that looked like legs. Belit stepped away as I continued to clean away the soil, fascinated by my treasure.

"It looks exactly like a man," I said, knowing the more defined the root's image, the more powerful its magic. "And it's large, Belit."

"I've never seen one larger." She began packing the supplies.

"How does the mandrake reveal the gods' plan for me?"

She whirled on me, eyes now black and narrowed with hate. "The gods gave you the most powerful mandrake I've ever seen." Belit snatched the root from my hand. "But *I* am chief āšipūtu, Meshullemeth. Don't forget it."

I saw the first sign of fear in my teacher. Insecurity. I answered quickly, "Belit, I don't want to be Nasseh's āšipūtu. You'll always be my teacher."

Seeming appeased, she shoved the mandrake back into my hands. "We'll dry the root for a month, crush it to powder, and you'll use it for the rest of your days on special occasions—as I used my powder in your tea tonight." Using her precious mandrake powder to help me was a twisted sort of kindness.

We returned home in silence, but at the courtyard gate Belit spoke. "Your mandrake proves the gods have chosen you for great things. You will be queen someday, Shulle—but don't ever cross swords with me."

I tried to swallow but couldn't remember how. "Yes, Belit."

We proceeded to the house, and she opened the door. "Shulle?" Abba called from the gathering room.

"Yes, Haruz," Belit shouted back, hurriedly removing my shoulder bag and discarding our supplies in Dohd's study. "We've returned." She gripped my face between her hands and hissed, "Remember, his life ends if he discovers your training."

Abba appeared in the hallway. "It's before dawn. Where did you take her, Belit?"

The woman squared her broad shoulders before answering. "If you must know, your daughter began her courses of the moon tonight. She woke me like a screeching cat. Had you never taught her, Haruz?"

I ducked my head, mortified that she would mention private female matters to Abba.

"Oh, I . . ." Abba cleared his throat.

"I took her outside the city to show her how women properly dispose of their menstrual rags and maintain your Hebrew Law."

"Fine then." Abba's footsteps faded down the hall, and his chamber door slammed shut.

The reality of the life thrust upon me settled into my gut. Abba would never turn from his antiquated beliefs in Yahweh, nor would he accept the gods I served. He'd hate me if he discovered I believed the starry hosts held more power. It was better that he go. Safer that he go.

Dohd appeared at his study doorway and grinned. "Excellent excuse, Belit." I covered my face, humiliated further. Dohd held out his hand. "Let me see her mandrake."

I tried to rush past him, aching to find solace in my chamber, at least until I must ready myself for today's class and pretend my whole world hadn't changed.

But he grabbed me and pulled me into a tight embrace. I tried to push him away, but he was surprisingly strong—and I was too exhausted for another battle.

My arms and legs went limp. He cradled me to the floor, smoothing my hair while I rested my head against his shoulder. Belit stood over us, holding my mandrake aloft.

"It would appear the gods have favored you tonight, my girl," Dohd said. "The first night in the Grove is difficult for any woman, but it becomes a pleasurable thing."

I sat up, pulling my knees to my chest. "Please, Dohd. I can't go back to the Grove. I can make Nasseh depend on me without . . ." My cheeks burned with shame, and I buried my face.

He forced me to look at him. "Training in the Grove is a privilege,

Meshullemeth. An act of worship to our gods. You must learn it well so *you* are the priestess to lead King Manasseh in his first sacrifice when the time comes." He chuckled, brushing my cheeks. "It's only your silly training in the Law that makes it seem shameful."

If it wasn't shameful, why did I need mandrake powder to get through it? "Why can't I wait until Nasseh and I are husband and wife? The Law doesn't seem so silly about that."

"Yahweh hates pleasure, my girl. Just look at the Law's restrictions, placing chains on the poor and stupid to keep arrogant Yahwists in power."

I nodded, too weary to argue. "I'd like a little rest before class this morning."

"Of course," he said. "Belit will wake you when it's time to break our fast, then you'll need to say goodbye to your abba. I've hired someone to transport him back to Jotbah."

I wanted to argue. Wished Abba could stay. But my shoulders slumped with a new heaviness as I walked to my chamber. I was giving up my abba in exchange for an enormous task from the gods—and a mandrake root.

Would Nasseh really want to marry me someday? He was still just a boy with a fascination for toys. He'd kissed me and declared his love—even said he would marry me—but last week he'd declared his love for boats and animals. He could recite huge passages of Torah but didn't know the language of the heart. The thought of marrying him was more than unsettling.

I pushed open my chamber door and fell onto my mat. Tears stung my already swollen eyes at the thought of saying goodbye to Abba, but I must focus wholeheartedly on my task. I didn't want to wander forever in the netherworld.

8

My son, if sinful men entice you,
do not give in to them.

PROVERBS 1:10

687 BC, One Year Before Hezekiah's Prophesied Death

Hezi propped his elbow on the table and yawned as he dipped a healthy portion of yogurt into his bowl.

Zibah reached for a boiled duck egg and cracked it—with zeal. "You could at least show some level of concern that our son is being drawn into rebellion by a beautiful girl. King Solomon would have been Israel's greatest king had he not been drawn into sin by his wives, you know."

"Nasseh is eleven, Zibah." Hezi's half-lidded eyes rose to meet hers. "He barely notices us, let alone girls."

"Not girl-zzz, Hezi. A girl. Shulle." She added cream to her gruel, trying to steady her hand. "He notices. Believe me. You know I love Shulle, but she's become a negative influence, causing Nasseh to question Yahweh's laws and His goodness."

Tears caught in her throat, and Hezi set aside his spoon. "Every man—especially a king—must search his heart to discover what he believes about Yahweh, my love. Nasseh is no exception. He's simply forced into these decisions younger than most." He waited for her to look at him before he continued. "Eliakim says he's the most intelligent boy he's ever seen. High praise from our best engineer." He picked up his spoon again and started shoveling his yogurt as if he were digging a ditch.

"I'm not talking about Nasseh's ability to build tunnels!" Zibah slammed her hand on the table. "He said he didn't see the need to sacrifice a Passover lamb, and he's refused to tend it in his chamber."

A storm brewed behind her husband's dark eyes. "Our son is a tender-hearted boy who struggles every year when I must kill our Passover lamb. I have one year left, Zibah. One year to prepare our son to rule the nation— before Yahweh takes me away." His voice broke, but he cleared his throat and continued what was becoming a tirade. "We must protect Nasseh from evil influence. Yes. Of course. But surely, a girl with a few challenging opinions in an environment of prophets and faithful Yahwists is a little turbulence our son should be able to overcome."

Zibah felt almost silly for her concerns. Almost. What was logic when compared to an ima's instincts? "I'm simply saying Nasseh's age makes it prudent to institute some guidelines for class discussion."

A knock interrupted them, and Hezi looked relieved. He kissed the top of her head on his way to the door. "You're a good ima," he said. "If you believe Shulle is becoming a distraction, set whatever parameters in place you feel necessary."

He set aside their partition, power radiating from him as he walked. His gait was that of a soldier, light in step yet confident in every stride. More handsome than ever and kinder than any man she knew, he was still the only man she'd ever loved—even when she wanted to strangle him.

Hezi opened the door and spoke in low tones. When Abba entered, the dark circles bruising the fragile skin under his eyes proved he'd had a sleepless night. Hurrying from the table, she offered her arm for support as they walked to the middle couch in the gathering area.

"I've been tormented by a vision all night long," he said, sitting heavily. "I can barely speak of it, but I must. Please, children, sit with me." His blue-veined hand motioned toward the couch on his right.

Hezi's apprehension mirrored Zibah's, but she was the one who spoke the obvious. "I'm not sure anything you say could be worse than Hezi's death already prophesied."

Abba lifted his head, his cheeks wet with tears. "In last night's vision,

I saw Manasseh as king, shortly after you died, Hezekiah." He shook his head and looked away, covering his trembling lips.

Zibah felt the blood drain from her face. "What, Abba? Say it."

He squeezed his eyes closed and turned back toward them. "Manasseh will turn away from Yahweh and follow the false gods of many nations. He will judge me false and saw me in two until I am dead. And then he'll kill more Yahwists in a rage that reaches heaven." His features hardened, eyes boring into Hezi's. "He will lead all of Judah into sin more grievous than any king before him and stir Yahweh's wrath until it boils over."

Silence magnified the horror of her abba's unthinkable words. Zibah stared at his drawn features. "You *saw* all this in a vision?" Her last words escaped on a sob.

The prophet's hard stare reverted to the look of a loving abba. He could only nod his affirmation. His message delivered, grief poured out in waves, shaking his shoulders. Both Hezi and Zibah knelt beside him, their eyes locked in astonished despair.

Zibah shook her head, fighting her own tears as if reversing their flow could rescind the vision. Hezi's eyes flowed like the Gihon spring, dripping through his beard and onto his robe. His head wagged, as if there were fighting thoughts behind his turbulent gaze.

Oh Yahweh, no! Zibah realized his intentions before he spoke the words.

Hezi squeezed his eyes closed and cried out toward heaven, "Yahweh, you cannot ask me to kill my only son." He heaved a great sob. "I would be no better than my abba Ahaz." He collapsed on the tiled floor, inconsolable.

Abba grabbed his shoulders and shook him. "Hezekiah! No! Listen to me! You will *not* sacrifice Manasseh for my sake."

Zibah could only sit back on her heels, covering nightmarish gasps at the childhood memories of children thrown into the fires of a giant idol.

"Do you hear me, Hezekiah? Nasseh will live, and I will die in the way foretold." Abba spoke quietly, having gained Hezi's attention. "Yahweh did not give me the vision to prevent it but to prepare us for it." He looked at

Zibah. "This is my calling, daughter, to die with Yahweh's testimony on my lips."

Her vision tunneled. Abba and Hezi seemed far away. Zibah clutched at the couch. Surely, this was a nightmare. She'd wake in Hezi's arms, and he'd tell her she needed to drink more water with her wine.

"Zibah. Zibah, my girl." Abba stood over her, eyes still red-rimmed.

"This is real, isn't it?" she asked.

Nodding, Hezi whispered, "But we can't linger there now, my love. Eliakim and Shebna are waiting in the hall with Nasseh for this morning's meeting. Should I send them away?"

In the haze of Abba's prophecy, Zibah forgot she'd demanded Nasseh meet this morning with his teachers regarding his comments about Passover. She turned to Abba. "I don't want you to be a part of challenging Nasseh's bad attitude and Shulle's negative influence." She helped him to his feet and hurried him to the door. "If we tell Eliakim and Shebna about your vision, they can help us work with Nasseh to keep him committed to Yahweh—"

"No, my dear." He halted her hand as she reached for the latch. "We dare not mention the vision to anyone. Not yet. Continue seeking wisdom as you normally would, and Yahweh will make it clear when we're to reveal the vision." Abba removed a small cloth from his belt to wipe beneath her eyes—no doubt correcting the kohl her maid had applied before breakfast but which her tears had hopelessly smudged.

Hezi opened the door and greeted their guests while Abba bid everyone farewell, offering a poor night's sleep as his excuse to return home. Zibah saw the whirling flail from the corner of her eye but couldn't force herself to look at her son. Swallowing a lump the size of a boulder in her throat, she stared at her sandals when Nasseh's personal guard escorted him into the chamber. How could her gentle boy harm anyone? Her son who refused to tend a Passover lamb because his Abba must kill it in four days for what he called an *outdated* celebration?

"Thank you for coming," Hezi began as Eliakim and Shebna chose opposite couches in the horseshoe-shaped sitting area. Nasseh sat on the

crimson rug between them, and Zibah followed her husband to their customary central settee. "We'll try to gather the facts quickly so we don't
impose on your class time for the day."

"I eat gruel in the morning," Nasseh said, rocking as he twirled the
flail. "Why bread and cheese today? I eat bread and cheese at midday. Will
we have gruel at midday? I don't want to be late for class." Shebna knelt
beside him and whispered something. Nasseh's rocking lessened, and a
slow smile softened the wrinkles on his forehead. "Shulle likes candied
dates."

Zibah lifted her brows at her husband. Did he see the influence even
the girl's name had on their son?

"Zibah and I are committed to ensuring that Nasseh remains wholly
devoted to Yahweh," Hezi began. "Evidently, Shulle's maturing opinions
and her beauty have become a distraction to him."

"Shulle is very beautiful," Nasseh said, still rocking. "She doesn't like
Passover either."

Hezi's thigh tensed against Zibah's, and she finally felt a measure of
vindication. "Tell Abba how you know she doesn't like it," she said gently
to their son.

"Saba Isaiah read the Law, 'Tell the whole community of Israel that on
the tenth day of this month each man is to take a lamb for his family, one
for each household,' and Shulle asked why Yahweh makes us love a lamb
before we kill it. Saba frowned, but I smiled because Shulle asked what I
wanted to know."

"You see?" Zibah whispered to Hezi.

But he looked at her as if she'd turned into a camel. "Haven't questions always been the best way to educate? Didn't you and I question your
abba with far more challenging ideas when we were Shulle's age?"

"But that's different." Zibah's voice rose, and she turned to the other
two men—who had also been childhood classmates. Their smug expressions were infuriating. "There's a difference between *asking* a question and
questioning Yahweh's laws. This isn't the first time Shulle has planted seeds
of doubt in Nasseh's mind about Yahweh's goodness. Nasseh," she said,

feeling her emotions spiraling into panic, "tell your abba what Shulle said about Adam and Eve in the garden."

"Perhaps I could help shed light on that," Eliakim said, retrieving a stack of parchments from his shoulder bag. "After yesterday's rather upsetting discussion on the Passover lamb—"

"I don't want to kill our lamb," Nasseh interrupted.

Hezi left the couch and knelt beside their son. "Nasseh, I don't want to kill the lamb either, but we do it once a year to an innocent lamb so that our guilt can be taken from us. Now, let Lord Eliakim speak." He nodded to his friend but remained at Nasseh's side.

Eliakim handed the parchments to Hezi. "After Shulle asked her difficult question and Nasseh made his unsettling statement, I found the two of them huddled in the corner after class looking at these drawings."

Zibah's curiosity propelled her off the couch to see what was enthralling her husband and son. Nasseh tapped one of the drawings. "It's a chuppah," he said, and then began reciting, "'My heart is stirred by a noble theme as I recite my verses for the king . . .'" Zibah gasped at the beautifully sketched kohl drawing of a chuppah—a wedding canopy—under a starry sky.

Hezi sorted through the other parchments as Nasseh continued reciting the wedding psalm. "Who drew all these?"

"Shulle drew them, my king," Shebna answered. He'd been uncharacteristically quiet and even now sat as stiff as a measuring rod without elaborating on the other parchments in Hezi's hands.

"She's incredibly talented," Hezi said, still inspecting her work. "The chuppah and temple done in kohl. This beautiful garden drawn in pigments. And maps—she's drawn several maps that give both scope and depth to the nations and seas."

Eliakim leaned over, tugging four parchments out of Hezi's hands. "These are the ones I believe we should address." He held out the garden and chuppah drawings, and the third was a sketch of a girl—a stunning likeness of Shulle.

"Shulle smiles a lot." Nasseh tapped the girl's self-portrait. "Shulle and

Kenaz are my friends. Shulle draws pictures, and Kenaz throws rocks with a sling."

"What about this garden, my king?" Eliakim showed him the other parchment. "What did Shulle teach you about the garden and the temple?"

Nasseh pointed to the garden and spoke as if reciting. "In the garden, man's fellowship with Yahweh was broken." Then he pointed to the chuppah drawing. "But through marriage, Yahweh unites man and woman, and they join Him in the creative act by producing new life." He turned to Hezi. "I will marry Shulle, and she will make an heir to Judah's throne, Abba."

"Nasseh, we must choose your wife carefully—"

"And then a man and his wife are reconciled to Yahweh through their sacrifices at the temple." He pointed to Shulle's lovely kohl depiction of Solomon's temple, and Zibah's heart softened.

She turned to Shebna, who still sat sullen and silent. "How long did Shulle work on these drawings, Shebna?"

"She's been working on them for weeks, my queen." His words were clipped, his tone as chilled as Mount Hermon in winter. "We felt the visual and tangible might help King Manasseh grasp abstract concepts. We also hoped the maps would help him see where Judah fits among the nations of the world." He aimed a pointed stare at both Eliakim and Hezi. "Forgive my niece and I if we've overstepped while trying to prepare our young king to look beyond Judah's borders." He shot off the couch and started toward the door.

Eliakim caught his arm and spoke gently. "I commend Shulle's methods and her message, Shebna, but I believe her presence in class has become a distraction and detriment to our king. *You* can teach Nasseh with Shulle's drawings." He turned to Hezi and Zibah. "It's time to be very clear with Nasseh about his *friendship* with Shulle."

Zibah exchanged a knowing glance with her husband's best friend before Hezi gathered the parchments and stood to usher Nasseh's two instructors out the door.

"Thank you for your candid insights," he said. "Nasseh and I will determine if Shulle remains in class and will communicate our decision by tomorrow."

The abrupt end to the meeting left Zibah unsettled. Nasseh's rocking said he felt it too. She sat beside him on the crimson rug and joined his rhythm. Silent. Ready to listen—as Shulle did.

"Shulle stays," Nasseh said when the door clicked shut behind their guests.

Zibah knew better than to argue. "You and your abba can discuss it later, love."

Hezi rejoined them, still sorting through the parchments. He sat on the rug, spreading out Shulle's drawings in front of them. "Which do you like best, Nasseh? Which is your favorite?"

"Shulle." Nasseh pointed to the girl's likeness.

Hezi chuckled. "Yes, Shulle is very pretty, isn't she?"

"Shulle stays," he said again, hands fisting. "Shulle stays."

Zibah sent an I-told-you-so glance toward her husband, but he shook his head—a clear signal she must keep silent.

"Which map do you like best?" he asked their son.

Nasseh stopped rocking and fisting, growing very still while he studied the maps. Finally, he traced his finger along the coastline of the Great Sea, naming each nation. "Phoenicia, Judah, Philistia, Egypt. Shebna teaches about the sea. I want to go, but I'm afraid. Shulle said she would go with me so I could see the sea." He laughed at the words and clapped in rhythm. "See the sea. See the sea. See the sea."

Hezi placed a kiss on Nasseh's head. "I believe we've made a good decision, my son." He met Zibah's gaze, his eyes misty. "We all need friends to help us overcome our fears. You will see the sea, Nasseh, and Shulle stays."

9

For the sins of their mouths,
  for the words of their lips,
  let them be caught in their pride.
For the curses and lies they utter.

PSALM 59:12

I'd waited in our classroom with Yaira and Kenaz while Dohd attended the meeting in the king's chamber. I knew it was about me. I'd questioned Passover too boldly yesterday. Tried to sway Nasseh too quickly. His heart was already tender toward the lambs. Why had I pushed? Dohd had sent me to my chamber without my evening meal and told Belit I'd embarrassed him in class. She smuggled in raisins and nuts when she woke me for our nighttime lessons.

But Dohd was still angry after this morning's meeting. Maybe even angrier. When class ended, I offered to help pack his shoulder bag. He waved me away with little more than a grunt.

On our way home, we passed through the market, and I looked for my troublesome beggar. After my horrendous day yesterday, he'd mocked me for reading one of Dohd's scrolls. "Teaching a girl to read is like training a dog to sing," he'd said. So I asked Belit for a special curse I could try on him this morning—she provided me with a whispered incantation and powder to toss over the coins I dropped in his basket. My reward would be seeing his breath fouled so much that no one would give him offerings.

But now, the filthy mat he usually occupied sat empty.

I tugged on Dohd's sleeve. "Wait. I need to check on something." He scowled, but I was determined to know if my curse had worked.

Approaching the sandal-maker's booth, I offered a respectful bow and asked, "Where is the man who begs by your stall?"

He looked first at Dohd, then back at me. "If you would have come before midday, you could have paid for his burial." My blood ran cold. "He seemed fit as a fig tree yesterday—except for his crooked legs, of course—but fell over dead this afternoon."

How could my curse meant to foul his breath take his life?

"I suppose we must forgive the debt he owed us." Dohd lied so easily.

I couldn't hide the tremors beginning in my chest and spreading to my arms and legs. Dohd fairly dragged me while hissing his threat amid the market noise. "Gather yourself, or I'll use the strap on you when we get home."

Teeth clattering, I gulped deep breaths to regain composure. As Dohd greeted a passing nobleman, I silently recounted the recipe of the powder and the words of my incantation. What had I done wrong?

Dohd released me, distancing himself. Was he afraid or angry? Would he really beat me? I hadn't felt Belit's strap since before my Grove training—and Dohd had never hit me. But I'd never killed a man either. For which transgression would I be punished? Murder or my boldness in class?

After a silent walk home, Dohd and I reached the courtyard, where Abba and I used to lounge under the myrtle tree. It had been our meeting place each afternoon, where we discussed what I'd learned in class. I missed him desperately, and his messages had diminished to every few months—though I wrote him a scroll every week.

We crossed the threshold, and Dohd shouted, "Belit! Get in here." Pulling me into his study, he shoved me onto a cushion. I waited in silence, eyes downcast.

Belit arrived, wiping her hands on a dishcloth. "Why are you home early?"

"Tell her." Dohd practically spit the words at me.

"My curse killed the beggar."

"Not that. Tell her you may be banned from class. Tell her what you said to Nasseh about the—"

"I only did as Belit instructed!" The accusation seemed to suck the air from the room.

Belit glared at me. Dohd glared at her. I closed my eyes, silently praying to Ishtar for protection against the violence that was surely about to visit me.

"Get the strap." Dohd's voice was a low growl.

Belit left the study, while I waited in silence, keeping my eyes closed. I wouldn't let him see my fear.

I heard her sandals slap against the tiles. She grabbed my arm and lifted me to my feet. "Bend over the—"

"No." Dohd edged between us and extended his hand to Belit. "Give me the strap." She offered up the long piece of leather that bore pearl-sized metal studs. "It is you, Belit, who will bend over the desk."

I stepped back, unable to believe what I was seeing. Belit's large frame bowed over Dohd's desk.

She kept her eyes fixed on him even as her hands met the top of the desk. "I won't be held accountable for every word I speak to the girl, Shebna."

He whirled the strap in a full arc and brought it down across her back. She pressed her mouth against her shoulder as if to keep from crying out.

I covered a cry. "Please, Dohd, it wasn't Belit. I shouldn't have—"

"What about the beggar?" he whispered in Belit's ear. "Did you purposely give Shulle the wrong incantation or too much of an herb to kill the man? To shake her confidence?"

"No," Belit hissed. "Shulle hasn't yet harnessed her powers. I suspect it's also true of her tongue."

Dohd swiveled his head to appraise me, his eyes like razors scraping at my imperfections. Without warning, he swept his arm in a circle again, bringing the strap down against Belit's arm.

She bit back a cry. I grabbed his arm to restrain him. "Please, Dohd. I'll be more careful with my curses."

He shoved me away. "I don't care about your curses! I want you to be queen!" And with another whirl of the strap, he began a blur of brutal fury.

"Stop! You're killing her!" I tried to push him away but finally laid on top of her, bracing myself for his next blow.

"Get out of the way!" He stood over me shaking, this little man barely taller than I.

Belit rolled to her side. "Get off me," she said. Welts and cuts oozed through her clothing.

Dohd dropped the strap, grasped my collar, and pulled me to within a handbreadth of his face. "I love you, Meshullemeth, but I won't let your carelessness jeopardize our future. Belit will bear the pain for every mistake you make. Take her to your chamber and count her wounds—because if you're banned from class, she'll have more to tend tomorrow."

Belit groaned, trying to stand. I placed her arm around my shoulder, and she cried out. "I'm sorry," I whispered.

I shuddered—Belit was as vulnerable as I in this world of gods and kings.

"You'll need to fix the evening meal, Shulle, since Belit seems unlikely to do so." Dohd positioned a cushion behind his desk, reached for a scroll, and began reading. "And you can bring me a cup of wine before you tend her wounds. All that activity made me thirsty."

In that moment, I'd never hated anyone the way I despised Lord Shebna.

~

Sleep held me a willing captive, though I grew aware of someone in my chamber.

"Wake, Shulle. You must wake."

I jolted upright and focused on Belit's mat across the room. She lay quiet, her wounds bandaged with turmeric and honey.

"The king has summoned you, Shulle." Dohd's voice was a purr.

I screamed, scooting away until the wall stopped my retreat. Hugging my knees tight, I glanced at Belit and back to her abuser.

He lifted a dim lamp in one hand, illuminating his unnatural smile. "I love you more than the day I first saw you, and I'll protect you from harm." He moved closer. "Sometimes we must protect each other because we're family, you and me. The only family we have."

"I have Abba." I lifted my chin.

"No, Shulle, I'm afraid you don't." The lamp flickered, casting ghoulish shadows across his face.

Panicked, I reached for the box where I kept the scrolls Abba had sent me. I grabbed the last one, dated over two months ago, and a wave of nausea stole my words.

"You look pale, my girl."

"What have you done?" I said in barely a whisper.

"I've done what was necessary." He pushed a different box toward me. Opening the lid, he revealed every message I'd written to Abba—all unsent. "I couldn't allow your abba to think you missed him even a little, or he would have found his way back to Jerusalem." He pointed to my box of letters. "But I allowed you to read his messages. You see? I'm not heartless, Shulle."

My fears gave way to a sense of betrayal. "How dare you—"

He grabbed my robe and pulled me to within a handbreadth of his face. "My brother is alive only because I allow it. Your abba will remain safe in Jotbah if you do as I say. Is that clear?" Hate burned through my veins but leaked out in tears. I nodded. "Good," he said with a smile thoroughly evil and true. "Baka, Nasseh's personal guard, is waiting in my study to escort you to the young king's chamber. It seems the gods are giving you a chance to sway the king before the classroom decision is made. King Hezekiah was delayed in court, so he and Manasseh couldn't have had time to collaborate about your class attendance. We still have time."

Was he completely mad? "You are asking me to seduce the eleven-year-old king and believe his righteous abba will allow me to remain in the classroom?"

"Don't be stupid, Meshullemeth," Dohd snapped. "Hezi need never know."

"Of course, he would know. Nasseh can't keep secrets."

A shadow of fear darkened his features just before he grabbed my arm and hauled me toward the door. Belit's head rose from her square of lamb's wool as we left the chamber, but it seemed she was too weak—or too afraid—to intervene.

Dohd dragged me down the hall and into his study where Nasseh's guard waited. "Why is my niece being summoned to King Manasseh's bedchamber?"

The man answered with a sneer. "A king commands, and we obey, Lord Shebna—without question."

Dohd's grip on my arm tightened, and he turned slowly to face me, his back to the guard. "Remember, Shulle, your abba and I love you. Family protects each other."

And suddenly I knew. Dohd wasn't afraid for me. He feared his end if I betrayed him—and Abba was his security that kept me faithful. Burdened with reality, I feigned an embrace and whispered, "Someday, you'll be sorry."

He kissed my cheek and turned to Baka. "No need to whisper, my girl. Baka and other faithful Grove worshipers anxiously await Manasseh's sole reign. Baka realizes he could be escorting the next queen of Judah."

The guard bowed slightly and extended his hand, as if I didn't know the way to the palace. "My robe!" I looked down at my blue linen, soiled with Belit's blood and turmeric powder. "I can't go to the king's chamber like this." I hurried to my chamber and changed into my green robe. Belit was asleep, but I kissed her forehead. She was warm but not feverish. A good sign that her wounds weren't festering.

On my way through the courtyard, I grabbed a few myrtle leaves and rolled them between my hands. The oil made my hair smell nice for Nasseh, and it helped dull the city stench as Baka and I walked in the damp, night air. Though I'd seen this man every day for as many years as I'd attended class with Nasseh, tonight was the first time I'd ever heard him speak. And I'd never seen him at the Grove. "Tell me, Baka, how long have you worshipped the starry hosts?" I heard nothing but our sandals slapping the cobblestone street and assumed the gruff soldier had refused to answer.

"Since my wife died." Shocked by his gravelly voice, I turned and saw his jaw muscles flexing. "If Yahweh could kill 185,000 Assyrians and give Queen Zibah a son, why wouldn't he save my wife?"

My cheeks warmed. "Have we worshipped together, Baka?"

"Oh no, my lady. Only the wealthiest noblemen sacrifice offerings in your tent." He stood a little straighter. "But I can assure you, I've been faithful and will teach our king to perform the rites properly when the time comes."

When the time comes.

"Baka, why do you think Nasseh summoned me to his chamber in the middle of the night?" We passed through the deserted market and into a darkened alley behind the palace.

"King Manasseh doesn't sleep much," he said finally. "I *think* he just needs a friend." Baka led me to a shrouded entrance, and we began our climb up a narrow, private staircase. My legs burned by the time we reached the top. We entered a small room furnished with only a table, washbasin, lamp, and a straw mat. "This is my chamber," he said. "King Manasseh waits beyond that door. I'll make sure all is well before you enter." Baka disappeared through the door to Nasseh's room, leaving me alone.

Curiosity made me impatient, so I lifted the latch and slowly poked my head inside. A giant hand seized my wrist, and I stared up at the now friendly guard whose grin was almost as wide as his shoulders. "I guessed correctly," he said, opening the door wide. "The king summoned you to play Hounds and Jackals." Nasseh and Kenaz sat on opposite sides of a game board, gleefully unaware I'd arrived. Baka bowed. "It will be an honor to someday call you my queen."

"Thank you." I wasn't sure what else to say. "Does Nasseh know you worship the gods?"

He smiled. "No, but I'm following your example and planting seeds of doubt."

"I'm sure you've done a fine job, Baka." I stood on the threshold between the unadorned servant's quarters and the magnificent chamber of the king, beginning to comprehend the enormity of my part in a plan so much larger than I. Dohd and Belit often said I wasn't alone, that all those in the Grove had a part to play in freeing Judah from Yahweh's chains. Baka was proof they spoke truth. My imaginings of the efforts to free Judah had been like the servant's chamber—simple and stark—when in reality the transition would require commitment as vast as the king's chamber.

"Shulle!" Nasseh jumped to his feet but didn't approach me. He smiled, but fisting betrayed his nerves. "I'm king and can do anything I want," he said. "And I can't sleep, so I want to play Hounds and Jackals with my friends. You look pretty even at night. Kenaz's eyes are bloodshot, and he yawns a lot. He said he's losing because he doesn't think as well when he's tired, but I think I'm just better at Hounds and Jackals."

By the time he finished his nervous chatter, I'd reached the sitting area. Kenaz stood and greeted me with a smile. "We've played three games while waiting on you."

"You can go now." Nasseh had become extremely agitated, rocking and fisting, eyes darting everywhere but at Kenaz and me.

I exchanged a questioning glance with Kenaz and got a shrug in return. "I just arrived, Nasseh. Do you want me to leave?"

"Not you," he said. "Kenaz can go. He's been here long enough. I want to talk with Shulle alone."

Kenaz looked first at me, his cheeks blooming instantly crimson, and back at Nasseh. "Summoning us in the middle of the night is unusual, Nasseh, but it would be inappropriate for you to meet with Shulle alone in your chamber."

"Baka is here," he said. "I am king. I do as I please. Good night, Kenaz. You need to practice Hounds and Jackals so you're a better opponent."

"Nasseh, I don't think I should leave—"

"Baka, I need my basin!" Nasseh's voice rose in near panic, his agitation growing. "Kenaz can go! I want my basin!"

"Shh, Nasseh." I began humming the fish song and nodded Kenaz toward the large double doors I assumed led to the harem. "I'll only stay long enough to calm him," I said to the king's cousin. "I'm his friend just like you, Kenaz. There's nothing inappropriate about it." I chuckled, keeping my tone light. "Besides, you know Nasseh can't lie or keep a secret. Ask him in the morning what happened."

I resumed the fish song, and Kenaz answered with retreating footsteps. When the door clicked shut, Baka placed a small table with a basin on it beside Nasseh and emptied a pitcher of water into it. He then sprinkled a pouch of dried myrtle blossoms on top, their aroma filling my senses. After hanging two towels on a bar attached to the table, he disappeared into his chamber.

Nasseh submerged his hands, closed his eyes, and sighed. "When I can't hear your fish song, the water is almost as good."

Staring at the floating myrtle blossoms, something I couldn't express flooded my heart. "Nasseh, myrtle blossoms are my favorite."

"I know," he said, opening his eyes but focusing on the basin. "After you came to class that first day, I went for a walk in the Garden of Uzza and realized you smelled like myrtle blossoms. I started requesting myrtle blossoms in my washbasin."

"Nasseh, you were only five when I came to your class."

"But I'm smart, Shulle. I always know more than people think I do."

It was true. "May I wash my hands too?" I placed my hands in the water without waiting for his response. Our hands brushed against each other, familiar and tender.

Finally, he said, "Did you know the tides of the sea are determined by the moon and stars, Shulle? The wind and waves obey them."

I picked out a blossom and touched it to his cheek, his nose, his lips. "Yes, Nasseh, and did you know both Assyrian and Babylonian kings gain clear answers through an āšipūtu—someone who consults the starry hosts?"

Surprised, he lifted his eyes to meet mine, but only for a moment. "I want you to advise me, Shulle. Forever. Maybe you should be an āšipūtu." Turning away, he grabbed a towel, dried his hands, and sat down beside the game board. "Do you know how to play Hounds and Jackals, or must I teach you?"

"You must teach me, my king." Sitting down opposite him, I only half listened while contemplating the similarities between the stark servant's chamber and the unadorned innocence I'd glimpsed through the windows of Nasseh's soul. His innermost self bore the same unadorned efficiency—a table and washbasin but no tapestries to hide selfish motives. His every thought lay exposed by unfiltered words, and every word was unmitigated truth. In contrast, Dohd and others in Judah's court thrived on lavish deceptions. I was but one piece of furniture in their elaborate decor. I wanted no part in their grand plan. I just hoped to protect this tender boy who wanted nothing more than to play with his friends because he couldn't sleep.

I noticed the brightening sky through the balcony curtains, and Dohd's threat replayed in my mind. *Your abba will remain safe in Jotbah if you do as I say.*

I had to leave with a promise. "You say you want me with you forever, Nasseh, but if I'm banished from our class, I must return to Jotbah and marry."

Startled, he abandoned his instructions and met my gaze again. "You will remain in class, and you will marry me."

"Your abba would never allow you to marry me, Nasseh," I said gently. "We'll have to wait until you reign alone." He looked away at the mention of his abba's death. His rocking started again, and I gathered his hands in mine. "I've heard of a Babylonian āšipūtu in Jerusalem. Perhaps she could overpower Isaiah's curse on your abba and defeat Yahweh."

He stopped rocking but didn't look up. "You think Saba Isaiah cursed my abba? And you're willing to fight Yahweh to save him?"

Caution halted me. Compassion prodded me. Though I truly believed Yahweh and his followers were destroying Judah, I couldn't risk discovery or endanger Nasseh with too much truth. "I believe in you, Manasseh ben Hezekiah. And whether your sole reign begins in one year or ten or twenty, I will stay beside you." I cradled his cheeks and kissed his forehead.

He sat back, grinning. "When I marry you, Shulle, we will kiss like Abba and Ima."

I giggled. "Yes, Nasseh—"

"Lady Shulle." Baka cleared his throat, standing a few paces away. "The sun will rise shortly. It's time for goodbyes."

Nasseh reached for my hand as I stood to go. "I'll see you later—in class."

"Thank you." I gave him another peck on the cheek. It was only a boy's promise, but Nasseh was a boy like no other.

10

Now then, my sons, listen to me. . . .
Keep to a path far from her,
　　do not go near the door of her house,
lest you lose your honor to others
　　and your dignity to one who is cruel.

PROVERBS 5:7–9

For the second night in a row, Zibah had lain awake, battling fear about her son's future. She'd prayed, begged, and cajoled the Maker of the heavens, but still Yahweh remained silent. *Why won't You show me how to protect him?*

When Hezi woke, he seemed agitated too. His court cases ran late last night, and he'd come to their chamber after Zibah was already in bed. She'd feigned sleep, refusing to ask the question burning on her heart. Refusing to ask, that is, until they sat down to break their fast. "Why did you give in so easily to Nasseh and allow Shulle to remain in class? You didn't even consult me."

"I consulted my co-ruler, and Judah's *kings* made their decision. We must rule together so he'll learn how to rule alone."

"He's a child, Hezi. You must—"

"He's brilliant, Zibah, and he's in authority over every person in that classroom—including you." He popped a candied date into his mouth and chewed while finishing his rant. "Perhaps if you would actually *listen* when he spoke instead of trying to make him say what you want, you'd discover he has interesting things in his head." He shoved his plate away and left the table.

"That's not fair, Hezi." Zibah chased him toward the door. "How much time do you spend with him? How often do you listen? Don't tell me what's in his head when I'm the one who—"

He grabbed her, startling her to silence. Searching her eyes, he covered her mouth with an impassioned kiss until his tension eased. He pulled away but tenderly cupped her cheeks. "You're right. What I said wasn't fair, but it's true of us both. We *both* need to listen more to our son. We're losing him, Zibah. I feel it, too, but I don't think removing Shulle—the only one who understands him—is the way to win his trust." He brushed her lips with a second kiss. "I'm sorry. I hate fighting with you, but I've got an early hearing in court."

And he was gone. Men always left with the last word, and Zibah was tired of it. She called for a messenger and wrote a quick note to summon Shebna before class. She downed her last bite of gruel and still no Shebna. She called for another messenger, then saw her son's tutor strolling toward her chamber. Finally!

Fury clipped her words. "Inside, Shebna." One of her guards started to follow, but Zibah stopped him. "I'll speak with Lord Shebna alone." The guard raised his brows but closed the door. She never met with a man alone in her chamber—unless it was Abba or her brother, Jashub. "I must ask you to remove Shulle from class. My son can't see the wisdom of it, so we must make the decision for him."

Shebna cocked his head. "Is King Hezekiah also unable to see your wisdom, Queen Hephzibah? I was told Shulle will remain in class."

"Who told you?"

"Shulle—after King Manasseh told her—when he summoned her to his chamber last night."

Dread closed Zibah's throat like a coiling snake. "What?"

"The young king couldn't sleep, so he summoned *both* his friends— Kenaz and Shulle—to his chamber last night to play Hounds and Jackals. While Shulle was there, he told her she would remain in class. We assumed King Hezekiah was in agreement." He wrinkled his brow. "Why would you—an adoring ima—ask me to remove one of your son's only two friends?"

"This isn't a game, Shebna." She stepped away, hiding her indecision. Abba said they'd know when the time was right to reveal his vision. Surely, if Shebna knew what was at stake, he'd be vigilant. "Abba experienced a vision two nights ago that will affect us all after Hezi's death." Zibah looked to see his reaction.

The man offered a patronizing smile. "My queen, you realize Isaiah's prophecies aren't always correct. Please don't allow his ravings to upset you so."

Her anger flared at the pomposity of the male species. "Nasseh will someday saw Abba in half, Shebna. Should I or should I not be upset about that?"

Eyes narrowing, he changed from fawning tutor to furious protector. "Manasseh would never do such a thing! You of all people know that your son, though not demonstrative in his emotion, is never intentionally cruel." He scoffed. "Isaiah is wrong. He's been wrong before, and he's wrong about his grandson. Isaiah ben Amoz should be ashamed."

Zibah suddenly wondered if Shebna was a better ima than she. But Abba's visions were accurate. "He was right when 185,000 Assyrians died outside Jerusalem's gates."

"And he was wrong when he thought Hezekiah was the anointed king described in his prophecies."

She refused to calculate Abba's wins and losses. "I will remove anyone or anything that is detrimental to my son's devotion to Yahweh, and I believe Shulle is making him question Yahweh's goodness."

"And as his ima you have every right to your opinion, but please don't allow Isaiah's prejudice against me to punish my niece. Your abba wields his prophecies as a political weapon whenever he disapproves of—"

"That's not true!"

"It is true, and you know it!" Shebna paused and massaged the back of his neck. "Please forgive me, my queen, but allow me one question." He looked up, and Zibah nodded. "If you're so certain Isaiah's vision is true, how will removing Shulle from Manasseh's presence prevent it from happening?"

Abba's words rang in her memory. *"This is my calling, daughter, to die with Yahweh's testimony on my lips."* Was there truly nothing she could do to stop it? Zibah turned away again, refusing to let him see her despair. He was right. In all of it. And she should never have told him about the vision. "You may go, Shebna."

She heard the chamber door close and fell to her knees. *Yahweh, how can Abba's death at my son's hand be Your will?* Hearing nothing but silence, she felt as if she'd been washed into the darkness by a giant wave.

PART 2

Manasseh was twelve years old when he became king, and he reigned in Jerusalem fifty-five years.

⸏ 2 KINGS 21:1 ⸏

11

Observe . . . and celebrate the Passover of the
LORD your God, because in the month of Aviv
he brought you out of Egypt by night. Sacrifice . . . an animal from your flock or herd at
the place the LORD will choose as a dwelling for
his Name. Do not eat it with bread made with
yeast, but for seven days eat unleavened bread.

DEUTERONOMY 16:1–3

Spring—686 BC, Twenty-Ninth Year of Hezekiah's Reign

N asseh stood at his bedchamber window, looking out over the
Garden of Uzza. Matti was supposed to arrive at dawn. He
was late. Dohd Matti was always late. Nasseh liked prompt.
"Any word on Abba's condition?" he asked his steward.

"King Hezekiah has made a miraculous recovery, my king." He hurried to Nasseh's side, keeping his voice low. "Lord Shebna spoke with the
new physician moments ago. The man removed Lady Shulle's charm from
beneath your abba's pillow before it was detected. Her incantations were
effective, my king. Lord Isaiah's curse has been broken."

The good news lessened the prickly feeling on his cheeks and quieted
the noise in his mind. Cat purred in the sun beneath his gentle strokes. "I
mustn't tell Abba about Shulle's charm. She got it from the Babylonian
āšipūtu in Jerusalem when I was scared and asked her to find a cure. I must
not tell the secret. How can I—"

"Shh, my king." The steward slipped a robe around his shoulders as the noise in Nasseh's head grew louder. "Think about today's Passover celebration," the man said, brushing cat hair off his shoulders.

"I hate Passover." He stroked Cat harder. The Passover lamb in the corner of his chamber bleated, grating on his nerves. "Did you feed the lamb yet?"

"Not yet, my king." The steward continued dressing him, choosing a jeweled belt, collar, and metal cuffs.

"Don't forget to feed it."

"I wouldn't dare, my king."

Nasseh had lived with the animal's stench while tending it for the last four days as the Law required. Cat licked her paws. Why couldn't sheep be as clean as cats? "Passover is an obsolete festival to an impotent god imposing archaic rules intended to control the masses."

"Well said, my king."

Nasseh stepped away from the steward's brushing, eyes averted. "Do you like Passover?"

"I don't like that you must kill the lamb today, my king, when you feel so strongly against it."

"I don't want to cut its throat!" Nasseh shouted above the clamoring in his head. "I'd rather worship Gula, the healer, since she saved Abba from Yahweh's curse."

"Shh!" The steward hushed him, and Baka appeared at the curtain.

"My king, you must whisper," his guard commanded.

Why must he whisper when there was an āšipūtu in Jerusalem who had proven stronger than Yahweh? When Abba fell mortally ill four days ago, Ima was certain Saba Isaiah's prophecy was being fulfilled. But the prophecy of fifteen years ago was imprecise. Did the countdown begin the day that prophecy was given? Or was it to be figured on the years of Abba's reign? How would death come? Another illness? A miraculous conveyance like the prophet Elijah's fiery chariot? But if the starry hosts proved more powerful than Saba's tired prophecy and worn-out god, Abba could live a normal life span.

"I don't want to whisper, Baka. I want Abba to live."

His guard approached and braced Nasseh's shoulders. "I pray your abba lives a long life, my king, but until you reign alone on Judah's throne, you must never speak of any god but Yahweh. Promise me."

"What if we speak of gods in our classroom? Sometimes Shebna teaches us of other gods and—"

He sighed. "Never speak of another god as more powerful than Yahweh, Nasseh, or of your desire for other gods. It's not safe."

The steward approached with an uncovered pot of vinegar. Cat hissed and absconded as the man dipped a cloth in the stinking liquid. "You have a few blemishes, my king."

He dabbed Nasseh's chin. *Blemishes.* Nasseh was a blemish in Abba's legacy, an inferior child to humble the "second Solomon." Inferior in Yahwists' eyes, but in Shebna's eyes Nasseh was exceptional. Worthy of Judah's throne. To him, Nasseh wasn't a second anything. "Shulle and Kenaz are my friends."

"Indeed, they are." The steward dabbed more vinegar around his nose. "Master Kenaz is close as a brother, and Lady Shulle is a beauty." The steward lowered his vinegar pot and offered a polished bronze hand mirror. "There. Your blemishes will be gone when Passover begins at twilight."

"Where's my favorite nephew?" The booming voice preceded Dohd Matti, Abba's brother, through the curtain. He halted, mouth agape. "I'm sorry, sir. I must be in the wrong chamber. I was looking for the boy king, Manasseh, but I must have stumbled into a man's chamber."

"Dohd Matti, it's me. Nasseh."

His smile dimmed. Was he angry or sad? Shulle's drawings couldn't make that distinction, so Nasseh still had a hard time differentiating.

"I was teasing, Nasseh." He crossed the room with arms open for an embrace.

"No, thank you." Nasseh stepped back to avoid contact. "A bow will suffice."

Matti's smile flattened again. Twice now. Not a good reunion. "You've grown a half cubit since I saw you last Passover. You're massive, boy. No soldier in his right mind would dare cross swords with you."

"I'm skinny and barely reach Abba's shoulder." Why did Matti lie so frequently? "How was your journey from Lachish? What did you bring me this year?"

"Because you are twelve and a child no longer, Manasseh ben Hezekiah, I brought a gift only a man would appreciate." He called out an odd-sounding word, and a red-haired woman appeared at his side. "I found her in a captive train on my way home from Egypt last month. She can be your first concubine."

Nasseh saw only the silver rings on her toes and bangles on her ankles. "I don't want a woman. I want Shulle." He hurried to his washbasin, splashing his hands amid the myrtle blossoms and rocking from left foot to right. "Tell her to go, Matti. Tell her to go."

Sandals shuffled. Whispers. "She's gone, Nasseh." A hand rested on his shoulder. "She's gone. I'm sorry. I liked girls by the time I was twelve."

"I like *one* girl," Nasseh said, head still lowered. "Shulle."

"So I'm gathering, you sly dog." He wrapped Nasseh's neck with one arm and ruffled his hair.

"I'm not a dog." Nasseh shrugged him off but couldn't stop a smile. Dohd laughed loud and long. Nasseh didn't mind this time. Matti was the only one besides Shulle who treated him like a man—like a king—not a child. "What else did you bring me?" Nasseh asked.

"What makes you think I brought you something else?"

"You always bring me many gifts."

"Baka!" Matti shouted and pulled back the curtain. "I brought this." Nasseh's guard appeared with a shiny sword, perched like a newborn on extended hands. "It will protect you in battle," Matti explained, "but I've brought something far more valuable." He removed a small, embroidered pouch attached to his belt. "Since you're a man, you must learn how to keep secrets."

"I'm already keeping one secret. Abba was sick from Saba Isaiah's curse, but Shulle found an āšipūtu and put a charm under his pillow that broke Yahweh's power."

Matti's eyes bulged. "That's quite a secret," he said, looking at Baka and back at Nasseh. "You should definitely not tell anyone else. I like Shulle more and more, but if you hope to win her heart, you'll need this." He placed the bag in Nasseh's hand. It was heavy.

Nasseh opened the cinched string at the top and withdrew a figurine of a woman, hands cupping large breasts. His cheeks felt warm and prickly. "What is it?"

"Ishtar, patron goddess of love and war." He slapped Nasseh's back again. "You'll need her favor when you love a woman, but you must never tell anyone I gave her to you."

Nasseh carefully replaced the goddess into her ornate pouch. "Thank you, Matti. I have something for you too."

"A gift? For me?" Matti clapped, then he rubbed his hands together. He was three times Nasseh's age but more like a child. "What is it?"

Nasseh hid his new golden goddess and retrieved the forbidden item from a basket underneath his bed. "The cooks refused to serve me anything with yeast because of Passover, so Shulle brought this sweet bread last night when we played Hounds and Jackals." He offered up the small folded bundle. "She made it with candied dates—her favorite thing in the world."

"I thought you were her favorite thing in the world." Matti unwrapped the forbidden delicacy, took a bite, and groaned at the sticky goodness. "This is far better than my gifts." He bowed. "Thank you, my king. I'm humbled by your thoughtfulness."

Nasseh studied his face. Was he being silly again? Lying? Or serious this time?

He finished the bread and wiped his mouth. "Are you sure this Shulle is the right woman to be your queen?"

"Absolutely. Shebna says every king must have one wife he trusts."

Matti laughed so loud, the priests at the temple probably heard him. "Never trust a woman, my boy! Never."

Nasseh waited until Matti grew quiet. "I trust Shulle completely, Matti. She is beautiful, but she is also kind."

A strange expression wiped away Dohd's smile. "You're a good kid, Nasseh. Did you know that?"

"I'm a man, remember?"

Matti drew him into a tight hug, and Nasseh allowed it. Only for a moment. Then he nudged him away. "I asked Abba again if you could stand with us in the temple's inner court, but he said no. Only kings and priests in the inner court."

"Of course. I'm only a prince. I'll stand in the portico with your ima and her family." Matti's voice had gotten louder, which Shulle said was a sign that a person was angry.

Nasseh looked into his eyes. "I'm sorry they hate you, Dohd."

He smiled. Why would he smile about that? "Yes, Nasseh. They hate me." He jostled Nasseh's shoulder. "I should go and officially greet my big brother, but I'll cheer you on from the portico while you preside over your first Passover."

He left quickly, and Nasseh took his new sword from Baka. "I want a jeweled leather belt made for this, but I'll use a borrowed belt for the ceremony at dusk."

Baka bowed. "The priests won't allow a weapon into the inner court, my king."

"I am king, and I will wear a sword. We'll hide it under my outer cloak at my back."

Baka left, and Nasseh's steward resumed his preparation. "Don't forget to feed the lamb," Nasseh reminded him.

"I wouldn't dare, my king."

"I hate Passover."

"Hmm. Perhaps someday you'll abolish it."

The thought had never occurred to him. "I wish I could abolish it before I have to slit that lamb's throat at twilight."

12

Hezekiah sent word to all Israel and Judah . . .
inviting them to come to the temple of the
LORD in Jerusalem and celebrate the Passover
to the LORD. . . . in the second month.

2 CHRONICLES 30:1–2

Zibah had dismissed their servants earlier, providing her and Hezi with a quiet afternoon alone after his four-day bout with the mysterious illness. They lounged on the couch together. She could see that Hezi's eyelids were heavy with fatigue. "Are you sure you feel well enough to attend tonight's Passover celebration?" she asked.

He sat up and scrubbed his face. He'd met with his younger brother earlier. Even at his strongest, a reunion with Mattaniah was draining. "Watching Nasseh preside over his first Passover will be life giving, my love." With a sigh, he glanced at her with a wry grin. "I'm glad Matti lives in Lachish and that we've chosen Eliakim and your abba to be Nasseh's advisors when I'm gone."

Zibah shot off the couch to choose a robe for the ceremony, ignoring the morbid comment. Couldn't they celebrate his miraculous healing and enjoy one day without the shadow of uncertainty? She was nervous enough about Matti's visit. They suspected he followed in his abba's footsteps and dabbled in pagan worship, but there had been no proof when Hezi investigated claims against him. Each Passover Hezi considered ordering him to remain in Lachish since he seemed to loathe celebrating with the family, but the memory of their ima's return to Yahweh late in her life made Hezi continue reaching out to Matti's lost soul. Since Matti had never married, Nasseh was a tremendous joy in his lonely world.

"Did Matti say what present he brought Nasseh this year?" Indecision kept her staring at four silk robes in her wardrobe.

"Let me help you choose." He hopped off the couch, obviously avoiding her question about Matti's gift, and grabbed the red robe. Nudging her toward the full-length bronze mirror, he held it up in front of her. "What do you think?"

She glared at him in the reflection. "The gift."

He grinned and placed the light blue robe in front of her, effectively wrapping her in both arms. "You're right. Red is too bold for Passover. Matti gave Nasseh a Hittite sword. Blue is peaceful."

"No, Hezi!" She broke out of his grasp. "Nasseh can't keep a sword in his chamber."

"The peaceful blue robe it is." He kissed her nose. "Our son begins military training as soon as the feast ends."

She turned away.

He rested his hands on her shoulders. "He's growing up, Zibah. You must let go. He is king—*your* king—and now a man of age. You no longer have the right to command him."

"But he's my *son*!" She whirled on him, the heat of a furnace burning in her veins.

Her husband's quivering chin betrayed his emotion. "Nasseh will always be our son, Hephzibah, but our time to train him is swiftly coming to an end. We must place him in Yahweh's hand and trust the only one who can teach him from the inside out."

Zibah fell into Hezi's arms, holding him like the lifeline he was. One month ago, he'd begun the twenty-ninth year of his reign—the last of Yahweh's fifteen-year gift. Abba's prophecy had given no detail about the exact date or circumstance of Hezi's death, so when the high fever came on the night they'd chosen the Passover lamb, Zibah was certain Yahweh would take him. After a few days of delirium and suffering— another miracle. *How much longer now, Yahweh?* The questions had become an insatiable worm, eating away at her nerves, her strength, her sanity.

"Do you remember the first Passover we celebrated together?" Hezi whispered.

She laughed through her tears and pulled away from him, wiping her eyes. "Yes. It was awful!"

"Yes, I suppose it was in some ways." He laughed with her. "You were desperately angry that I'd invited our northern tribes because of what they'd done to your parents—"

"And because I still carry the scars of their captivity." She pulled up her sleeve, exposing the brand of a pagan god burned into her flesh by enemy soldiers when she was a little girl.

He lifted her arm to his lips and kissed the hideous mark. "My scars are on the inside," he said, "but our scars made that first Passover richer, Zibah. The blacker the darkness, the brighter God's spark."

She kept her head bowed. "I fear your death will be a darkness that swallows me whole."

He swept her into his arms. "Yahweh will protect and provide for you, my love. He will be your Sword, your Shield, and your—" He gasped. "He's your Bridegroom, Zibah. Remember the promise?" He stared down at her with awe, but all she felt was rising resentment.

"Those are fine words, Hezekiah, but you'll be in paradise, and I must live here without you."

"I've read your abba's account of *Hephzibah,* the prophecy he was given the night he renamed you. Do you remember what it says?"

"Of course, I remember."

"Say it."

She hesitated, stubborn in her grief.

"Say it!" he insisted.

"I don't remember every word."

"If Nasseh were here, he could recite it for us." They chuckled together.

She began speaking the parts of Abba's prophecy she could recall. "No longer will you be called *Ishma* or your land deserted; but you'll be named *Hephzibah* and your land called Beulah for the Lord will take delight in you. As a young man marries a young woman, so your Builder will marry you . . ." Her breath caught. "My Builder. Hezi. Yahweh will be my Builder—"

"And then the Lord said," he continued for her, "'I have posted watchmen on your walls, Jerusalem; they will never be silent day or night. You who call on the LORD, give yourselves no rest, and give *him* no rest till he establishes Jerusalem and makes her the praise of the earth.'" He lifted her hands to his lips. "When I leave you, Zibah, watchmen will be posted on the walls around you, interceding day and night. Your Bridegroom will never leave you, but neither should you give Him rest until He fulfills every good promise He's so graciously given."

Whispered affection, a husband's strong hands, and a wife's soft touch drew them together in the one-flesh expression that had carried them through both sorrow and celebration. Today, when life felt too short, they let the shadows grow long before leaving their bed to commemorate the day in their nation's history when Yahweh took Egypt's firstborn sons to ransom His people from bondage.

Hezi placed the gold crown on his wife's head. "We must pray for our son, my love. I can tell Nasseh is nervous about making the sacrifice for our household this year."

Zibah had sensed their gentle son's reluctance as well—another reason the vision of him ordering his saba sawn in half seemed too outrageous to imagine. They left their chamber and reached the end of their private hall at the exact moment Nasseh led their family's Passover lamb down the harem stairs. His guard corralled the animal from behind while Matti, Jashub, Yaira, and Kenaz followed at a distance, careful to mask their amusement.

Nasseh met his abba's gaze for a moment but quickly looked away. "I'll be glad to be rid of this beast." His bluster was undoubtedly a cover for his apprehension.

The royal family exited the palace through the servants' entry and meandered north to the Gate of the Guard, a private entrance for the king's household and Levites serving at the temple.

Zibah and the others halted as Hezi, Nasseh, and their lamb prepared to enter the inner courts. She squeezed her husband's hand. "We'll meet you in the banquet hall after the sacrifice. Cook has prepared enough to include Abba, Eliakim, and his family as well."

She bent to kiss Nasseh's forehead, but he pulled away. "Ima, not in public."

"Forgive me," she said. "You've been my child for twelve years. You've been a man for considerably less time. Give me time to adjust." Bowing to her son, Zibah exchanged a knowing grin with Hezi and led the others toward the outer court.

Eliakim leaned over the stone railing of the southern portico and waved to them. "We're up here with Lord Isaiah." Zibah led her brother, Yaira, and Kenaz up the stairs to join the others on the elevated porch.

From their bird's-eye view, they watched pilgrims pass through every city gate for the highest and holiest celebration of their year. The sun was sinking below the horizon, the time for sacrifice drawing near. Lambs bleating and the crowd's loud hum was enough to set Zibah's teeth on edge. She looked for Nasseh on the inner court below to gauge how he was managing the noise and confusion.

He and Hezi climbed the steps of a giant platform on which the brazen altar was elevated atop even more stairs, making its flames visible and the aroma of sacrifice rise high enough to reach all those gathered to worship. Hezi engaged the high priest, Azariah, in conversation as they stood on the platform, while Nasseh craned his neck toward the eastern portico. Zibah followed his gaze and spotted Shebna chatting with other noblemen, but Nasseh's eyes were locked on Shulle—as they often were.

Yaira leaned over, raising her voice to be heard above the noise. "Has Hezi told Nasseh yet about the match he's considering with Pharaoh Tirhakah's daughter?"

She shook her head. "No, but he must tell him soon. The longer he waits, the more devastated both Nasseh and Shulle will be. I fear they both have unrealistic expectations of a relationship beyond the classroom."

"A similar situation occurred with a prince named Hezekiah and his classmate Ishma." Yaira's smirk disarmed Zibah, but before she could fuss, the shofar sounded, drawing their attention back to the altar.

Mattaniah hurried up the portico stairs, huffing and bedraggled as if he'd just risen from his bed. "I'm sorry I'm late," he said, squeezing past everyone to stand next to Zibah. His eyes were bloodshot, and he smelled of stale wine. Eliakim, his wife, and three sons lined the rail on Zibah's right, their family a modicum of grace and peace. Zibah breathed a heavy sigh, wishing for the kind of peace Abba spoke of in his prophecies. She let her eyes wander back to the annual reminder of Yahweh's rescue from bondage.

"And when your children ask you, 'What does this ceremony mean to you?'"—Azariah's voice poured over the gathering, amplified by the bowl-shaped walls of Hezi's addition to the courts—"then tell them, 'It is the Passover sacrifice to the LORD, who passed over the houses of the Israelites in Egypt and spared our homes when he struck down the Egyptians.'"

The high priest, Hezi, and Nasseh stood at the edge of the raised altar. Hezi gave Nasseh his dagger and held the lamb while Azariah placed a golden bowl beneath its throat, waiting for Nasseh to make the cut. Instead, Judah's co-ruler discarded the dagger and—in a single, fluid motion—produced a sword concealed beneath his cloak, surprising both priest and king.

Zibah cast an accusatory glance at her brother-in-law, but Matti held up both hands. "I didn't know he'd bring it to the ceremony."

The crowd's single horrified gasp drew Zibah's attention back to the altar. Her first sight was the lamb scampering free of Hezi's grasp. Then her husband teetered on one foot at the platform's edge, arms extended like a dove in flight. His body fell slowly, as if reluctant to embark on the fated journey. He reached for Nasseh on his descent from the altar platform—the height of three grown men—before crashing, headfirst, to the limestone floor.

The air was silent, except for the bleating of Passover lambs. Hezekiah ben Ahaz lay motionless on the inner court. There was no question. Zibah's husband was dead.

In the blink of an eye—ready or not—Yahweh posted His watchmen and became her Builder.

The sound of rending garments, magnified by thousands, seemed to be the sound of her own chest being torn. Wailing assaulted her from all directions. She covered her ears and crumpled to the portico floor, gasping great gulps but getting no air. Then her mind seized one thought.

"Manasseh!" Zibah shot to her feet and gripped the railing. How would he cope?

Her son stood like a stone at the edge of the platform, sword still in his hand, staring down at his abba.

She pushed past her family. "Get out of my way!" She shrugged off hands that grabbed at her as she skittered down the portico steps. Chaos erupted around her. More wailing. Voices shouting Hezi's name. Screams. Zibah rushed toward the inner court's gate but stared through the iron bars at a commotion at the south gate. She could see that Manasseh was fixated on something, sword still in his hand. He followed two temple guards toward the eastern gate.

"Nasseh!" Zibah's cry was lost in the tempest of confusion. And then she saw her son's only focus amid the turmoil. Shulle, held between two temple guards, screeching his name, kicking and clawing to reach him. Nasseh's normally placid face was twisted with rage as he neared the guards restraining her. He raised his sword.

"Nasseh, no!" Zibah screamed and turned away.

The crowd again grew still, and the sound of a sword clanging on stone mingled with Shulle's whimpering. Zibah forced her eyes open and found Nasseh holding Shulle in his arms. Four unharmed guards knelt before him, heads bowed. Relief flowed through her like an ocean tide—until Judah's king escorted Shulle *through* Yahweh's holy inner court, making a wide arc around Hezi's lifeless form toward the gate meant for royalty.

Zibah stepped back, allowing the guards to open the iron gate, and she reached for Nasseh's arm the moment he stepped from the temple court. Pulling away, he shouted, "This is the last Passover Judah will ever celebrate!" And he marched with Shulle toward the palace.

13

Manasseh was twelve years old when he became
king, and he reigned in Jerusalem fifty-five years.
His mother's name was Hephzibah.

2 KINGS 21:1

I thought I'd broken Lord Isaiah's curse when King Hezekiah's illness left him, but the moment I saw him stumble backward, I knew. Yahweh had somehow overpowered Gula, the merciful healer, in the heavenlies.

Would Nasseh blame himself—or me?

When he approached me in the temple court with his sword and two guards, I worried he might arrest me. Instead, he came to save me—and suffered public humiliation because of me by being disarmed by temple guards. I had no idea he'd take me through the inner court. No idea he'd shout at Queen Zibah or cease future Passover celebrations. I couldn't look at the dear woman. My heart broke for her and her son.

Baka followed Nasseh and me from the temple, through the royal garden, into the servants' entrance, and up the back stairs. Nasseh's focus remained forward, his expression calm, but his whole body shivered like a leaf in winter winds.

When we entered his private chamber, Baka dismissed all the servants and spoke to his chamber guards outside the main door. Nasseh stared out the open balcony. Silent.

I could almost hear Belit's voice. *Now is the moment for which you've been trained.* Without speaking, I slipped my fingers into Nasseh's hand. He didn't embrace them but neither did he resist. I led him to his bedchamber. The black cat sunbathed in the window. Nasseh pulled me to-ward it and began stroking its back while gazing at the garden below. I removed his outer cloak and hung it on a peg. Then his belt, his gold collar, necklaces, bracelets, and crown. Finally, I pushed the heavy dark-purple robe from his shoulders. It fell to the floor with a thud.

His eyes squeezed shut, and in his thin linen tunic, he looked like any other twelve-year-old boy. The tear rolling down his cheek, however, re-minded me he was also a son who had lost his abba. I knew that bone-deep ache.

The silly fish song played in my mind. Distraction. It was a glorious balm to heal—or at least to help forget. I attempted a broken melody through a throat tightened by emotion and led Nasseh to his bed. I pressed on his shoulders. He sat, gazing at the floor, shoulders rigid.

I filled his water basin from the pitcher beside it, slung a towel over my shoulder, and knelt before my king. Lifting his right foot into the basin, I began washing the dirt from his feet. After wiping them dry, I pushed aside the basin and pressed a kiss against each knee.

The silly song had become a repetitious hum. A chant allowing my thoughts to run free. I had defiled the temple by walking across the inner court. Would Manasseh be disciplined? Would I? Nasseh was king. Who could condemn him? But the priests could condemn me.

I startled when he touched me, and the fish song died on my lips. He pulled me onto his bed, and we lay on our sides, facing each other.

His eyes followed the path of his finger, which traced my arm, my shoulder, my jaw. "I killed my abba, Shulle." Words as lifeless as his expression.

"No, Nasseh. It was an accident. He stumbled."

"Abba always held the lamb *and* made the cut." He lifted himself on one elbow, still tracing the lines of my form. "I was too weak to do either. If I were stronger, the lamb would be dead and my abba alive." He squeezed his eyes closed. "Saba Isaiah said his god would kill Abba. I just never thought he'd use me to do it."

I wanted to reassure him, but Belit said to never argue with powerful men, so I swirled his dark-brown curls around my finger, allowing my touch to comfort him.

His eyes found mine. "The temple guard tried to keep you from me, Shulle. He'll pay for taking my sword." He looked away, but I'd seen something dangerous. "I'll never show weakness in front of my people again."

"You weren't weak, Nasseh. You stood up to—"

He sat up, turning his back. "When the thirty days of mourning for Abba are complete, we'll marry." He paused before adding. "If you'll still have me."

Had I truly heard the words? "What if your ima or saba Isaiah forbids it?"

He scooted off the bed and returned to the window, his fists clenching nervously. "I am a man now, Shulle, the sole reigning king of Judah. No one forbids me anything."

The statement drew me off the bed, and I slid my arms around his waist. "I would be honored to be your wife, Manasseh ben Hezekiah."

The sound of wailing grew louder, drawing our attention out the window. The Passover crowd wandered the streets, robes torn, dirt and ashes on their heads. Nasseh reached for my hand. "Stay with me, Shulle. I don't want to be alone."

I squeezed his hand lightly. "I'd like that very much." My life task was well on its way, but I was surprised to discover I needed Nasseh as much as he needed me. "What would you like to do to pass the time?" He had been pleased with my kisses, but it hardly seemed right to take our first taste of pleasure on the day of Hezekiah's death.

He released my hand and moved toward the curtain. "Baka! Shulle and I will play Hounds and Jackals. Fetch the board and pieces." He glanced at me. "After I beat you soundly in a few rounds, I want to hear all you know of this Babylonian āšipūtu and her gods. Yahweh is no longer the god of Judah, Shulle. I will maintain our nation's traditions but seek the world's most powerful gods."

Baka arrived with the game board and pieces. "Thank you," I said.

"Would you bring us a fresh basin and pitcher of water with myrtle blossoms?" I'd noticed Nasseh's agitation increasing again. Setting aside the board, I took his hands in mine and rested my forehead against his shoulder. "Now that you are the sole ruler of Judah, I can confess to you, my king . . ." I felt his muscles tighten, but I continued, "Dohd Shebna's maid is the Babylonian āšipūtu, and *I* am her apprentice. I can teach you everything about the powerful starry hosts."

14

Do I eat the flesh of bulls
 or drink the blood of goats?
"Sacrifice thank offerings to God,
 fulfill your vows to the Most High,
and call on me in the day of trouble;
 I will deliver you, and you will honor me."

PSALM 50:13–15

Dust danced in dawn's soft rays intruding through the balcony curtains. Yaira lay on Hezi's side of the bed, snoring. Zibah faced her, exhausted from her first long, dark night as . . .

A widow.

She couldn't bring herself to say it aloud. *Yahweh, are You truly with me?*

Silence answered, and a gaping emptiness threatened to swallow her. Had she merely conjured a promise from Abba's well-phrased prophecy about God being her Builder? Anger stirred her sorrow. She hated death, and this morning—Yahweh forgive her—she even hated the temple's bronze altar.

Yaira stirred. Eyes blinked open. Sorrow shadowed her features in the morning's half light. "Shalom, my friend." She laid her hand against Zibah's cheek.

Zibah nudged it away. "There is no shalom. Why offer a lamb when the psalm says, 'Do I eat the flesh of bulls or drink the blood of goats?' Why was my husband on that elevated altar, Yaira, if Yahweh doesn't need blood? Why did my son tend a yearling lamb, dreading the moment he'd slice its throat and watch it die?" A new flow of tears cut the rant short. "He watched his abba die instead. I see nothing good Yahweh can *build* with blood and sorrow."

"Shh, my girl." Yaira pulled her into an embrace and called for the maid. "Get the physician."

Zibah closed her eyes and surrendered to the ache inside her, barely aware of the voices and activity around her.

"Zibah, sit up now." Yaira's voice again.

She obeyed but kept her eyes closed.

"Rest now, my queen." The palace physician poured a foul-tasting potion down her throat. "You need to sleep."

She wanted to rant at him about bulls and goats and altars and blood but too soon felt herself floating. Weightless. Passing first through a dark haze and billowing gray clouds, Zibah emerged into a brilliant light. Driven to her knees, she covered her eyes and heard a voice like the sound of rushing waters—powerful but as soothing as Hezi's arm around her shoulders. The Voice was a shout that sank gently into her soul.

Sin is a mortal wound all men bear. You now feel the grief I endure each time My children sin. Yet if I came near to comfort while sin still stained, My holiness would destroy them. Love compels Me to both break your heart and engage your faith with the bloody, noisy, noxious purification that mirrors but a glimpse of My pain. I don't need blood, but I must have your heart. I must have Manasseh's heart. I have given him a heart to build, and I will be his Builder. But first, I must seize his heart.

The Voice ceased. The Light remained. Zibah slid from her knees to her belly, stretching her hands overhead to bask in its warmth and worship the One who had deigned to speak so clearly. Who was she to have questioned Yahweh? Who was her son that the Almighty would build him up and capture his heart? *O God, my God, You are the Rock on which I'll stand all the days of my life.*

All too soon, Zibah woke to a sun-brightened chamber and Yaira spinning wool beside her bed. "I thought you might sleep all day." Even in her best friend's presence, loneliness threatened to bury her.

"I had a vision," Zibah said, sitting up against the plentiful cushions behind her. "I was in Yahweh's presence, and He promised to build up Manasseh and capture his heart."

Yaira set aside her spindle, her brows pinched. "Then we have another promise to which we'll cling." Doubt curved into a sad smile, and she picked up her spindle to resume her task.

Zibah slid out of bed and rang the bell for her maid. Only the certainty of Yahweh's vision would sustain her through Hezi's loss. Some would blame Nasseh—perhaps even Nasseh himself—and many would challenge his insolence toward the priests and Yahweh's temple.

Zibah meandered over to the wall peg where her casual robes hung and sorted through them to find the sackcloth. Nasseh must cut short the Passover celebration and declare Judah in mourning for the next thirty days. She pressed her forehead against the peg. He knew the customs, but he'd never presided over a burial—especially the burial of a king. Or his abba.

Yaira's soft voice interrupted. "I'm going back to my chamber, but I can walk across the hall anytime. Day or night."

Zibah hugged her, fighting more tears. "Thank you, my friend. What would I do without you?"

Her maid arrived with comb in hand. Zibah walked past the partition tucked in the corner, unnecessary this morning since Hezi and his steward weren't here. She sat on her stool in silence while the maid loosened her braid and drew the ivory comb through Zibah's long curls.

Nasseh should know about her vision, that she'd heard his name on Yahweh's lips. That Yahweh promised to be his Builder, not hers, with all that Abba's prophecy entailed. The thought dulled her pain on the bleakest day of her life.

Her mind wandered to Nasseh's erratic behavior at the temple. No doubt, after watching his abba fall, he'd been overwrought and acted without forethought. With Hezi's advisors to guide him, Nasseh could salve his relationship with the priests and temple guards. Few people heard his hasty declaration about Passover, and the nation could celebrate next month—after they'd mourned Hezi's death.

Her maid finished weaving a new braid and covered her head with a sackcloth scarf. Forgoing lotions or perfumes as part of mourning shortened Zibah's time to ponder, so she stood to look in the full-length bronze mirror. Was she ready to face her son? Would he see her swollen, red eyes as condemnation? *Yahweh, give me wisdom to lead him as he leads Your people.*

15

When that day comes, you will cry out for
relief from the king you have chosen, but the
LORD will not answer you in that day.

1 SAMUEL 8:18

Nasseh woke to the sound of purring and found Cat curled up
on the pillow beside his head. "You're spoiled," he whispered
and turned over to watch Shulle sleep. She was pretty. And
smarter than Kenaz. She was better than him at Hounds and Jackals too.
She'd won twice last night out of twenty-seven games. While they played,
she told him incredible things about a world of gods and goddesses that
gave him hope for Judah's new future.

Rolling to his back, he released a long sigh. Shulle was a woman, and
he was now a man. A king. In a month he would be her husband. She
would expect him to give her a child. Even the gods expected the intimate
act as part of worship in their sacred Grove. Baka had described how ba-
bies were made. Matti had talked about a king's duty to lie with many
women in order to build a strong legacy.

Shulle was a priestess. She'd lain with many men already. Yahweh said
that was bad, but Shulle wasn't bad. Nasseh realized his hands were keeping rhythm with the noises in his head again and concentrated on relaxing
them. Yahweh and Shulle couldn't both be right. Yahweh killed Abba;
Shulle had tried to save him. Saba Isaiah told Nasseh all the bad things
that would happen to Judah because of their nation's sins. Shulle and
Shebna said the starry hosts gave worshipers pleasure and rewarded kings
for valor and honor.

Though he knew Ima, Kenaz, *Doda* Yaira, and Dohd Jashub loved

Yahweh, Nasseh was certain they would still love him if he chose to seek other gods for Judah's future. They would be angry, but Shulle promised there were many other people who would be happy—grateful even. Many people would praise Nasseh as a good and worthy king if he declared Judah's freedom to worship any god. Matti would certainly be pleased.

He turned on his side toward Shulle and touched her throat, letting his finger linger at the slight indentation at its base. The softness of her skin made warmth in his cheeks spread. Like sitting in front of a fire too long. His cheeks had also warmed when the temple guards took away his sword. The memory of Shulle screaming in their grip stirred something in his belly—sort of like when he thought of never seeing Abba again.

"Shulle, wake up." He shook her shoulder hard. "Wake up!"

"What's wrong?" She sat up. "Are you all right?"

He sat up too, crossed his legs, and rested his forearms on them. "Which emotions make my cheeks warm?"

Her lazy smile made her even prettier. "Many emotions can warm your cheeks." She laced her fingers in his and kissed them. "Tell me the circumstance, and I'll be more specific."

He pulled his hand away. "Like now."

She sat up. Kissed his cheek and left a trail of kisses down his neck, intensifying the burn. "I suspect that emotion is desire," she whispered. "Is there another time you felt your cheeks warm?"

He pushed her shoulders back. "I did not feel desire when the guards knocked my sword from my hands. My cheeks warm, but my stomach hurts when I think of it."

Her smile flattened. "I'm sorry, Nasseh. That's embarrassment. Some might even call it shame, but you are Judah's king and should never feel embarrassed or ashamed."

"Why must I feel at all?" He glanced at her, immediately recognizing the sad frown.

"If you couldn't feel, my king, you would never know love." She reached for his hand again and placed it over her heart. "Sometimes warm cheeks mean love, like the love you had for your abba."

"Abba's death was worse than I imagined," he said. "Why can't I cry? Ima will want me to display grief at Abba's burial. If I don't, others will think I'm not sad, but I am." He squinted, trying to squeeze out tears. It didn't work. When he closed his eyes, he saw Abba fall from the altar platform. And he saw faces in the crowd focused on him, the strange boy who killed their beloved king. He opened his eyes to see tears on Shulle's cheeks. How did she cry so easily?

"You'll cry when you're ready." She turned his hand over and kissed his palm. "A king cries after his tasks are complete."

He stole a quick glance at her. "You will be a wise queen like my ima."

She wrapped her arms around his neck and pressed her lips against his ear. "I love you, Manasseh ben Hezekiah."

Only Abba and Ima had ever said those words to him. He placed one hand on her back and patted. "I love you, Meshullemeth bat Haruz." The mention of her abba resurrected a memory. "Does your abba still live with you and Shebna? You never speak of him."

"My abba went back to Jotbah a long time ago." She snuggled close. He didn't mind. She smelled like myrtle blossoms and sunshine. "I'm so sorry your abba is gone, Nasseh. He was a good man and a great king."

"I will miss talking with him." Nasseh twirled a single ringlet of her dark hair. "The Yahwists called him the second Solomon, but I don't think Abba was as wise as Solomon. As you said last night, Solomon worshipped his wives' foreign gods, but Abba couldn't see Yahweh's faults."

Shulle released him and met his gaze. "You can be greater than Solomon, Nasseh. Why force the people to worship a god who killed their king? Break the high priest's chains. Show Judah the freedom of our starry hosts and become even greater than your abba."

Nasseh's cheeks warmed again, and his stomach felt like grasshoppers had taken up residency. Add sweaty palms and a heartbeat like a camel's trot. *Desire,* Shulle had called it. He desired her, yes, but he also desired to be a great king. "Judah will openly seek gods from every nation," he said, pulling her closer. "I'll never be a second anything, Shulle."

His body was responding to her nearness in other ways as well, making him wonder if the grieving laws of abstinence were a tradition worth keeping or a Yahwist chain to be broken. A loud knock at his chamber door interrupted further deliberation.

"Who is it?" he shouted.

"Your ima wishes to see you immediately," his guard said, the familiar clanging of his weapons approaching Nasseh's bedchamber curtain.

Panicked, Shulle pulled aside the curtain and started to scoot off the bed. "She can't find me—"

"Shulle!" Ima looked startled, then angry. "Why are you both wearing only your tunics?"

"Why have you come so early, Ima?" Nasseh asked.

Shulle tried again to hurry off the bed, but he grabbed her arm. "Please," Shulle said, her eyes full of tears. "Let me return to Dohd's house and retrieve my things. You and Queen Zibah have much to discuss, Nasseh."

"She is now the queen mother, Shulle, and we can send servants to fetch your things. I meant it when I said I didn't want you to leave me." He kept his head bowed but addressed Ima. "Shulle is to be my wife after mourning Abba for the customary thirty days. We'll sign betrothal documents today, marry the day after mourning is complete, and celebrate our wedding feast for thirty days more. It's all decided."

"All decided? You are my son!"

Shulle placed a hand on his chest. "Please, Nasseh. I should go."

Before he spoke, Ima took charge. "My personal guard is waiting outside the chamber, Shulle. I insist he escort you home."

She bowed slightly. "Thank you, my queen."

But Nasseh caught Shulle's arm. "The *queen mother's* guard may escort you home, but you will come back to me tonight." With noise blaring inside his head, he pulled Shulle against him, kissed her hard, and released her.

"Yes, my king," she whispered, then hurried out of his chamber.

Forcing his hands into calm, Nasseh drew a deep breath and faced Ima. No circle drawing could have conveyed her sadness. For the first time, tears stung his eyes. "Come, Ima," he said, moving toward the audi-ence chamber. "Sit with me on the couches."

Ima sat on the middle couch. Nasseh halted where he stood. If he was to become her king, he must begin now.

"What?" she asked.

"No one sits before the king."

Though still frowning, her expression had changed somehow. Lips drawn into a thin line, she rose slowly, staring at him. Nasseh sat on the couch next to the place where she'd been sitting.

She resumed her seat but looked at the balcony curtain. "I came to tell you that Yahweh has a good plan for you, Nasseh. He wishes to be—"

"I'll have nothing to do with the god who killed my abba," he said flatly. "Saba Isaiah has spoken fine-sounding prophecies that have never come to pass, and those that did come true proved destructive to Judah's well-being."

"Nasseh, you can't—"

"I can do whatever I wish, Ima. I am Judah's king."

She sighed loudly. "I realize you are king, my love, but every king—no matter what his age—listens to his advisors."

"I attended some council meetings," he said. "Abba listened, as will I, but they always did what Abba said because he was king."

She shook her head before he finished—as she always did. "Nasseh, they listened because he was an *experienced* king, familiar with laws and customs you simply don't know yet. For example, you've never planned a king's burial. We should have hired the professional mourners already."

He lifted a hand to silence her shrill voice. "I'll send for mourners, Ima, and Abba's burial ceremony will be spectacular. My new advisory council will—"

"New? Why must you—"

"I'll inform you of burial plans by sunset." He stood, offering his arm.

Grudgingly, she stood, and he walked her to the door where Baka waited. When she faced him, her cheeks were wet with tears. "Please,

Nasseh. Don't reject Yahweh. He didn't *kill* your abba. He *healed* him fifteen years ago and gave us you."

Nasseh pulled her into his arms, remembering Shulle's counsel that Ima needed hugs now that Abba was gone. "It's not I who rejected Yahweh, Ima. He cursed me with oddities that shame me and then used my weakness to kill Abba."

"Nasseh, no!" She pulled away. "That's not true!"

Patience spent, he said to Baka. "See that the queen mother is moved to a chamber of her choosing in the harem. I want my personal belongings in the king's chamber by nightfall. And summon my tutors, as well as Dohd Jashub, Dohd Matti, and Kenaz. Today, we'll plan a burial *and* a betrothal."

16

Blessed is the one
>who does not walk in step with the wicked

or stand in the way that sinners take
>or sit in the company of mockers.

PSALM 1:1

One Month After Hezi's Burial, Iyar

Onan, the queen mother's personal guard, escorted me to Dohd Shebna's home. Like a foreboding shadow, he walked three paces behind and two paces to my right through the palace halls, into the market, and around the horseshoe-shaped streets.

"Thank you, Onan," I said when we reached the courtyard gate. "You may go."

He inclined his head slightly and left without a word.

I searched the house and found Belit sleeping in our chamber. Happy for the solitude, I searched through our food basket and found leftover bread and a wineskin to enjoy beneath the shade of my myrtle tree. I unfurled a reed mat, then lay beneath the tree and inhaled its sweet aroma, aching for Abba's presence. In the year since discovering Dohd intercepted all my letters, I hadn't written Abba another. But when life's questions rumbled like thunder in my mind, I sat under the myrtle tree and imagined the wisdom he might have shared.

I rolled myrtle leaves between my hands and closed my eyes, allowing the fragrant oil to fill my senses. Would I still live in Dohd's house when the white blossoms of summer covered the tree? Or when the purple-black berries of autumn teased the birds to its branches? Nasseh said I'd be queen and Judah would seek the gods, but how could he make it so when he was still a child in so many ways?

Mourners' wails seeped into my consciousness, and I covered my ears, loathing the undignified profession. Queen Zibah would never walk through the streets howling, tossing dust and ashes over her head. She hadn't even rent her neckline when she'd witnessed King Hezekiah's death. Even her grief was elegant—until she saw me in her son's bed, both of us wearing only our tunics. Her expression turned to granite as she appraised me.

Would she ever look at me with tenderness as she'd done when I was a child? After my Grove training commenced, her tender smiles had turned to stares, condemning my slightest mistake. *Why does it matter?* As long as I became Nasseh's bride, why must I gain her approval? I didn't *need* it, but I longed for it. As surely as I longed to see Abba again. Perhaps one of Belit's love potions could help me regain her favor.

If her charm couldn't save King Hezekiah from Isaiah's curse, could a potion work on the queen mother? The thought felt like a betrayal, but if Yahweh was as weak as Dohd and Belit claimed, why did King Hezekiah die—in spite of Belit's strongest magic that healed his pre-Passover illness?

"There she is." Dohd's jovial tone scattered my thoughts. "The new Queen of Judah."

I shaded my eyes from the afternoon sun. "Stop teasing."

He tossed a gold neckband in my lap. "Consider it a down payment on your bride price."

I caressed the etched floral pattern, and a thousand questions distilled into a single word. "When?"

"Come inside. We have much to discuss." He was already walking toward the house shouting, "Belit! Wine and bread. Now!"

I scurried to my feet and arrived in the gathering room as he settled on his cushion. Belit looked as if she'd just awakened and placed three cups on the leather mat. She filled each one with undiluted wine as I sat at Dohd's right.

I shoved mine away, too nervous to drink. "Tell me everything."

"The king wants you to move into the harem immediately, but I refused."

"What?" I turned to Belit, hoping she'd support my outrage. "How can I complete my task if Dohd ruins all the work I've already done?"

She waved off my concern. "A farmer need not buy the cow if he gets her milk for free."

I'd given three years of free milk in the Grove and finally found a "farmer"—no, a *king*—who wanted me. "Why wait and risk his change of heart?"

Dohd touched the gold neckband I'd placed around my neck. "Do you really think after Manasseh has loved you so long, he would let anything stop the wedding? Making him yearn for thirty days will stoke his fire. You'll be chaperoned in his presence until the betrothal contract is fulfilled—which will also improve the queen mother's opinion of you."

I nearly groaned at the mention. "Did you meet with Queen Zibah? Does she hate me?"

"She is no longer *Queen Zibah*," he said. "You may call her Queen Mother. And yes, I met with her. She's too distraught over her dead husband and wayward son to hate you."

"Dohd! Be kind." I nudged his arm. "How would you feel if someone you loved died before your eyes?"

He held my gaze, and I braced myself for his wrath. "*You* are the one I love most, Meshullemeth. I will always protect you."

His glistening eyes looked so sincere. I looked at my fumbling hands, forcing myself to remember his repeated lies and betrayals.

He cleared his throat and said, "Mattaniah is the queen mother's current target of wrath. She blames him for giving Manasseh the sword before he was 'trained in its proper use.'"

Belit's cynical laugh drew my attention. "Prince Mattaniah is an ignorant toad. The perfect diversion."

Dohd ignored her, reaching for a piece of stale bread. "Shulle, you must find a way back into the queen mother's favor. You'll spend every day in her chamber, doing whatever eases her sorrow. Every evening, I'll escort you to the king's chamber, where we'll share meals with members of his council."

"What have I to do with the king's council?" I'd hoped to spend more time alone with Nasseh.

"Absolutely nothing." Dohd grinned. "But you'll distract Nasseh while I bend each council member to my will." He bit off a chunk of bread. "Tonight, for example, you and I will meet with the king and Mattaniah, who is acting as Abba of the groom. Mattaniah and I will negotiate bride price and dowry. King Manasseh will sign the ketubah and seal the agreement with the traditional gift of a gold ring for his bride."

I tried not to squeal but clasped my hands together, wondering what a ring would feel like. "Manasseh said he'd marry me the day after mourning ended."

Dohd nodded with a smile that felt more like family and less like business. "The king has decreed it."

"That's . . . That's thirty-one days!" I leapt from my cushion and threw my arms around his neck. "Thank you, Dohd. Thank you. Thank you."

"Do I get any credit?" Belit sat with her arms crossed.

In the awkward silence, I walked around our leather mat and knelt beside her. "You've taught me well, Belit." I lifted the back of her hand to my forehead, the sign of fealty to a sovereign. "Without your wisdom, I could not have won Nasseh's heart."

She yanked her hand away and looked at me with searing yellow eyes. "Remember, when you and Shebna sit with noblemen night after night, I who showed you the stars can also deliver you to darkness."

"Get out." Shebna's voice was sharp as a blade.

Belit raised her brows over half-hooded eyes. A silent dare.

"I mean it," he said. "Go to your chamber if you can't celebrate when we've won this victory together."

I felt a measure of relief as she left the room. "She's feeling left out, Dohd. Perhaps you should talk with her."

"Belit knew her part in our rise to power would change when you married Manasseh. She works behind the scenes with potions and spells. I work in the throne room with a king and his council."

"So you believe Manasseh will restore you as palace administrator in place of Eliakim?"

"He already has."

His smug declaration made me uneasy. How had he manipulated Nasseh so quickly? "Congratulations. How did you manage it?"

"When Nasseh called for his three tutors, his two dohds, and Kenaz, he asked one question: Who supported his decision to marry you? Isaiah and Eliakim disagreed emphatically. Mattaniah and I were elated. Kenaz, of course, supported Manasseh but cautioned him to regain the support of Yahweh's priesthood before moving forward. His dohd Jashub suggested the young king wait until he'd ruled the nation at least a year before attempting to rule a wife."

"Rule me?" I bristled.

Dohd waved off my comment and leaned forward. "Eliakim and Isaiah disqualified themselves with their disapproval. Jashub was saved by his humor and was given the position of Manasseh's chief scribe. Kenaz will serve as friend of the groom but was given no official place on his royal council. He'll likely serve his abba among the scribes."

I studied his triumphant expression with growing concern. "How did he decide between you and Prince Mattaniah to replace Eliakim as palace administrator?

"He asked us one more question: Which Assyrian god or goddess is most powerful?"

I silently sorted through the ones I'd been taught, happy I didn't have to answer. "Which did you choose?"

"I remained quiet while Mattaniah named nearly every god in their pantheon incorrectly. His indecision and stupidity would have made anything I said sound brilliant." Dohd laced his fingers behind his head and leaned back as if he owned the world. "I answered, 'Nusku, Assyria's fire god, the messenger through whom all other gods communicate.' Then I turned to Mattaniah and added, 'The ability to control communication is the most powerful role in the pantheon, much like a palace administrator in a king's administration.' Nasseh made me his fire god and designated Mattaniah chief counselor. But Hezekiah's brother knows I bested him today." He drained his cup of wine and poured another.

"So, that's it then? You've been restored to power. You've gotten your revenge on Lord Isaiah and Lord Eliakim." He'd been so good at pretending to truly care for Nasseh—and me—that moments like these unnerved me. I rose silently, hoping his overabundance of wine would help mask my departure.

"Oh no, Shulle." He took another long drink. "I've only just begun."

I retreated around the corner and yelped when I nearly tripped over Belit.

"What is it?" Dohd shuffled to his feet.

"A lizard." I waved him back to his cushion, hiding the eavesdropper behind me. "Enjoy your wine. I'll ask Belit to dress me for tonight's dinner."

"Wear your best robe, my girl." He plopped onto his cushion. "When Nasseh signs the ketubah, you are bound as Judah's queen. I'll use the thirty days' wait to negotiate even more advantages."

I turned toward the hallway again, and Belit was gone. If Dohd wished to cross swords with her, let him. I knew the power of her dark arts; maintaining Belit's favor was every bit as important as regaining the queen mother's.

"I've decided to offer incense at the altar in the Grove." I crossed the gathering room to snag a basket. Thankfully, Dohd ignored me. "I'll be back in plenty of time to prepare for tonight's dinner." He drained the wineskin into his cup as I walked toward the courtyard.

I inhaled the sweet scent of my myrtle tree, clearing my mind, then traversed the familiar path out the Corner Gate. Passing the caves, I meandered along the hillsides. Everything looked different in daylight, but the poplar grove was easily recognizable. Colorful silk scarves fluttered in the breeze from myriad branches. I'd tied many of them myself, lifted into the trees by strong and devoted worshipers who had bestowed expensive scarves on me—a priestess who couldn't keep their gifts. Since Nasseh would allow free worship, perhaps I should take a few home to Belit. A peace offering.

"I thought I might find you here." Lord Isaiah sat on Baal's sacred altar.

"How did you—" I looked on the paths behind and ahead. No temple guards to arrest me. Still, I pointed to my empty basket. "I was collecting herbs."

"Are you a priestess, Shulle?"

Icy fingers of dread snaked around my throat. "Why would you ask such a thing?"

"I know power-hungry people lie to young girls and force them to do unthinkable things."

His eyes bored a hole into my soul, so I looked away—toward the gleaming palace. I thought of the young king I'd soon marry, and a burst of confidence loosened my tongue. "It's Yahweh and his followers who force people to do the unthinkable, Lord Isaiah." I met his condemning gaze. "Yes, I am a priestess. Dohd Shebna and his Babylonian āšipūtu, Belit, have taught me all I need to know to break Yahweh's chains on this nation."

His features softened, and his rheumy eyes grew moist. "Oh, sweet Shulle. I'm so sorry for what they've done to you."

I'd expected hate, not pity, and when he reached for my hand, I stepped back. "Why did you come here?"

He stared at me, those penetrating eyes exposing every debasing act I'd performed in this grove. "Did you know Shebna is from a prominent Levite family that served faithfully for generations in Yahweh's temple?"

"Of course, I know, but did *you* know the abuse both Dohd and Abba suffered at their 'faithful' abba's hands? It's why Abba and I lived as paupers in Jotbah."

"Will you blame the whole tribe of Levi for a single wicked man?"

"I blame Yahweh and those who use his laws like a strap to wound innocent people."

"Innocent?" Lord Isaiah stood and ripped one of the scarves from a branch, holding it over his eyes. "Shebna wants you to see his life through a colored filter. Yes, his abba Joseph banished him from Levitical work in the temple, but wasn't it through hardship that he rose to positions of power?"

I'd never considered that. "But Yahweh stole his position as palace administrator and gave it to Lord Eliakim. You were the one who pronounced the judgment."

He lowered the scarf. "Shebna hardened his heart, Shulle, blaming God for poor choices he and others made. Your dohd knows Yahweh is the one true God but refuses to serve Him because he's angry."

"Angry at you," I clarified.

"Angry at me and Eliakim." His lips pursed together as if trapping warriors behind them. After five long heartbeats, his full assault commenced. "A few years after Shebna was demoted to secretary, my wife Aya died. I'd been at the palace all day, and we had only one servant at the time—who said Shebna had shared a cup of mint tea with Aya in the courtyard that afternoon."

I felt the blood drain from my face. My heartbeat sped. I knew what he was going to say.

"Shebna poisoned my wife, Shulle. But because we had only one witness, the Law says he couldn't be convicted of murder. A law I taught him as a boy in my class."

The words hit me like a blow, and I reached for a tree to steady myself. "Surely, your wife was just old. Perhaps sickly." But Dohd was capable, and I knew the potions Belit would have given him to use in a cup of tea.

The old man's eyes held no judgment. "Shebna is a master of deception, Shulle. I think you're beginning to see it. But Nasseh trusts him completely. I see the way you look at my grandson, and I believe you truly care for him—unlike Shebna who only wants to use him to gain power."

"I do care." Throat tight, I could say no more.

"Yahweh created us in His image—to love and be loved. Nasseh has chosen you as his wife, but I'm not sure he fully understands how to love a wife. And how can you, after being subjected to acts of humiliation in this grove, understand the love Yahweh intended for one woman and one man?" He nodded at the tent at the head of the Grove, my altar to Ishtar for the past three years. "Since you're of marriageable age, I suspect you've been groomed by the finest noblemen, but you haven't known a man's *true* love, Shulle."

Mortified, I walked a few steps away so he couldn't see the crimson burning my neck and face. "My abba loves me, Lord Isaiah, and so does Nasseh. Though they show love differently than most, they feel it as deeply as you and I do."

He rested his hand on my shoulder. "I don't doubt yours or Nasseh's capacity to love—only the ability to love as husband and wife *right now*. He listens to you, Shulle. You taught him to speak as a child. You've helped him understand and express his emotions. You've even strengthened his confidence to speak to crowds in the Throne Hall. You're his dearest friend, but while he grieves his abba's death, Nasseh needs the love of *family*." He stepped around to meet my gaze. "Please, Shulle. Ask him to postpone your wedding for the traditional year of a betrothal."

"That's why you came today." Rage bubbled up, burning my throat. "Why must you control him? Control me?" I shouted. "We will be married when Nasseh chooses, not when you or your Yahwist friends decide!" I stomped away, leaving my basket.

"Wait! Shulle," he cried. "Please, listen—"

But his words died away as blood pulsed in my ears. The Yahwists would say anything—do anything—to retain power over Judah and keep me from becoming Nasseh's queen. But what about Dohd? Hadn't he also done awful things? *Did he really kill Lord Isaiah's wife?*

I had little time to consider the implications. The sun hung low over the western hills, and in a very short while I'd be legally bound to Judah's king. Tonight, in a small and private ceremony, I would become the betrothed Queen of Judah.

17

Hezekiah rested with his ancestors and was
buried on the hill where the tombs of David's
descendants are. All Judah and the people of
Jerusalem honored him when he died. And
Manasseh his son succeeded him as king.

2 CHRONICLES 32:33

Two days later

Nasseh proved true to his word and planned a royal burial rival-
ing any in Jerusalem's history. Zibah and her son rode on white
donkeys behind the ox-drawn cart bearing Hezi's spice-laden
bier. The royal family walked in two rows behind them. Abba Isaiah,
brother Jashub, Yaira, and Kenaz followed first. Prince Mattaniah and
Shebna flanked the newly betrothed Shulle in the second row.

After Zibah's devastating confrontation with Nasseh, she'd run to
Yaira's chamber and fallen into her arms. "All I feared about Shulle was
true," she'd said through sobs. "She's captured Nasseh's heart and already
turned him toward pagan gods."

Yaira suggested a good thrashing for them both, lightening the mood.
Then, as usual, she added her steadfast wisdom. "Yahweh promised to be
Nasseh's Builder and capture his heart, Zibah. Perhaps it came in such a
vivid vision to sustain you through troubling days ahead."

Yaira didn't know about Abba's dream, of his prophesied horrific
death. The thought of it sent a shiver through her. *Yahweh, please! I can't
lose Abba too!*

Mourners' wails brought her back to the moment, and the slow, somber beat of a funeral dirge accompanied the burial parade through Jerusalem's southernmost gate. Halting outside the city at the tombs of King David's descendants, Zibah dismounted and followed six soldiers who carried Hezi's flower-covered bier into the cave. His body was placed on a hewn-rock shelf, where it would return to the dust from which all men were formed, and then his bones would be transferred to a sarcophagus—a stone box like the others lining the walls of the cave.

Nasseh placed his hand at the small of her back. "Come, Ima. Abba wouldn't want you to linger here." It was a small but tender touch. Such a grown-up gesture. He was changing too fast.

She touched his cheek. "Abba wouldn't want you worshiping pagan gods either." He ducked his head, stormed past his white donkey, took Shulle's hand, and walked back to the palace with her—leaving Zibah to return to her new chamber alone.

The next morning, she rose early, and Yaira joined her to begin the third official day of grieving. Professional mourners began their wailing outside her balcony just after sunrise. A knock at her door sent her to her feet.

Nasseh entered without invitation. "Good morning, Ima." He strode into the chamber, Shulle beside him. "My bride-to-be will spend her days of mourning with you while the counsel and I prepare for our wedding. I'm sure you and Yaira have much wisdom to impart before we begin our life together." He kissed Shulle's cheek and left.

"Wait, I—," Zibah sputtered, but the door clicked shut.

Shulle stood, head bowed. "I'm sorry, Queen Mother. I can leave if you'd like."

More manipulation. "If you leave, Nasseh will be angry that I didn't welcome you. Congratulations. You have won my son's allegiance, but you've lost your soul to false gods." Her venom tasted bitter, but she had no mercy for a deceptive heart.

Shulle retreated to a corner with a spindle and basket of wool. Zibah sat on her stool beside Yaira, who looked at her as if she'd kicked a stray cat.

"You can't let Shulle work silent and alone," she whispered.

"I can and I will," Zibah said, grasping the shuttle on her loom. Yaira snorted her disapproval but also kept silent until a servant brought their midday meal.

"Come, Shulle," Yaira said. "You must eat something." The girl left her corner, picked up a few dates, a small loaf of bread, and a handful of pistachios. Then she turned back toward her corner.

"You may join us if you like," Zibah said, pulling a third cushion closer to the table.

"Thank you, Queen Mother." Shulle sat, twitchy like a skittish fawn.

Zibah's cheeks warmed as her fury pressed into challenge. "Look me in the eye, Meshullemeth, and tell me one thing you haven't lied about in the past seven years."

Shulle looked up, cheeks wet with convincing sorrow. "Abba and I came to Jerusalem with Dohd to escape unfair treatment in Jotbah and help Nasseh adjust to his role as king." She lifted her chin. "That is the truth."

"But it's not the *whole* truth, is it?" Zibah watched the girl's brashness wilt like a flower after a frost. "Have you always worshipped pagan gods?"

"No. I turned from Yahweh when the starry hosts proved themselves more powerful." She reached for Zibah's hand, her brow wrinkled with intensity. "Queen Mother, your god was once a champion of his people, but his power has dwindled. Nasseh is among those who have realized it and will lead Judah into greatness beyond what we've ever known. But Lord Isaiah was right when he spoke to me in the Grove on the day of our betrothal."

"Abba spoke to you in the Grove?" Zibah pulled her hand away.

"Yes, he said many things I didn't believe, but one thing was true. I love Nasseh as a friend. As deep and strong as that love is, it's not yet a love between husband and wife." She looked at Yaira and back at Zibah. "Both of you are good wives. I've seen the love you and your husbands share. Teach me how to love and be loved in that way."

Zibah stared at the girl, speechless. Shulle had manipulated her for so long. How could she ever trust her?

"Zibah and I believe Yahweh is the only God and powerful beyond compare." Yaira laid her hand on Zibah's arm as she spoke gently to the girl. "We can only share the love we've learned from Yahweh. It has very practical applications in our marriages that we'll be happy to share, regardless of your belief in other gods." She patted Zibah's arm. "Isn't that right, Queen Mother?"

Zibah wanted to scream, *No! I want her to leave Jerusalem and never see my son again!* Instead she breathed in Yahweh's strength and breathed out *His* calm. "Yes, of course. I'd love to tell you stories of how Yahweh strengthened the love between Hezi and me."

~

Zibah waited with Nasseh and Mattaniah under the chuppah in the Garden of Uzza. Shebna and Belit—the woman Shulle chose as her surrogate ima—led the bride down a center aisle. Close family members and Nasseh's royal council filled the benches. A quaint and quiet setting her son had planned to the last detail and managed with surprising calm. Though his hands were balled into fists, he breathed slowly, deliberately. He seemed calmer than his ima. *Yahweh, please use the wisdom Yaira and I shared with Shulle to draw her closer to You and love my son well.*

The moon and stars shone down on the audience, and four lonely torches made the jewels on Shulle's heavy veil sparkle. Upon reaching the chuppah, she began the walk of seven circles around her husband, symbolically drawing them into a new household. A family all their own.

What would they teach their children? Deception, bitterness, and false gods? Zibah pressed down her angst, as she'd been doing for weeks, with words from Abba's prophecies: *"You will keep in perfect peace those whose minds are steadfast, because they trust in you. Trust in the LORD forever, for the LORD, the LORD himself, is the Rock eternal."* She inhaled a sustaining breath and felt the warmth of Yahweh's presence soothe her.

Nasseh, however, grew restless as Shulle finished her seventh circle and halted beside him. He began rocking left to right, his hands now clenching and releasing to the silent beat of the torturous noise in his mind.

Zibah reached for his hand and whispered, "'My heart is stirred by a noble theme as I recite my verses for the king.'" Nasseh joined her recitation: "'My tongue is the pen of a skillful writer. You are the most excellent of men and your lips have been anointed with grace, since God—'" He pulled his hand away, features darkening. "I won't say, 'Yahweh has blessed me forever,' since he's cursed me since birth."

Shulle reached for his other hand, though her veil blinded her, and he cradled it as if it were a treasure. Zibah felt his rejection as deeply as the pain she'd heard in his voice. How long had he felt cursed by Yahweh—but never confided it?

Azariah, the high priest, began the wedding blessing and then asked Kenaz to read aloud the ketubah as friend of the bridegroom. The familiar words of the betrothal contract rolled over Zibah like balm. He hadn't completely abandoned Yahweh's traditions in his wedding. The chuppah symbolized Yahweh's promise to Abraham of numberless descendants. Shulle's heavy veil was a humorous memory of Jacob's mixed-up marriage to the wrong sister.

"And now the priestess Belit will pronounce her blessing," Azariah said.

Priestess? Horrified, Zibah turned to Abba, his features twisted in sorrow instead of the anger she expected.

Belit lifted the couple's hands toward the heavens. "Bind this union, O gods of night. Great stars Orion, Wagon, Ferry, and Centaurus lead our great king to the south and north, west and east, and make our great queen a mother of nations." Her eyes rolled back, and she began to twitch. "O mighty Ninsianna, holy torch that fills the heavens . . . Lady Ishtar, enforcer of divine justice . . ."

Nasseh's self-assurance turned to panic, eyes wide with fear. "Ima?" Zibah grabbed the couple's hands, hoping to break the witch's grasp, but Belit held them with something beyond physical power.

Her eyes flew open, the whites now blood red. "Step away, woman of God," she said to Zibah, then turned her bloody eyes on Judah's king. "The gods look favorably on your marriage, but you must travel."

"Travel?" Nasseh glanced first at Zibah and then back at the sorceress.

Belit spoke with a chilling smile. "The stars command a long journey and promise a strong alliance. But you must not linger in Jerusalem when the wedding feast is done." Her body sagged, and she released their hands, bracing herself against the table where the wedding cup of wine waited for the ceremony's end.

Shebna stepped to her side, supporting her as if she'd run a great race. When she looked up at Zibah, her black eyes were normal again but held a glint of triumph.

Hushed whispers rippled through the gathering, and then eerie silence prevailed. Zibah scanned the guests, waiting for someone to defend Yahweh. Abba shook his head with a barely perceptible *no*. Appalled, she looked to her brother. *Jashub, please.* No witch should rant at the wedding of Judah's king. Jashub, too, sat silent.

Finally, she turned to Yahweh's high priest. "Azariah, say something!" His lips hung colorless. Empty when they should have been full of truth and wisdom.

"Yes, Azariah," Nasseh said. "By all means, finish the ceremony so we can begin the feast." He turned to Belit. "And it would seem you and Shebna should begin planning a journey on which my queen and I will seal a strong alliance."

18

Take me away with you—let us hurry!
Let the king bring me into his chambers.

SONG OF SONGS 1:4

The moment Belit lifted Nasseh's hand and mine toward heaven, I knew asking her to serve as ima for the wedding had been a mistake. I'd hoped doing so would win her favor. When she accepted, she vowed to *"make it a day I'd never forget."* She'd done that and more. With a single divining, she'd inserted herself in planning our king's first diplomatic journey with influence greater than the king's counsel.

While still contemplating Belit's genius, I received the cup of wine passed under my veil, and the wedding ended with a final blessing from the high priest. I waited for Nasseh to take my hand and lead me to the wedding chamber amid rejoicing as I'd seen happen at other weddings. But there would be no hand holding or rejoicing.

Dohd nudged me forward and whispered. "Go on, Shulle."

"Hurry, Shulle!" Nasseh called from somewhere in the garden. Had everyone forgotten I couldn't see through the veil?

"I'll lead you to the king's chamber." Zibah leaned close. "A girl is nervous enough on her wedding night without having to guess where she's going." A soft hand slid into mine.

I wanted to thank her but didn't trust my voice. I trembled with gratitude and humiliation, eagerness and relief, fear and fury as I watched my feet all the way to the king's chamber. When we halted at the threshold, the stories the queen mother had shared about love and marriage came rushing back. Could Nasseh and I enjoy the same love and life she and King Hezi shared in this chamber?

"Thank you," I said, kissing her hand and hurrying inside before my questions tormented me further. My grasp of Zibah and Hezi's exquisite love was like my drawings of Dohd's memorable travels—all a dim substitute until personal experience made it vibrant and alive.

"You may go," Nasseh said.

My breath caught, thinking he meant me, but then I heard shuffling feet and the clanging of a washbasin and pitcher. The scent of myrtle. Washing hands. He was nervous too.

The click of a door closing. I waited. If I'd counted heartbeats, I might have reached a thousand. Still my husband made no attempt to speak or touch me. Some girls dreamt of this wedding week all their lives. Undisturbed, intimate bliss. But I'd been trained for it. Why was I standing here, waiting for Nasseh to be like other men? He was a king, but he was only twelve years old. Awkward, but brilliant. And I loved him. Someday, I'd love him more.

The sweat dripping down my back made the first decision easy. Grabbing my veil, I flung it across the chamber. Nasseh's startled look made me chuckle, which softened the tension on his features. He sat on one of the couches, frantically petting his black cat. His red, chapped hands proved he'd been washing his hands even more than usual.

Though I'd visited this chamber with Dohd every evening during the mourning period, Nasseh had surprised me with a few changes for our wedding week. "Beautiful new couches." I began my approach, and he began rocking. "Did you choose the purple to replace your parents' red ones?"

"Purple is the color of royalty," he said, eyes fixed on the new purple rug at his feet. "Tyre is the only source of the murex shellfish from which the dye is extracted and—"

"Nasseh." I touched his shoulder and halted his rocking.

"Yes?"

"I know about the dye." I slid onto the couch beside him, not sure if the cat or my husband would bolt first. "Tell me about the lovely curtains hanging around the bed. How did you decide on blue and crimson?" I reached over to pet Cat. "Ouch! She scratched me!"

"She only likes me." He chuckled and seemed to relax.

I scooted closer. "May I try to pet her again?"

He nodded and held Cat's front paws while I scratched behind her ears. "She likes that." After a few moments, he lowered Cat to the floor and cradled my hand without looking at me. "I love you, Shulle." He started rocking again. "It's time for my first sacrifice to the gods, isn't it?"

His voice was small, tentative. I felt like an ima, making him drink fish oil for an upset stomach. I tilted his chin up, forcing him to meet my eyes. "I love you, Nasseh, and you are Judah's king. You get to decide when we make our first sacrifice to the gods."

A genuine smile lit his eyes as he looked away. "You really love me?"

"Yes, my king." I laid my head on his shoulder and felt him relax.

"All right then." He grabbed my hand and shot to his feet, leading me toward his bed. "You will teach me the pleasures of sacrifice, and then we'll play Hounds and Jackals."

"What? I . . ."

He stopped beside the bed and began removing his jewelry, his crown, then his belt.

"Nasseh, wait. You must—"

His hands froze, head bowed. "Am I doing something wrong, Shulle? You must teach me with great detail if I'm to become proficient and build a household like the great King David."

In that fleeting moment of decision, I released the wedding night of my dreams to embrace the friend I loved and the king I hoped to empower. There would be no subtleties tonight. No flirting or innuendo. I took my time explaining my intentions, every moment and emotion, and then received my husband's first sacrifice to Ishtar.

His fiery passion passed quickly, and he immediately turned his back to me.

"Nasseh?" I touched his shoulder, but he shrugged me away.

"I'm tired," he said. "I want the tapestries open to see the moonrise."

Two heavy tapestries closed off the balcony and blocked the chill night breeze, but I dared not argue with a king. Scooting off the bed to open them, sudden weariness draped me like a wet blanket. I pulled the tapestries apart and then padded to the washbasin, splashed my face, and wiped away the artificial colors of celebration. Black kohl, green malachite, and red ochre stained my towel as witness against me. Abba had never seen the paints I wore in the Grove, but he'd soon discover that I was queen and helped Nasseh turn Judah away from Yahweh. Could he let go of those ancient beliefs? Trust the powerful starry hosts? Could the healing Nasseh would bring to Judah outshine the harm I'd done to Zibah and Yaira—and Abba?

Bile rising in my throat, I returned to my husband's bed and slid beneath the Egyptian linen, careful not to disturb the boy who reportedly slept so little. Back still turned, his quiet sniffs proved my man-child was hiding tears.

"Nasseh, tell me what's wrong." I leaned over his shoulder, but he shrugged off my comfort and drew Cat into his arms. I lay back on my feather-stuffed pillow, confused and concerned but too exhausted to delve deeper into my husband's complex heart.

The sound of birdsong seeped into my consciousness with the realization of morning light. I opened my eyes and found Nasseh propped on one elbow, staring.

"Your eyes are the same color as your hair. Do you realize you're beautiful?" He waited for an answer, no attempt at charm.

I covered my mouth to protect him from morning breath. "No, but I'm glad you do." I sat up, pulling my unruly mop of curls out of my face.

He sat up and kissed my cheek. "I've got every day planned out. First, we break our fast. Next, we play Hounds and Jackals." He reached for a scroll on his bedside table and unfurled it, pointing to the third item on his list. "Do you know how to throw a dagger?"

I giggled. "I can't say I've ever needed that skill."

"Well, I'm going to teach you."

I whistled my excitement and thought his eyes might pop from his head. "And you must teach me to whistle!"

He left our bed, washed his hands in the basin, dried them thoroughly, then flung open the doors of a large wardrobe. It was filled with every game, tool, and toy a twelve-year-old boy could wish for. In that moment, he was simply *Nasseh,* the boy I'd known and loved since he was five. The boy who had taken my hand the first day he met me—and spoken to me when he'd barely said a word to anyone else. No one had ever made me feel loved like Nasseh did.

I crossed the chamber, and interrupting his setup of Hounds and Jackals, I led him to the low table where we would break our fast. "I would marry you, Manasseh ben Hezekiah, whether you were a king or a pauper." He ducked his head, smiling, and I reached for a small silver bell to call the steward Dohd Shebna had promised would present my surprise. "I've arranged something special for this morning."

Nasseh's cheerfulness ebbed. "I eat gruel in the morning."

"I know, but—" The steward arrived with three bowls on a silver tray. He placed a bowl of warm gruel before each of us and a mounding dish of candied dates by my king. I picked out the plumpest one and fed it to him before he could protest. Eyes rounding with delight, he smiled, letting some syrup drip from his mouth. "They're my favorite," I said. "I thought we could break our fast with them every day of our wedding week."

"We'll have them three times a day!" He reached for another and then ordered bread, cheese, and dates for our midday meal before dismissing the steward.

He recited the day's schedule to me again, and the day progressed exactly as he'd planned. I taught him to whistle and skip. We threw daggers at a straw target he ordered brought into our chamber. And my hands grew weary from the many times I rolled knucklebones to play Hounds and Jackals. I even taught him to weave.

But when darkness returned, so did the dark cloud over Nasseh's spirit. He twirled and danced during the day but shivered with uncertainties at night. Why could he kiss away date syrup in the morning but recoil when I brushed his cheek in the moonlight?

After our second sacrifice to the gods, I heard again the telltale sounds of his breaking heart and couldn't bear the thought I had been the cause. "Nasseh, you've fulfilled your duties to the gods. We don't need to sacrifice again." I placed my hand on his back. He flinched but didn't pull away. "I can sleep on the couch."

He turned over suddenly, pulling me so close I could hardly breathe. "I loved Abba too much, and Yahweh took him away. If I love you too much, Shulle, Yahweh might take you too."

I curled my arms and leg around him, my hatred stirred for the god who had ruined so many lives. "We will fight him and his followers, Nasseh. Belit's dark arts are powerful, and I've won the favor of many noblemen as the high priestess in the Grove."

He pulled away, staring at me hard in the moonlit chamber. "You can no longer be a priestess, Shulle. You are mine alone, and any child you bear must be mine without question." He hugged me again, tucking my head beneath his chin.

His possessiveness warmed my heart yet chilled my bones. This boy wielded the power of a nation, but I had no intention of bearing his children until I was ready. "Of course, my king. I haven't served as priestess since our betrothal. I would never put King David's pure line of succession in jeopardy." But I would continue to use the herbal pouches that kept a man's seed from growing in my belly.

"Let's sacrifice to the gods again," he said. "All this talk of an heir makes me yearn for you."

My head throbbed with exhaustion from a week with this boy who barely slept. "Nasseh, I must rest before we make our appearance at the wedding feast today." I turned on my side and curled my arms around a pillow. "Aren't you tired?"

He rang the bell for the steward and washed his hands in the basin. "You rest, Shulle. I'll go to finalize the details of our journey with Shebna."

I was too tired to be offended that he was leaving the seclusion of our wedding week without me. There would undoubtedly be many traditions my husband would break in the years to come, but did it matter? Manasseh ben Hezekiah loved me, and I was his queen.

19

My son, do not go along with them,
    do not set foot on their paths;
for their feet rush into evil,
    they are swift to shed blood.

PROVERBS 1:15–16

The day I walked into our wedding feast on my husband's arm was the happiest day of my life. The cavernous courtroom had been transformed into a veritable garden.

Gasping, I halted at the threshold to take it all in. "Nasseh, did Eliakim build all these fountains?"

My husband stood taller. "Actually, I designed the plan, and Eliakim contracted the workers." We walked the center aisle among three bubbling fountains and grand columns carved into images of gods and goddesses from surrounding nations, all wrapped in trailing green plants. Nasseh trapped my hand on his arm and whispered, "Don't leave me, Shulle." His thumb danced to a nervous beat, eyes darting from dancers to musicians to raucous guests.

I hummed the fish song, the tune we still sang to calm his fears, while taking my first public walk as Queen Shulle. Men and women mingled at tables, a custom more Egyptian than Judean. Laughter and wine flowed freely. Musicians meandered and dancers twirled. Our family waited at a table on the dais, where two empty places beckoned us. My heart ached at the thought of Abba's absence. He should have been here, but Dohd had said no, refusing any discussion.

The queen mother and her relatives sat to the left of the king's purple cushion. An identical embroidered pillow waited beside it, the place of honor for his bride. Prince Mattaniah, Dohd, and Belit were seated to my right.

Nasseh nearly sprinted the final steps to the dais, and once seated he gulped great gasps of air. He rocked emphatically while washing his hands in the basin placed on the table for him.

I offered him his goblet. "Drink, my love." He downed the wine instantly. I set aside the cup, then turned him to face me. "Focus on me, Nasseh."

To my astonishment, he looked into my eyes. "I will focus on you alone."

And he did. All day long.

Ignoring all others, he talked to me as if we were the only two in the world. And I reveled in it.

Council members demanded his time. Dohd Shebna shooed them away. Prince Mattaniah told him bawdy stories. Nasseh ignored him. Belit tried to tend me, but Nasseh shoved her aside and demanded our privacy—in the middle of a feast.

I happily gave him my full attention. "You can deny anyone anything or grant anyone something," I said as he lifted my hand to kiss it. Only then did I chance a quick glimpse at his ima. Pale and sad, she hadn't even attempted to address her son. I prodded him quietly. "Perhaps you should go kiss your ima's cheek. She loves you so."

He shook his head. "Yaira will tend her. I'm Judah's king. I tend my wife and my nation." He brushed my cheek—a little rough, but a sweet gesture, nonetheless. I still worried. Zibah looked thinner. Gaunt.

By late afternoon, when bellies were full and eyelids heavy, Prince Mattaniah snored like thunder beside Belit, and she continued whispering with Shebna. Nasseh laid his head in my lap, focused on my ruby pendant while recounting how my dagger throwing could improve. I twirled a dark tendril of his shoulder-length hair and nearly choked on a sip of wine when a booming voice disrupted the peaceful hum.

"Listen, House of Jacob, to Yahweh's judgment on Babylon." Lord Isaiah stood at the head table, bellowing like a rutting roebuck.

"A noise on the mountains, like that of a great multitude! Listen, an uproar among the kingdoms, like nations massing together! The LORD Almighty is mustering an army for war."

Nasseh sat up, back rigid, muscles taut as a bowstring. He watched the reactions of the audience rather than offering a moment's attention to his saba.

"Ignore it," I whispered. "Everyone knows of your saba's lunacy."

Attention fixed solely on his guests, Nasseh's chapped hands clenched and released as the prophecy droned on.

"Babylon, the jewel of kingdoms, the pride and glory of the Babylonians, will be overthrown by God like Sodom and Gomorrah. She will never be inhabited or lived in through all generations . . ."

When Lord Isaiah showed no signs of stopping, Nasseh peered around me to Belit and nodded. She stood, cleared the table with one foot, and climbed atop it as if it were a perch—halting the old prophet's blathering. "Enough rambling from a doddering old man about an irrelevant god."

Isaiah's eyes narrowed, but rather than engage the woman, he lifted his hands toward heaven. "I remain faithful to Your will, Yahweh." He returned to his cushion with the help of the queen mother and Jashub, while Belit motioned to a white-robed priest, who'd been standing near a partition, to come forward.

The priest carried a small vial and climbed the steps of the dais. Bowing, he presented it to Belit who still stood on our table.

"In this flacon," she shouted, "I hold the most powerful elixir of death ever created." She cast a menacing glance at Isaiah and walked across platters, stepping on food, then stopped in front of him. The crowd gasped, but the old prophet never flinched. She uncorked the flacon and held it above his head. "You should be careful who you threaten with your useless words."

Isaiah held her gaze. "And you shouldn't gamble on a public exhibition. I won't die by your hand, sorceress."

She righted the bottle, seeming rattled by his confidence. Replacing the lid securely, she returned her attention to the audience and chuckled. "But why dampen a wedding celebration with an execution?"

Nasseh shot to his feet. "Yahweh's threats have devolved into an old man's bluster. Babylon was destroyed four years ago with armies Sennacherib gathered from many nations." He sloshed his goblet toward his saba. "Have you begun prophesying the past because you've failed miserably at foretelling the future?"

Shulle's cheeks flushed at the spectacle their royal table had made, but Nasseh continued shouting.

"Didn't you walk around naked and barefoot for three years, Saba, predicting Assyria would lead Egyptian captives 'naked and barefoot' to Nineveh? Assyria has never even crossed Egypt's border." He laughed, and most of the crowd joined him. Lifting his silver goblet, Nasseh coaxed others into his humiliating display. "Today, Judah celebrates the freedom to ignore Lord Isaiah's wearisome god and embrace any god we choose."

A loud cheer rose, but I kept my head bowed, focusing on the queen mother. She placed a protective arm around Isaiah and wept quietly, while Lord Jashub, Yaira, and Kenaz stared straight ahead, expressions well trained.

When the audience stilled, I looked up to see Belit emerging from the partition. She carried a wooden ship about the size of our cushions and exchanged a knowing grin with Dohd. My stomach clenched.

"I have a gift to present to my bride," Nasseh said, as Belit placed the treasure on our table.

Overwhelmed, I stood and hugged my husband. "Nasseh! It's lovely! I'll treasure it."

"This isn't just a toy boat." Nasseh continued speaking to the crowd while I inspected its cloth sails, wooden oars, and gold trim. "It's an exact replica of the ship on which my queen and I will begin our yearlong tour of nations. Egypt will be the first of our many destinations." My hand froze on an oar. "As you can see by the drawings the priests show you now, my new queen is a gifted artist—"

The unified "Ooh" drew my attention, and I watched ten priests stroll amid the tables displaying the maps and sketches I'd drawn for Nasseh through the years.

"A tour of nations?" I whispered.

He turned and grabbed my arms with quiet intensity. "Isn't it exciting? I've worked out all the details with Belit and Shebna. I've always wanted to see the sea. Remember, Shulle?" He laughed and danced a little to the rhythm of the words. " 'See the sea, see the sea'—remember?"

"Of course, my love." I wanted to be angry that he, Dohd, and Belit had arranged this journey without telling me. Had anyone considered how Nasseh would react to a change in schedule? To the unpredictability of travel? But asking such questions would ruin his excitement. I wrapped my arms around him and whispered against his cheek. "I'm so proud of you."

His arms tightened around my waist. "Did you see how people responded to the news of worshiping any god of their choosing?" His whisper was full of hope and promise. "I can do this, Shulle. I can be Judah's king."

He released me and lifted his goblet again. "Eat! Drink! We still have three weeks to celebrate before your king and queen begin their tour of nations." Another cheer erupted, reviving the musicians and dancers. The priests returned my drawings to Nasseh, and he showed me each of our destinations.

"We'll cross the Judean Mountains and Philistine plain to board our beautiful ship. From there it's a five-day sail to Pelusium, where we'll travel south on the Nile to meet Pharaoh Tirhakah in Memphis. After a brief stay, we'll retrace our journey north to Assyria's vassal nations and end our tour in Nineveh, meeting the great King Sennacherib face to face." He pointed to the mountain peaks I'd drawn as part of Assyria's capital.

I laid my hand on his cheek, gently pulling his attention from the parchments to me. "Travel is seldom predictable, my love. How will we maintain a daily routine?"

"Shebna promised he would research each location thoroughly so there won't be any surprises."

"Nasseh?" The queen mother stood behind us. "Your tour of nations is a lovely gesture for your bride, and I understand that you trust Shebna and want to see all the nations he's so vividly described. But please, son, listen to me. The Assyrians are a violent people. Your abba met the Assyrian king, Tiglath-Pileser, when he was a boy your age, and it changed him. Please, give yourself a few years before—"

"I am king, Ima." He stood, agitation growing, but he kept his voice low. "You can neither protect me nor command me. Now, sit down and maintain control of Saba. Another outburst, and I'll have him arrested."

After only a slight hesitation, she inclined her head. "Yes, my king." She returned to the cushion beside Isaiah, leaving dignity and grace in her wake.

Nasseh resumed his place beside me, and I slipped my hand into his to stop its spasms. "Like Dohd says, *A king need never raise his voice. His power is like a trumpet.*'"

A slight grin curved his lips and he reached for his wine. "No one tells me what to do."

The thought of traveling with him on a yearlong journey and having no one to help with his moods was daunting. I leaned over to Dohd, keeping my voice low. "I suppose you've placed yourself on Judah's throne while Nasseh and I travel?" It was more an accusation than a question.

"Prince Mattaniah will sit on Judah's throne, and I will accompany you and the king." He turned to me with a single lifted brow. "Belit has proven more cunning than I expected."

I glanced around Dohd and noticed Belit and Prince Mattaniah with their heads together, exchanging whispers. When had they become so friendly?

"She's captured Mattaniah's affection," Dohd continued, "and will no doubt try to rule him and Judah, but my spies will end her if she betrays me."

Leaving Jerusalem seemed suddenly appealing—if only to avoid the war between my two mentors.

When Nasseh and I retired to our chamber, he could talk of nothing but our travel plans. "After Egypt, we'll sail to Tyre and harvest purple dye from a murex shell. Then we'll buy silk in Damascus, sit in the lush shade of Tadmor's palms, and ferry across the Great River to Anatho's floating paradise before our final trek to Nineveh."

His eyes sparked with adventure, but practicality niggled at my excitement. The farthest my husband had traveled was a half day's excursion to Gibeon, where Yahweh had given Solomon wisdom through a dream. I'd made the four-day journey from Jotbah in a carriage, but neither of us had ridden a camel for weeks at a time or sailed the Great Sea.

"It sounds wonderful, doesn't it?" His eyes bright with anticipation, I dared not disappoint.

"It's beyond what I could even imagine, my love." I offered my best attempt at a smile and dropped my robe to the floor. "Shall we go to bed?" My nakedness still caused a flush on his cheeks.

Nasseh blew out the lamps and slipped into bed beside me, curling his body around mine. He was quiet for a few moments, then he finally whispered, "Thank you for loving me, Shulle." He turned over, and I soon heard the slow and steady breathing of restful sleep.

I slipped from our bed, retrieved the golden image Prince Mattaniah had given him, and cradled her in my hands as I returned to my husband's side to pray. *Ishtar, Queen of the Night, grant me your wisdom and power to both love and fight for my husband.*

⁓

Each day for the next three weeks, I watched Nasseh grow more confident and regal. Lifting his goblet each morning, he recognized ambassadors from visiting nations, making promises to visit their kings on our upcoming tour. Occasionally, I caught myself thinking King Hezekiah would walk into the courtroom. I'd glance at the queen mother and find her talking quietly with Lord Isaiah or Yaira. Fresh tears often stained their cheeks, and I wondered if it was grief over King Hezekiah's passing that haunted them or the swift passion with which our guests embraced the new gods and worship practices we introduced at the feast.

The Yahwists seemed to sequester themselves in a protective shell as the rest of Judah began breaking free of old rules that hung like a dark cloud over spring blooms. At sunset, on the final evening of our feast, our guests raised their goblets, then Shebna stood and pronounced the blessing:

"May the gods of every nation bless King Manasseh and Queen Meshullemeth. May you find favor in Philistia, Egypt, Syria, and throughout the Assyrian Empire at every temple, altar, and high place. And may the gods guide you into the strong alliance they've promised."

I lifted my goblet and emptied it to the dregs, peering over the lip to see Nasseh's Yahwist family standing but refusing to join the toast. Nasseh watched them, too, the public slight adding to his pain. It was the first time I feared for them. Nasseh loved his ima. Kenaz was as close as a brother. But the rest must learn to bow the knee or face the wrath of Judah's new king.

20

All night long on my bed
  I looked for the one my heart loves;
  I looked for him but did not find him.

SONG OF SONGS 3:1

Three Weeks Later, Sivan (June)

Zibah opened her chamber door, startling her guard with an early morning greeting. "Shalom, Onan. I'd like to visit the king and queen before they leave."

The man who had been captain of Hezi's guard bowed deeply. "Who would you like to visit first, Queen Mother?"

Understanding dawned with disappointment. "Which chamber in the harem did my son give his queen?"

"I'll take you to her."

Zibah followed the man who had guarded her chamber since Hezi's passing. She trusted him with her life because Hezi had trusted him so long. Onan paused outside the largest chamber, the one that had been Nasseh's—and had belonged to Hezi's ima before that.

Onan motioned toward a guard at Shulle's door, and the man pounded his spear against it before announcing Zibah's arrival. Shulle's invitation was barely audible.

"Thank you, Onan," Zibah said. "I can find my way back to my chamber." Stepping into the darkened room, she let her eyes adjust. The balcony curtains were drawn, and only a few lamps lit the cavernous sitting area.

"Come in, Queen Mother." A lone figure sat on the couch facing the balcony. "Have you come to say goodbye?" Shulle asked, sniffing.

All the pleading Zibah planned disappeared when she walked around the couch and saw Shulle's swollen eyes. "You've been crying a long time. Why didn't you share Nasseh's chamber last night?"

Shulle glanced down at the wet cloth in her hands. "Dohd Shebna wouldn't allow it. He told Nasseh a king needs a private chamber." She looked up then, eyes glistening. "Dohd and Belit conjured this whole tour of nations without even consulting me."

Relief washed over Zibah. "I'm so glad you agree. We can work together to convince Nasseh it's too dangerous to leave for a whole year this early in his reign. Besides, Mattaniah loves Nasseh, but he would cut off his own hand for the right price."

"You're wrong." The girl stood, suddenly defiant. "The journey will strengthen Nasseh's influence among world leaders, and Prince Mattaniah will maintain good faith here at home."

Zibah heard Shebna's coaching behind every word. "Will Belit also maintain good faith?" The question dimmed Shulle's confidence, giving Zibah fuel to continue. "If Belit openly practices sorcery, she'll threaten Yahwist lives."

"So, you admit the starry hosts are more powerful than Yahweh?" A surprising smugness narrowed her eyes.

"It isn't about power, Shulle. It's about freedom. Yahweh created humans, and humans created gods. Your gods enslave humans until Yahweh provides freedom through sometimes painful paths." Zibah offered her hand. "Will you help me prevent the pain my son may experience in Yahweh's battle for his soul?"

She folded her arms across her chest. "It's Yahweh who has chained Nasseh all his life, and Ishtar will help me win my husband's battle for freedom."

The words cut Zibah to the core. *Yahweh, only You can help me love this girl and place both her and Nasseh in Your hands.* Inhaling Yahweh's presence and exhaling her rising anger, she spoke with a calm she didn't feel.

"I don't want our last words to be cross." Zibah sat down on the couch, patting the spot beside her. "I have a favor to ask and a story to tell. Which would you like to hear first?"

Shulle's features softened, but she still seemed wary, walking over to open the balcony curtains. "I'll hear no more negativity about my husband, and we leave midmorning. If your story is short, you may proceed."

Haughty little snip. Perhaps she'd be more open to the favor after hearing the story. "This chamber belonged to Hezi's ima, Abijah, before it became Nasseh's. She and King Ahaz had a rather tumultuous relationship." Zibah left the couch to join Shulle near the balcony railing, gazing down at the Valley of Kidron below. "Abijah worshipped the goddess Asherah, involving Ahaz's other wives and many harem guards."

Shulle's head whipped around. "Abba told me King Ahaz worshipped pagan gods, but I never knew—"

"Not many people did," Zibah said. "When Ahaz died, and Hezi assumed sole reign, I discovered the queen mother's idolatry. She hated me with a passion, so I know a little about dealing with a difficult mother-in-law, Shulle." Zibah cradled the girl's hand and grinned. "Later in Abijah's life, she came to the realization that Yahweh loved her, and only then did she experience true joy."

The young queen slipped her hand away. "I don't need your god to be happy."

"What if you get to Egypt and Pharaoh Tirhakah believes Nasseh is spying for Assyria? He'll kill you both."

"Don't even say—"

"What if, when Nasseh arrives in Assyria, King Sennacherib accuses him of making a treaty with Egypt? Sennacherib would enjoy killing the son of Hezekiah, the only king whose city he never conquered. Yahweh killed 185,000 of his soldiers outside our gates."

"Stop!" Shulle covered her ears.

Zibah pulled her into a fierce embrace and whispered harshly. "I want you and my son to spend eternity with Hezi and me in the life beyond. That's the only true peace, Shulle. Peace that offers joy when happiness fails."

Shulle pushed away Zibah. "Where's the joy and peace your invisible god promised? All you do is cry over your wayward son and dead husband."

Stunned by the girl's venom, Zibah glared at the adversary she was determined to love. "I go to bed alone; I wake up alone. But I'm never really alone, Meshullemeth, because Yahweh is invisible. He is always with me."

The girl scoffed. "A quaint bedtime story for children, Queen Mother, but—"

"Stop it!" Zibah shouted, and the girl fell silent at her fury. "You know it's true. You see it in Yaira, my brother, and Kenaz. Though Abba is a crusty old prophet, even he exudes an unshakable peace no one can destroy. I grieve, yes, but I go on living. I miss Hezi, of course, because he shared my life, my breath, my soul. I feel like half of me is missing, Shulle, and I will never be whole again—until I see Hezi and Yahweh in the life beyond. But," she said, pounding her heart with each word, "I. Will. See. Him. Again."

Shulle's eyes glistened. "The paradise you speak of is too ideal. Too simple." She shook her head. "I don't know if Egypt's or Assyria's or Babylon's gods will meet me in the afterworld, but the life beyond can't be so simple. Not when this world is so complex." Wiping her face, she squared her shoulders and turned away.

Zibah saw the invisible walls go up. "Before I ask my favor, please accept my gift." No response. "Three things I learned as Hezi's queen. Number one: a king's council is never unanimous."

The girl grinned slightly. "Go on."

"Number two: no king is *always* right."

Shulle covered a lovely smile. "I'll use that one when Nasseh and I argue."

"Number three: Yahweh's prophets only speak truth, Shulle, and they've said my own flesh and blood will be taken captive to Babylon. Now, I must ask my favor. Please don't let my son visit Babylon's ruins on your tour of nations."

She rolled her eyes and turned away again. "Why would we go to Babylon? You heard Dohd. It's a heap of ruins."

"Promise me, Shulle."

"Babylon is not in our plan, Queen Mother."

Zibah paused. Dare she ask for one more thing? She laid her hand on Shulle's arm, and Shulle didn't pull away. "Abba has a gift for Nasseh," Zibah said, "but my son has refused to see him. Would you escort him to Nasseh's chamber?" She'd already started shaking her head. "Please. You don't realize how important—"

"And you don't realize how deeply Lord Isaiah hurt Nasseh."

"Nasseh will appreciate the gift Abba has for him. I promise."

Zibah waited silently until the hard lines around Shulle's mouth softened. "Have Lord Isaiah come here when he's ready, and I'll escort him to Nasseh's chamber."

"Thank you." She kissed her forehead and turned to go.

"I can't promise Nasseh will speak with him," she said.

Zibah looked over her shoulder as she opened the door to leave. "At least Abba's final words to Nasseh will be kind." Or so she hoped.

21

[Ahaz] . . . even sacrificed his son in the fire,
engaging in the detestable practices of the
nations the LORD had driven out before the
Israelites. He offered sacrifices and burned
incense at the high places, on the hilltops and
under every spreading tree.

2 KINGS 16:3–4

Four stewards packed Manasseh's robes and jewels. He moved toward the balcony to check the weather and bumped into three more servants. Desperate for fresh air, he looked to the sky. Cloudy. Hadn't Belit prophesied sun for today's travel? The noise in his head crescendoed, and he ran inside to the nearest corner, face against the wall. *See the sea. See the sea. See the sea.*

A hand on his back was too much. "Leave me!"

"Shh, Nasseh. It's me." Shulle said and began humming the fish song.

"Stop!" He whirled on her and then shouted at the servants, "Get out, all of you! Get out!" Ten people scurried like rats to their holes. "Why are they here, Shulle? Make them leave."

"They're taking your personal items to the caravan." She slipped her arms around his neck and began the fish song again.

This time he didn't resist. "I'm glad you're here," he said, burying his face in the bend of her neck. "I didn't like sleeping without you."

She swayed to the rhythm of the song but stopped singing. "Nasseh, I brought your saba Isaiah. He has a gift for you."

"You what?" Nasseh shoved aside Shulle as the old man stepped from the shadows.

"Shalom, Nasseh."

"Have you come to tell me what a worthless king I am?"

Saba's frown lines deepened. "You're not worthless, Nasseh. You're a treasure to me—and to Yahweh."

Nasseh studied him. Nothing was ever simple with Saba. "What do you want?"

"I've come to beg you to stay in Jerusalem—only for a year."

Nasseh scoffed. "Have you seen the caravan already packed and waiting outside? You're insane."

Saba chuckled. "You're not the first to suggest it." He took a step closer. "I know how much you loved your abba. Give yourself time to grieve. The law of Moses gives newlywed soldiers twelve months' reprieve from military service. Surely a king should receive no less to nurture his bride." He nodded and smiled at Shulle, but the gesture seemed misplaced on the normally frowning face.

"We'll nurture each other," Nasseh said, grasping Shulle's hand to keep his own from clenching. "And we'll measure the political climate of Assyria's vassal nations. If most seem submissive, we'll carry the report to Nineveh and curry Sennacherib's favor. If conditions are ripe for rebellion, well then—"

"Traveling with his new queen will seem entirely social," Shulle said, wrapping Nasseh's arm around her waist as if to further steady him. "We're very much looking forward to meeting Pharaoh Tirhakah."

Nasseh laughed. "Wasn't Tirhakah Egypt's general when Abba joined the anti-Assyrian coalition that prompted your three-year naked prophecy, Saba?"

Isaiah's droopy frown matched his sad eyes. "Have you even considered where your abba is now? What do you think happened when Hezekiah closed his eyes in this world and opened them in the next?" He stepped closer—too close—and Nasseh felt his stare like razors cutting his face. "You haven't had time to grieve," he said. "Please, Nasseh. Stay in Judah for at least six months, and wrestle with these questions."

"No!" He left Shulle's embrace and shoved past the old man, slapping his head to distract from the inner noise. "You don't know what waits beyond. No one knows."

"*Yahweh* waits beyond." His voice was close. "He waits beyond for those who live in faith. Faith that we'll see Him and those we love again. King David. Solomon. Uzziah, Jotham, and Hezekiah."

Nasseh whirled on him. "You left out Saba Ahaz."

"He wasn't faithful, son. Ahaz left only brokenness and destruction as his legacy."

"And what legacy did Abba leave? Me!" Nasseh pounded his chest, self-loathing fueling his rage. "I'm broken, Saba, but I will leave a better legacy than Abba. I'll go to Nineveh and face the man Abba hid from. When Sennacherib returned to Assyria after besieging Jerusalem, he inscribed on a monument that will endure for all time, 'I trapped Hezekiah like a bird in a cage.' *That is* Abba's legacy." Nasseh stepped closer, meeting the old man's gaze. "I will be more than Judah's second Solomon."

Saba's slap came without warning, leaving Nasseh's hair hanging in his eyes.

"Nasseh, I'm sorry. I . . ." Saba's voice shook. "I won't let you degrade your abba's memory. You were named *Manasseh* 'to remember' the near destruction your saba Ahaz brought on Judah and the powerful ways Hezekiah turned this nation back to Yahweh."

"I remember, old man." Nasseh raised his hand to cover the fire burning his cheek but didn't look at his saba again. "I remember your endless prophecies of doom despite Abba's faithful service. He was a caged bird, not just by Sennacherib but also by the merciless god from whom he begged for crumbs." Nasseh grabbed Isaiah's robe and shouted, "I will not be caged!" He shoved the old man away.

Shaking with rage, Nasseh watched Saba retreat toward a servant who waited at the chamber doors with a small basket. He retrieved the covered vessel and slowly walked back to Manasseh, placing the basket in his hands.

"I hope it brings you comfort on your journey," Saba said. "And perhaps reminds you that I love you." He walked away without waiting for a response.

Something inside the basket moved, and Nasseh was almost afraid to remove the lid. Had Saba gifted him a viper?

Shulle laid her hand on the basket. "Do you want me to open it?"

He shook his head, knelt, and placed the basket on the floor before removing the lid. A fluffy gray kitten climbed out, wakened by the light. Nasseh held it under his chin, staring at his chamber door. "He cannot buy my favor with a kitten after he killed my abba with a curse." Placing the kitten back in the basket, he handed it to Shulle. "Finish packing. I'm ready to leave Jerusalem."

22

[Manasseh] rebuilt the high places his father
Hezekiah had destroyed; he also erected altars to
Baal and made an Asherah pole. . . . He bowed
down to all the starry hosts and worshiped them.

2 KINGS 21:3

Jerusalem to Ashkelon to Pelusium to Memphis
Sivan (June) to Tammuz (July)

Nasseh insisted on riding his white stallion at the head of our caravan as we left Jerusalem. Dohd Shebna and I shared the royal carriage—with the new kitten—traveling behind the king's guard. My nerves were frayed after Nasseh's confrontation with Lord Isaiah, and I couldn't push the queen mother's words from my mind. *"If Belit openly practices sorcery, she'll threaten Yahwist lives."* Would Belit harm Zibah while we were away? Or Yaira?

I glanced at Dohd studying his scroll. I snatched it from his hand. "Did you kill Lord Isaiah's wife?"

Surprise shifted to annoyance. "What are you talking about?" He reached for the scroll, but I shoved it into the basket at our feet.

"Lord Isaiah said you poisoned his wife, and Queen Zibah thinks Belit might harm the Yahwists while we're away."

His eyelids lowered to half mast. "She isn't Queen Zibah anymore, and yes, Belit will likely call down a curse or two on the Yahwists, but I doubt she'll kill anyone." He picked out another scroll from his basket and resumed his study.

A cold chill raced through me, so I held the kitten close. "You didn't answer my first question. About Lord Isaiah's wife." He ignored me. And I knew. Lord Isaiah had told the truth. My dohd was a murderer.

I shoved aside a curtain in the carriage window. *Breathe. Breathe.* Had Dohd lied about everything? "I thought we wanted to make Judah better. Teach Nasseh about the true gods that could make him the greatest king in Judah's history."

Dohd set aside his parchment, looking at me with the tenderness I remembered from childhood. "At times like these, I see your ima's goodness in you, Shulle. Adnah would be proud of the young woman you've become. But as I've told you before, sometimes we must harm to heal."

"How could killing Isaiah's wife heal anyone? And explain why you would place an unbridled sorceress and a senseless drunk in charge of Judah while Nasseh visits volatile kings in unfamiliar lands?"

He clucked his tongue, making me feel like a child. "Do you think I made these decisions without considering every possibility before setting them into motion? Who do you think suggested this tour of nations as your gift? It was I who suggested Belit advise Mattaniah while we're gone." He leaned so close the kitten hissed, and I smelled wine on his breath. "Don't *ever* question me again, Shulle. You are my treasure, but at the first sniff of disloyalty—your abba dies. Do you understand?"

Barely breathing, I nodded. He grinned, resuming his seat and straightening his robe. "Now, would you like to hear the safeguards I've instituted while we scamper all over the empire?"

I nodded again, scooting to the corner of my bench, as far from him as possible.

"The first days of Manasseh's reign are most favorable for audiences with foreign kings. Most will think him harmless because he's young and rather . . . odd. Those who recognize his brilliance will assume the jackals on Judah's council will devour him when we return home. The faithful waiting in Judah will execute anyone who tries to steal Manasseh's throne—simply because they adored Hezekiah. Mattaniah, though a parasite, isn't clever enough to steal the throne. I've strategically placed spies around Belit, who *is* clever enough to steal the throne, to execute her if she betrays our goal."

"*Our* goal?" I asked cautiously, which won his approving smile.

"As you said, dear niece. We will ensure Nasseh becomes the greatest king in Judah's history—and it begins today. Judean troops will have completed construction of Asherah poles on every hillside and altars on every street corner in all Judean cities by the time we return from our tour. Judah's transition to free worship will appear to have taken place under Matti's guidance, not Manasseh's."

"But the Yahwist council members would never allow Matti to proceed with those changes." They'd vehemently objected to all Dohd's suggestions during our evening meals while the nation mourned Hezekiah.

"While you were celebrating at your wedding feast, your husband dismissed five Yahwist council members, relieving them of their royal duties, and appointed eight new members who you know *intimately* from the Grove." My cheeks flamed instantly. "Publicly, we'll emphasize the necessity for new members to stir lively debate," he said. "And if by some strange twist, the council adopts policies detrimental to our reforms, Mattaniah has the power—as acting regent—to overrule any decision."

"It appears you've thought of everything," I said.

He reached over to smooth my hair. "Of course, my girl. You can relax and enjoy the journey. Your only responsibility is to love your husband and give him fat little sons to fill the palace halls." With a satisfied smile, he sat back and unfurled the scroll in his hand.

I turned my back to him. The jostling of the carriage on rocky, wilderness terrain made sleep impossible, so I cuddled with the furry gray kitten, my only escape from a man I once thought I knew.

We traveled in rigid silence until nightfall. As soon as the carriage stopped, I flung open the door and saw two tents at the center of camp already set up by servants that our caravan master had sent ahead. My chambermaid waited beside a small, white tent with the flap open, but I chose instead to join my husband in the elegant white tent beside it.

Nasseh was tired and sore from his long day on the stallion. While we ate alone in his two-chambered tent, he paid more attention to the kitten than to me. I wanted to beg him to let me ride a stallion beside him—or better yet, to ride with me and the kitten in a sedan atop one of the camels. But Nasseh seemed to barely have enough strength to wash his hands and lift food to his mouth. I dared not complain about my golden carriage, but neither could I bear riding with Dohd for the next two days.

"I'm too tired to eat." He shoved his plate away, eyes drooping.

Hurrying to my feet, I cradled the kitten in one arm and helped Nasseh stand. We walked the few steps to his sleeping chamber, and I saw the pouch with the golden Ishtar lying beside his sleeping mat. Inhaling the sweet incense burning in the small brazier, I prayed to my goddess for favor and mustered my courage.

"May I wash your feet, my love?"

Nasseh barely nodded. I removed his crown, his sandals, and his robe. He lay on his sleeping mat, still silent, and I lifted Ishtar from the bag and placed her on the ground beside his head. Splashing cool water over his feet, I then massaged them dry with a cloth. Though I lingered, he didn't speak, so I set aside the basin and stood to leave.

"Stay." He caught my hand. "I want to hold you while we fall asleep."

Nasseh pulled me to his side, tucking the kitten under one arm and me under the other. My goddess watched over us till dawn.

When the three of us emerged from the tent in morning's light, Dohd looked on disapprovingly.

"Secure a camel with a canopied sedan," Nasseh told him. "Shulle and I will spend the remainder of this journey together."

Nasseh took the kitten from me while we waited. "What shall we name her?" He scratched beneath her chin.

I stroked her gray fur until she purred. "Adnah," I said.

"*Delight,* I like it."

A caravanner arrived with our dromedary and helped us climb into the sedan. Dohd looked up from the window of his carriage beside us and offered me a rueful grin. I laced my arm in Nasseh's, triumphant. Dohd may wield power over counselors and spies, but as long as I tended my husband's love, I was as safe as a camel in the desert.

On our third day of travel, we arrived in Ashkelon, the Philistine seaport conquered and lost by both Israel and Judah countless times in our history. Currently, it was under Assyria's rule. Our caravan master halted us near the central fountain, and Nasseh tapped our camel's front shoulder. The moment we dismounted, six dogs ran at us, barking and jumping. I screamed and sheltered Adnah in my arms. Nasseh drew his sword.

"No, my king!" Baka stayed Nasseh's hand, while six other guards encircled him, fending off the raving beasts by tossing pieces of dried meat as far as possible.

Now that the immediate danger had passed, Nasseh's anger ignited. "How dare you—"

Baka knelt, head bowed. "Forgive me, but the dogs of Ashkelon are sacred, my king. Had you injured or killed them, we would have been arrested or killed ourselves." Philistine soldiers surrounded our caravan, proving his words.

Nasseh sheathed his sword. "But the Philistine god is Dagon—with a fish's tail. Not a dog god."

"My king, are you well?" Dohd stood beside us, shaking. "The dogs won't harm you. They're sort of a good luck charm for the fishermen on the docks. The same thing happened to me the first time I visited Ashkelon."

"Then why was I not prepared, Lord Shebna?" Nasseh's glare assured him the question was rhetorical. "You promised to brief me on everything about a city before we arrived. Everything. Should I feed *you* to the dogs in Ashkelon and find someone more competent to brief me on my journey?"

Dohd bowed to one knee. "It won't happen again, my king. I've secured a room for you and your queen at the inn. It's barely more than a Sabbath's walk from here. Your meal has been ordered, fresh fish from the Great Sea and all the delicacies Ashkelon offers."

"Stand, Shebna," Nasseh said, eyes roving the seashore. "I want to know what kind of delicacies, the type of fish, and how many steps from the dining room to my bed. I mean *every* detail."

Shebna glanced at me, but I wasn't about to rescue him from his blunder. "If you and Queen Shulle will follow me," he said, "I'll ensure you're settled at the inn, and then I'll share every detail of the rest of our journey before your guards escort you to the dining hall."

Nasseh took my hand and waved at our shaken guide. "Go, Shebna. We'll follow you—for now."

～

The next morning, Nasseh and I recognized our ship in Ashkelon's port from our chamber's window. I lifted my wooden model while Nasseh marveled at the resemblance. "It even has the exact number of oars as the real ship," he said, tucking Adnah beneath his chin.

I still worried how so much wood, metal, and people could float, especially if the early summer clouds in Ashkelon's gray sky turned to winds and rain.

"We're well into the month of Sivan, Queen of Judah." The ship's captain spoke in perfect Akkadian, the language of trade. "A month ago, I wouldn't have tried it, but the clouds are a gift from the gods. They'll keep us from baking on our five-day journey."

Two days later, when our ship was tossed on waves higher than second-story balconies, Nasseh threatened to have the captain executed. By morning of our third day, however, the Great Sea was smooth as glass, and Judah's king leaned over the railing in utter delight to feel the oars' spray.

"Look, Shulle," he said, letting the salt water wet his dark curls. "We're doing it."

"Doing what?" All we'd done for the past two days was fill the waste pot with vomit.

"Seeing the sea!" He stood on the deck, arms open wide and twirled. My gleeful husband was realizing his dream.

For the remainder of our voyage, we hardly left the deck. Under the sun, we enjoyed slick-skinned fish speeding past us, each one as big as a man. They leaped in perfect arcs, sometimes in formation, delighting even the stodgiest sailors. Adnah hated getting her paws wet but loved the fresh fish the sailors fed her.

Under our starry hosts, I taught Nasseh prayers, and the captain explained navigation by the stars. Each night, when the sailors retreated below deck and we lay alone beneath our shelter, we spoke of his reign, his dreams, and his fears. Adnah lay between us, soaking up our love, giving us hers. For all my husband's bluster at Lord Isaiah about uncaged greatness, he was as afraid as I of meeting Pharaoh Tirhakah.

When we docked near Pelusium, the fortress city at Egypt's northeastern border, Nasseh bid farewell to the ship's captain and our sailors. He'd captured their respect and gained more confidence on this first leg of our journey. He insisted on leaving the ship first, but when he stepped from the gangplank, his sandal sank in black muck. So much for the gallant farewell. Pelusium—Egyptian for "ooze"—was aptly named.

Though activity hummed around us, Dohd pressed Nasseh and me through the sweaty mass of humanity in the shoreline market and then south toward our next ship. "Keep your arms folded across your chests," he shouted above the din. "Don't stop for any child beggars. They'll rob you blind."

We were surrounded by a hundred of our royal guards. How could any children get to—

"Please, my queen. Just a scrap of bread?" A dirt-smudged face with sandy-brown eyes stared up at me, scratched Adnah behind the ears, and melted my heart.

I reached down to ruffle his hair. "How did you know I was a quee—"
Quicker than a gasp, my gold bangles were off my wrist and in his hands,
and the sandy-eyed urchin slipped between a guard's legs.

"Stop him!" Dohd shouted.

"Let him go." I chuckled, and Nasseh laughed too. "Perhaps he'll buy
supper for his family," I said, receiving a chastising glare from Dohd.

But Nasseh drew my hand to his lips. "You'll make a gracious queen."
The love in his eyes was worth more than a thousand bangles.

Our sandaled feet were a muddy mess by the time we'd tromped
through tall grass and reeds to climb a gangplank. "There must be some
mistake." I stopped at the base of the footbridge. "There's not enough
water to sail." The flat-bottomed, narrow barque sat in water no deeper
than my knees.

"Have you forgotten all our lessons?" Dohd's tone felt hotter in the
glaring Egyptian sun. "We've arrived during the final days of *Shemu*—
harvest season—when the Nile is at its lowest. The oarsmen must walk the
banks and pull us with ropes for most of our journey to Memphis."

"I thought you exaggerated." Dread made me sound squeaky.

Both Nasseh and Dohd fell into a fit of laughter, but I saw nothing
funny about dozens of men dragging us down a muddy gulch for twelve
days. Half the length and width of our previous ship, the single-deck
barque would be our only shelter from the glaring sun on the crocodile-
infested Nile. Rowing benches were arranged aft to propel us; three private
cabins sat in the center; and canopied lounging couches awaited our leisure
on the bow. Half our guards accompanied us while the other half boarded
a second barque with the bulk of our personal items.

I tried not to complain, but after inspecting the sparse single mattress
and washbasin in the chamber I would share with Nasseh, I joined the
men on a couch to watch our oarsmen begin the journey. A hundred men
took up their positions on the banks beside us and began the arduous
journey under Egypt's blazing sun. "Will they really do this for the whole
twelve days?"

"They'll rest at night," Dohd said. "No one travels the Nile at night."

"Why?" Nasseh asked as he took Adnah from my arms. I wasn't sure I wanted to know the reason.

"It's too dangerous," Dohd said. He then quickly described the hemp ropes secured to the starboard and port sides, each as thick as a man's forearm, used to drag our boat. Nasseh seemed content with Dohd's diversionary tactic, and I certainly wasn't going to dwell on the dangers.

Five days into our journey, our oarsmen were exhausted. Only one afternoon had we encountered enough water to float, so the poor men had literally tugged us the whole way. Nasseh and I began distributing water skins for the midday break, and like a mother hen, I watched our oarsmen all afternoon to make sure none fainted from the heat.

Dusk settled over the riverbed, and sweat glistened on our faithful oarsmen's backs. "Must we continue to Memphis?" I asked Dohd. "How can they continue like this for another week? Isn't there somewhere else we could go until the inundation swells the river?"

"It will be at least three weeks before the season of Akhet *begins,* and we have no idea if the floods will rise slowly—or too quickly and make traveling even more dangerous."

Like Nasseh, he wasn't going to budge on the schedule. "How long will we stay— Oh, no!" I screamed, covering my eyes, but not before I saw a monstrous crocodile clamp onto an oarsman's legs. The creature pulled him into the riverbed ahead of our barque.

"Don't look away!" Dohd's angry voice startled me, and I uncovered my eyes. He had yanked Nasseh's hands away from his eyes and now lowered his voice. "Your guards will think you weak. A man rushes toward violence. A king revels in blood." Dohd pulled him to his feet and nudged him toward the bow.

Eyes wide, Nasseh stood fast, looking to me as if waiting for permission. Dohd's glare told me I dare not interfere. "Go, Nasseh. You can prove yourself to our men."

Nodding, he followed Dohd. I picked up Adnah and buried my face

in her fur, listening as men's panicked cries turned to cheering and victorious song. When the noise finally calmed, I lifted my head, and found
Nasseh running toward me, wide eyed with wonder.

"You should have seen it, Shulle. It happened just as Shebna said. The
giant crocodiles began feeding at dusk, but to think we actually saw one
hunt and eat its prey."

Prey? It was one of our oarsmen!

Before I voiced my disgust, Dohd arrived and circled Nasseh's shoulders. "You proved yourself courageous in a crisis, my king. Your men have
seen you revel in the kill. Congratulations."

"Thank you, Shebna." Nasseh looked over his shoulder at the guards
still recounting the incident as if he longed to join them.

"Go back to your barbaric soldiers," I said. "I want nothing to do with
men who celebrate a senseless death." I couldn't stop shaking.

Nasseh studied me and then said, "I think you're afraid, Shulle. But
we're safe. We've dropped the stone anchor for the night, and every oarsman will line the deck with a spear in hand."

Barely holding back tears, I whispered, "How many more days until
we reach Memphis?"

"I already told you." Dohd's words were clipped, glare threatening.

I walked away before tears humiliated me.

For the remainder of our journey, I spent as little time on deck as possible. Perhaps only the oarsmen and Adnah were more relieved than me to
see Egypt's capital city when we docked seven days later. Relieved, that is,
until I saw Pharaoh Tirhakah and the two hundred soldiers he brought
to meet our barque. I could only hope we brought enough gifts to appease him.

23

Such are the paths of all who go after ill-gotten gain;
it takes away the life of those who get it.

PROVERBS 1:19

Memphis, Egypt
One Month Later, Ab (August)

Nasseh woke under the sheer linen draped over his bed, marveling at the horde of mosquitos outside it. They'd attacked like an invading army with the inundation—only two weeks after Tirhakah and his troops swarmed the dock at Memphis to welcome Judah's king and queen. Nasseh swatted the netting, watching the pests scatter, remembering his fear.

Pharaoh's expression had looked like chiseled granite. Tirhakah was a head taller than Abba. His gold collar and white kilt gleamed in the afternoon sun against sweat-glistening black skin. Chariots lined the dock, and every driver's face looked as angry as his king's.

"You are a small boy" were Tirhakah's first words when Nasseh debarked. He barely reached the Egyptian's armpit. "But to visit Egypt requires a big man's courage."

Nasseh dared a glance at his face and interpreted a twitch at the corner of his mouth as a smile. He'd instantly liked the man. When the inundation raised the Nile to record-breaking levels, depositing fertile silt into Egypt's dark soil, Tirhakah told him he deemed King Manasseh's visit a good omen.

The memory pleased Nasseh as he rolled on his side and watched his wife sleep on her stomach, Adnah curled in the bend of her arm. The kitten had grown fat on Egypt's plentiful mice, and the Black Land's magic had seeped into Nasseh's soul. Shulle was less enamored. Thousands of gods dwelt in Egypt, but she insisted on worshiping only the starry hosts. Nubian royalty, pyramid tombs, and barley beer captured Nasseh's attention, but Shulle drew only sketches of home.

And she'd been worried about *his* adjustment to change.

He lifted a dark curl from her cheek—gently, so he wouldn't wake her. She was so beautiful. While sailing the Great Sea, he'd asked Baka if Shulle was a goddess. His confidant assured him Shulle was human, but Nasseh still wasn't convinced.

He reached for the vial of lemongrass oil before leaving the safety of their linen cocoon. Smearing it on his arms and legs, he recalled his ima and abba kissing and hugging. As a boy he'd thought a kiss or hug built love like bricks built a house, but Shulle said love was more like the smell of myrtle blossoms. Not so easily built or torn down, love sort of drifts into place. He smeared a layer of pungent oil on his chest and clutched at the ache. Did the ache mean love was drifting into place?

Safely armored with oil, Nasseh emerged from his linen cocoon and padded down two steps to the sitting area in their private villa. Adnah followed, stretching, yawning, shaking out her paws. Far more social than Cat, she divided her attention between his villa and Shebna's next door, spoiled by the house slaves, who left dried fish for her. The slaves had placed dried fruit and nuts on a table for Judah's king to break his fast. Nasseh grabbed a handful of pistachios and raisins, then meandered toward the open courtyard and down a path toward the Nile. He halted at the edge of the tiles, of course, not wishing to tempt the crocodiles he'd seen lounging in the reeds.

When they'd docked a month ago, he thought Tirhakah might be like a crocodile, waiting to snap him in two. But the pharaoh had treated Nasseh kindly, inviting him to observe his court rulings; Tirhakah was a patient teacher who explained his decisions. He was very wise—which meant Nasseh should take his advice and marry many women. Would Shulle be angry if he did? Would Tirhakah be angry if he didn't?

Shulle's chin rested on his shoulder, startling him. Nasseh turned, offering the remainder of his pistachios and raisins. "You would make a good spy."

"Not very good if I didn't notice when you slipped out of bed." She took a few raisins. "How long have you been awake?"

"Not long, but I must prepare for today's hunt."

"I'll ask my maid to braid and cover my hair so I can accompany you."

"It's for men only," Nasseh said. "We'll be back in time for tonight's banquet."

She smiled, but her eyes filled with tears. Why must Shulle's smiles be so complicated? "I need to start packing for our departure tomorrow." She started to walk away.

"Tirhakah says I should take another wife," Nasseh blurted out. Shulle stopped but didn't turn. He added, "He will present her to me at tonight's banquet."

Shulle reached down to pick up Adnah and buried her face in the cat's fur.

Nasseh closed the distance between them and tried to tilt her chin up, but she wouldn't look at him. "I need to read your face."

She lifted her eyes, her cheeks wet with tears. "Why must you read my face? Would you want me to marry someone else?"

"Why would you marry someone else, Shulle? Only kings need to build a household."

"Ugh!" She shoved his chest. "King Tirhakah isn't always right, Nasseh. You don't need more wives to build a household."

She was angry, just as he'd feared. Would Tirhakah be even more angry if Nasseh refused his advice? At the moment, facing Pharaoh's army seemed preferable to enduring Shulle's tears. Like a coward, he hurried into the villa. "Steward! Ready me for the day. Now!" He sat on a stool and washed his hands in a water basin with floating lotus pedals. The dry

Egyptian heat had caused his hands to crack and bleed. He'd mastered most of his other tics—rocking on his feet, clenching his fists—but nothing calmed him more than the feel of water trickling over his hands.

"Let me help you." Shulle's soft touch in the basin soothed him. "I miss the myrtle blossoms, don't you?"

His chest ached again. How could he become Judah's greatest king if he didn't make the right decision? "It's not just Tirhakah," he said. "Shebna also says I must build my house quickly. We've been married three months, Shulle, and you're still not with child."

With a single finger, she traced a trail of fire from his wrist to his earlobe and then pressed her lips against his cheek. "It's only three months, my love. These things take time."

A groan escaped him, and his body burned. He slid his fingers through her dark curls and kissed her.

"Would you like me to return later?" The Egyptian steward had appeared, and Nasseh released his wife as if she'd scorched him.

"No!" he shouted, rocking from foot to foot. Shulle reached for his hand, but he recoiled. "Wait. Just wait." Taking several deep breaths, he concentrated on calming himself. He couldn't keep relying on Shulle.

She stood beside him, head bowed. "Please, Nasseh. Promise me you won't take another wife."

She was crying again, sniffing and wiping her face. How could he deny her? But neither could he reject a gift from Pharaoh.

Abba had married only Ima, but they had only one son. A great king had many sons. *Normal* sons. Saba Ahaz married many wives, but stories of their infighting seemed worse than the uncertainty of a lone son. Shebna said concubines were a better idea.

"All right, Shulle. You'll be my only wife."

She nodded and tentatively slid her arms around his waist. The warmth of her in his arms was better than soothing his hands in water.

"Take another walk with me in Pharaoh's gardens today," she whispered.

He pulled away from her embrace. "I'm hunting today. You may join

Pharaoh's wives in the harem. They've offered to teach you their linen-making process. Now, go." He waved her away as he'd seen Tirhakah do his women.

She frowned and his stomach clenched, but he'd done nothing wrong. Hadn't he succumbed to her wishes even though the King of Egypt advised otherwise? Tirhakah said Shulle possessed a strange power over him—even asked if she'd used her dark arts to cast a spell. Nasseh assured him Shulle would never betray him like that. But she'd become the ache within, a common part of his existence. Tirhakah said a king must sample many delicacies and allow no woman to rule him. Perhaps the great pharaoh could explain if the ache was Shulle's rule or love.

⁓

This morning's discussion with Shulle had confused Nasseh, weakened his confidence even, but the day-long hunt with Tirhakah and his men proved Nasseh must silence some of his teachers. "The only people qualified to teach you now," Tirhakah had said while standing over a lion he'd just killed, "are other rulers who display exceptional authority and vigor."

Rulers like Tirhakah, who commanded noblemen and soldiers alike but also laughed with them like friends.

"Nasseh?" Shulle hurried to catch up with Nasseh's long strides toward the palace entrance. After the hunt, he'd determined she would ride in a separate coach for tonight's banquet, decreasing her opportunities to *instruct* him. She looped her arm around his. "You're smiling. I hope you're thinking of me."

"Actually, I was recalling how that lion somersaulted when Tirhakah's three arrows hit their mark and—"

She shuddered and said, "Please don't tell me any more."

Happy for the silence, his thoughts wandered toward home as they entered Pharaoh's palace. He wished Kenaz were here for sword drills and wrestling. And Abba . . . though his stomach tightened every time he thought of him, he wished Abba could help him become the greatest king of Judah. Nasseh enjoyed making sacrifices and playing games with Shulle, but she wasn't qualified to *teach* him anymore. He must measure the kings he met on their tour as right or wrong, good or bad, and the great ones would become his teachers.

Music blared as they neared the banquet hall, and the pungent fragrance of wax cones made Nasseh cover his nose. Shulle lowered her head, allowing a servant to place the scented wax amid her coiffed hair and crown.

Nasseh swatted away the cone meant for him. "I won't go through the torture of washing my hair again." And he most certainly wouldn't wear a ridiculous wig. "Shulle, you'll sit at the end of the table this evening, beside Tirhakah's queens." He kissed her cheek and passed her off to a guard, then he began his procession up the aisle toward the royal dais.

Nearly every guest wore the scented wax cones so Egypt's unrelenting heat would melt the herbal aroma into their braided, beaded, and cropped wigs. Nasseh strode past the table where Shebna was seated. He wore the most hideous cropped wig, wax dripping down his forehead. Nasseh laughed as he passed his teacher and climbed the three steps to join Tirhakah's table.

The god-king wore no wig. His head, shaved bald, was covered with the distinguished *pschent,* the double crown that declared him ruler of both the Upper and Lower Black Land. Four wives sat on his left in marriage order with an empty cushion awaiting Shulle.

"Sit, my friend." Tirhakah motioned to the cushion on his right as Shulle took her place on his wives' left.

Nasseh sat and inclined his head. "I'm deeply grateful, good god, for the wisdom you've imparted during my visit." He reached for a handful of almonds, realizing he'd likely never see Tirhakah after their barque left Memphis tomorrow.

Pharaoh jostled Nasseh's shoulder. "Did your pretty wife tell you about this afternoon's excitement in the harem?"

"She didn't seem excited when I returned from our hunt." In truth, Shulle had barely spoken a word while their servants prepared them for the banquet.

"Perhaps you haven't heard my good news yet." Pharaoh turned to a guard without waiting for a reply. "Bring in my new son."

Nasseh shot another glance at Tirhakah's fourth wife, one of his three half-sisters. Her stomach still looked round. Surely, she hadn't—

But the unmistakable cry of a newborn rent the air, propelling the three sister-queens to their feet. The youngest queen swayed, her face as white as her linen robe. When she stood, she was undeniably thinner, and her full attention seemed locked on a nursemaid emerging from a side door, holding a small bundle. The nursemaid approached the royal dais.

Mesmerized, Nasseh watched the squalling infant transform Tirhakah —a hardened warrior—into a gentle abba. His large hands gently received his tiny, naked boy, and at his abba's touch, the prince became a squirting fountain. The quick-thinking nursemaid tossed a scrap of linen over his little spout, while the guests erupted in laughter. Even mighty Pharaoh laughed and buried kisses in his son's neck.

Nasseh's chest ached again, much like he'd felt this morning when looking at Shulle. He'd wondered if it was love, but how could he love an Egyptian baby at first glance? What made his pulse beat behind his eyes and wish someone showered him with the extravagant delight Tirhakah showed for his son? Had Abba ever celebrated him with such abandon? Had Ima ever loved him without demands?

Tirhakah raised the child over his head and shouted above the roar. "To the mighty gods of Egypt, I introduce my son, Nesishutefnut. Mighty warrior. Strong of heart. Quick of mind. Devoted to the gods." Lowering him, Tirhakah gazed on the infant with an indecipherable expression.

Without warning, he pressed the babe against Nasseh's chest, leaving him no option but to cradle the squirming, mewling thing. Nasseh touched his little hand with one finger. The warmth of his skin was startling. His softness. Vitality. Nasseh looked again at the young queen and back at Tirhakah. "*This* was inside her?"

Pharaoh chuckled low. "Yes, my young friend. Queen Taka is my gift from the gods, and she gave me a son that I must now protect." He took the baby back and cradled him in one arm, while clamping his other large hand on Nasseh's shoulder. "You came here out of curiosity—to meet a king who joined forces with your abba against Assyria's tyranny. Now—so my spies tell me—you will visit other nations and end your journey in Nineveh. Is this true?"

Nasseh's heart raced. Shebna had advised against revealing their itinerary to Pharaoh, but he couldn't lie to a man he so admired. "Yes, it's true."

Tirhakah squeezed his shoulder hard. "I fight to protect what is most important. This child and many others are the reasons I will never submit to Assyria's yoke. King Sennacherib cares nothing about family or honor."

Something stirred in Nasseh's belly. Deeper than hunger. Stronger than the ache. "Someday I too will have sons to protect."

"Indeed, you will." Tirhakah released Nasseh's shoulder and turned his attention to the banquet guests. "King Hezekiah was a noble man, and I have found his son a worthy successor. So worthy, in fact, that I offer a daughter of Egypt to help build his house and strengthen the bond between our nations."

The back doors of the hall opened, revealing a beautiful Egyptian escorted between two soldiers. As dark as the night with eyes like the stars, her skin glowed as if stroked by the gods. Nasseh realized he'd been staring and recovered with a slight incline of his head. "Your gift is too generous, good god, strong ruler of the Two Lands and glorious father of your people. I will treasure the offspring of Egypt that will someday fill the halls of my palace."

Nasseh felt a slight tug on his sleeve and found Shulle standing behind him. "What about your promise?" she whispered, eyes flooded with tears.

The banquet hall grew quiet, and Nasseh felt Tirhakah's disapproving stare. "Sit down, Meshullemeth." He nudged her toward her cushion, but she wouldn't budge.

"Where will she sleep tonight?" she pressed in a strangled whisper.

Patience spent, Nasseh motioned to Shebna. "My queen is feeling ill. Please escort her back to your villa so she can rest peacefully tonight, Lord Shebna."

An Egyptian guard escorted Shulle to Shebna's table. Both wore deep frowns, but their journey to Tyre began tomorrow, and two weeks' travel would give everyone time to adjust to his new rules.

Pharaoh's gift knelt at Nasseh's feet, her black eyes both lovely and inviting. "I am Panya."

Nasseh reached for her hand, escorting her to his cushion. "I will treasure you, Panya, because you were a gift from a great man." The words were forced, as would be the actions required of him this night. But he would fulfill his duties and sow his seed in the fertile soil of this Egyptian maid.

24

They made me jealous by what is no god and angered me with their worthless idols. I will make them envious by those who are not a people; I will make them angry by a nation that has no understanding.

DEUTERONOMY 32:21

The Journey to Tyre
Next Day

I reclined on Dohd's sitting-room couch with two thick slices of Egypt's cucumbers pressed against my swollen eyes while servants loaded our belongings onto the barque. Sleepless tears had done their damage, but it could have been much worse. Dohd's anger had exploded when we returned to his villa last night, and for the first time I feared for my life.

He dismissed the servants and then dashed a water pitcher against the wall, barely missing my head. "Are you incompetent or barren? I saved you from my wretched brother and made you a *queen,* and you can't even bear a child?" He ripped his wig to pieces and released a guttural howl that sent tremors down my spine.

"We've only been married three months," I ventured, knowing now I must never reveal the herbal pouches I'd been using.

He covered the distance between us in three long strides, and I braced for a blow. It didn't come. I opened my eyes and recognized my own insecurities in his wild-eyed stare. "If you were pregnant by now—as I'd planned—you would give birth in Assyria. What if the Egyptian gives him a son to celebrate in Nineveh?"

"But Nasseh promised he'd never take another wife," I said to reassure myself as much as him. "She'll be a concubine, and a concubine's child isn't an heir."

His grimace eased. "What makes you sure he'll keep his promise?"

"You'll convince him," I said, hoping to stroke his ego.

He turned away. "He's a child and a king, Shulle. It's an unwieldy combination."

I now understood. Fear of his waning influence had driven him to this rage.

"Nasseh loves me, Dohd. Let him breed his Egyptian, and he'll return to me."

He whirled; eyes sharper than blades. "Your confidence betrays your stupidity, girl. If the Egyptian shows any sign of controlling him, you will use your dark arts to dispose of her *and* any offspring. Do I need to remind you whose life is at stake?"

Last night's threats echoed into daylight. How could I even be sure Abba was still alive? I pressed harder against the cucumber slices. I could never use black arts to purposefully harm another. The beggar in the market had been a terrible mistake—too many herbs in an advanced potion. More tears festered, and I threw the cucumbers across the chamber.

I called the maid to come ready me for our departure. By the time I finished dressing, Adnah had come to Dohd's villa and servants loaded the final supplies onto our barques. I toted our kitten to the docks and avoided Nasseh during the departure. We set sail under the stoic watchfulness of a gracious but harsh people. I went immediately to the canopied couches, escaping Egypt's punishing sun. Nasseh and Dohd stood nearby, discussing the journey's details, while the Egyptian beauty lingered near the cabins.

I watched her as she grieved her homeland. Tears, like jewels, tumbled down her ebony cheeks. She was about my age and looked even sadder than me.

I turned away. I didn't want to feel sorry for the woman who'd slept in my place last night. I'd noted Nasseh's reaction when he first saw her. Mesmerized. So enthralled, he hadn't even realized I was standing behind him, tugging on his sleeve like a child begging for scraps.

And now we ignored each other? I had to do something to breach the walls this concubine had already built between us. I released Adnah to prowl the deck as I pondered when the real trouble began, reflecting on our conversation yesterday morning. Tirhakah's wives. Building his house quickly. Then the hunt. Why had he insisted on traveling separately to the banquet? He was at least civil until he saw Tirhakah's newborn son.

An abba's love for his son.

Understanding struck like lightning when I remembered Nasseh's expression, watching Tirhakah's affectionate dedication of his son. Nasseh missed his abba and had latched onto Tirhakah like a leech in an Egyptian marsh—caring more about pleasing him than appeasing me. The realization didn't mend my heart, but it explained the distance between us. I even admired Tirhakah's commitment to family. He was fierce but loyal. Independent but loving. Perhaps someday I could overcome the fear of dying on the birthing stones as my ima did and give Nasseh the heir he desired. At the thought of Ima, I needed the namesake kitten in my arms. I rose from my couch and nearly bumped noses with Panya.

"Forgive," she said in stuttering Akkadian. She held Adnah in her arms. "Your cat very beautiful." Her eyes shimmered with unshed tears, and my heart softened.

"Please, sit." I offered the couch next to mine. "Tell me about your family in Memphis." We would sail on this small barque for at least six days and another eight on the larger ship to Tyre. I should at least be civil.

"My family lives in small village near Pharaoh's home in Napata, far south, near fourth cataract of Nile." Sadness darkened her features. "Traveling to Memphis was new experience, so traveling more north will be . . ." She turned away, and the rest of my hard heart turned to yogurt. As difficult as last night had been for me, it couldn't compare to what Panya was experiencing.

I squeezed her hand tightly. "King Manasseh is kind." He heard his name and looked our direction, silent questions written across his handsome features. My heart tumbled in my chest, and I knew then I'd come to love him as his wife. "My husband is a kind man, Panya. He'll provide a good home for you and your children."

Nasseh approached, and I quickly relinquished my couch, my magnanimity spent. "I'm sure the king wishes to be alone with you, Panya." With a curt bow, I hurried to my cabin before tears betrayed me. Falling onto the thin mattress, I silenced my sobs in a pillow and let the rhythmic pull of the oars rock me into a fitful sleep.

"Shulle?" A knock accompanied Nasseh's timid voice, and then the pressure of his hand on my arm made me bolt upright.

"What?" I stared into his startled face.

He placed Adnah in my arms and sat beside me. "I thought you might miss her since she spent last night . . ." He looked away.

"Since she spent last night with you and your concubine." Adnah's purring made me regret the venom in my tone. "The kitten was your gift, my king. Thank you for sharing her with me."

He laid his arm around my shoulder and pulled me toward him, kissing the top of my head. "Adnah was a gift I didn't ask for—like Panya. Can't they both be our friends?"

I squeezed my eyes shut, happy my head was bowed. "If you wish it."

Adnah squirmed out of my arms. He chuckled as she escaped to the deck. "Good. I wanted to be alone with you anyway." He released me and tilted my chin up. "I like being with you."

Five simple words opened the floodgates, and I clung to him. "I love you, Nasseh."

"My chest still aches for you, Shulle." He rocked me like a child. "That hasn't changed, but the way you treat me must."

I pulled away, confused. "The way I treat you?" Indignation dried my tears.

He entwined our fingers and looked at them while explaining. "I sent you to Shebna's villa because you challenged me publicly. Both you and Shebna have helped me learn, but now you must obey me—or bear the consequences."

I swallowed the justification burning my throat. Had reminding him of his promise been overbearing? Then Dohd's words echoed in my mind. *"A child and a king . . . an unwieldy combination."* Anger would only escalate to conflict. I must rely on the weapon I knew best.

I traced his jawline, but he captured my hand and held my gaze. "We will sacrifice to the starry hosts again someday—when I will it." He drew my hand to his lips and kissed my palm. "For now, I wish to tell you what I learned in Egypt and hear what you think."

Humiliated, I choked back tears and leaned against the wall beside him, listening as he recounted his love of the Black Land and respect for Tirhakah. He talked long into the night, describing each day's discoveries from his impeccable memory. He'd become Nasseh again—the boy-king I loved. I realized now that his rejection of my advances hadn't been meant to hurt me. He was simply finding his new role as king and trying to make me his queen, not his teacher. And I loved him for it.

"I'll evaluate the kings in every city," he said as moonlight glowed through my cabin window. "And I'll model the good qualities in the greatest kings of all nations."

I rolled over, hovering above him. "I'll help in any way I can." I pressed my lips against his.

Like a long-legged spider, he slipped from beneath me. "It's late," he said, ducking out of the cabin. "Good night, Shulle." The door slammed shut.

Frustration sent my fist into the wall. Was he going to Panya's cabin next? Angry tears robbed my sleep. The next morning Panya had swollen eyes matching mine. Nasseh had spent the night on deck with Adnah.

Shebna seemed the only well-rested nobility on board. So went our cramped six days on the Nile.

~

When we finally boarded our larger ship in Pelusium, the freedom of the Great Sea felt like a new beginning. If Nasseh was determined to model the finest qualities of the greatest kings, why wouldn't I adopt the grace and elegance I'd so admired in Queen Zibah? Hadn't she shown extreme kindness to me even when I'd betrayed her trust? Had I any right to treat Panya so poorly when her circumstances were no more of her choosing than mine were?

On the second day of our eight-day sail to Tyre, Panya spotted my drawings in Dohd's basket of scrolls. Too shy to ask him about them, she whispered to me. "You ask if I see his pictures?"

"Of course," I said. "Or perhaps I could simply draw one for you."

Wonder flickered on her features before sadness returned. "I have no skill to make king love me."

Indeed, Nasseh had gone to her chamber only twice since we'd left Egypt. I hurried to my cabin to retrieve some supplies and began our lesson. Mixing her kohl makeup with a little water, I used the frayed end of a stick to draw a simple sunset shedding its light over a rippling sea. I added seagulls circling a ship in the distance.

"Oh, Shulle." Panya gawked as if my poor attempt was a mural on Pharaoh's palace walls. "Look, my king!" She snagged Nasseh's arm as he walked past our couches.

His annoyance disappeared with a second look at my drawing. "It's our ship," he breathed and turned an appreciative smile on me.

"Take it," Panya said, offering it with her head bowed. "My queen is the greatest of women." After he'd disappeared with the parchment, Panya hurried to explain. "If I want the king's admiration, I can't steal it from you. I must find my own way to win it."

I looked into the eyes of a woman I could truly call *friend*. "Give him a son, Panya. You'll win Nasseh's admiration, and I'll be there to welcome him into our family."

That night, I informed my husband he must share his seed with Panya each night of our remaining sail to Tyre before coming to our small tent on deck. It wasn't a command or instruction—as he'd made clear I was no longer his teacher or peer. It was, I told him, the knowledge of a priestess, trained and skilled to know the courses of a woman's body in sync with the waxing and waning moon.

"Panya will be most likely to conceive if she feels relaxed and loved," I coaxed, lying beside him one night.

"You don't mind that Panya has my first child?" his voice barely a whisper.

Tears threatened, and I chose my words carefully since I still wasn't ready to risk my life in childbirth. "I love you, Nasseh, and I want you to build a great household." Rising on my elbow, I placed myself between him and the stars he was counting. "Our love is a gift from the gods, Nasseh. I am yours and you are mine—in a way no one else will ever compare."

He pulled me into his arms. "Tirhakah said few women understand a king's burden to build a harem. It's good that you do. You are the gods' best gift to me."

Under the starry hosts, we sacrificed for the first time in too long. When our passion was spent, I lay in the bend of my husband's arm and stroked the golden image of my patron goddess. "Someday, Ishtar will give us a son, Nasseh." When she removed my fear and filled my heart with courage.

～

We dropped anchor a safe distance from the reefs that surrounded the heavily fortified island of Tyre and tendered ashore in smaller boats. Panya and I sat on a middle bench. Dohd and Nasseh shared a bench in the prow, while six royal guards rowed our lead tender to shore. Adnah, although accustomed to our ship, climbed onto my shoulder and hid under my hair at the sight of water all around us.

Our captain explained that King Baal maintained his palace and trade on Tyre's island while using its sister city's mainland location as a staging point for his caravans. "Your long journey will require significant planning and supplies," he'd told Dohd. "Curry favor with the king and then hire his best caravanner."

When our small boat sliced into shore, Tyrian soldiers surrounded us, demanding to know our business. "The king of Judah brings gifts for King Baal." Dohd's calm reply earned an immediate escort to the palace through the market's haggling merchants. My hopes of hunting murex shells and making the famed purple dye were dashed. I looked longingly back at the rugged shore and stumbled, falling against Dohd. "Watch where you're walking," he hissed. "You're a queen, not an urchin."

Nasseh cooed at the kitten I held. "Silly Shulle could have dropped you. She must be more careful." He returned to his march, and I fumed quietly beside Panya. Was I now relegated to cat keeper when meeting foreign kings?

We followed the soldiers out of the busy marketplace, up a steep grade, and to the jewel of Tyre—the palace of Phoenicia's wealthiest king. Its mosaic floors, ivory-inlaid doors, tapestried walls, and embroidered furniture did make me feel more urchin than queen. Ostentatious in both style and color, the interior's deep purples, rich crimsons, and brilliant blues surged into a panoply of visual delight.

We waited at the rear of a throne room twice the size of Jerusalem's while Dohd spoke in hushed tones to a scribe seated behind a desk. The scribe pressed marks into a wax tablet and passed the message to his assistant. Skirting the edge of the crowded courtroom, the assistant slipped the wax tablet to the king's herald who then whispered to King Baal. The king waved away the petitioner before him, saying something about thirty days in the palace dungeon.

The man wailed as two guards hauled him away, but the herald's introduction was louder. "I present to our great King Baal these four worthy guests: King Manasseh of Judah with his ambassador, Lord Shebna; accompanied by Queen Meshullemeth and an Egyptian concubine." The herald bowed, and King Baal rose to descend the dais. Everyone in the courtroom bowed—except for us.

I wasn't sure what to do. Bow or walk? Nasseh and Dohd stepped forward, and for the first time that morning, I was happy to follow. Adnah crawled up my arm, hiding beneath my hair.

"You are most welcome, young king." Baal offered his hand as if Nasseh should place it on his forehead in fealty.

The nerve! But sinking dread drained my outrage when I remembered half our royal guard were on the ship with the supplies. The other half had been detained at the palace entrance. Who would protect my husband if he didn't show the homage demanded?

Nasseh reached for the king's wrist, locking it in a warrior's grasp. "It is a pleasure to meet the man my abba spoke of so highly." Surprise and respect warred on King Baal's face. "Even now," Nasseh continued hurriedly, "my captain unloads the finest wine from Judah's vineyards and the purest oil from our olive presses to honor Phoenicia's most gracious king." My husband inclined his head slightly, the only bow he offered. King Manasseh of Judah owed fealty to only one king—and it wasn't Baal of Tyre.

25

> Because of this our hearts are faint,
> because of these things our eyes grow dim.
>
> LAMENTATIONS 5:17

From Tyre to Anatho
Ab (August) to Tishri (October)

Everything Nasseh had admired in Pharaoh Tirhakah—his devotion to family, his quiet power, and his soldiers' loyalty—found its antithesis in Tyre's King Baal. "We were fortunate to escape with any silver in our pockets," Nasseh told Shebna as the older man squirmed on his stallion. Shebna groaned and shifted again. "Why are you moving around so much?"

"Men weren't . . . *fashioned* . . . to sit on a horse, my king."

"You need different clothes?"

"Not *fashion,* my king—like clothing—but I meant—" He shook his head. "It is . . . um . . . uncomfortable for me to ride a horse, my king. I prefer the carriage."

"You and I will ride horses so Shulle and the two concubines can enjoy the comfort of the carriage." Though neither Shulle nor Panya had seemed eager to share the carriage with King Baal's gift.

The Tyrian girl was rather rough—even carried her own dagger that his guards confiscated as she entered Nasseh's chamber at the inn last night. Hopefully, his seed would grow in her quickly so he wouldn't need to couple with her often. Shulle said it was too early to tell if Panya was with child. He agreed with Tirhakah's wise advice, but he'd much rather spend time planning the journey with Shebna and sacrificing with Shulle. It was *her* face he saw no matter what woman lay in his arms. Neither Panya nor the Tyrian girl—what was her name—made his chest ache.

"My king!" Shebna shouted.

Nasseh must have missed his call several times, but Tirhakah said no one should shout at a king. Nasseh turned his head slowly in silent censure.

Shebna's down-turned brows relaxed. Shulle said that meant calming. "Forgive me for shouting." Shebna inclined his head slightly. "I simply wanted to congratulate you on your dealings with the very slippery king of Tyre. You showed restraint and wisdom beyond your years."

"By *restraint,* you mean I controlled my tics?" Tirhakah taught him that by merely staring at subordinates, a king can cow them into submission.

Shebna shifted on his stallion again. "Well, more than that. I . . . uh—"

The staring worked. "Thank you, Shebna. I'm learning to manage my oddities."

"I would be pleased to continue our lessons—not instructing you on actions of state, of course—merely to inform you on other kings' decisions so you might learn from history."

"That's the reason I've asked you to ride beside me. Proceed."

"You're the only king to undertake this sort of bold journey. Most send ambassadors with gifts and the authority to form alliances. But you, because of your youth and brilliance, can appear quite innocent while using your intellect to build wealth, reputation, and a burgeoning household."

"Unless every king takes as much from me as King Baal of Tyre."

"You were wise in your dealings with Tyre," Shebna countered. "You unloaded most of our wine and oil, retaining enough to gift the King of Damascus while keeping our caravan light for the journey. We have ample funds to replenish our gift-stock with Damask silk, and the trade agreements you established with Tyre will spread Judah's inland products through coastal lands as far as Greece and Rome. You even gained another concubine by proclaiming Judah's new freedom to worship gods of every nation." He shook his head and laughed. "An experienced foreign minister couldn't have done more, my king."

Nasseh bristled. "Why are you laughing if I did so well?"

Shebna sobered. "I'm not laughing *at* you, Nasseh. I'm bursting with joy and pride because you've exceeded my highest hopes." The words hit Nasseh like cool water on a hot day. "Your abba would be proud too."

"Don't say that." That awful prickly feeling stung his cheeks—like the day the temple guard took away his sword. Abba would think it wrong to have two concubines, but Tirhakah would be proud. "Do you think Shulle is proud of me?"

Shebna was quiet. Nasseh glanced over quickly and saw him smiling. "Shulle is always proud of you," he said. "She loves you very much."

"I know." Nasseh could always trust Shulle.

~

The Damascus and Tadmor kings were no better than King Baal of Tyre. All three grumbled mildly against Assyria, but none possessed the strength or determination to rebel against King Sennacherib. Nasseh bestowed his gifts, made his treaties, and received a concubine from each king, making the promise that his offspring would worship the gods of their homeland.

After more than three months of travel—the last forty days on horseback—the caravan crested a hill and saw the legendary city of Anatho below, an island paradise in the center of the Great River between desert hills. Nasseh was ecstatic. "I'll race you," he said to Shebna. Before the old man could respond, he clutched his reins, swatted his stallion, and shot down the hill.

Nasseh halted just short of the ferry dock, and Shebna arrived spitting dirt. "I've already arranged passage," he said, leaving his stallion to a servant boy. "The ferry will carry twenty men at a time. Or ten men and five pack animals."

Nasseh dismounted and waved over the gold carriage, then opened the door and assisted his five women down the steps. The Tyrian came first, face pinched and crimson. "It's hotter than a bread oven in there. I won't ride with these cows another day."

The Damascan and Tadmorian concubines were next, sober and soaked with perspiration. Panya emerged, skin glistening and eyes downcast. Finally, Shulle appeared, her cheeks the color of ripe apples, hair hanging in ringlets around Adnah. "Nasseh, my love, it would be cooler on camels. Truly, Panya is with child and she can't—"

He lifted his hand to silence her and stared at Panya's belly. "With child?" Laying his hand on the concubine's stomach, he noted her slight smile. "Does it pain you?"

"No, my king—well, a little sick sometimes, but no pain."

Nasseh turned to the docks. "Shebna!"

The man rushed over, out of breath. "I've arranged for you, me, and Shulle to take the first ferry so we can go to the inn immediately and clean up. We'll be able to present your gifts to Anatho's king this afternoon."

"The women must ride on camels."

Shebna frowned. "They must ferry over to the island, my king. They can't ride camels across the Great River."

"I'm not an imbecile," Nasseh said. "When we leave Anatho, the women will each ride a camel with a canopied sedan. Except Shulle and Panya will ride together."

Shebna's face paled. "I'll do what I can, but camels are in short supply on an island, my king."

"Find a camel for my queen and Panya. I'm going to be an abba, Shebna."

Nasseh insisted Panya ride the ferry with him, Shulle, and Shebna. He placed her in a room next to his at the inn. While his steward prepared him for the meeting with Anatho's king, the noise in Nasseh's head grew louder and more chaotic. What did he know of being an abba? What if Panya's child was broken like him?

By the time he, Shulle, and Shebna stood at the entrance of Anatho's small courtroom, Nasseh heard nothing but the chaos inside. Shulle shook his arm and turned his face toward her. He watched her lips move but heard no sound. Losing control, his hands started spasming, and he rocked back and forth. He couldn't meet Anatho's king like this.

"King Manasseh!" The herald's voice added to his panic.

"Shulle, I can't." He turned to flee, but a deep voice from the throne stopped him.

"King Manasseh, are you aware that King Sennacherib sent a personal message to your Lord Shebna?"

The crashing cymbals in Nasseh's mind settled to distant echoes. He turned to find Anatho's king approaching. "If I were you, King of Judah, I'd want to know why my ambassador received a private message from Assyria's king." He offered Nasseh the sealed scroll.

Shebna—a man full of words—was sullen and silent. "What have you done?" Nasseh hissed.

Anatho's king leaned close, keeping his voice low. "I can see you weren't aware of the correspondence. You should know this is the fourth message in two months I've couriered between your ambassador and Assyria's king." He stepped back and frowned at Shebna. "An ambassador who loses his king's trust doesn't live long."

Nasseh crushed the scroll in his hand. "Thank you for your warning," he said. "I'll be more cautious in the future about who I trust."

The king braced Nasseh's shoulder. "Keep whatever gifts you planned to give me and add them to those you planned to offer Sennacherib. We must all appease him, my friend."

Nasseh inclined his head to the second honorable man he'd met on his journey and left the courtroom. His guards, Shulle, and Shebna fell in step behind him.

"My king," Shebna said, hurrying to keep pace. "Please let me explain."

Nasseh lifted his hand, motioning to his personal guard. "Baka, keep him quiet until I give him permission to speak."

When they arrived at the inn, Nasseh left the guards outside, allowing only Shebna and Shulle into his room. His queen sat on a cushion beside a low table, and Shebna stood like a naughty child near the door.

Nasseh unsheathed his dagger to dislodge the scroll's wax-seal and then threw the parchment at Shebna. "Read it—out loud."

"First, let me explain—"

"No! I'll hear no more lies. Read!"

Lifting it with a trembling hand, he began:

Sennacherib, the great king of the universe, king of the four quarters of the earth; the wise ruler and favorite of the great gods, guardian of the right, lover of justice; who comes to the aid of the needy, who turns his thoughts to pious deeds; perfect hero and mighty man . . .

To the little man of Judah.

You will bring your king to Babylon, the pile of ruin and destruction, where he will see what my mighty power has done; where he will atone for his father's folly and pledge his fealty in blood. Waste no time, or I will bring him here in chains.

Nasseh felt the blood drain from his face. "You've handed me over to my executioner."

Shebna shook his head violently. "No, Manasseh! He's summoning you to Babylon to introduce you to his heir."

"Admit it!" Nasseh shouted. "You planned all along to deliver me to Sennacherib and take my throne."

Shebna fell to his knees, clasping pleading hands. "Please believe me. Prince Esarhaddon will soon be named heir to Assyria's throne, and you'll be the first vassal king to pledge fealty to him. It's an honor, my king. This meeting will make you memorable to Esarhaddon."

"Get out," Nasseh said, feeling his control waning. "Get out now!"

"My king, I know it seems frightening now, but it's a foundation for a powerful union—"

"Guards!" Nasseh couldn't stop rocking. "Guards! Guards! Guards! Guards!" He grabbed his ears, unable to bear the chaos.

"Shh, I'm here." Gentle hands covered his. A familiar melody. "The fish and the frog swam round and round." Rocking. Rocking. "He's gone, Nasseh. It's just you and me now." His breathing slowed, but he still couldn't bear to open his eyes. She pressed a kiss against his forehead. "Baka will help us. We can trust Baka."

He pulled Shulle close, burying his face in her neck. "If Shebna is lying, Shulle, promise you'll use your dark arts to destroy him." When she didn't answer, he squeezed her tighter. "Promise me!"

"I'm sure he's not lying, Nasseh."

He thought of the crocodile attack on the Nile—the sheer power of the predator against its prey. He'd thought Tirhakah was a crocodile when he'd first met him, but he *knew* Sennacherib was. Shebna had made Nasseh prey. How could he tame Sennacherib?

He began humming the frog song, and Shulle joined him. Rocking and singing. Thinking and planning. His soldiers would fight Assyrians. They weren't afraid of blood. Fight chaos with chaos, and the gods would offer peace. But could a fish fight a crocodile?

26

Marduk-Baladan son of Baladan king of Babylon
sent Hezekiah letters and a gift, because he had
heard of Hezekiah's illness. Hezekiah received
the envoys and showed them all that was in his
storehouses. . . . Then Isaiah said to Hezekiah . . .
"The time will surely come when everything in
your palace . . . will be carried off to Babylon. . . .
And some of your descendants, your own flesh
and blood who will be born to you, will be taken
away, and they will become eunuchs in the
palace of the king of Babylon."

2 KINGS 20:12–13, 16–18

From Anatho to Babylon
Tishri (October)

Dohd traded our gold carriage for three camels—with sedans—
and additional gifts for the King of Assyria. Nasseh's women
left Anatho in relative comfort for our thirteen-day march to
Sippar, the gateway to Babylon. With every step I heard Zibah's plea:
"Don't let my son visit Babylon's ruins on your tour of nations." How
could she have known we'd be diverted there?

Dohd vowed he hadn't planned to go there until he'd learned Sennacherib appointed Esarhaddon, his youngest son, as governor of the re-
claimed city. Our visit couldn't be the fulfillment of Yahweh's prophets,
since they'd foretold Hezekiah's descendants—which meant Zibah's, his

only wife's, too—being led to Babylon as captives. Nasseh would arrive as a king on a stallion.

Yet the pall of fear gnawed at us all.

Though we traveled past fascinating plants, animals, birds, and trees along the shoreline of the mighty Euphrates, the constant threat of a surprise attack made our vigilant travel seem endless. When we finally reached Sippar, Babylonia's first trade town where the great river branched into tributaries, our soldiers forfeited pleasures in the city to guard their king in camp.

I ate the evening meal with Nasseh's women around a separate fire and then waited in his tent until he'd planted his seed with the scary Tyrian concubine. I was relieved when he returned to me—even though he fell asleep within moments. I stared at the man-child I loved, listening to his slow, even breaths, while trying to push away images of him in his concubine's arms. Three of the women spent our evening meals quietly mocking Nasseh, while Panya and I held hands in dignified silence. My Egyptian friend had become as dear as the nearly grown kitten I held close.

I woke the next morning to Adnah's purring—and an empty mat beside me. Nasseh was already waiting at Sippar's dock for our first *quffa* ride. With incredible efficiency, our captain loaded soldiers and supplies on twenty round reed boats. Smaller, and not as spectacular as our ship on the Great Sea, the quffas were more agile on the river.

Nasseh barely spoke when we made camp that night. He and I ate together in front of his tent, hard cheese and dried fruit purchased from Sippar. His hand spasms had grown more frantic as the day grew long, and in the absence of a basin, I'd poured ten skins of water over them.

"Might I prepare my king for his meeting King Sennacherib?" Dohd's voice startled me. He approached from the shadows and bent to one knee less than an arm's length away.

Nasseh began rocking, and I refused to let Dohd upset him further. "How dare you even say that name in Nasseh's presence. Sennacherib's savagery is legendary. Staking prisoners on tall poles like wildflowers, while King Hezekiah lay dying in his bed. Leave, Dohd. Now!"

With eyes fixed on Nasseh, he pretended not to hear me. "Remember, my king, Sennacherib left 185,000 dead troops outside our gates and retreated to Assyria. Jerusalem remains the only besieged city he could not conquer, and your abba was one of two kings Sennacherib could never subdue."

Nasseh pulled a blanket around his shoulders as he rocked. "Yes, Shebna. It's clear to me why Sennacherib would consider me—the son of King Hezekiah, his one unconquered foe—such a great prize."

"No, no, my king." He sat, without invitation, on the opposite side of the fire. "I've obviously failed to explain the grander picture. Remember the Babylonian envoys that came to pay homage shortly after your abba's illness? And Isaiah's ridiculous prophecy that Hezekiah's descendants and all he owned would someday be marched as captives to Babylon and made eunuchs?"

Nasseh stopped rocking and shot a cutting glare at Dohd. "Are you preparing me by frightening me?"

"Of course not, my king, but I believe you'll be less afraid when I finish my explanation." Dohd cleared his throat and continued. "After King Marduk-Baladan and his envoys left Jerusalem, they were returning to Babylon when Sennacherib's troops attacked them here in Sippar. One of Baladan's generals, a man your abba Hezekiah had welcomed to Jerusalem, captured and killed Sennacherib's firstborn son—the crown prince."

I gasped, but Nasseh raised his head slowly, disturbingly calm. "My abba welcomed the man who killed Sennacherib's crown prince?" Nasseh repeated the facts as if etching them into his mind.

Dohd nodded. "Eleven years ago, Sennacherib meted out his revenge by destroying Babylon. Razed it. Burned it. Left it abandoned. And he never named another crown prince from his remaining sons." Leaning forward, Dohd pinned my husband with a stare. "A few months ago, Sennacherib appointed his youngest son, Prince Esarhaddon, as governor of Babylon—if the prince could rebuild it."

"Why rebuild after eleven years? Why invite Hezekiah's son to the new city?" Nasseh scanned the stars. "To show the gods I'm weak and inferior?"

"No, my king. Think. Think!" Dohd raised his voice, and Nasseh flinched. "If Sennacherib wanted us dead, he could have done it in a million ways by now."

I was tired of Dohd's manipulation. "Then Sennacherib made his son governor of a pile of rubble. How does that make Prince Esarhaddon anything but a bad joke?"

He ignored me, his eyes fixed on Nasseh. "I perceive understanding on your features, my king. Explain it to her."

Nasseh's rocking had suddenly calmed, and he wore a wry grin. "Sennacherib is testing Esarhaddon by making him governor. He'll watch the way his son rules through adversity. He'll measure his son's ability to lead by stripping away entitlement."

Dohd applauded. "Yes, my king. Now, why did Sennacherib invite you to Babylon?"

The flame of our campfire reflected in Nasseh's eyes. "Since he never conquered Jerusalem, I've never witnessed the havoc his army can reap on a great city. He's teaching me, Shebna. He's a teacher."

"Yes, my brilliant king." Dohd sat back with a thud. "*And* I believe Sennacherib understands Judah's strategic trade location and seeks a strong alliance between his soon-to-be crown prince and the *only* vassal king he invited to this meeting."

Nasseh sat taller. "It is Sennacherib's heir who will rule the empire for most of my reign."

"Wait!" I said, fearing Nasseh had succumbed too quickly. "Sennacherib hasn't actually named Esarhaddon his heir. He's simply the governor of Babylon."

Dohd's eyes blazed. "He appointed Esarhaddon governor but will announce him as crown prince publicly—as soon as it's safe to do so."

"Safe?" Nasseh asked.

"There are rumors the king's older sons war among themselves, but they're unified against Esarhaddon because he's stolen their abba's favor.

Sennacherib knows making his crown prince governor of Babylon—an ancient jewel far from Nineveh—is the best protection."

Nasseh had completely stopped rocking. "Prince Esarhaddon and I are the future of Assyria and Judah. *He* is the king I must evaluate as a mentor to make my reign great."

"A mighty reign it will be, my king. Never doubt it." Dohd hadn't yet learned the value Nasseh placed on silence.

"You should have informed me of these things *before* you wrote to Sennacherib."

"You're right, my king." Dohd bowed his head. "Forgive me."

"You must rebuild my trust, Lord Shebna, but I'll give you another chance—if we live through tomorrow's meeting."

Dohd kissed Nasseh's hand and struggled to his feet, bowing again before hurrying away. Nasseh watched him disappear amid white tents and the dark night. I turned toward our tent, exhausted by every encounter with my dohd Shebna. Nothing from his lips was ever completely true.

"Shulle." The timbre of Nasseh's voice halted me. His hands massaged my shoulders, and I stifled a moan. He pulled aside my collar and placed a single kiss where my neck met my shoulder. "If Shebna's right, our lives could change tomorrow with special favor from the emperor. If he's wrong, tonight could be our last night together before we close our eyes in death."

A shiver overtook me at the uncertainty of our life beyond death. I turned suddenly to face him. "Aren't you afraid of dying?"

His desire-laden eyes widened with surprise. "A little, I suppose, but I don't want to discuss it now." He took my hand, leading me into his tent.

"What do you think lies beyond, Nasseh?"

He faced me in the glow of a single lamp and stared like a man already dead. "There is no life beyond."

How could he say such a thing? Every nation believed in *something* after death. "We have to believe if we die tomorrow, there's at least a chance I'll see you again. Don't you want to see your abba?"

His eyes narrowed, and the muscles in his jaw tensed. "You will never speak to me again of the life beyond, Shulle." He swallowed hard. "Leave me."

Horrified at the coldness in his voice, I reached for his arm. "Nas—"

"I said go!"

I hurried outside and slipped into Panya's tent next door. She was already sleeping soundly, so I snuggled under her extra blanket and spent what might be my last night on earth wishing the queen mother were there to tell me stories of Yahweh's paradise—a place I once thought too simple to be true. In the yawning uncertainty of a dark tomorrow, simplicity was what I desired most.

⌣

When we boarded the quffas the next morning, Nasseh wanted me beside him but didn't want to be touched. He wanted to talk but insisted I be silent. He enjoyed sailing but complained about the quffa. Too small. Too wobbly. He was constantly fisting, pacing, rocking. I resorted to the only comfort left, placing Adnah in his arms and retreating to the other side of the round boat.

Our kitten's calm purr and presence seemed to soothe him in a way that logic couldn't. Bracing himself against the rail, he buried his face against her fur and closed his eyes. He'd explained the inner battle once, how he needed his full capacity to overcome when the inexplicable noise rose inside his mind. As I watched him now, I remembered Abba's reactions when life's struggles became overwhelming. I had been Abba's kitten—the calming presence that soothed and the warmth that brought comfort. How I wished I could shelter Nasseh so he could somehow be at peace. The queen mother had said as much to me many times. She'd suggested Yahweh as the answer. I knew better.

Only Nasseh could calm Nasseh.

"We're beginning our approach!" Our quffa captain shouted to the vessels behind us. Nasseh's momentary rest ended, and he hurried toward me, panic in his voice. "We must have a signal, Shulle. Some way you can alert me if I'm acting like an imbecile. I can't appear weak to the king of the world."

"Nasseh, you'll be fine."

"No!" he said, holding Adnah close. "A signal. Squeeze my hand or wink if I show my . . . deficiencies."

I grasped his face between my hands, but he shoved them away. So, I leaned as close as he'd allow. "You are not deficient, Manasseh ben Hezekiah. Do you hear me?"

He stared at a distant nothing. "If they kill me, Shulle, I won't see Abba."

Now I was even more confused about his beliefs on the life beyond. "What do you mean?" But he gripped the railing, moving back and forth in tortured rhythm. It was useless to ask him questions now.

As we sailed deeper into the city's canal system, I was stunned by the destruction. Giant building stones lay scattered like children's toy blocks. Broken-down walls and burned-out homes whispered of a once-grand city far beyond Jerusalem's splendor.

Our quffa captain docked in stagnant water at a quay. "This is as far as I go." His face looked haunted, and I wondered how many friends and family were buried in the city's rubble.

Camels and pack animals waited on shore for the transfer of our supplies, but Nasseh was too anxious to wait for the quffas to be unloaded. "Let the guides bring the supplies later. My entourage marches now." Baka led twenty men, Dohd, Manasseh, and his five women, while our remaining eighty soldiers provided rear guard. Mice in a lion's den if Sennacherib chose to attack.

We walked a distance equal to the entire wall surrounding Jerusalem before finally cresting a hill where we looked down on Babylon's ruins. Panting and dripping with sweat, I nearly fell to my knees. A city twice the size of Jerusalem lay decaying like a body, weeks dead. Armed guards surrounded small areas of construction that sprang up like resurrected flesh. Devastation and hope lay before us. Which would rule our future?

Within a single heartbeat, a long, shrill whistle drew my attention to a heap of rubble no more than a stone's throw to our right. Two men sat atop enormous black horses, flanked by a dozen armored warriors. A blur of snarling fur, muscle, and teeth sprinted toward us.

Nasseh saw it too and reached for his sword—but dropped Adnah in the process. Our cat yowled and darted through our guards' legs. I screamed, and Sennacherib's leonine beast focused its pursuit on our helpless feline. The hunt was over before I could cover my eyes.

"Nooo!" Hysterical, I shook and shrieked. One of our guards pinned my arms to my sides and clamped his hand over my mouth. My eyes pleaded with Nasseh, who stood rigid beside me. He stared slack jawed at the empty space that separated our group from the monstrous dog that had returned to its master, its prey already devoured.

Dohd stood behind my husband, bracing his shoulders and whispering frantically against his ear. "He's testing you, Manasseh. Sennacherib holds our lives in his hands. Don't react. Think! This is the moment you decide—are you a boy or a king? Will you be manipulated, or will you control the situation?" Dohd released Nasseh and stepped back, awaiting his response.

I shrugged from my guard's grasp as Nasseh's silence lengthened. Still rigid, except for both hands fisting wildly, Nasseh took his first step toward the two men on horseback. The man-eating hound growled, and I squeezed my eyes shut. Assyria's king said something in Akkadian, and I opened my eyes. The dog quieted, laying his head between his paws.

Nasseh halted at the base of the heap and bowed, focusing on the dog. "Sennacherib, king of the universe and the four quarters of the earth,"—his voice was loud but trembling—"wise ruler and favorite of the great gods, guardian of the right and lover of justice, who comes to the aid of the needy, who turns his thoughts to pious deeds; a perfect hero and mighty man—I, King Manasseh of Judah, greet you." Nasseh's perfect recitation of the titles written in Dohd's scroll cracked Sennacherib's chiseled expression.

"It's plain you've been reading your steward's messages, King Manasseh."

"My officials are loyal or they die, mighty king, as is the practice of any great ruler." He paused, and I marveled that he could put together two coherent words, let alone speak confidently in this moment. "I will show my loyalty by showering the great Sennacherib with gifts from Egypt, Phoenicia, Lebanon, and Syria as well as sharing my insights about each nation's loyalty to Assyria's empire. However, it would seem, great king, you've offered me a decidedly inhospitable welcome." He motioned toward the beast lying beside Sennacherib's mount. "Did you or your dog have a personal quarrel with my cat?"

An undeniable grin broke the Assyrian's granite countenance. "Cats come from Egypt. Anything from Egypt offends me."

He looked over Nasseh's head, inspecting our ranks. His eyes lingered too long on Panya. I stepped in front of her.

Sennacherib returned his attention to my husband. "I see Tirhakah gave you a Nubian woman. Egypt is the only nation that still refuses to bend the knee."

"My saba Isaiah refuses to bend his knee to anyone but Yahweh," Nasseh said. "I'd gladly feed him to your dog."

Sennacherib's brows rose, and he choked out a laugh, shoving the shoulder of the second man on a matching horse. He chuckled, too, his angular features and bushy, black brows identical to the king's. I was certain he was Prince Esarhaddon.

"You can keep that crusty old prophet," Sennacherib said, still chuckling. "My dog would much rather eat the advisor who welcomed the Babylonian envoys to Jerusalem." Eyes narrowing, he leaned forward on his stallion. "I won't tolerate disloyalty from you, infant king."

Nasseh motioned toward our whole contingent. "You may have anyone or anything in this caravan, King Sennacherib, if it proves my loyalty. Claim whatever you wish." He spread his arms wide toward us. "He or she is yours."

Terror shot through me. *Anyone?* Panya nudged me aside, placing me behind her back, while it seemed our whole retinue held its collective breath. The moment passed when Prince Esarhaddon nodded approvingly to his father.

"My son believes you are worthy to rule Judah when I go to my fate and reach the seven gates of the netherworld." Sennacherib appraised the guards standing behind us. Would this madman send his dog after our soldiers next?

"I leave for Nineveh tomorrow," he said, "and will take everyone in your company with me. You will remain in Babylon with Esarhaddon for two days of training. If at the end of that time my heir still believes you are a worthy vassal king, he'll bring you to Nineveh for the coronation feast, at which time I'll publicly announce Esarhaddon as crown prince."

He turned then to his son. "Perhaps Judah's king can teach your warring brothers a little about loyalty."

He addressed our hundred men. "If you learn well from my captains, you'll return to Jerusalem with the skills of the fiercest warriors in the world. If you don't learn well, you won't return at all." Without another word, Assyria's king turned his horse away with gentle pressure against its sides. I marveled at his care for the stallion and his whistle, calling his monstrous dog to follow.

Dohd wrapped his arm around my shoulder, and only then did I realize he was shaking too. "Come, Shulle. We'll travel upriver with our guards and supplies."

"But we can't just leave Nasseh," I said, peering over my shoulder as Dohd led me away. Esarhaddon had dismounted and now stood beside Nasseh, two heads taller.

"We *must* leave him," Dohd said, "and our king will win the respect of Assyria's crown prince—because Judah's future depends on it." The tremor in his voice drew my attention, and I noted the deep creases between his brows and tear stains on his cheeks. Nasseh would hold Dohd responsible for my safety and that of the concubines—especially Panya's—on our twenty-day journey to Nineveh.

Unbidden, Isaiah's prophecy came to mind and Zibah's warning to avoid this place. *But Nasseh hadn't been led captive here in chains,* I reasoned silently. So why did I feel like we were all Sennacherib's prisoners?

27

Let no one be found among you who sacrifices
their son or daughter in the fire, who practices
divination or sorcery, interprets omens, engages
in witchcraft, or casts spells.

DEUTERONOMY 18:10–11

Nasseh willed his body into stillness while Sennacherib and his beast rode away. The noise in his mind clanged like a thousand bells, but Shebna was right. He must learn to control himself. *Control the situation. Be a king.*

"King Manasseh!" Prince Esarhaddon shook his shoulder. How many times had he shouted over Nasseh's thoughts?

"Are you all right?" he asked.

"No. Your abba killed my cat."

The prince frowned and nodded, watching his abba retreat with a large retinue of troops. "Every ruler must instill fear, Manasseh." He pointed to three Assyrian soldiers overseeing a portion of reconstruction on Babylon's wall. "Do you see those men over there?"

One of the men noted his attention and rushed over, falling to one knee. "How may I serve you, my prince?"

"Alorus, what would you do if I commanded you to kill the six slaves under your commission?"

The soldier looked up with a troubled expression. "If you commanded it, I failed you already. A good soldier knows his commander's mind with only a glance."

Nasseh noted the smile on Esarhaddon's face, and with a barely perceptible nod, the prince sent the man back to work. "My father rules with cruelty, Manasseh." Esarhaddon began a leisurely stroll as if in a luxurious garden, not a fallen city. "His ways are extremely effective, as you yourself witnessed, but the gods have favored me with wit and weapons. I prefer respect to fear and will build an even greater Assyria than my father."

Nasseh looked up at the giant of a man. "I, too, wish to be greater than my abba."

"Then we have much in common already." He stopped walking and clapped a massive hand on Nasseh's shoulder. "Our spies tell me you have a brilliant mind and are—how should I phrase it—untethered by social norms. Is this true?"

Untethered by social norms. Coupling the elegant phrase with *a brilliant mind* almost made Nasseh's oddities sound positive. "Yes. Both are true."

They stood within a few paces of a larger group of soldiers. Esarhaddon's pointed stare brought the commanding officer over to bow before him. "How may I serve you, my prince?"

"Are you committed to serve Assyria at any cost?"

"I am, my lord."

He merely looked in the direction of another soldier, and the man scurried over like a child begging bread. "How may I serve you, lord prince?"

Esarhaddon's features darkened into something Nasseh couldn't understand. Neither did the soldier because the prince finally spoke. "Kill your commander."

"Lord?"

In that fleeting hesitation, Esarhaddon drew his dagger—and slit the man's throat. Stunned, he clasped the mortal wound and fell at the prince's feet.

Esarhaddon leaned to within a handbreadth of the commander. "Are you still committed to Assyria, no matter the cost?"

"Without hesitation." The commander nudged aside his soldier with his foot, then knelt and pulled at his collar to expose his throat. "I'm honored to meet my fate at your hand, my prince."

Nasseh could hardly breathe, appalled yet transfixed by a prince whose men were honored to die at his hand.

Esarhaddon wiped the bloody dagger before sheathing it and patted the man's shoulder. "Stand, my friend. You bring honor to your unit." He reached into a pouch at his waist, drawing out seven silver rings. "You and your comrades may mourn your friend for seven days. Make sure his soul gains passage over the Khuber River so that he enters the seven gates. The dread gods must judge him fairly."

"May Ishtar bless you, my prince." The commander received payment with a reverent bow.

Esarhaddon wrapped his arm around Nasseh's shoulders. "I will teach you the difference between intimidation and instilling fear, Manasseh. As my chosen vassal, you'll need to learn both, but you'll come to discern which is appropriate to use in a particular moment. Hesitation is *always* intolerable—as I demonstrated. It reveals either slowness of mind or a propensity to rebel."

"I understand." Nasseh glanced at his hands.

"Why are your hands red and chapped?" Esarhaddon released him, stepping toward a third group of construction workers. "Is it a disease?"

"No, my lord prince! I wash my hands quite often. It's one of my *untethered social norms.*" A grand revelation halted him. "I haven't needed to suppress any compulsions since you and I began talking." And the noise in Nasseh's head had hushed to whispers.

The prince studied him with lifted brows and a grin. "Perhaps the gods are already smiling on us. You may call me Esar when we're among my troops but Prince Esarhaddon when members of Nineveh's court are present."

Heartbeat racing, Nasseh's palms grew sweaty. "I'm honored, Prince Esar. And you may call me Nasseh."

Esar continued teaching, and Nasseh soaked in his insight as if it were water on dry ground. How had such a disastrous first meeting become the key to Nasseh's new reign? This prince of Assyria—this soon-to-be ruler of the empire—could most certainly make him the greatest king ever to rule Judah.

Some of Nasseh's most loathsome oddities—his inability to relate and difficulty showing emotion—were traits Esar lauded as characteristics of a great king. Nasseh had refused to be a mere second Solomon, but he would gladly become a wise second Esarhaddon—and would willingly pledge fealty.

~

The two days of training in Babylon had sped by too quickly, but valuable instruction had continued on the twenty-day march to the capital with five hundred of Esar's troops. On the last night of their journey, Nasseh sat opposite the prince at the private cook fire outside their neighboring tents. "I want to repay your kindness, Esar. Let me send a thousand of my best men to Nineveh."

"Keep your men, Nasseh. You'll need the ones who return with you to train others to fight like Assyrians." Always teaching, he pointed to the soldiers still scurrying around camp. "Do you remember the first night of our journey, when I appointed twelve men to travel ahead and prepare camp—tents, cook fires, and water drawn for your tent and mine? Every night since, they've done it without being told. Anticipating commands, Nasseh. It's what separates good soldiers from great ones, and you must be willing to winnow your men without regrets."

"I will, Esar."

He'd *winnowed* over thirty of his own men in the three weeks Nasseh had been with him, but hundreds of Babylonians from outlying towns and villages had begged to replace them. He was like a flame, drawing moths to his light on their glorious march to Nineveh.

"Truly great rulers are efficient beyond this world, Nasseh." He poked at the dying embers of the fire. "Just as we prepare the camp ahead of our arrival, we mortals—made by the mixture of dust and blood from the rebellious god We-ilu—must prepare for the life to come."

Nasseh remained silent, as he'd done every time Esar discussed his burial beliefs.

"Why are you fluttery like a woman when we speak of death and burial, Nasseh?" His frown showed deep lines of frustration. "A king—more than any other mortal—must sacrifice to the gods, build his house, and prepare the offerings to be made after he meets his fate."

"I don't wish to speak of the dead for risk of stirring the spirits who still wander aimlessly." Nasseh used Esar's own beliefs against him, but Assyria's prince grinned at him—too clever for the trick.

"Then we won't speak of those already dead. We'll consult the starry hosts about our deaths because the gods of night hold the power of conception—and it's our children who will make offerings after our burials to maintain our pleasures in the life beyond."

"My Nubian is with child," Nasseh confided, "but she's only a concubine."

"My mother was a concubine."

Nasseh tried to mask his surprise, keeping his tone level. "The son of a concubine will be Sennacherib's heir?"

Esar laughed, warming Nasseh's cheeks with his mocking. "If only you mastered your reactions as handily as the dagger and sword. My mother is no longer a concubine but the king's favorite wife." Nasseh glanced up, and Esar's broad smile calmed him. "Mother is the main reason I'm the chosen heir. The women who share a king's bed affect him profoundly—whether he admits it or not."

"My queen is my favorite."

"She's stunning. If you ever tire of her, I'll take her off your hands."

"You'll stay away from her." Nasseh's fury rose before reason.

Esar's smile faded. "You've just revealed your weakness, Nasseh. Every king has one."

"Shulle is my strength." How could he make Esar understand? "My abba loved me, but Yahweh took him away. The thought of losing Shulle . . ." He could barely even speak of it. "It haunts me."

"Then she is worse than your weakness." Esar leaned forward. "She's your curse, and a curse must be broken."

"You will not harm her!" Nasseh shot to his feet, but Esar grabbed his arm.

"You misunderstand me, Nasseh. Sit down."

Eyes averted, Nasseh obeyed. Hands fisting wildly, he heard the chaos rumble in his head. He could barely think, barely breathe. "You mustn't hurt her Esar. Please."

"Listen to me!" Esar shook him, shouting above the roar. Nasseh forced his eyes open but stared at the ground. "You will take a Babylonian wife," Esar said, squeezing his shoulder hard. "I'll choose her myself. Someone to teach you to worship the starry hosts."

"Shulle teaches me. She's a gifted āšipūtu, taught by a Babylonian sorceress." Nasseh's words came out like a whine. "I promised I'd never take another wife."

Esar resumed his seat but remained silent so long that curiosity drew Nasseh's attention. Assyria's prince watched him with an unreadable expression. If Nasseh failed to anticipate his command, would he—? Esar's fingers stroked his dagger. Nasseh closed his eyes and waited for the strike.

"I'd heard Lord Shebna provided your queen with a Babylonian education," Esar said, "but she's not *Babylonian*. You will understand the difference when I present your Babylonian wife in Nineveh." A slight pause, then, "Look at me, Nasseh." Esar gripped the hilt of his dagger, and Nasseh understood the prince's intention. To refuse the gift meant immediate execution.

"I'm humbled by your generosity, my prince, and most grateful."

"You're not grateful yet, but you will be." Esar grinned. "Only a Babylonian mother is more treasured than a Babylonian wife," Esar continued, "and I have both. My mother Naqia is the reason I'll be king. My father treasures her above his other wives because she has divined both his greatest victory and the day of his death."

"How can anyone divine the day of death?"

Esar's frown told Nasseh he should have posed the question more cautiously. "Queen Naqia accurately predicted all my father's military successes, proving herself as the greatest āšipūtu in Assyria. That's why he trusted her to choose the empire's successor." He pressed his fist against his heart and bowed slightly, then straightened with a grin. "My mother also chose a Babylonian wife for me, who she's training to be equally wise and powerful. I have been considering this for some time. I choose Gemeti for you, Nasseh. She'll divine the gods' will but also teach you the regal bearing of a king."

Bristling, Nasseh had no use for another teacher. "Shebna and Shulle teach me the ways of kings, and I already have a *Babylonian* āšipūtu in Jerusalem. I will welcome Gemeti to my harem and treat her with the respect she deserves as my most revered concubine."

"Gemeti will be your wife," Esar said flatly. "You need not make her your queen—yet. However, by retaining Shulle as queen, you place both her future offspring and Gemeti's at odds from the moment of their birth. I have nine brothers, Nasseh, and I've known nothing but their hatred all my life because we compete for our father's attention and favor and ultimately—his crown."

Nasseh had always wished for brothers. Even a sister might have been nice. But Esar's normally pleasant features were unmistakably angry. If Nasseh was forced to compete for Abba's crown, surely a more perfect sibling would have won Judah's throne. "I will accept Gemeti as my wife, Esar, and try to accept her counsel." And he would, but he would never let Shulle leave his side.

~

Nasseh arrived in Nineveh on the sixteenth day of Heshvan, under the starry host of the Crab and Esar's patron god, Marduk, three days before the evil nineteenth day. "Every tragedy in my mother's life and mine has fallen on the nineteenth day of a month," Esar said as they entered the gates of the astounding city. "I sent a messenger to my mother each day of our journey with updates on our travel. I'm sure it's her incantations that brought us safely to Nineveh under the stars most powerful for laying foundations. I believe our nations have a great future."

He appeared so pleased that Nasseh kept his doubts to himself, choosing instead to focus on Assyria's impressive capital. "Of all the cities we've visited on our tour, even Memphis and Tyre can't compare to Nineveh."

Esar pointed to the soaring mountains that formed the eastern ramparts of the city. "See how the rushing streams flow naturally into the river inside our walls? And how the impenetrable walls surrounding the other three sides, guarding our farmland within the gates, make Nineveh virtually impervious to military siege?"

Nasseh gawked at the wonders all around, thinking of his teacher, Lord Eliakim. Even Judah's greatest engineer couldn't have conceived this city. The gargantuan wall stretched around the sprawling city on the banks of the Tigris River, as high as two of Solomon's palaces and as thick as fifty camels end-to-end.

The caravan began its long, dark trek through the city's main gate, more like a tunnel than any normal entry. Torches lined the inside walls, though the sun shone outside. "This is beyond imagination!" Nasseh exclaimed, "I wish Eliakim were here to see this."

"Eliakim?" Sudden recognition lit Esar's features. "Oh yes. The man responsible for Jerusalem's underground tunnel that brought water from outside your gates to a cistern inside the walls." He chuckled. "Yes, my father wishes he were here too. He'd like to skin him and feed him to his dog."

Startled by the remark, Nasseh bristled. "He was my abba's best friend."

Esar's humor faded. "Kings have no friends, Nasseh. They form alliances." He winked and resumed a grin. Shulle told him people often winked when they were teasing—lying in jest. Of course, kings had friends. Esar had spent three weeks with him. Learning, laughing, talking of their families and future. "Since you're so enamored with our city," Esar said, "I'll arrange for a tour tomorrow."

"It's barely after midday. Why can't you show me now?"

The prince's shrill whistle called a swarm of guards to surround them as they continued into the city. "I'm sorry, Nasseh, but because I've openly shown you favor, my brothers will make you a target. We'll find out how many of your guards survived the training and form a full protective detail for you by tomorrow."

"What? I don't under—"

"I'll assign my personal guards to accompany you tonight, both inside and outside your chamber."

"What about Shulle?" Nasseh asked. "Has she been protected?"

Esar fell silent, returning his attention to the wide, bricked street leading to the grand palace ahead. Nasseh's pulse raced. What had happened to his queen while he'd meekly trusted Sennacherib's son?

"Please," Nasseh said quietly. "Are my people safe?"

Esar nodded. "My father told you he'd train your men as he trains all soldiers—challenging the best to excellence and killing the rest. Your wife and advisor have likely been waiting in separate chambers under guard. My brothers wouldn't shame our father by attacking your people under his protection." Finally, he looked Nasseh's way again. "But now, you're all mine to protect. If my brothers can kill anyone under my protection, it discredits me before the king publicly names me his heir."

Nasseh swallowed.

"I'll do my best not to let that happen, but may I offer a word of caution?"

"Yes, of course."

"If my brothers see your preoccupation with the little Hebrew queen, even my father's protection wouldn't be enough to save her."

Nodding, Nasseh worked hard to gather enough spit to swallow again. He followed Esar into the royal stables, passing off his reins to a stable boy.

Esar's hand landed on his shoulder. "My guards will escort you to your guest chamber. You'll find a washbasin and a fresh set of clothes for tonight's banquet. After you've refreshed yourself, you'll be escorted to my room. I'm anxious for you to see your gift."

Head bowed, Nasseh heard Esar's footsteps recede as an impenetrable circle of eight guards surrounded him. "This way, your majesty." He followed blindly, silently repeating the prince's instructions to occupy his mind. *You'll find a washbasin. I'm anxious for you to see your gift.* The washbasin he could enjoy, but would the prince so quickly force a new wife?

Mosaic tiles led him into a guest chamber more lavish than his own in Solomon's palace. Gold trimmed every piece of furniture, and inlaid ivory and ebony accents created a manly decor to accompany the various beast heads hanging on walls.

The assigned guards waited as he soothed his shaking hands in the cool, scented water, and they noted his readiness without being told. Four men preceded him out the door, while four guards followed down a wide staircase and a narrow hall with doors lining each side. No doubt military housing for Assyria's royal guard. They emerged into a separate wing with a circular receiving area, where guards stood at attention beside four double doors. Nasseh was led to the first doorway on the left, and without a knock the doors opened to him.

"Welcome." Esar walked toward him, arms open wide, but Nasseh was too stunned to reply.

The room was no larger than his own guest chamber, but the furnishings were stark. A single straw mat, a lamb's wool headrest, and two goat skins lay in one corner. In another corner was a washbasin and stand with a single wardrobe beside it. Four ragged cushions lay haphazardly on a worn tapestry in the center of the room.

"You're staring, Nasseh." Esar's low chuckle proved he wasn't angry. "My mother taught me that living simply made one stronger." The prince motioned to his modest sitting area. "Choose a cushion, Nasseh, and let's talk about your most important task of all." He wore an unbelted robe and stretched out on his side with a cushion tucked under his arm. Nasseh mirrored his posture while a serving maid poured wine into two gold goblets. Esar waved her away.

Nasseh sipped the wine. "What is my most important task?"

"I'm sure your mother is still grieving King Hezekiah. With you traveling, is she able to make adequate provision for his life in the netherworld?" He took a long draw of wine from his goblet but stared at Nasseh over the rim. He set down the goblet. "We have temples for all the nations' gods in Nineveh, so you can take your offerings to whichever god you choose."

After three weeks with this deeply religious prince, Nasseh's trust in the starry hosts had never been stronger—nor his confusion about death greater. "How can you know which nation's beliefs of the netherworld are true, my prince?"

"You have a strong mind, Nasseh. You know every nation's beliefs about the afterlife are similar. Simply choose one and believe." He shrugged as if the decision was no more than choosing a scarf for his wife in the market. "Even the Hebrews' own father Abraham came from the land of Chaldeans, the Babylonians' ancient ancestors, and would have agreed that the living must provide for the dead who pass over a river from this life to the next."

Shame burned Nasseh's cheeks. "Yes, but when Abraham emigrated to Canaan, he rejected the teachings of the Chaldeans."

Esar's expression changed to sudden horror. "Are you saying neither you nor your mother have made offerings for King Hezekiah's afterlife?"

"My ima believes Abba closed his eyes in this life and was immediately transported to the presence of Yahweh, the only true God. She believes Yahweh rewards those who serve Him in this life with an eternal life in paradise—without offerings by the family after death. In fact, such rituals are considered an abomination."

Esar shook his head like a disapproving ima. "If what you say is true, then your abba is doomed as an etemmu—a ghost—who wanders in darkness. You're his only child, Nasseh, and even though you're a king, you could never provide all his needs for an eternity of pleasure. It's shameful,

Nasseh. King Hezekiah was a worthy king and should have gone to a better fate."

The weight of his pronouncement felt like a death sentence. "I've failed in the most important task."

Esar clanked his wine goblet, drawing Nasseh's attention. "No, my friend. The most important task is to build a household that will secure *your* journey across the demon-infested River Khuber. I won't see you succumb to the same fate as your father, regardless of your mother's beliefs. A king must always honor his mother, but your eternal destiny must take precedent."

Prickly flesh raised over Nasseh's whole body. How could he honor Ima and yet prepare for a netherworld she branded as blasphemy?

Esar clapped his hands, startling Nasseh. "I can see I've ruined your welcome to Nineveh. No more talk of death," the prince said, jumping to his feet. "It's time for your gift." Nasseh's eyes slid shut, dreading the introduction of his Babylonian wife.

A strange sound forced his eyes open as a golden ball of fur jumped into his lap—a miniature replica of the beast that had eaten Adnah.

"He's twelve weeks old," Esar said, "and you may name him whatever you wish."

Nasseh patted the wriggling animal and tried to keep his face away from its slobbery tongue. "In Jerusalem, cats roam the palace, and dogs scavenge for garbage in the streets." The little beast's razor-sharp teeth bloodied Nasseh's finger. "Esar, get him off me!"

The prince set aside his wine and lifted the dog—already the size of a small child—into his arms. "I know your introduction to my father's Assyrian Shepherd was a bit harsh, but it's an intelligent, loyal breed that makes a fantastic war dog."

Nasseh couldn't deny their ability to kill with precision.

The prince set the dog on the floor and gripped his braided leather collar with one hand while raising a fist in the air. *"Kammusu,"* he said sternly—the Akkadian word for "sit." The puppy obeyed immediately, his frenetic activity ceasing like Nasseh's controlled tics.

"You see?" Esar said. "They're incredibly smart and very lovable."

"When they aren't killing cats or people?"

"Yes, well . . ." The prince splayed his fingers in front of the dog's face. "*Ā.*" The dog remained perfectly still while Esar settled on a cushion beside Nasseh. "I'll begin with an apology. My father doesn't believe in *pets*. I grew fond of a garden lizard once, but Father found me feeding it one day and made me watch while he skinned it."

"So, King Sennacherib prefers dogs to lizards?"

"Father has no use for any animal that can't hunt or kill on command. King Sennacherib shows no sentiment and takes no leisure—which is why his wives and my brothers hate him."

"But you don't?"

"I feel sorry for him." Esarhaddon said. "Mother taught me to love him."

"My ima has been trying to teach me to love. It's quite complex."

Esarhaddon laughed. "On this we agree, young king. My mother won Sennacherib's heart because she's the only woman who never deceived him. I'll forever thank her for my crown." He drained his cup.

"My ima is also a great woman." Nasseh suddenly wished she was there. "I think your mother and mine could be good friends."

The prince made a kissing sound and patted his chest. The puppy romped at him, biting and ripping his sleeve. "What will your new master name you, little boy?"

"I'll call him *Ra`ah.*"

Nasseh said, hoping a Hebrew name might make him more acceptable to Ima. "It means 'shepherd.'"

"Perfect." Esar shoved the dog playfully at Nasseh and crossed the chamber to refill his goblet. "Perhaps when I sit on Assyria's throne, it will be safe for our mothers to meet. Until then, you'll use the training I provide to rule Judah as my father wishes."

The dog squatted, leaving a wet spot on the prince's tattered cushion. Nasseh laughed. "I hope your training includes teaching the dog not to do that, or my ima will skin me and Ra`ah both."

28

In the fourteenth year of King Hezekiah's
reign, Sennacherib king of Assyria attacked all
the fortified cities of Judah and captured them.

2 KINGS 18:13

Nineveh, Assyria
Shebat (February)

My journey to Nineveh had proven less terrifying, but lonelier,
than expected. Sennacherib had separated Dohd Shebna and
me right away, and he placed each of Nasseh's women in
separate tents when we camped, with guards forming walls around each
shelter. Travel imposed similar segregation with Dohd and our Hebrew
guards dispersed among Sennacherib's troops while we women rode camels in silence at the front of the procession. Our guides and caravanners
obeyed the Assyrians without question, making twenty days of travel in-
furiatingly efficient. By the time we reached Nineveh, I ached for a familiar
face or the throaty sounds of our Hebrew tongue.

That was three months and eleven days ago.

I despised Sennacherib with every fiber of my being. If there was a
drop more of hate left in me, it was reserved for his son, Esarhaddon, who
I'd watched from my balcony each day walking in the royal gardens with
my husband. For the first month, I also hated Nasseh, but remembering
his trusting nature, I could only focus my loathing on the Assyrians who
had undoubtedly bent his will to theirs by now.

"Would you like your hair plaited or flowing, mistress?" Tonight's maidservant asked in perfect Akkadian. They'd sent a different maid each day, and none were allowed to tell me their names.

"How do the other royal women wear their hair for evening banquets?"

Her eyes sparked with a little life. "The older women wear it plaited and twirled in all manner of shapes, but few royals are as young as you, mistress. Perhaps we could let your lovely curls flow freely." Her cheeks bloomed pink as she reached for the hand mirror and placed it before me. "Forgive me if I've spoken out of turn."

I set aside the mirror and faced her. "Quite the opposite. I'm grateful for your conversation and value your candor. Why don't you prepare me for tonight's banquet as if I were your friend, not a stranger from a foreign land."

Her eyes shimmered as she placed the mirror in my hands again. "You will be magnificent when you meet the Assyrian court on your last night in Nineveh."

I swiped at my eyes, appreciating the boost in confidence. Tonight's banquet would be the first time I had been allowed to leave my chamber. I'd enjoy the revelry of the banquet tonight, and tomorrow, when we left this god-forsaken city, I planned to spit on its streets and hope to forget I had ever been here.

My maid reached for the kohl pot to begin my eye makeup and released a little gasp at the stack of parchments beneath it. Inspecting the drawing on top, she looked at me. Then back at the drawing. And back at me. "Who drew this portrait of you, mistress?"

"I did."

"How . . . You did?"

I chuckled. "I sat in front of the mirror, opened my kohl pot, and used that stick in your hand to draw. A solid line here. A few smudges there." The cascading curls were no doubt the reason she knew it was me. Though my captivity had been unrelenting, the maids somehow found blank parchments for me each day so I could at least stay busy.

I showed her the kohl stains on my hands and nails. "I'm afraid I'll need a little extra scrubbing to prepare me for the banquet."

"Mistress," the maid said, staring at the parchment. "Your face matches the sad girl in the drawing."

I looked in the polished bronze mirror and studied the face staring back. How would Nasseh interpret such a face after more than three months apart? I couldn't allow any misunderstandings. Forcing my lips into a smile, I turned to my maid. "There. Better?"

"Beautiful." Her kindness felt like a splash of cool water.

When Nasseh's guards arrived at dusk to escort me, my smile was authentic. The ten men were as efficient as every other Assyrian. Working in perfect concert, two walked ahead with eyes roaming; six formed a circle, swords drawn; the other two provided rear guard. If I were such a treasure, why had they cooped me up in a chamber for three months?

When we emerged from a labyrinth of halls that made a spider's web seem simple, I gasped at the canyon of elegance. Golden pillars supported a circular rooftop that pointed like the cedars of Lebanon toward the center.

"Magnificent," I whispered, skimming the beauty only a moment before landing on a grander sight. "Nasseh." His name tasted like honey. I saw only his profile while he waited beside gigantic cedar doors. Though I'd noticed changes in his appearance while I watched him from my balcony, now standing close, I could see he'd grown taller. His shoulders were broader too. Head bowed, his hands were fisting. He was nervous. My palms were sweaty too.

I took two steps toward him and halted at the sight of a pacing dog. Panic crawled up my arms. "I can't go any closer," I said to a guard. I'd seen the puppy grow too week by week, walking with the prince and Nasseh in the garden. Though smaller than the beast that killed Adnah, the dog's markings were identical, and its head reached Nasseh's waist. "You must send it away before I approach King Manasseh."

"The dog Ra'ah belongs to your husband," he said without expression.

"You will continue. King Manasseh is waiting." His piercing eyes left no room for discussion.

As I approached, the dog's ears perked, and it began to growl. I released an uncontrolled whimper at the same time Nasseh saw me.

"Ra'ah, *ahu*," he said, spreading his fingers in front of the dog's face. Without expression he extended his right arm to me. "He knows you're a friend now. He won't harm you."

The mammoth puppy no longer growled but seemed to keep a wary eye on me as I rested my hand on Nasseh's arm. "You look lovely, Shulle." He then faced forward and without expression. Right foot first, as we'd been taught, we began our march into the crowded banquet.

I cursed the thick robe beneath my hand, wishing I could feel the warmth of my husband's skin against mine. "I've missed you," I whispered.

He remained silent, more regal than I'd ever seen him. His dog pranced at his left. I trembled at his right.

I felt the measure of every eye as we walked the center aisle, approaching the empire's most powerful men. King Sennacherib sat with his eleven sons on an elevated dais. I recognized only Esarhaddon, of course, who stood like a proud abba, waiting to greet Nasseh. We stopped at the edge of a crimson carpet.

Nasseh removed my hand from his arm and bounded up the steps into Prince Esarhaddon's embrace. Even the dog was welcomed to the dais, while a guard escorted me to a table of sour-faced women with plaited hair in all manner of shapes—as my maid predicted. I was the only one with curls cascading around my shoulders and down my back. The only one fighting the roar in my ears and black spots in my vision. *He barely spoke to me. Why?*

With a smile etched in stone, I nodded to the seven women at my table but was greeted by only one. "I'm Queen Naqia," said a gray-haired, round woman wearing a simple gold crown. "You can ignore the cows at this table. If they pretend to like you, it's only because they want your jewels when you're dead." I covered a real grin and felt the balm of a kindred spirit. "I'm happy to finally meet you, little queen. My son believes your husband will make a fine ruler someday."

This was Esarhaddon's mother? "He is already a fine ruler," I quipped with equal spunk. "He will be great someday."

She waved over the wine steward and chose a larger goblet for me. "Tonight will be a long and difficult evening for you, girl. Drink up while I explain how to survive a powerful king's household." When I hesitated, she put the full goblet in my hand and tipped it toward my lips.

I drank while inspecting the other six women. They were models of elegance. Naqia was the least regal royal I'd encountered but the most engaging.

"Both my husband and my son have taken notice of your young husband, Shulle—may I call you Shulle?"

Already feeling the effects of strong wine, I set aside the goblet. "Of course. What shall I call you?"

"In public, you are to call me Queen Naqia. When this night is over, you will write to me often and call me friend. Now, here is both good news and bad news for you, little Shulle. Both my men are confident Manasseh will lead Judah as no other king before him."

Perhaps the wine had done more damage than I thought. "Why would that be bad news?"

"When much confidence is given, much is required."

"Manasseh is brilliant, Queen Naqia. He will not disappoint."

She laughed too loud, and I winced. Scanning the crowded hall, I expected every face turned our way with mocking ire, but others seemed deaf to her bawdy behavior. "Everyone disappoints my Senn," she said, finally calming. "But he's more likely to forgive those who prove true." So began the advice of Sennacherib's wife, who poured both wine and wisdom into me when no one else would even look at me. "Make friends with his dog," she said. "If you can win the dog, you'll win the man."

"Nasseh doesn't even like dogs," I whispered in confidence. "He prefers cats."

"That puppy will eat cats for dinner." This time Naqia's cackling drew King Sennacherib's attention. He gave her a loving wink.

"Isn't he a marvel?" The warmth in her tone startled me. "I've loved him since the moment he took me to his bed."

Took her to his bed. No wedding? "You're fortunate your parents betrothed you to a man you loved."

Again, her laughter carried. "I forget you haven't been privy to palace gossip. I became Senn's *wife* two months ago—after he named Esarhaddon governor of Babylon. I've been his concubine for nearly thirty years." She lowered her voice and nodded toward the others at our table. "I've always been his favorite because I love Senn, the man—not Sennacherib, the king." Naqia fixed her eyes on the king of her heart, a look of longing as unchecked as her laughter. "All kings are ruthless and powerful. The other wives love his power and reap his cruelty. I love the *man* and welcome his tenderness."

I stared at the king I'd been taught to hate. Though I hadn't experienced his barbarity during his siege on Jerusalem, I had no doubt Sennacherib was more monster than man. "I mean no disrespect, Queen Naqia, but I don't believe all kings are ruthless. I love Nasseh as both a king and a man. He need not be *ruthless* to be a powerful king."

She looked at me like a warrior ready for battle. "Did you know your husband's concubine gave birth to her first child last week? A girl." Her harsh tone sent fear coursing through me.

"Nasseh has always been kind to Panya."

"Your husband gave the baby to one of Senn's sons who was especially angry that he'd been passed over as heir to the throne. Manasseh's firstborn daughter will be a concubine when she comes of age—or sooner if she's as lovely as her mother."

"He wouldn't." I felt suddenly light-headed.

Naqia lifted a single brow. "As I said, young queen, *all* kings are ruthless. You must find a way to love the man, or his cruelty falls on you."

The wine gorged in my throat, and the room began to spin. Naqia shoved a plate of quail eggs toward me. "Eat something. You mustn't make a scene." I obeyed, and she began naming the princes on the dais, matching them with their mothers seated at our table. "These women don't know what real love is," she said. "They know lust for power, and that's what they've taught their sons. You, little Shulle, must teach your sons to love. That's how they win their father's favor and become an heir."

I drained my fifth goblet of wine. "I don't want a child." I gasped and met Naqia's shocked expression, realizing I'd told the queen of Assyria my darkest secret.

She glanced at the other wives. Deep in conversation, they were oblivious to the prize gossip that had slipped past them unnoticed. *Thank the gods.* "Too much wine can ruin years of hard work," Naqia said, nudging my empty goblet out of reach. "My son assures me your husband adores you—to a level of distraction. Pretending barrenness keeps him chained for a while, but don't pretend too long."

Perhaps she could say something to allay my fears. "I don't want to die on the birthing stones like my—"

She lifted her hand in warning, but a semblance of pity bunched her brow. "Every woman fears childbirth, but you must remember the words I'm about to speak, little Shulle. In the days ahead, your courage must rise above your insecurities so you can fight for the man you love—and the children to come from your womb."

The foreboding in her tone sent a chill through me. Why must I fight for Nasseh? For children not yet born?

"Discover what *you* love, Shulle. Discover your passion, and do it with all your heart. Only then can you excel and snare your husband's notice. Only then can you offer your unique gifts to your husband as I have and never doubt his love again."

"Nasseh loves my drawings, and he often asks me to interpret the stars for him."

"Those are things you do for *him*. What makes *you* feel alive, little queen? Only when you find your pure pleasure—and do it so well it reveals your true nature—only then will you become irresistible to your husband. Irreplaceable to your king. What connects you to something greater than yourself?"

"I don't know, Naqia." I'd never been connected to anything greater than Dohd and the purpose of winning Nasseh's love. "What makes you irresistible and irreplaceable?"

"The starry hosts speak to me in ways that are—unusual."

"I, too, have been trained as an āšipūtu." My new mentor offered a pathetic smile, revealing my pathetic comparison. "Belit says I'm good at it, but I don't love it as you say you do." The thought of connecting so intimately with the gods intrigued me. I pondered my life, searching for anything so satisfying.

"You're getting it," she said, staring deep into my eyes. "If Nasseh is to be yours, you must love him with the very best *Shulle* the gods created." She framed my cheeks with her hands. "But first you must discover what your best is, darling girl."

The swirling noise of music and dancing suddenly quieted. Naqia tapped my shoulder and motioned to Esarhaddon who stood beside his father at the front of the dais. "My handsome men." She wiggled her eyebrows, and I laughed, partly from the wine, partly at the antics of this woman who'd so quickly become my friend. She motioned to the wine steward again. "Leave the wineskin. She'll need it."

Dread prickled my cheeks when I saw King Sennacherib rise from his cushion. "Tonight," he began, "we celebrate Nisrok's new temple and my faithful priests who serve." Twelve bald priests in white robes stood at the table beside us, bowed to the king, and received the compulsory applause of a bored crowd.

Esarhaddon stood with his father, and the audience stilled. "Also, we celebrate the Crown Prince's return to Babylon tomorrow," Sennacherib said. "He goes to govern a city that, like our great Huma and the Phoenix, will rise from ashes to become great again. And when I go to my fate, Esar will rule my great empire with his father's iron fist and his mother's silk scarves." He lifted his golden goblet to Naqia and then clinked it against Esarhaddon's before draining it to the dregs.

The crown prince stood to raucous praise, and for the first time I spotted Dohd near the back of the crowded hall. Nasseh's concubines were seated at the table with him. Was a place at the women's table to be Dohd's humiliation? Had they all been held captive like me until this evening? But Panya was missing. Was she still locked away?

"Indeed, we will see Babylon rise again," Esarhaddon shouted over waning applause. "It will become the strongest vassal nation in our empire. Tonight, I introduce King Manasseh of Judah, a dedicated vassal whose trade routes are critical for Assyria's expansion."

Esar coaxed him to stand, whispering something that prompted Nasseh to speak. "Thank you, Prince Esarhaddon and King Sennacherib," he said, with a quick bow but remained focused on his dog. "Thank you for your hospitality and for the new member of my family, Ra'ah, which in my language means "Shepherd." He whispered something to the puppy, who then perched on his hind legs and pawed at the air as if fighting. Nasseh feigned a beating, and his antics won the crowd. My husband bowed, smile affixed but eyes still averted. "In honor of Assyria's great king and prince, I've ordered a monument built in Jerusalem's temple unlike any the world has ever seen. And following the example set by this great city, Jerusalem will honor all the gods of Assyria's empire."

Applause exploded as Esarhaddon wrapped his arm around Nasseh's shoulders. Lifting his hand for quiet, the crown prince added, "With Judah's strategic partnership, the empire's expansion toward Egypt is sealed. As a gesture of good faith, we offer our good friend Manasseh one of Babylon's royal daughters as his honored wife."

The double cedar doors opened at the rear of the hall, and a willowy, dark-eyed beauty appeared between two royal guards. Veiled and dressed in Tyrian purple, she was as mysterious as she was alluring. Gasps and whispers were drowned out by my frantically beating heart.

"May I present Gemeti," Esar continued, "daughter of Babylon's royal family. Though presented to King Manasseh on his first night in Nineveh, Gemeti is presented publicly tonight to show her great respect for the king she now loves and serves." He turned to Nasseh, grasping his wrist in a soldier's clasp. "May she bring not only beauty but also an heir to your throne as we build Assyria's great empire."

As the woman passed our table on her way to the dais, the aroma of her lotions overwhelmed me. Naqia leaned close. "Remember, little Shulle. Find your best, and love Manasseh with it. Other stars might twinkle in his harem, but you can still be the only moon in his night sky."

I squeezed the stem of my goblet and watched my husband's face brighten as he removed his new wife's veil. He'd broken his promise. Taken another wife.

And she was the brightest star I'd ever seen.

29

In the ninth year of Hoshea, the king of Assyria captured Samaria and deported the Israelites to Assyria.

2 Kings 17:6

Drunk and wounded, I was escorted from the banquet to my chamber, where my maid waited with warming stones for my bed and even warmer news for my heart. "I've been given to you as a gift, mistress, if you'll have me." Eyes lowered and wringing her hands, she added, "My name is Adnah."

Instantly sober, I studied her in torchlight. "That's a Hebrew name." I was too astonished to mention it also belonged to Ima and our kitten.

"My ima was taken prisoner fifteen years ago," she said, "when King Sennacherib attacked Bethlehem. She died giving birth to me." Her story held too many coincidences to be true. "I would be most grateful to return with you to the land of her birth as your lifelong servant."

Though I didn't believe her story, the scars on her face and extremities proved at least part of her life had been difficult. Had she been sent to infiltrate Judah's royal household? Nothing in her appearance confirmed her claim to Hebrew heritage. Lighter skin and silky, black hair looked distinctly Assyrian. Her doe eyes brimmed with tears while she rubbed a scar on her left hand and awaited my answer. How could I deny her the escape our caravan could provide?

"You may come to Jerusalem as my serving maid," I said coolly, "but only if you tell me your real name and who forced you to lie about it."

The shock on her face transformed to genuine indignation. She squared her shoulders and swiped away tears. "Thank you for your kindness, Queen Shulle, but if you cannot trust me, binding ourselves for a lifetime would be torture for us both." She bowed respectfully and set about preparing me for bed in a silence thick with tension.

I considered every schemer capable of such a plot. Perhaps Sennacherib or the prince sent her to spy, or one of their guards. I might have considered Dohd, except his authority had obviously been stripped, or he would never have been content to sit with Nasseh's women at the banquet. Would Nasseh have sent her? The thought of his growing ruthlessness generated a chill. And then I remembered Naqia, not a schemer, but a friend.

"Are you a gift from Queen Naqia?"

"I would have been her gift—if you had trusted me. My ima was the queen's handmaid, and it was she who named me Adnah—since the queen's ima was Hebrew as well."

"Naqia?" I turned on my stool. "Part Hebrew?"

Fear darkened Adnah's features. "I thought she would have told you at the banquet. She is descended from Israel's kings, her ima taken prisoner in the exile of Tiglath-Pileser."

I left the stool and stumbled toward my bed, mind reeling. What sense could be made of the broken lives before me? Were the gods scheming? If so, to what purpose?

"My queen?" Adnah supported my arm until I fell on the bed. She gently rubbed my back. "Please forgive me for upsetting you. What may I do to help?"

I turned on my side to face her and saw strength in her kindness. "Tell me why the gods have separated me from my husband while keeping me a prisoner in this chamber. Why did they show me the monster Sennacherib through Naqia's eyes as a loving husband? Why give me a half-Hebrew queen as a friend whose wisdom I value more than gold?" I brushed the girl's cheek, unable to stem my tears. "And what god would be so kind to give me you—a maidservant who bears the name of my own ima who died to give me life?"

Adnah's eyes widened to match her joyous smile. "There is only one God, my queen, who loves His people enough to pursue you with such powerful detail. Yahweh must have a mighty plan for you, indeed."

I moaned at the irony and surrendered to the wine, too weary to consider the implications of Yahweh's power if Adnah's words were true.

~

Adnah and I were packed and ready to begin our journey to Judah before sunrise. I'd warned her never to mention Yahweh in my presence again or speak his name to *anyone* else in our caravan—at least until I was reunited with my husband and could assess the climate of his new reign. My chamber guards came midmorning and escorted us to a camel in the middle of the caravan. Travel in the canopied sedan was bearable, but with only two stops for personal needs, we ached for rest by the time darkness fell.

Upon reaching camp, an unfamiliar Assyrian soldier tapped our camel's shoulder for dismount. "Why haven't I been assigned a contingent of Hebrew guards?" I asked in a tone sharper than intended.

He peered down at me as if I were a salamander. "Because they are the king's guard. Follow me, Queen Shulle."

Dignity bruised, I obeyed without further comment and was led to an unadorned tent with sparse furnishings: two reed mats, each with a lamb's wool headrest, one large bowl on the dirt floor with a pitcher, and two cups, two bowls, and two spoons.

I lowered the flap and found the guard standing at attention beside me. "Your personal items will be delivered momentarily," he said, "and your maid may fetch water and the evening meal from the central tent and cook fire. King Manasseh has requested your company for this evening. When your maid finishes preparing you, I will assess your appearance to ensure you will please the king. Only then will I escort you to his tent."

Words escaped in choked disbelief. "You. Will. Not. Assess—"

"We will prepare quickly, my lord." Adnah grabbed my arm and pulled me inside.

I turned my indignation on her. "How dare you? I am Judah's queen, and you're both under my command."

Head bowed, she stood wringing her hands again. "I beg your forgiveness, my queen, but he is an Assyrian and *not* under your command." The gravity of my ignorance struck me like a blow. "Please be cautious with the guards, my queen. There was talk among the palace servants before we left of treachery against King Manasseh and his household because of Prince Esarhaddon's favor. The other princes would kill to discredit their brother."

She grabbed our bowls and pitcher, slipping away before I could ask questions or even consider the far-reaching implications, but one realization came immediately. My months of captivity in Nineveh's palace may have been for my protection, not harm or humiliation. Could my seclusion have been motivated by love and not hate?

Adnah returned with two steaming bowls of venison stew, a warm loaf of bread, and a pitcher of fresh water. We ate ravenously, then she loosened my hair from its braid, and I donned the simplest linen robe in my wardrobe. If my husband chose an unadorned tent for his queen, he would receive an unadorned queen for this night.

"You are stunning," Adnah whispered when she'd finished pinching my cheeks to give them color.

I peered at my dull reflection in the hand mirror and recalled Naqia's words. *"Rise above your insecurities so you can fight for the man you love—and the children to come from your womb."* I hadn't been with Nasseh for months. He was thirteen now and married to the Babylonian Gemeti. Undoubtedly, trained as a priestess as I'd been. But she was older. More experienced. Would I still please him?

During the day's travel, I'd seen Gemeti at the front of the long caravan. I tried not to stare at her. Or notice the way she and Nasseh talked most of the day.

Adnah placed her hand over mine. "You're shaking, my queen. How can I help calm you?"

I gave her the mirror, then straightened my robe. "Thank you, Adnah. You may call the guard to assess me."

She ducked under the flap, and the Assyrian filled our small space. I focused on his bronze breastplate while his eyes roved over me. "Come," he said finally. The single word completed my degradation.

I followed a man I didn't know and couldn't trust, remaining vigilant as we walked through camp. Tents stood in rows like spokes of a wheel around a central cluster of three pristine white shelters and a utility tent where slaves still worked feverishly to cook for hundreds.

I bumped into my guard's armored back when he stopped abruptly. He turned slowly, amusement lifting his brows as he motioned toward the largest white tent. "Your king awaits."

The urge to slap him nearly got the better of me—but I wasn't sure if Nasseh would protect or arrest me. I wanted to believe my months of seclusion were a kindness, but I wouldn't know until I entered that tent. So I glared at the cheeky guard and said, "I hope the gods repay your wife or your daughters with the same kindness you've shown me." I ducked into the tent before he could retaliate and stood in the dim glow of a single lamp.

"How can you be more beautiful in a simple robe than in the finery of last night's banquet?" Nasseh's whisper came from the shadows. Blood pulsed in my ears. And then he was there. His hands settled on my waist.

"You're taller," I said, quaking.

He smiled and kissed my nose. "How can you still smell like myrtle leaves?"

"The maids brought them each day." Only now did I realize he'd sent them. "Was it you that—"

"I missed you too," he said, touching my hair, my cheeks, my lips—as if he wasn't sure I was real. "I couldn't say it last night in front of Esar, but I missed you, Shulle. I love you so," he whispered against my neck, and we sank to our knees.

A sudden *swish, thunk* startled us apart—an arrow buried in the tent pole above our heads. A mortal cry outside the tent doused our passion, and in an instant Nasseh stood over me, sword drawn.

"Ra'ah, stay!" he said, moving toward the chaos exploding outside.

"You can't leave me here with this monster!" I grabbed his hand, and the dog lunged toward me.

"Ra'ah, friend!" Nasseh splayed his hand between us. Hysteria claimed me, but Nasseh grabbed my curls and pulled my head back. "Ra'ah is the only thing standing between you and the real monster outside who wants us both dead." He released me and scratched behind the dog's ears. "Ra'ah, protect."

When he left, the guard who escorted me fell through the flap, eyes lifeless and staring, an arrow buried in his heart.

I covered a low wail. The hound growled, sniffed the dead man, and looked back at me. Terrified, I froze, certain the beast preferred a fresh kill over dead soldier meat. But Ra'ah padded to my side, circled twice, and lay down beside me, resting his huge head in my lap. Paralyzed, I listened to the angry shouts outside the tent and prayed the gods would protect the boy, now Judah's king, who had rushed to the fray.

The night stretched long, and my eyelids grew heavy. When the noise subsided, I longed to peek through the tent flap, but Ra'ah's bulk was too cumbersome to move. When he finally released me from the role of human pillow, I retreated to Nasseh's reed mat. The moment I lay down, my protector snuggled up against me, releasing a great sigh that flubbered his lips.

I tried but failed to suppress a grin. "That was a poor attempt at a monster sound." I turned on my side, placing my arm over his chest, feeling the day's weariness descend like a drawn curtain.

"Shulle, my girl. Wake up." Dohd bent over me, gently rubbing my shoulder. "I'm to escort you back to your tent."

I blinked and sat up quickly, looking around Nasseh's empty chamber. "Where's Ra'ah?"

Dohd chuckled. "I thought you might ask about your husband first."

I threw my arms around his neck, overcome by emotion. "Is Nasseh all right? I've missed you."

"King Manasseh discovered and executed the attackers." He patted my back awkwardly. "And it's good to see you as well."

I released him, sensing a significant change in his demeanor. "Are you well, Dohd?" I searched his face for unspoken answers and found him much aged since we'd last spoken. Three months seemed a lifetime.

"There is no time for trivialities, Meshullemeth. The king has ordered me to escort you to your tent." He grabbed my arm, but I'd endured more terse commands than I could bear.

I wrenched free of his hold and sat down on the mat. "Before I leave this tent, I will hear a report on Panya, the other concubines, and why Nasseh and I were nearly skewered in the middle of his well-guarded camp."

Dohd towered above me, the lines on his face etched deeper and the spark in his eyes dimmer. "Panya is dead by her own hand, and Manasseh was forced to relinquish three of his concubines to appease Prince Esarhaddon, who wanted him to spend more time with Gemeti."

"Panya dead?" The only two words I could squeak out.

"Poisoned herself with oleander."

I squeezed my eyes shut and shook my head. "What happened to the concubines Nasseh relinquished to the prince?"

Dohd hesitated. "They were given to the king's other sons."

"Like Panya's baby daughter." His face registered the surprise I'd hoped for. "Naqia told me of the hideous trade. Was it your idea, Dohd? Have you stooped to the level of Sennacherib's depravity?"

He crouched beside me, the fragile skin beneath his eyes puffy and dark. "Welcome to royalty, my girl. Life has a price—the death of those less important. That baby and those concubines are the reason you're alive. Esarhaddon's disgruntled brothers would be rid of Manasseh and anyone precious to him." Dohd turned his back and cleared his throat. "When his spies saw the king call for you on our first night of travel, you became their prime target."

The hair on the back of my neck stood at attention. "Did they find all the traitorous guards?"

He sniffed and turned to face me again, a carefully chiseled calm in place. "Some, but likely not all. King Manasseh asked me to give you this and escort you back to your tent." He handed me a small scroll and swept his hand toward the tent flap. "Please read it after you get back to your tent. I have much to accomplish before we begin this morning's travel."

The scroll almost burned my hand, demanding to be read, but I acquiesced and returned to Adnah who'd been waiting in our tent on the edge of panic all night. Almost sunrise now, she fell on me weeping. "I heard the commotion, the guards searching tents, and then the executions. I thought the spies had killed you."

I shared the information Dohd told me, which didn't bring comfort to either of us, and then unfurled the small scroll to read it aloud:

Manasseh Ben Hezekiah to his wife and queen, Meshullemeth bat Haruz. The words written herein by my own hand prove this decision is my own and final. Because any display of my favor places those who receive it in grave danger, we will in future meet only in public ceremony and maintain a distance that suggests strife between us until Prince Esarhaddon inherits his father's throne. You'll have more freedom than I allowed in Nineveh, but your life must be preserved at all costs—even at the price of separation. Farewell, my love, until Sennacherib meets his fate and crosses the River Khuber.

I lowered the scroll, feeling the ripping of my soul as the rending of a garment. As I suspected, my imprisonment in Nineveh had been motivated by Nasseh's desire to protect me, but he had now imposed an enduring banishment beyond repeal.

"You must rest, my queen." Adnah took the scroll from my hand, led me to the straw mat, and covered me with a woolen blanket. "I'll wake you when the caravan is ready to begin the day's march."

Closing my eyes to the sounds of a waking camp, I pondered what my days would be like without Nasseh to talk to, laugh with, learn from. Would Belit still fill my nights with lessons under the starry hosts? *"Until Sennacherib meets his fate and crosses the River Khuber."* Had Nasseh discovered the keys to death's mystery? Had he sent similar messages to Gemeti and his one remaining concubine or only to me? Would he isolate himself from the queen mother and other family members as well? So many questions lingered, but an exhausted yawn drew me into oblivion.

30

Therefore the law is paralyzed,
and justice never prevails.
The wicked hem in the righteous,
so that justice is perverted.

HABAKKUK 1:4

Jerusalem, Judah
Spring 684 BC, Two Years After Hezekiah's Death

Gemeti groaned in her sleep and rolled over, taking most of Nasseh's bed covers. She was beautiful, but she wasn't Shulle. And her breath stank of onions and garlic. Nasseh slid out of bed and padded across the cool tiles to his balcony. Ra'ah followed him like a good shepherd.

Winter's breath still nipped on the breeze, but tomorrow's ceremony at Solomon's temple would ensure Ishtar's return from the netherworld with spring's warmth and new life. At least, those were the words Gemeti had helped him prepare for his speech. Then she'd demanded he bed her.

It wasn't his fault her womb was empty. His concubines had given him two children with another on the way. *I gave away my first child.* The thought still sent prickly heat up his neck, but he fought it with reason. Nasseh had proven his loyalty to Esar when a servant brought news of Panya's healthy delivery. He and Esar had been walking in the garden, when his friend posed the question he asked the soldiers in Babylon. "Are you committed to Assyria, no matter the cost?"

"Yes, my prince," Nasseh answered without hesitation. Esar watched the messenger leave the garden and returned a silent stare at the new abba. Knowing Esar's mind, Nasseh ordered Panya's baby be given to the Assyrians, and he never saw his first child.

The sound of revelers in the street below offered welcome distraction. After a year of Nasseh's reforms, his city had nearly recovered from Matti's poor management. When the royal caravan returned from Nineveh, Jerusalem's slovenly condition matched Matti's drunken sway. Belit stood beside him, wearing more jewels and finery than the queens of Egypt and Assyria combined. Nasseh didn't need Gemeti's coaching to see they'd enjoyed his absence.

Three cubits to the left of Matti and Belit waited Ima, Saba Isaiah, Dohd Jashub, Doda Yaira, and Kenaz. Waving. Smiling. Shouting at his approach. They were noticeably happy about his return.

Nasseh dismounted and locked eyes with Commander Baka, now trained as an Assyrian warrior. Without further communication, Baka followed two steps behind Nasseh and ascended the palace stairs with him. Nasseh waved to shoppers in the Upper City market and continued to the platform, where Matti opened his arms wide. "My favorite nephew returns."

Nasseh halted. Silent. Stiff. He glanced at Baka, then at the guard behind Matti's right shoulder. Before Nasseh's gaze returned to Matti, his guard fell, grasping a fatal belly wound.

"What . . . I . . . ," Matti stammered.

"I won't tolerate mediocrity, Matti, but I will treasure my family at all costs." He looked at Belit, who raised her chin. Gemeti had proven ineffective in divination, but she taught him how better to understand people. Belit's raised chin could signal defiance—or prove her strength. "You aren't my family, Belit, but your skill makes you valuable. For now."

Nasseh moved down the greeting line to Ima, her smile replaced with tears. He wiped them away and kissed her cheek. "Don't cry, Ima. Prince Esar taught me that honoring and protecting my ima must be my highest priority—second only to pleasing King Sennacherib, of course." He offered Saba Isaiah a cool nod. "Sennacherib killed your kitten."

Saba's brows rose, and he seemed at a loss for words. Dohd Jashub grabbed Nasseh's hand. "We're happy you're home safe, Nasseh. That's what's important."

Kenaz embraced him. "I've missed you, Cousin."

He shrugged off the touch but couldn't stop a smile. "Are you married yet?" The family chuckled.

Nasseh turned to the crowded street below. His royal guard, trimmed from one hundred to fifty by Assyria's rigorous standards, formed a shield around the palace entrance.

"Good people of Jerusalem," he said, addressing the throng. "Your king has returned from a long absence as an abba returns to his children. After gaining wisdom from the greatest king on earth and winning the favor of mighty Sennacherib, the king of kings, I will raise Judah to its highest splendor. Judah is now a free nation. Free to trade. Free to celebrate. And free to worship gods from every nation." He lifted his sword, the sing of it causing those near him to step back. "Let every man fight for Judah's fellowship in Assyria's great empire. Celebrate! Find the loveliest priestess, and worship at the nearest altar!"

The cheer that rose still rang in Nasseh's ears even now, a year later, as he watched moonlight celebrations in the street below. Since his return, the city thrived in trade, and the image Nasseh had commissioned while in Nineveh stood as testimony of Judah's free worship. At the private unveiling earlier today, Nasseh entered Solomon's temple for the first time since Abba's death. Yahweh's vile altar and its platform had been removed, and in its place stood the bronze creation Nasseh saw in a dream. Taller than three men, the image bore the faces of a bull, a lion, an eagle, and a man. No matter which temple gate people entered or which deity they served, the amalgamation represented the deity of any nation—and every offering made to it would help ensure Abba's rest in the netherworld.

"Would you approve, Esar?" Nasseh spoke to the moon, already well past its zenith. Only silence answered on this night when sleep was as distant as his only friend.

Returning to his chamber, he shouted over his second wife's snoring.

"Gemeti, return to your chamber." He walked past the bed to his sitting area, where a basket of scrolls waited.

She rose languidly, her silky black hair hanging in clumps over her face. "Nasseh, I was sleeping soundly. Why can't I stay?"

"A king needs privacy. Esar and Shebna agree," he said without looking up. "Queen Shulle and I will lead the procession to the temple for the official dedication. You'll follow, accompanied by Lord Shebna, as usual." He began reading the scroll with this week's financial report. Trade had increased with improving weather.

Gemeti stroked his cheek and nearly sent him through the ceiling. Standing with dagger drawn, he faced his startled wife. "You will leave my chamber, woman. I will not say it again."

Tears formed, and her chin quivered. "Why must you treat me worse than your dog? I only want to be near you."

"You want to rule me," he said. "And train me, which has been most beneficial, Gemeti, and I thank you." He sheathed his dagger. "You are my second wife but occupy the best chamber in my harem. I shower you with gifts and give you a monthly stipend. You are well cared for, as I promised Esar, yet you have fulfilled none of your vows to me. Belit exceeds your āšipūtu talents by far, and you have yet to produce a child."

"I should at least appear on your arm at the front of the procession. What kind of queen is Shulle if you don't even lie with h—"

Nasseh gripped her throat, thumb pressing on the spot Esar said could kill within heartbeats. "If you wish to live, you will never speak of Queen Shulle to me again." He released her, and she sagged to the floor. "If walking with Shebna displeases you, *wife,* you may skip the processional altogether and stand with my concubines on the portico. It matters not to me." Returning to his couch, he picked up the scroll and continued reading. The chamber door opened and closed.

Blessed silence followed. He studied the finances, pleased to have restored the palace treasury after Matti's extravagant spending. "I will make you proud, Abba," he whispered, wondering if an etemmu had ears to hear.

31

Let us discern for ourselves what is right;
let us learn together what is good.

JOB 34:4

Instead of plaiting or binding my spiraling curls, Adnah threaded a tendril through a bone needle and pulled it alternately through a pierced pearl then a sparkly bauble, painstakingly creating glimmering tresses down my back. Cat prowled around our ankles, the finicky feline who had taken up residence in my chamber when Ra'ah had taken over Nasseh's world. Adnah picked up another pierced pearl, concentrating on her masterpiece in silence.

"There," Adnah said, primping the final curl. "You'll be the talk of the dedication ceremony."

I groaned. "The gossips need no more fodder." I peered into the hand mirror wishing my marriage wasn't the central focus of Judean society. "I wish I didn't have to attend the dedication at all while Nasseh still ignores me."

My maid's deep sigh caught my attention, and I noticed splotches forming on her neck in the mirror's reflection. "Adnah?" I turned and startled her. "Forgive me. I'm sure celebrating an image in Yahweh's temple will be difficult for you."

She stepped back, wringing her hands. "Mistress, I have a request."

"Name it, my friend." I leaned back on the couch, closing my eyes so she could apply my makeup.

"I'd like to remain in the chamber." The steady touch of her hand lined my lashes, but her voice trembled.

I nudged her hand away and sat up. "The king commanded everyone to attend, Adnah."

She set aside the kohl pot. "I fear he'll also ask *everyone* to bow to the new image, my queen, and in all good conscience . . ." She squared her shoulders, eyes sparking. "I cannot. I will not."

Torn between loving my friend and fearing Nasseh's reprisals, I lay back on my couch and closed my eyes. I couldn't be angry with Adnah. It was her strength I admired most. It was her Hebrew heritage that connected us. But it was Yahweh that always divided us.

I opened one eye. "I can see you're not well, Adnah. You should go to your chamber and rest—all day."

A wry grin replaced her belligerence. "Thank you, my queen." She kissed my cheek. "Perhaps I'll feel better for our evening spinning and weaving with the queen mother and Yaira."

I watched her hurry away. "I hope we all feel better this evening," I whispered. Zibah, Yaira, and the other family Yahwists had expressed their own fears, but they couldn't hide in their chambers during this morning's dedication at the temple.

Returning to my task, I picked up the applicator to finish the line of kohl above my right eye.

"I've been patient." Belit barged into the chamber, jolting my hand and sending a line of kohl up to my eyebrow. I wiped away my miscue, working to calm my nerves.

"It's been a year, and it's clear you've lost Nasseh's affection." She stopped beside me and stabbed her fists at her hips. Cat hissed and hid under my bed.

"Good morning, Belit." I had tried a dozen chamber guards, but not even Assyrian-trained cutthroats dared stop her. "I'll win back Nasseh's affection," I said. "You'll see."

"Ridding ourselves of his Babylonian wife will help." She withdrew a pouch from her pocket. I reached for it, but she slapped my hand and revealed its contents: oleander seeds and a few pieces of bark. "Incantations, spells, curses, assassins—all good options—but oleander is quick and easy. Visit Gemeti's chamber after the ceremony. Grind the seeds into powder and sprinkle it into her tea. Then slip the bark in her incense altar on your way out. You must act before a child swells her belly, or I fear you'll lose courage, Meshullemeth."

I'd been finding excuses to keep Gemeti alive since Belit first saw her. "If she dies under suspicious circumstances, Nasseh will know you or I had a hand in it and will be forced to deliver one of us to Prince Esarhaddon." I crossed my arms. "Would he sacrifice you or me to account for Gemeti's death?"

I knew by her twitching cheek that the bluff had worked. "Before you returned from Nineveh, I would have been certain he'd sacrifice me." Her grin sent a chill through me. "Now, I'm not so sure."

If she sensed weakness, I might find oleander in my tea. "Why do you think I chose this tiny chamber? I may have lost Nasseh's affections for now, but I've gained the queen mother's by cultivating her friendship and Yaira's."

"Phssht!" Belit waved away my reasoning. "You're Judah's queen, Meshullemeth. You need an heir in your belly, not a chamber next to the king's mother."

I counted to ten before answering. "Both Sennacherib and Crown Prince Esarhaddon have a reverent respect for Queen Naqia, and Nasseh has embraced that reverence for his own ima. I show the same deference to maintain his favor." I dared not admit that I'd chosen the chamber next to Zibah and across from Yaira because a year away from them proved how precious they were to me.

Belit stared into my eyes, her yellow flecks beginning to pulse. I turned away quickly then heard the sound of her low chuckle. "Resist if you like, Meshullemeth, but if you refuse to dispense of your rival, you must help me dispose of mine."

"No, Belit." She and Dohd's feud had escalated. "I won't get involved in your private war."

"Ah, but you're already involved, little Shulle."

"I'm not *little* Shulle anymore."

Eyes narrowing, she peered into my soul. "I'll get what I want with or without your help. Why not join me and seize the rewards?"

If she could get what she wanted without my help, why had she come to my chamber? "Our weekly lessons under the stars are essential to me, Belit, but right now I don't have time to talk. My maid is ill, and I have much to do before I join Nasseh for the processional." I cradled her elbow, escorting her toward the door.

She shoved me away. "You don't have the heart of an āšipūtu, Meshullemeth. If you will not do what must be done, tell me now, and I'll be done with you."

I knew exactly what *done with you* meant, rehearsing the names of the poisons on her shelf. "While you have the luxury of focusing on dark arts alone, Belit, I live in a world of complex relationships and political maneuvering." I stepped closer, meeting the yellow-eyed witch without flinching. "If a queen could gain power with a potion or incantation, many in Nasseh's court would be gone by now. You are not *done with me*. It is I who will finish you if you betray my trust."

Belit smiled at me with perfect, white teeth. "Better. Now, turn your anger on the Babylonian wife, and win back your king." She opened the door and left me exhausted.

Pressing my back against the cedar panels, I closed my eyes and released a sigh. How different were the two worlds in which I lived. Zibah and Yaira, so peaceful and loving. Belit, Dohd, and Nasseh, so angry yet fearful. I pushed myself toward my makeup table, dreading this morning's dedication, where those two worlds were about to collide.

32

Moreover, Manasseh also shed so much
innocent blood that he filled Jerusalem
from end to end—besides the sin that he
had caused Judah to commit.

2 KINGS 21:16

Nasseh stood at the foot of the harem stairway, waiting for the
royal family to descend. Old habits resurfaced, and he caught
himself clenching and unclenching his fists. Gemeti had
taught him chants to soothe the noise in his head, although nothing
worked as well as Shulle's fish song. But those days were gone.

He looked to the top of the stairs, and there she stood. It had been
weeks since he'd seen her. Reminding himself to breathe, Nasseh forced
his body into calm indifference and looked past his queen. Gemeti followed, joined by Matti and Belit. Then Ima with Dohd Jashub, Doda
Yaira, and Kenaz. Saba Isaiah would likely meet them at the temple.

His eyes betrayed him, wandering back to Shulle. Light framed her as
she approached. He looked away, pressing a fist against the ache in his
chest.

A moment later, Shulle's tender touch on his shoulder. "Nasseh, are
you well?"

He jerked away as if a lightning bolt had struck him. "Fine!"

Startled, she lowered her eyes. "Forgive me . . ." The pink glow in her
cheeks faded to gray.

Hating himself a little more, he offered his right arm. "You look lovely,
my queen."

She placed her hand on his forearm without reply, and they began their march to the temple. Ra'ah paced a circle around them, creating distance between the royal couple and the gathering crowd. Since the night he'd guarded Shulle in Nasseh's tent, he'd adored her. "I think he likes you better than me," Nasseh whispered, cautious not to appear too friendly.

"If you mean the dog likes me more than you do, I agree."

"No, I mean—" He glanced over and saw her blinking away tears. *Stupid. Stupid, Manasseh.* He kept his voice low. "I would give half my kingdom to hold you in my arms, Shulle, but the danger is still real."

"And I would gladly give my life to feel your arms around me." She held her head high. "But you have made the choice for me, so I have no husband. No love."

"It won't always be this way," he said, fire rising in his cheeks. Should he tell her they caught an assassin in the harem hallway last week? Would she appreciate his protection then?

"I know the season will pass." She squeezed his forearm, a silent and cautious show of affection. "I only hope you'll remember me when it's over."

If she only knew how she pervaded his thoughts and haunted his dreams.

Passing through the first temple gate, they entered the crowded outer courts, where his royal guard created a safe space for Nasseh and Shulle to lead the royal procession through the second gate. The once-forbidden inner courts were now opened to nobility, who stood shoulder to shoulder near the large new platform constructed for the king and his honored guests.

He scanned the inner courts for Saba Isaiah but still saw no sign of the old man. Esar's words rang in his memory. *"Are you committed to Assyria, no matter the cost?"* Nasseh looked briefly over his shoulder to ensure the others would follow as he alone ascended the dais. With the protections he'd set in place, his family would be safe if they followed.

Wild applause met him when he reached the top step. Nasseh turned to soak in the adulation, searching again for Saba in the crowd. The familiar gray beard, furrowed brow, and intense stare were nowhere to be found. Nasseh gave up. A king's protection could stretch only so far.

Shebna stood beside the image with Azariah, the high priest. Though Azariah was responsible for promulgating Yahweh's archaic traditions during Abba's reign, he'd atoned for his crimes by drafting a decree for Nasseh to sign and seal. The order had been sent over a month ago to every city in Judah:

> *King Manasseh ben Hezekiah, Ruler of Judah, Son of David.*
> *May every man, woman, and child receive ample blessing for*
>   *your obedience and torture beyond imagining if the slightest*
>   *detail is ignored.*
> *On the fourteenth day of Nisan, one representative from each*
>   *municipality will bring to Jerusalem's temple: oil, grain,*
>   *silver, and gold in proportion to the citizenry of each location.*
>   *Henceforth, such provisions will be offered monthly to the*
>   *bronze Image of Four Faces to ensure mighty King Heze-*
>   *kiah's eternal rest and pleasure beyond the River Khuber*
>   *and to establish his eternal glory among the spirits of the*
>   *netherworld.*
> *So says King Manasseh, loving Abba to his people, great*
>   *deliverer of Judah.*

Scanning the crowd, Nasseh delighted that his people had not only obeyed but had sent far more than one representative from every city. The crowds in the courts and porticos spilled out into the streets. Excitement stirred the air and ignited the chaos in Nasseh's mind and body. Using every trick he'd learned to force calm, he vowed silently, *I will be the king you trained me to be, Esar.*

Baka stood beside the steps to assist the rest of his family onto the dais. When Nasseh reached for Shulle's hand and kissed it, the cheers grew deafening. King and queen bowed in gracious recognition, but the moment Gemeti and Belit stepped onto the platform, hecklers began their taunts.

When Baka helped Ima and Doda Yaira climb the steps, reverent silence settled over the audience. Then a lone voice, hidden among nobility in the inner court, began humming one of David's psalms while the rest of Nasseh's family positioned themselves behind him. Judah's king stood defiantly silent—and found Lord Eliakim with his family in the inner court. All singing with tears streaming down their cheeks.

"Enough!" Nasseh shouted, releasing Shulle's hand and motioning to Dohd Jashub and Kenaz. "You will record every detail of this day's ceremony as we begin a new era in Judah's history." As chief scribe and his assistant, Nasseh's uncle and cousin would be useful—and safe.

Stepping to the edge of the platform, Nasseh began the long-awaited dedication. "Men and women of Jerusalem, Judah, and all nations under the starry hosts—I, King Manasseh, welcome you to the new temple of Jerusalem!" More applause, and Nasseh felt its pleasure like honeyed wine. "Today, we gather to right a great injustice that occurred in this place two years ago. I was but a child when the great Hezekiah died in these very courts. No provision had been made for his journey across the River Khuber because of the archaic superstitions of Yahwist tradition."

Nasseh realized he was shouting and reminded himself of Shebna's advice from long ago. *A king need never raise his voice; his authority is a trumpet.* He nodded to his old teacher and high priest, who unveiled the bronze image. The covering billowed to the ground, and the crowd gasped. Whispered awe fluttered through the courts and porticos. It was the response of Nasseh's dreams.

"My abba will wander in darkness no longer," he said in a controlled tone. "Worshipers from every nation will be welcomed by the face of a god they recognize, and every offering will ensure King Hezekiah's pleasure in the life beyond."

Nasseh glanced at Jashub and Kenaz, making sure they recorded each word in the annals of Judah's kings before he made the announcement that would change the trajectory of their nation. Their heads bowed,

Kenaz pressed a metal stylus into a wax tablet while Jashub scribbled furiously with quill and pigment on parchment.

Lifting his hands, Nasseh commanded silence. "Since your enthusiasm matches my own, I now give you the opportunity to prove your commitment to Judah's future." He shifted his attention over the heads of the nobility—a trick Gemeti taught him—to appear as though he looked at their faces. "Everyone within the inner court will approach the image, kiss the base, and bow in worship. If any should refuse, their rebellion will be treated as treason, for which the penalty is death." A panicked hum rose among the Yahwists, and Nasseh found Eliakim in the crowd. Locking eyes for only a moment, he ensured his old teacher heard the simple solution. "For those who wish to worship Yahweh, you must still bow and kiss the image. You may adhere to your archaic notions of one god as long as you don't impede our nation's progress or my abba's peace."

Without hesitation, he descended the stairs and approached the base bearing hooves, paws, claws, and human feet—corresponding to the four faces. He bent and kissed the human feet, silently apologizing to Abba, then knelt with his head bowed. A line of royal guards formed between him and the anticipated stream of worshipers.

The sounds of shuffling sandaled feet mingled with sniffles and sobs. Thankfully, Belit's rattling voice began a familiar Babylonian chant, easing Nasseh's tension and drowning out the vocal resistance. Stubborn in his posture, Nasseh refused to lift his head for the troublemakers. He would answer their complaints soon enough. Time passed. The sun beat down. His knees ached and sweat dripped down his back by the time a guard tapped his shoulder.

"It's time, my king."

Nasseh raised his head and looked first at the platform. To his great relief, his family remained there in safety—as planned—with Baka blocking the steps. Nasseh looked next toward the northwest corner of the inner court.

"No," he whispered, stumbling back a step. Hundreds of stubborn Yahwists awaited promised execution. He'd thought the threat would be enough. Or the promise of Abba's rest. He'd built goodwill with a year of prosperity. Searching the faces, he found men and women he'd known all his life. There were children and infants. And Eliakim. His wife and children.

"Are you committed to Assyria, no matter the cost?" Esar's words played again in his mind. *A strong king displays his power.* Nasseh chanted silently as he walked toward the condemned. *A strong king displays his power. A strong king displays his power.*

One day, on a training field, Esar had lined up hundreds of soldiers— perfectly trained warriors—and killed them one at a time until Nasseh was willing to draw his dagger across a man's throat. *A strong king displays his power.* Every decision had purpose. Every death meant better life. *A strong king displays his power.*

He stood in front of Eliakim. "You realize I won't spare you because you were Abba's best friend." *"Kings have no friends. . . . They form alliances."*

"I know, my king, but I beg you to save my wife." His whole body shook in fear.

"Where is Saba Isaiah?"

Eliakim's lips pressed into a thin white line.

"You know but won't tell me? Is he hiding like a rat in a hole?" Nasseh shouted. He glanced at Eliakim's wife, and Baka instantly appeared with a dagger poised at her throat. "Why not tell me where he is and save your wife?"

Eliakim reached for her hand and closed his eyes. "Hear, O Israel: The LORD our God, the LORD is one. Love the LORD your God with all your heart and with all your soul and with all your strength." Others began the recitation with him. "These commandments that I give you today are to be on your hearts."

Fury rose at the sound of the Torah, and Nasseh covered his ears. "Now!" Releasing his guards to their gruesome task, Nasseh ran from the place Abba's blood had been spilt.

A strong king displays his power. For you, Esar. For you, my friend.

33

The wicked draw the sword
and bend the bow
to bring down the poor and needy,
to slay those whose ways are upright.

PSALM 37:14

Curled up in the corner of my balcony, I couldn't stop shaking. With Nasseh's guards barricading the platform stairs, the royal family was forced to witness every moment of the temple carnage. I pressed my fists against my eyes, trying to erase the images, but they were seared into my mind. Nauseous, I released a low moan and stared at the stars in eerie silence. No revelers danced in the streets. The temple torches were extinguished. I pulled Cat closer, taking comfort in her gentle purring.

"Mistress . . ." Adnah appeared, startling me and sending Cat scampering into the chamber. My maid covered me with a blanket, tucking it around my shoulders and under my chin. "It's too cold for you to be out—"

"You were wise not to attend."

She sat beside me. "I've been with the queen mother in Lord Jashub and Yaira's chamber. The physician gave Mistress Zibah herbed tea to calm her, but it hasn't helped." Adnah sighed. "She's shaking too."

"I saw life drain from Lord Eliakim's eyes." I let my tears fall and turned to my friend. "Gemeti and Belit laughed as they chanted, while I retched. They were chanting together, Adnah. Belit hates Gemeti, but in the violence, they've become friends." Shaking my head, I looked into the night sky again and found Pleiades, the cursed god Bel, Babylon's patron. It was his madness that reigned today in the Babylonian women. "My āšipūtu skills are almost as powerful as Belit's, but if she and Gemeti join against me, I'll die in the fray."

"True." Belit's presence startled us both to our feet. "Has little Shulle finally realized she must use her power to fight?"

I shoved Adnah into the chamber to remove her from danger. "I use my skills to *protect*, Belit. Why must everything be a fight?"

"How can you ask such a question after seeing today's slaughter?" She stepped closer, eyes pulsing. "Who will protect you when Nasseh makes Gemeti queen and orders *your* execution?"

Panic, quick and feral, churned in my belly. He wouldn't—would he? "You must help me," I said. "Nasseh still loves me." I reached for the small parchment I hid in my pocket each day.

"Mistress, no!" Adnah cried from the doorway.

I handed the yellow-eyed sorceress Nasseh's message from the night we were almost killed in his tent. "Our separation is a ruse."

Admiration dawned as she read proof of my husband's love. "Not many people surprise me," she said, returning the parchment to me. "But you and our king have been successful at this deception. If you and I combine our skills, we could help Nasseh rule the empire."

The ridiculous comment and Adnah's grim expression ignited immediate regret. "If you betray us, I swear by the gods of every nation Nasseh will hand you over to the Assyrians for a fate far worse than any that could be conjured by the dark arts."

She looked up, her eyes the color of the sun. "You're ready, Meshullemeth. You and I will step into the fire of sorcery and spread its flames across Judah."

34

And what does the LORD require of you?
To act justly and to love mercy
and to walk humbly with your God.

MICAH 6:8

Zibah sat between her nephew, Kenaz, and Yaira, staring at the food Adnah had placed before them.

"Zibah, you must eat something." Jashub reached across the cozy table. "We're all grieving our friends, but we must focus on the peace they now enjoy, not on the violence that took them to paradise."

Zibah lifted her wine with a trembling hand but quickly set it back on the table and forced herself to look at her brother. "What about the families that remain? The Yahwist noblemen who felt slighted because there was no room for them in the inner court but are now praising God for sparing them. I saw some of them slip out before the guards closed the outer courts. Why were we and others saved but Eliakim and some of our friends butchered like meat in a market?" Zibah covered a sob.

Jashub pushed food around on his plate, but Yaira pulled her into a fierce embrace. "*Why* questions lead only to doubt. Only *Who* questions build faith. *Who* is sovereign over the kingdoms of earth? *Who* spoke light into darkness? And *who* promised to capture and build Nasseh's heart?"

Kenaz said quietly, "I don't understand what happened to Nasseh in Assyria." He'd been utterly silent during today's events, while his metal stylus pressed names into a wax tablet—a memorial to those slain in Yahweh's name. "I believe Nasseh still has a conscience. He ran to his chamber when the killings began. I heard some guards talking about it."

"It was that Assyrian crown prince, Esarhaddon." Yaira hissed his name. "And Shebna has manipulated our Nasseh for years. He's a brilliant boy but has never perceived ulterior motive or innuendo."

"Stop it!" Zibah struggled from her friend's embrace. "Nasseh knows right from wrong, Yaira, and he's responsible for his choices. He's naive, yes, but today my son *chose* to do the unconscionable—and he knew it was wrong." Silent stares met her declaration, and the consequences for her son hit like a boulder into her chest. She could barely breathe the words. "Nasseh declared *my* God his enemy today. How can I love this stranger? I will never kiss the idol. Abba Isaiah will never bow—" Gasping, she stared at Jashub in horror. "The prophecy."

"What prophecy?" Kenaz asked, but Yaira looked away. Jashub had evidently confided in his wife.

"Your saba foretold his death a few years ago," he explained to his son. "Nasseh will judge Abba as a false prophet and have him executed."

"No!" Kenaz jumped to his feet. "No! Nasseh would never—"

"Kenaz." Jashub spoke softly. "What does the Lord require of you?"

"No, Abba. I will not recite it."

Jashub moved his plate aside and stood to meet his son face to face. "We learn the Truth in daylight so we can walk in darkness. Yahweh's words to Micah are the wisdom we need to live under Nasseh's reign." He placed a firm hand on his son's shoulder. "Say it with me. 'What does the LORD require of you?'"

Tears formed on Kenaz's dark lashes as he followed in a gravelly voice. "'To act justly and to love mercy and to walk humbly with your God.'"

Jashub pulled him into a crushing hug. "No matter how our king acts, we act justly, *we* love mercy, and *we* walk humbly." He turned to Zibah and added, "And we love him because somewhere inside that stranger is the Manasseh God gave you."

Jashub's words penetrated her pain. *The Manasseh God gave you.* Yes. He'd been a miracle after countless miscarriages, born after Yahweh extended Hezi's life. *Why, Yahweh? Why give me a son so evil he would destroy everything Hezi built for You?* Yaira was right. *Why* questions served no purpose.

"I need some time alone," she said. Jashub helped her to her feet. "Thank you for your encouragement."

She started across the hall to her chamber, but the sight of Shulle's doorway stopped her. The young queen had declined their invitation for the evening meal. Adnah said she'd been as upset as the rest of them by today's violence. Though everything inside her screamed to be alone, Zibah had grown to love this girl and love began with the sacrifice of time. *Yahweh, give me words to speak when I have no comfort to give.*

As she approached the Hebrew guards, one bowed and spoke before she reached them. "I'm sorry, Queen Mother, but Queen Shulle is gone for the evening."

Normally, she wouldn't have pressed, but he seemed anxious, which Zibah thought odd. Because the guards were Hebrew and not among Nasseh's trained goons, she forced her will. "Where has she gone?"

"She left with Lady Belit." He exchanged an uneasy glance with the other guard. "Her lessons with the sorceress last well past the moon's zenith."

Zibah's raw heart received the news like vinegar on a wound. Had Shulle's affection for the past year been manipulation rather than friendship? "Please don't mention my visit to the queen." Yahweh promised to capture her son's heart, but what about the little thief who'd stolen Zibah's? What had Yahweh planned for Shulle?

Weary beyond exhaustion, Zibah slept fitfully. Hellish dreams of Nasseh covered in her friends' blood sent her bolting upright in bed, shrieking. The guards outside her chamber rushed in at least four times until, finally, Onan graciously sat outside the closed curtain of her bedchamber. She trusted him with her life, but could he save her from her son?

Yahweh, please, give Your peace to wash away the violence that's stained my spirit. She began reciting Abba's prophecies, though at first bits and pieces were all she remembered. In the twilight of slumber and wake-

fulness, her mind's eye traveled over a stunning piece of parchment as if
she were reading it from a scroll:

*For to us a child is born, to us a son is given, and the govern-
ment will be on his shoulders. And he will be called Wonderful
Counselor, Mighty God, Everlasting Father, Prince of Peace.
Of the greatness of his government and peace there will be no
end. He will reign on David's throne and over his kingdom,
establishing and upholding it with justice and righteousness
from that time on and forever. The zeal of the LORD Almighty
will accomplish this.*

Warmth seeped through her, bone deep and calming. She knew the
prophecy spoke of an eternal King who would restore Israel's perfect relationship with Yahweh, but could it also be another promise that Nasseh—
her prodigal—would continue David's line in faithfulness someday?
Surely not after all the evil he'd done. But a whisper breathed over her
weary spirit. *"The zeal of the LORD Almighty will accomplish this."* Shalom
settled over her with understanding. Even as Yahweh would position all
nations of the world to produce His eternal king, His zeal for her son
would accomplish His perfect plan in Nasseh's life. With a deep sigh, she
closed her eyes again and let sleep take her away.

The first hints of consciousness dawned with a glow brightening her chamber. Next came the uneasy sense that she wasn't alone, a vague dread that
grew with the memories of yesterday's loss. She wiped moisture from her
eyes before they'd even opened.

"Good morning, Ima." She was startled upright, and the sight of
Nasseh seated by her bed sent her shooting backward against her headboard. Sorrow darkened his features. "You're the only person on earth who
need not fear me. Even if Esar hadn't told me to love you, I'd never let my
guards harm you."

Drawing up her knees, she wasn't convinced. "What do you want, Nasseh?"

"Esar taught me many skills in Babylon before—"

"Why would you go to Babylon when you knew Abba's prophecy?" She forgot one terror and gasped at the other.

"It wasn't a fulfillment of Saba's prophecy, Ima. I wasn't taken captive there. I was taught how to lead. How to be a man. A king. And when my friend Esar took me to Nineveh, he taught me how to love and protect my family as well as rule a nation. Esar adores Queen Naqia. She's a strong woman, like you. Her abba was a priest at Dan, taken in the Assyrian deportation under Tiglath-Pileser. I think you'd like her. Esar says someday you'll meet her."

Zibah stared at her child. The scraggly hairs on his chin and sinewy muscles in his shoulders pointing to the man he would become. He was so loving in this moment. So heartbreakingly precious to her. Forcing herself to remain on the bed, she resisted the urge to hug him fiercely. Instead, she relaxed her legs, tilted her head, and patted her heart, the singular sign of affection shared only by the two of them—and Hezi.

He lifted his chin, as if to rebuff the gesture, but his lips quivered, and he tapped his heart in return. Inhaling deeply, he looked at the ceiling, swallowed back tears, and whispered, "I wish Abba were still here." He pressed his face into her mattress, shoulders shaking in silent grief.

No matter what he'd done—or what he would do—she was called to love him as Yahweh loved His rebellious and wicked people. Daring to touch him, Zibah placed a trembling hand on his black curls and prayed. *Yahweh, he is Yours. I cannot fix him. I cannot lead him. Only You can capture his heart and rebuild all that is broken inside him.* Closing her eyes, she wept, repeating the passages hidden in her heart from the Torah, Psalms, and prophets.

When Nasseh's crying stilled, he lifted his head, stood abruptly, and wiped his face.

"Are you all right?" Zibah asked, scooting off the bed. "Would you like to break your fast with me?"

He took a step back, his hands fisting nervously. "No. Thank you. I wanted to inform you my men found Saba and his prophets hiding in caves south of Bethlehem. He agreed to surrender all his scrolls if I let the others go." He wiped his nose on his sleeve. "Saba will be executed in the Garden of Uzza before midday. You should stay in your chamber." He started toward the door—almost running.

"How did you find him?" She choked on the words.

Nasseh stopped but didn't face her. "Shulle divined it. Belit is teaching her a new level of sorcery." And he was gone.

Stunned, Zibah had no breath. No tears. After this day, she would have no abba. Her son, once precious and loving, was now bent on evil and destruction. Her eyes fell to the tear stains on her mattress, and she ached to understand him. He said he missed Hezi, but how could he if there wasn't a drop of righteous blood left in Nasseh's veins? Did he feel remorse for the innocent people he'd murdered yesterday? Any guilt in ordering his saba's execution? Closing her eyes against the pain, she pictured the Garden of Uzza, the place where Hezi built her dovecote years ago. The place she often prayed.

The place she would witness her abba's death.

He would not die alone.

Zibah rang the bell for her maid and shouted on the way to Jashub and Yaira's chamber. "Prepare my sackcloth robe. We begin thirty days of mourning." Neither Abba nor Yahweh would be mocked today.

35

In the year that King Uzziah died, I saw the
Lord, high and exalted, seated on a throne;
and the train of his robe filled the temple.

ISAIAH 6:1

Next Day

For the second morning in a row, I led a royal processional with
Nasseh—this one much smaller since half the royal council was
dead. My silent husband was pale as we marched to his beloved
garden amid a morning mist that chilled my bones.

Perfect, I supposed, for an execution.

Thirty benches waited in neat rows split by a central aisle. A scene
eerily similar to our wedding, except instead of a chuppah waiting at the
front of the gathering, a strange-looking tree trunk lay on a table, guarded
by a line of royal guards.

Far-fetched tales spread like a wildfire through the palace about
Lord Isaiah's early-morning capture. The one Adnah shared seemed
most likely—though still hard to imagine—since Isaiah lay in that tree
trunk like an Egyptian mummy in a coffin. Yahweh's prophets had been
hiding in caves and fled capture when Judean soldiers drew near. Lord
Isaiah sheltered in a partially hollowed-out cedar, and according to the
rumors, the tree miraculously grew branches like fingers that encased
him—to protect him. The soldiers felled the cedar below the prophet's
feet and topped it above his head, then toted the whole trunk to the
execution.

Nasseh and I halted at the front benches, staring at the rumor proved true. "Did you protect him with a spell or incantation, Shulle?"

"I don't have that kind of power." My wonder slipped out on a whisper.

We sat on the bench beside Belit, her cheeks as gray as the clouds above us. Last night's training session was the reason we were here. It began as an innocent divining, when I noted the city of Bethlehem and caves in the sheep's liver. Belit took the information and turned it into a betrayal. Making an excuse about feeling ill, she insisted we return to the city and went directly to Nasseh's chamber, telling him I'd divined Isaiah's location in Bethlehem. Nasseh sent his guards immediately and credited me with the find.

I glanced past my husband and saw Zibah and her family seated on the bench to our right. They'd glared at me as we approached. Evidently, they credited me with the find as well. I wanted to crawl under the bench.

Nasseh stared at the cedar trunk, refusing to even acknowledge his family. Neither did he notice Gemeti, Matti, or Dohd on the other side of Belit, all fidgeting and whispering with the council members behind us. Did they hope I'd hear their whispered praises? I no longer wanted to be a great āšipūtu like Belit—now that Yahweh had so boldly displayed his power.

The sound of clanking chains broke the silence. I looked up to see soldiers wrapping the tree with heavy chains. Did they think the prophet would burst out? I supposed after what they'd witnessed while apprehending him, they could leave nothing to chance.

Nasseh stood and approached his Yahwist family. "Kenaz, what did Moses say about those who gaze upon Yahweh's face?"

I cringed at my husband's cruelty. Who was he to test the faithful about their god? Lord Jashub intervened before his son's glare brought more trouble. "Moses said no man could see the face of Yahweh and live."

"Yet in the sight of many witnesses," Nasseh said, pointing to his saba, "Isaiah ben Amoz, proclaimed in prophetic office, 'In the year that King Uzziah died, I saw the Lord, high and exalted, seated on a throne; and the train of his robe filled the temple.' Claiming to have seen the face of the Lord—and yet lived—Saba either lied about his vision or made Moses a liar. Regardless of which crime he committed, Isaiah ben Amoz has condemned himself to death by your own Yahwist law." His recitation was flawless. His compassion absent.

Lord Jashub stood, the tenderness on his features more disarming than anger or accusation. "I will not defend Abba, my king, for fear that in doing so I would heap more guilt on your head since you still refuse to believe." He offered a respectful bow, leaving Nasseh's shoulders slumped with unspent bluster.

"My lord king," one guard shouted, "the tree glows but doesn't burn." The row of guards stepped back, and the audience rose in wonder. An ethereal glow radiated around Lord Isaiah, drawing every spectator toward him like moths to a flame. The cedar trunk was three-quarters intact but had grown latticed fingers of protection around the prophet's body. His face shone, and I shot a panicked glance at Belit. She rolled her eyes and returned to our bench, feigning disinterest in a power she'd always contended was inferior.

Others slipped away, leaving Judah's king to confront the power of a god in his prophet. "You have committed treason, Isaiah ben Amoz." He leaned over his saba, shouting. "By conspiring with Yahweh's prophets to undermine the freedom of worship declared by Judah's throne. Have you any defense?"

I watched in silence as the light grew brighter. We shaded our eyes. Undaunted, Nasseh took a step closer, but I stepped back. "As ruler of Judah . . . and vassal of mighty Assyria . . ." He spoke haltingly and stepped even closer, fascinated, and then addressed one of the frightened guards. "Fetch a two-man saw. Because his god hid him in a tree, you will saw him asunder until he's dead."

The guards scurried to obey, and Nasseh turned to face the shaken audience. "I hereby judge Isaiah ben Amoz a false prophet by his own archaic laws and a traitor by the laws of my new kingdom." He resumed his place beside me as two guards arrived with the large saw, lifted it over the tree, and set its blade in the wood that enfolded Isaiah's abdomen.

Before their first pull, Isaiah's weak voice split the tension, "King Manasseh, Yahweh condemns your plans to build more pagan altars in His temple. They'll be destroyed during your lifetime."

Nasseh's face drained of color. The guards manning the saw cast him a questioning look.

"And Topheth," Isaiah added, his voice stronger now. "Does Prince Mattaniah know you've drawn plans to rebuild Topheth—the same pagan furnace where King Ahaz sacrificed his and Hezekiah's older brother?"

Matti shouted, "Nasseh would never rebuild that monstrous—"

"Quiet." Nasseh's clipped word was terrifying. He returned to the tree and leaned over it, hissing, "I will build many altars and worship any god I wish. I will be Judah's greatest king, and you, Saba, will be forgotten the moment I leave this garden."

A brilliant light flashed from the tree, and Isaiah's hand emerged, gripping Nasseh's arm. I heard the old man's whisper but couldn't distinguish his words. My husband struggled to free himself yet seemed to be transfixed by the old prophet's message. When silence fell, Isaiah released him, and Nasseh rushed back to our bench, leaving the executioners as unsettled as their king.

Looking first at each other and then at their comrades, none were willing to make the first cut. Lord Isaiah's reedy, old voice began the same psalm the Yahwists had hummed at yesterday's dedication. Thunder rumbled in the distance and worked a chill through my veins.

"Nasseh, please stop this," I whispered, grasping his hand.

Prince Mattaniah leaned around the others. "Give the command, Nasseh. Silence him or I will."

Nasseh stared. Eyes forward. Another defeat in what should have been victory.

"Begin!" Matti said to the guards. Each man holding a handle, one man pulled while the other pushed in a quick, fierce thrust. I buried my face, waiting for the agonizing wail—that didn't come.

The old man's strains of praise grew louder, and I lifted my head. My wonder was reflected on the gawking faces around me, including the soldiers still sawing. As Isaiah's blood flowed, he sang a psalm he'd taught our class:

> I will sing of your love and justice;
>   to you, LORD, I will sing praise.
>   I will be careful to lead a blameless life—
>   when will you come to me?

"Silence!" Nasseh leaped to his feet. "You will be silent!"

But Isaiah shouted, "The faithful should flee to Tyre and Sidon—nations less idolatrous than Judah will become."

Nasseh lunged across me and grabbed Belit by the throat. "Make him stop."

"I cannot," she gasped. "I've never seen a power so strong." Nasseh shoved her away, and she fled the garden—beginning a mass exodus of terror. Matti and Dohd remained but sat on the end of our bench like dead men, creating distance between them and their raging king.

The soldiers, still sawing, were transfixed by Isaiah's face. Zibah and her family now gathered round, repeating the psalm with him, undaunted by the gore. Nasseh rose from our bench, and I followed, steadying myself by grasping his hand. As we approached, Isaiah's voice faded to a whisper, and I saw the shining glory leave his face in the horrifying silence.

The two soldiers let the saw fall to the blood-soaked soil. "You promised us a place with kings in the netherworld," one of them said without pretense.

"And you promised the new gods wouldn't judge our deeds," said the other. "As long as those living provide for us after we're dead."

Zibah, standing beside the second man, placed her hand on his arm. "There are no other gods but Yahweh, soldier, and He judges the heart and deeds of *every* man—in light of your knowledge and faith. But He is gracious and forgiving to those who seek Him. He is the mighty God who spared my abba from unimaginable pain." Turning to Nasseh, she tugged at the collar of her sackcloth robe, dried tears on her cheeks. "I'll mourn the customary thirty days, my son, but I don't grieve for Abba. I've witnessed the power of his eternal peace. From this day forward I mourn for Judah because we are all poorer for Abba's absence." She walked around the table to kiss Nasseh's cheek and mine and led Jashub and his family out of the garden.

Nasseh stared silently at his saba's empty shell. I noticed Dohd and Matti's approach but blocked their progress before they could torment my husband with manipulation and lies. "Leave. Both of you. Now." Their objection consisted of a brief hesitation. Then they scurried away like night creatures in the light.

Nasseh and I were alone now. His royal guard had deserted him. Palace gossip labeled his hysterical retreat from yesterday's temple massacre cowardly. Weak. He'd hoped today's decisive execution of a high-profile family member would help regain their respect. But Yahweh's display of indomitable power had been a blow. A second man-sized mistake from the adolescent king. Sennacherib's spies would report it. Prince Esar would know. Would there be ramifications?

I no longer knew the man-child before me. Egypt had changed him. Assyria ruined him. Yet somehow—I still loved him. Somewhere, behind the unfathomable decisions and unconscionable behavior was the tenderhearted boy whom I loved and who loved me like no one else. Slowly, timidly, I placed my hand in his. "I'll walk you to your chamber."

He nodded and followed meekly, silence and sidelong glances accompanying us. His guards opened the double doors, and he seemed surprised when I turned to leave.

"Aren't you coming in?"

I glanced at his Assyrian guards, unsure if I should continue the role of a spurned wife. "Are you commanding it of me?"

The abrupt question seemed to remind him of our ruse. "Don't get used to it." He closed the door behind us, and I felt the sting of his venom even knowing it was contrived. Suddenly awkward, I lingered at the doors while he continued to his favorite couch. A fleeting memory of playing Hounds and Jackals during our wedding week lightened my heart.

"Sit with me, Shulle." He patted the place beside him, and I sat stiffly on the opposite end. "Thank you for helping me find Saba," he said, reaching for my hand. "Perhaps you'll become my chief āšipūtu like Queen Naqia is to Sennacherib. I would never have been able to root out Yahweh's prophets without your skilled divining."

I removed my hand, the reminder twisting like a knife in my gut. "What I saw this morning in the garden proves Yahweh is real, Nasseh, and He's more powerful than anything Belit has taught me." His eyes held warning, so I chose my next words carefully. "I need not *exclude* Yahweh to continue training with Belit nor must I worship Yahweh *alone* to deepen my friendship with your ima. Remember, you said at the dedication that as long as Yahwists don't discourage the worship of other gods, you have no objections to their Hebrew God."

"I have many objections to the Hebrew god," he said, studying me. "But as long as you never leave me, you may worship any god you like." He brushed my lips with a kiss. "And when my friend Esar is king of Assyria, you and I will be together again."

PART 3

Manasseh led [the people] astray, so that they
did more evil than the nations the LORD had
destroyed before the Israelites.

2 KINGS 21:9

36

Why do you make me look at injustice?
Why do you tolerate wrongdoing?

HABAKKUK 1:3

Jerusalem, Judah
681 BC, Three Years Later, Tebet (January)

Adnah! Cat is giving birth under my bed!" I shouted for my chief handmaid, and our two delightful girls came squealing toward the yowling feline. We'd rescued two nine-year-old urchins from their abusive abbas in Jerusalem's Lower City—and they'd become our whole world.

On the day after Isaiah's execution, I'd awakened to the inglorious sound of Cat's first birth experience—under Adnah's bed that day. Thrilled as we were to witness the event, we were ill prepared to be kitten caregivers and made a hurried trip to the city market. While shopping, we witnessed a man beating his little girl. I knew the importance of a loving abba, and Adnah knew the sting of a captive's abuse. Our rage was satisfied when my guards arrested the man, and Adnah and I returned from the market with two baskets, three blankets, and a frightened six-year-old girl named Penina whose ima had died in childbirth. Penina's best friend Jericho lived a similar nightmare and joined our little family a few days later—her abba also now a servant in the palace prison.

"I think Cat's having a second one!" Jericho squealed.

"Here it comes, Adnah!" I shouted, chuckling at both our girls' backsides in the air. "Hurry!"

My friend nudged me aside, basket and blanket in hand. "Why must I hurry? We dare not bother her while she's delivering."

I linked my arm around hers. "I know. I just didn't want you to miss it." Cat's previous offspring had been placed in good homes throughout the city. Without even realizing it, I'd stumbled headlong into the unique passion Queen Naqia encouraged me to find during that long-ago banquet. Caring for my girls and watching them care for the kittens had given me the greatest joy of my life.

Penina and Jericho had also created a bridge to the queen mother, who knew most families in both Upper and Lower Jerusalem and had known their abbas as boys. She and Yaira were civil to me after Isaiah's execution, but they poured their love into our little delights as they'd done with me. Meeting together each day, we taught the girls to spin, weave, embroider, and sew.

After a few weeks, we'd had an especially pleasant day. I sent Adnah and my delights back to my chamber to prepare for our evening meal and lingered in the queen mother's chamber. Swallowing my fear, I attempted to explain my involvement in her abba's arrest.

"Belit was instructing me on the prayer to the gods of the night while inspecting the sheep's liver," I began rambling. "After the evening star had risen, Belit said to address the deity, Ninsianna, in its male manifestation instead of its female form. So I invoked his power by making an offering of bat's blood and goat's hair and asking him to place a portent of well-being in his servant Utu—which then led me to see Bethlehem in the sheep's liver. We weren't even talking about Isaiah. But Belit's skills are more refined than mine, and evidently, she saw something about Isaiah *and* Bethlehem in the sheep's liver and told Nasseh that *I* had divined it, but really it was she who—"

"Stop, Shulle!" Zibah squeezed her eyes shut. "Don't you grow weary of it all?" She opened her eyes and looked deep into my soul. "Are you still training with Belit?"

I hesitated—but refused to deceive her. "Yes, but not every night—as I had planned."

"Why not worship one God, Shulle?" Her voice held more pity than anger. "Didn't Abba's death convince you Yahweh is stronger than any stars He hung in the sky?"

"It convinced me He exists. A fact I doubted before that day." My words weren't cunning or cautious, but they opened her heart to me. For three years now, she and Yaira had loved me like they were my imas—despite the pain I'd caused.

"I heard the commotion," Zibah said, hurrying into my chamber. "Is Cat having her kittens? Two more families have already requested one."

"She's pooping out her third," Jericho said, hazel eyes sparkling with mischief. "Can I show King Nasseh the new kittens when he visits tonight?"

Ima Zibah knelt beside the girl with the stiffness of age and drew her into a hug. "With eyes like those, few people will refuse you."

"Don't encourage her," I teased. "You know the rules, Jericho. When the king comes to visit Cat, you go to the queen mother's chamber for a snack. He wants Cat's full attention since he only sees her once a day."

"I think he wants your full attention." Penina wiggled her eyebrows.

I ignored her and stood, dusting cat hair from my robe. "Let's give Cat some privacy while we focus on today's lessons. Queen Mother, would you like to join us? Adnah is teaching Penina and Jericho to paint henna on my hands and feet."

"I want to paint the queen mother!" Jericho practically tackled Zibah as she tried to stand.

"You plaited her hair last time," Penina whined.

"You may each paint one foot." Zibah put her arms around their shoulders and guided them toward the balcony couches.

Adnah and I followed. My chief handmaid was a brilliant teacher, training our girls with the skills that could someday place them in the finest homes in the Upper City. Yahwist families, of course, because they had a reputation for being kind, hardworking, fair, loyal. The remnant that survived the temple massacre wore their faith like a tunic—an ever-present but hidden mantle.

"I heard the king's dog ate a rat in a single bite," Penina said while cleaning dirt from under Zibah's nails.

"I saw the king's bodyguard playing with the beast outside our balcony," Jericho said, "and it was taller than the guard when it stood on its hind legs!"

Penina dropped Zibah's hand and looked at me. "Would the king bring his dog to our chamber, Mistress?"

"No, love. King Manasseh comes because he loves Cat and her kittens. He would never bring Ra'ah to my chamber." The cats were a pathetic excuse for my husband's nightly visits, but I didn't care what brought him. His continued obsession with my safety seemed extreme, though he assured me of the necessity. Granted, Assyrian guards remained in Jerusalem—men Esarhaddon called his *representatives*—but they were spies. One of them accompanied Baka each evening when Nasseh came to my chamber. The two guards even listened to our inane talk of cats. A ridiculous charade, but if it was the only way I could enjoy my husband's presence . . .

"I heard spies spotted Yahweh prophets near Shunem," Jericho was saying.

Zibah and I sat up, exchanging uneasy glances. "Say that again, Jericho." My tone was harsher than I intended.

The room fell silent, and Jericho bowed her head. "Am I in trouble?"

Zibah grabbed her arm. "Tell us what you heard."

"Zibah." I removed her hand from Jericho's arm, and the queen mother's features softened.

"Forgive me," she said softly to the girl. "I'm not angry. I'm afraid for the prophets, love. They're my friends."

Jericho looked at me as if asking permission, and I nodded, coaxing. "I was in the kitchen when Lord Shebna's steward told the cook that spies had spotted Yahweh prophets hiding near the forests of Shunem." She swallowed hard and glanced at Ima Zibah. "Lord Shebna sent more spies yesterday to confirm it and hopes to capture the prophets by week's end."

Zibah began shaking her head, tears gathering on her lashes. Adnah guided our girls toward her small chamber. "Take them to the garden," I suggested. "It's too nice to be cooped up indoors."

My chamber door closed, and Ima Zibah blinked, sending a stream of tears down her cheeks. "You must speak to Shebna. Nasseh promised he'd leave the prophets alone if Abba gave his life."

"If I get involved, it could endanger Penina and Jericho." Using my delights as an excuse was disgraceful but true. I'd lived at peace for more than three years by choosing neither Yahwists' extremes nor Belit's excesses.

Zibah's features hardened. "Why were Shebna's spies looking for the Yahweh prophets?"

"Why were the prophets hiding if they've done nothing wrong?"

But we both knew the answer. Nasseh yearned for Esarhaddon's approval and would eradicate any threat to Judah's peace with Assyria. Though he'd promised to spare the prophets, their continued prophecies against Assyria—and Nasseh's dearest friend—became justification for Judah's king to rescind his promise.

"I'll find a way to warn the prophets myself." Zibah wiped her cheeks and stood with the elegance I so admired.

"You know how to contact them?"

Her glare fueled my shame. "Do you really want to know?"

I hesitated, wishing I were brave. "No, Queen Mother, I don't."

She inclined her head and started toward the door but halted with her hand on the latch. "At some point, Shulle, you must choose to which god you will kneel."

"Actually, I don't."

I expected her to argue. Perhaps even spew angry words. Instead she left without a backward glance and left me drowning in her goodness.

When Nasseh arrived after the evening meal, I was quiet and withdrawn while my maids cleared the dishes. He waved them away before their task was complete and didn't even look at the kittens. Pulling aside the veil of curls that hid my frown, he asked, "Why are only your dishes on the table? Didn't Ima join you as usual?"

"Your ima and I had a disagreement this morning. Perhaps she chose Yaira and Jashub's company to mine."

"Whatever it was, you should apologize," he said. "She and Yaira are grieving."

"Grieving?" Dread rose. He hadn't mentioned Jashub's or Kenaz's names. "Why are they grieving?"

"Shebna discovered Dohd Jashub conspiring with Yahweh prophets in Shunem. Jashub will be executed at dawn—privately, in the palace dungeon. We don't need another mishap like the one with Saba Isaiah."

Mishap. Was that what the king called Yahweh's display of power? I schooled my emotions and trained my expression to show just what my king needed to see. "I'm sure you have acted wisely, my love, and I will apply your advice to my relationship with the queen mother." Zibah could never forgive me a third time. I'd stolen her son. Killed her abba. And because of my selfish fear, I refused to help protect Yahweh's prophets—making me complicit in her brother's execution.

Nasseh rose from the couch, kissed my forehead, and walked away. "I have much to do. I'll see you tomorrow night."

I sat alone in my quiet chamber, listening to the subdued chatter of my little girls with Adnah next door. Loneliness seeped into my bones. I'd given up Abba for Nasseh. Nasseh had given up me for Assyria. Would anyone give themselves up for me?

37

You, Lord, are forgiving and good,
abounding in love to all who call to you.

Next Day

Nasseh donned his outer cloak to meet winter's chill and stepped onto his balcony to watch the sun rise. When the golden orb crested the hill above the Valley of Kidron, he asked himself for the hundredth time which gods were responsible. Did anyone really know? "I must execute the man I respect most, who believes only one god does everything." He scratched behind Ra'ah's ears. "Why couldn't Dohd Jashub continue to worship Yahweh quietly? I can't let him go unpunished after finally regaining my guards' confidence."

He would need every man in Judah to join Esar's troops if news from his spies proved accurate. Sennacherib was dead. Murdered by two of his sons while worshiping in the temple of Nisrok. They'd sealed off the capital and taken command of the army, leaving Esar cut off from his rightful throne.

Nasseh rang the bell for his steward, who appeared immediately. Silent and efficient, the boy had lasted three months. Perhaps he'd let this one live.

Dressed now in a simple linen robe, gold crown, and his sword, Nasseh emerged from his chamber. Baka and five other guards joined him. "Esar's Babylonian army is a fraction of the troops his brothers command in Nineveh," Nasseh said. "Judean troops and the Assyrians here in Jerusalem must be ready to assist if Esar calls us to action. Summon my council to meet following Jashub's execution."

"Yes, my king." Baka cleared his throat. "Have you considered the winter weather?"

"I have, Baka." Nasseh stopped, and the men nearly bumped into him. "If it were summer, we'd already be on our way to Babylon."

"Yes, my king."

Nasseh resumed his hurried pace, and his faithful escort followed, winding through halls, into the stables, around a corner, and down the prison stairs. Dank and dark, the narrow stone stairs seemed like a passage to the netherworld. Though he knew the proper offerings had been made, Nasseh still imagined Abba waking from his fatal fall in a place like this.

They wouldn't make the same mistake for Dohd Jashub. Though Ima and Doda Yaira would no doubt protest, Nasseh would insist Kenaz provide offerings to the gods after his abba's death. Ima had forbidden it for Saba Isaiah, but his passing was—different. Nasseh reached out to lay his hand on Ra'ah's head. Death must first get past Ra'ah, his shepherd, a comforting thought, considering the dog's ferocity and size. Nasseh still feared the netherworld, but his growing household reassured him. His concubines had given him two sons and three daughters, and Gemeti had finally borne a son. He'd need more sons to secure his peace in the netherworld, but someday Shulle, too, would—

The princes killed Sennacherib!

Nasseh stopped his descent.

"My king, are you all right?" Baka laid a hand on his shoulder.

"They no longer need to kill us," he whispered. If Sennacherib's sons seized the throne, they no longer needed to discredit Esar to gain it. Killing Nasseh and Shulle would serve no purpose—and Assyria had far greater problems now than Judah's vassal king and queen.

But he could hardly rejoice on his way to Dohd Jashub's execution. Heart racing, Nasseh continued down the stairs and reached the landing, where he lifted a torch from its holster. "Only you, Baka. We need no witnesses for this." His other guards bowed and returned up the stairs. He and Baka continued past cells carved into palace bedrock, then down a smaller, circular stairway into the torture and execution chamber. The prophets had been executed as a group upon their arrival, but Dohd Jashub was royalty. His passing over the Khuber River must be controlled and peaceful.

A rat skittered over his foot. He pressed his back against the wall, taking deep and calming breaths. The filthy creatures seemed the common resident of every dark hole in every nation.

"Are you well, my king?"

"I'll be better when we leave this dungeon." Noisy chatter rose from the chamber below. When he descended the final step and rounded the corner, the execution chamber was full. "My explicit instruction, Shebna, was no audience!"

"Short of putting your ima, doda, and cousin in chains, my king, I'm not sure how I could have kept them away." Shebna tried to bow, but there was no room.

Ima gouged him with a glare. "You had no qualms about putting my brother in chains, Shebna."

"I have no qualms about putting self-righteous subversives to death," he barked back.

"*You* are the subversive, Shebna!" she spat.

"Enough!" Nasseh rubbed his temples, the noise in his head louder than the raised voices in the chamber.

Ima scooted between bodies to stand beside him. "Please, Nasseh, Jashub needs to see our faces until he looks on the face of Yahweh in the heavenlies."

"Have you heard the news about Sennacherib?" Her startled look was answer enough. "Two of his sons assassinated him while he knelt before Nisrok. In what heavenlies did he open his eyes?"

"In the fires of Sheol, my son." No hesitation.

"How can you be so certain, Ima?"

"Because it's the place reserved for those without faith in Abraham's covenant."

Nasseh wrapped his arm around her shoulders and kissed her forehead. "It's the answer I would expect from someone who has never left Judah." He turned to Dohd Jashub, held in chains between two guards. Esar said sometimes belligerence is rooted in ignorance and must be plucked before healthy ideas can grow. "Because you, too, have only known the teachings of Saba Isaiah, your death will be quick, Dohd." Nasseh turned away. He had no wish to witness this execution.

"Nasseh, wait," Jashub pleaded. "May I say something to you?"

"Please, my king." Kenaz's hand on his shoulder halted him "Let Abba speak to you this last time."

Grudgingly, Nasseh turned to face his dohd.

"The prophets who died this morning did not hate you," Jashub said. "I do not hate you. Yahweh does not hate you. No matter how many Yahweh followers you kill, we'll scream forgiveness from our graves because you are a son of David, God's king. May Yahweh deal with you as gently as you will allow, while He draws your heart back to Him."

After a glance at the executioner, Nasseh turned his back.

"Nooooo!" Kenaz screamed as Nasseh walked away.

Baka lunged to restrain Kenaz, who clawed at Nasseh from the guard's iron grasp. "I will never forgive you, Nasseh. Never!"

Nasseh's internal struggle was equally frenzied. "You *will* forgive me, Kenaz." He crossed the two steps between them and met his gaze. "And Baka has let you live—because even he knows we are cousins and friends. Forever."

He hurried away before Kenaz could say anything else he'd regret. Or anything Nasseh would be forced to punish. His family was upset. Understandably. But he'd told them not to come. It wasn't his fault Dohd conspired with the prophets.

He would send Doda Yaira a bottle of perfume and Kenaz a basket of dried fruit and nuts. Everyone liked fruit and nuts.

During times like these, Nasseh wished for Abba's presence most. The great King Hezekiah would know how to make Kenaz forgive him. A strange thought occurred. Kenaz no longer had a father. Neither did Prince Esar. Would Assyria's crown prince wish for a confidante like he did?

Nasseh's legs burned as he marched up the circular stairs, but by the time he was reunited with Ra'ah, he'd decided on a letter of condolence to Esar and a basket of dried fruit with a hint of oil for Kenaz. Shebna could arrange it. And Nasseh would have Shulle read the letter before he sent it. She knew Nasseh's heart better than anyone.

Shulle. Tonight, she was his again. Openly. Always. Without restraint.

38

Pray for the peace of Jerusalem!
    "May they be secure who love you!
Peace be within your walls
    and security within your towers!"

PSALM 122:6–7

Adnah, the girls, and I were waiting in Yaira's chamber when she and Kenaz returned after Jashub's execution. We'd prepared food to nourish their bodies, burned incense in the comforting aroma of lavender, and kept their brazier fires burning to dull the chill of Jashub's absence. It was the least I could do since my refusal to speak to Dohd had caused their heartache.

The moment Yaira entered the chamber, I broke into sobs. "I'm so, so sorry."

She grabbed me in a ferocious embrace. "Don't you dare lighten the Accuser's burden by carrying his guilt. We have the story of Job to show us there's a battle in the heavenlies and an Accuser who deserves the blame." She kissed my cheek and held me tighter. "Jashub died doing what he knew was right—and I love him for it." Her voice broke on the last words, and Kenaz wrapped his arms around us both, weeping and broken.

When our tears ran dry, we stepped back, bonded by the cleansing. I had sent Penina and Jericho back to our chamber, but Adnah remained to offer Kenaz a piece of cloth, embroidered with his abba's name. "I don't know how to read," she said, "but Queen Shulle helped me. I know it can't replace your abba, but if you carry it with you, it can remind you of him."

"Thank you," he said, his hand grazing hers when he received it from her. "I'll treasure it." Their gaze lingered, and something passed between them. Adnah had admired Kenaz since she'd arrived with me from Nineveh, but he'd been too busy with court business to notice her.

I kissed Yaira's cheek and Kenaz's. "Please send your maid if you need anything at all. Adnah or I will be over this evening to serve your meal."

Yaira grabbed my hand. "My queen, we have a maid who can serve our meals."

"But we're family." I squeezed her hand and left quickly, before more tears robbed the moment of calm.

The afternoon passed quietly. We continued our normal schedule, and then I began preparing for Nasseh's nightly visit. Each time Jericho attempted to apply makeup to my eyes, however, tears washed it away. Finally, she gave up.

Adnah returned from Zibah's chamber with news that the queen mother would eat alone. I didn't fault her. She had every reason to hate me. *Don't you carry his guilt.* Yaira's insistence that an *Accuser* was responsible for Jashub's death, not me, had been balm to my soul, but I suspected Zibah disagreed. Adnah and the girls were invited to share their evening meal with Yaira and Kenaz, while I sat alone in my chamber with Cat and a basket of kittens. Refusing to dwell on sorrow while waiting for Nasseh, I pinched my cheeks for color and forced down some warm stew on this cold night.

After a few bites, the chamber door opened, and my husband appeared. Never a knock. He was king, after all. To my surprise, he came alone.

"Where's Baka?"

He handed me a scroll without answering. "I've written a letter of condolence to Esar. I wanted you to read it before I sent it."

"A letter of condol—" Realization dawned. "King Sennacherib died?"

"Murdered. His two oldest sons. In Nisrok's temple."

"That's awful! Has Prince Esarhaddon executed them?"

The spark in his eyes dimmed. "Esar is trapped in Babylon, and his brothers sealed off Nineveh. I must help him gain the throne, Shulle. I've encouraged him in the letter. His abba was killed unjustly. As was mine.

The gods have ordained a struggle for him. As they have for me. I feel certain he must struggle through the winter journey to claim his throne."

His passion sent me to the scroll. It was as if Nasseh had opened his wrists and bled on the page, his deepest pain an offering to a man he knew for a few months four years ago.

"Nasseh. Beloved," I said, forming my words carefully. "I see the depths of your heart in these words." Why would he send a written document, making himself vulnerable to a prince who was currently an enemy to the new rulers of the empire?

Before I could form the warning, he devoured me with a kiss, pressing me back against my couch. "Nasseh, wait." I pressed against his chest, caught off guard by his desire. His arms locked around me, lean and sinewy from training. Panic rising, I struggled against him, confused and afraid. "Nasseh, stop! Listen, please!" I began to flail and kick, the fear of every man who hurt me polarizing in that moment.

He shoved me onto the floor, standing over me, panting. "What is wrong with you?" He touched fresh scratches on his cheek.

"I'm sorry," I sobbed. "I don't understand." I bowed my head and tried to gather my wits. The chamber door slammed.

My body tense, mind sluggish, and emotions unraveling, I tried to piece together the broken shards of this night. Was I married to a monster? *"All kings are ruthless."* Queen Naqia's words came rushing back. How could Nasseh express such empathy for an Assyrian prince he'd known for a few months but no remorse for killing Jashub, a man he'd adored his whole life? And why grieve deeply one moment and treat me like a prostitu—?

Sennacherib is dead. He came without his guards.

The broken shards came together. My husband had spent all day contemplating the impact on our lives and our restored freedom, while I, on the other hand, spent the day caring for his grieving family. He'd given me no time to process the change. But what could I say to heal my seventeen-year-old husband's wounded pride?

I groaned, using my dressing table to help me stand. The kohl pot and applicator lay amid a jumble of other supplies like buried treasures, and I realized I must *show* Nasseh the difference between his logical mind and my emotional need. Grabbing two blank pieces of parchment, I hurried out of my chamber, hoping my prize student would let me teach him one more lesson.

39

Whoever would foster love covers over an offense,
but whoever repeats the matter separates close friends.

PROVERBS 17:9

All day, the image of Jashub's execution replayed in Zibah's memory. Her brother's death wasn't the miraculous transportation Abba's had been. Though it was quicker, it was harsh. Constrained. And her fault. Why had she sent him to warn the prophets? Just because he'd played the spy during Hezi's reign didn't mean he had the same talents twenty years later.

Zibah couldn't bear another moment in her stuffy chamber. She needed air, no matter how biting the winter winds. Wrapping herself in her cloak and a heavy blanket, she tugged at the decorative wooden planks that held her balcony tapestry in place for winter, breaking it free. As she stepped onto her balcony, the wintry air felt refreshing to her swollen eyes.

She slid down the wall, sitting down hard on the stone balcony, and looked up at the stars. How could Nasseh believe each one was a separate god? The legends of deific squabbles changed with each generation's retelling. How could her brilliant son believe such far-fetched tales when the simple truth had been given to his ancestors for the redemption of all nations? *Oh, Yahweh, how many more must die before You capture and rebuild his heart?*

A shooting star raced across the sky. What would have normally caused her spirit to brighten, tonight only stirred more questions. Why were all the good men being killed? How could she look Yaira in the eyes again? Would Kenaz ever forgive her?

"Ima?" Her son's voice sounded small behind her.

Her emotions too drained to be startled, she was too full of despair to answer.

He crouched beside her and pointed to the sky. "See? The constellation of the dog goddess Gula, the great healer. But it's overshadowed by the constellation of Erra, the Tail, god of mayhem and upheaval. That's why this trouble has come to our family." He rested his elbows on his knees and clasped his hands. "I know you believe Yahweh is the only god, but many ancient texts tell similar legends. Moses's creation story, for example. I could bring my Babylonian scroll if—"

"I've read the Enuma Elis, Nasseh. Our father Abraham rejected the Babylonians' account of creation when Yahweh called him to the Promised Land." She looked at her son. "Please leave me alone." She'd never denied him anything. Perhaps it was time she start.

"Don't be sad, Ima." He cupped her cheek, something *he'd* never done before. "The prophets are gone, so we can move forward with tolerance and freedom. You can choose any one of those stars to worship, any god from any nation."

Righteous anger sharpened her tongue. "Perhaps you could escort me to one of the altars, and I could make a personal offering to a shrine priest?"

He stiffened and said, "Ima. You have a guest." Then left her.

"Good evening, Zibah." Yaira peeked from behind the heavy tapestry. "May I sit with you?"

Zibah looked up at her friend, throat too tight to speak, and opened her blanket in silent invitation. Yaira sat, and they wept in each other's arms—healing tears that needed no words.

"He came to my chamber," Yaira whispered, "with a basket of grain and some dried fruit. I think it was his way of apologizing."

Zibah sat back and wiped her face on the blanket. "How could everything have gone so wrong, Yaira? When I told you and Jashub about the prophets, I never expected . . ." She shook her head, words inadequate to express her emotions. Sorrow. Anger. Fear. Uncertainty.

"It was Jashub's choice to warn the prophets, Zibah." Her friend looked at the stars. "Can you imagine the joy of his reunion with Hezi and his abba? Yahweh is their comfort—and ours—until we see them again someday."

A sigh escaped before Zibah could capture it. "I'm trying to focus on eternity, Yaira, but I'm worried about our sons. Nasseh because he rejected Yahweh and Kenaz because of his zeal."

Yaira's strong arms wrapped her like a cloak. "We'll hold each other tonight and trust Yahweh to hold on to our boys for eternity.

40

Place me like a seal over your heart,
    like a seal on your arm;
for love is as strong as death,
    its jealousy unyielding as the grave.
It burns like blazing fire,
    like a mighty flame.

SONG OF SONGS 8:6

"Call for my concubine," Nasseh said as he marched past his chamber guards.

"Which one, my king?"

"It doesn't matter."

He slammed the door and slapped an Egyptian vase from its stand. It shattered against the wall, but the destruction gave little relief. Ra'ah cowered in the corner. Hands fisting violently, Nasseh paced.

What more could the gods expect of him? What more could his guards demand? His family? His queen? He killed the prophets to show the gods his devotion. He killed Dohd Jashub to prove ferocity to his guards. He gave Doda and Kenaz a peace offering, hoped to make love to his queen, and attempted to encourage Ima. None of it was enough. He picked up another vase and threw it at the wall.

"Nasseh?"

"What?" He whirled on Shulle, ready to banish her from his presence, but the sight of her gutted him. Her hair still askew from his awkward attempt to bed her, she was barefoot, without makeup, and as beautiful as he'd ever seen her. He turned his back, afraid she'd see the absolute power she held over him. "You made your feelings quite clear, Shulle. There's no need to—"

"May I draw for you?"

He felt her presence behind him. Close. Too close.

"Please, Nasseh. There's something I need to show you."

He squeezed his eyes shut, determined to deny her. She'd humiliated the king of Judah. "Draw if you must."

She touched his shoulder, and he jumped like a maiden. Ra'ah growled, responding to his tension. "Ra'ah, friend." He splayed his hand, and the dog retreated.

"Will you sit with me on the couch?" she asked.

Pushing. She always pushed. He followed her and sat, while she began her stupid drawing.

Placing her kohl pot on the floor, she dipped the applicator in it and drew a single circle. "See how this circle is a clean, black line?"

"Are you going to draw eyes and a smile? I'm not a child, Shulle." Her eyes glistened, and he hated himself more.

"You're a man, your majesty. A king, who deals with every manner of *hard, difficult, unforgiving* decisions every day." She drew solid marks through the circle for every word she emphasized. "You use *logic* and *reason* to balance *power* and *justice*. You keep your emotions in check all day long." She made more random marks with chosen words and then looked at him without threat. "Would you like to see what my day looks like on parchment?"

Nasseh gave a single nod.

She set aside the first parchment and reached for a blank canvas. Dipping the other end of the applicator, the end with frayed bristles, into the pot, she scattered brushstrokes that seemed like a disorganized glob. But she used her thumb to smudge highlights and shadows as she spoke. "My day is a blending of lives," she said. "My life with others—Adnah, my girls, your ima and the rest of your dear family." A mountain scene emerged as she dipped the handle of the applicator in the kohl again and drew a single straight line, cutting through the smudges. "My day also includes Belit and Dohd Shebna, meeting their expectations which, as you can imagine, requires a bit of your kind of thinking."

"You've ruined it." He stared at the hideous black line marring the lovely mountains.

She dipped her thumb into the kohl, lifted his hand, and pressed the black powder against his thumb. "The most important blending, my king, is my life with yours." She held their hands together and looked into his eyes. "When you came to my chamber this evening, my day was full of smudges. I didn't know all the straight lines you'd drawn in your day. Only after you left did I connect those lines and understand what Sennacherib's death meant for you . . . for me . . . for *us*." She brushed her lips across his and breathed the words, "I would never deny you, my king. It is my pleasure to love you."

His chest began to ache—a sensation he hadn't felt in too long. He'd been so busy meeting the demands of Gemeti and his jealous concubines he had forgotten the exquisite fullness of Shulle's love. The tenderness. The playfulness. The joy. The ecstasy. He welcomed her into his arms and let their passion unfold.

Dawn came too soon, and Shebna arrived for the daily briefing. Shulle covered herself, and Nasseh placed the condolence letter in his hand. "Make sure this reaches Prince Esar safely, my friend. He must know I share the heart of a son who lost his abba too soon. That's all for today." He looked back at Shulle. "My queen and I deserve another wedding week."

41

> One day, while [Sennacherib] was worshiping
> in the temple of his god Nisrok, his sons
> Adrammelek and Sharezer killed him with the
> sword. . . . And Esarhaddon his son succeeded
> him as king.
>
> ISAIAH 37:38

Shebat (February)

More than three weeks had passed since Nasseh sent his letter to Esar. Because my husband knew the couriers' routes and travel times, his mood darkened each day beyond the anticipated reply from his *friend*. How could I gently remind him that Judah was one of Assyria's smallest vassals? Expecting Assyria's crown prince to answer a letter during such political upheaval was like an ant asking a bear to carry a crumb in a dust storm.

While my husband brooded about Esar, I worried about Naqia. Was I being equally silly? When we first left Nineveh, she wrote letters to ask about Adnah, to ensure her happiness in the land of our shared heritage. Within a few short months, however, the letters grew more personal. The candid relationship begun at a banquet in Assyria deepened through written correspondence—but I'd received nothing from her since Sennacherib's death.

When I asked Nasseh about Naqia's whereabouts, he seemed surprised. Why would his spies report on Assyria's queen? I tried to divine her as alive or dead, but the starry hosts were divided—one reading good news, the next reading doom. I surmised because Assyria and Babylon were divided, the gods had split as well. Belit said I was the one divided from spending too much time with Yahwists.

Rumors about the Assyrian conflict circulated as the weeks wore on. Traveling merchants kept us connected to the world outside Judah's borders. While purchasing cat supplies in the market, Adnah and our girls heard Queen Naqia survived in Nineveh though her beloved Senn was killed. A month later, I received a short missive written in her own hand: *Safe. Grieving. Strong.* And I knew my friend would not let her son be defeated.

A heavy rap on my door disturbed my afternoon brooding. When I sat up, Cat bounded off my couch to hide as Nasseh rushed through the door with Ra'ah at his side.

I shrieked as the dog lunged toward Cat.

"Ra'ah, leave it." The beast skidded as if an invisible chain yanked him back. Ra'ah showed his disapproval with a terrifying growl.

Shaken, I begrudged a moment of admiration for the well-trained animal. "Why would you bring him to my chamber? You know Cat—"

"I've heard from Esar." Nasseh crossed the chamber in five long strides and presented an unfurled scroll. "Read it aloud." He paced, and I began.

From Esarhaddon, rightful and true King of Assyria.

To Manasseh, King of Judah and most honored son of Hezekiah.

King Sennacherib's mighty god, Nisrok, carried your letter on powerful wings to Babylon during my deepest sorrow. I prove my determination to avenge my great father's murder by making sacrifices to the gods of every nation.

Your letter came the next day, proving the sovereignty of Ashur, Sin, Shamash, Baal, Nabu, Nergal, and Ishtar. You are witness to the power with which they have clothed me to reclaim my father's house and my priestly office.

By the time you read this, I've become a fierce lion, marching on my enemies in Nineveh with troops from Babylon, Persia, and Elam, who have followed me into the ferocity of winter's blast without concern for horses, weapons, or food. Ishtar, the mistress of onslaught and battle, the lover of my priestly office will war at my side.

Dread knotted my stomach as I set aside the parchment. "Please, Nasseh, sit down and talk to me."

"No! I will not sit while my dearest friend is fighting for his rightful throne!" More pacing. Fisting.

His dearest friend? I chose my words carefully. "It would appear you've already done a great deal, my king." He halted his pacing, and I continued, "Your letter affirmed the gods' pleasure with Esar and propelled him toward Nineveh to seize his throne."

Nasseh knelt beside my bed, and Ra'ah followed, his black muzzle resting on my knee. Nasseh took the hand I'd rested on Ra'ah's massive head—and kissed it. "For your wisdom," he said. "Esar made sacrifices to *every* nation, Shulle. Did you see? I must make the same kind of sacrifices to ensure his victory in Nineveh."

Relieved he wouldn't be sending Judah's troops, I leaned up and kissed him. "And I think you are very wise."

"Good. Now, you must help me decide which of my sons to sacrifice."

"What? No!" I blurted. "You can't sacrifice your sons."

He stood and backed away. "I can and I will. As Esar did."

I slid off my bed to my knees, bowing to hide my panic. "Please, my king, forgive my ignorance. I'm unaccustomed to missives from other rulers, and I didn't realize Prince Esar had sacrificed children."

"He sacrificed to the gods of *every* nation, Shulle." Nasseh grabbed the scroll and tapped it. "His empire includes Ammon and Moab—and their gods Molek and Chemosh—who demand a child's pure blood during worship."

I looked up and forced calm. "But, my love, he didn't mention Molek or Chemosh."

"He said Baal. Tyre, also, offers children—" His brow pinched together. "I need not justify my actions to you."

"Of course not, my—" I doubled over, diverting a sudden wave of nausea.

He knelt beside me. "Shulle, are you well?"

I covered my face, rocking. "Sick. Feeling sick." Ra'ah towered over me, licking salty tears from leaking between my fingers.

"I'll send for my physician." His footsteps echoed in retreat. "Ra'ah come! Perhaps you're with child, Shulle. Too bad it can't be our son we offer tonight." The door slammed behind him.

I pressed a pillow over my face and released the shriek I could cage no longer. My monthly flow began this morning, and I'd been disappointed that I wouldn't bear his child. Now, determination coursed through me. I would never give him an heir if it meant my baby could be tossed in the flames. I set aside the cushion to search my trunk for the supplies I'd need to make herbal pouches. I'd used them for most of my marriage, and now I knew I'd need them again. No one need know. Especially the monster I called my husband.

42

[Manasseh] sacrificed his own son in the
fire, practiced divination, sought omens,
and consulted mediums and spiritists.

2 Kings 21:6

676 BC, Five Years Later

Nasseh paced across the front of the dais, the chaos in his head deafening. Was someone speaking?

"My king!" Adaiah, the royal treasurer, shouted but was cowed immediately by his king's hard stare.

"Is there an assassin approaching," Nasseh asked, "that you would dare raise your voice to your king?"

Adaiah left the council's gallery and fell to his knees beside the dais. "Forgive my impertinence, Lord King. My heart is devoted to Judah and to you. I'm a simple man who spends too much time with numbers, and frankly, my king,"—he looked up—"those numbers frighten me. The construction of Judah's altars and images in addition to King Esarhaddon's continuing demands have drained our resources. We've supplied Assyrian soldiers with clothing, weapons, livestock, oil, and even musicians for their entertainment. We simply cannot fulfill King Esarhaddon's most recent demand for more troops, grain, and animals in Sidon. Our current grain stores won't even feed Jerusalem for the remaining six months till harvest."

Nasseh soothed his hands in a basin of water on his way back to the throne. Three sleepless nights made it harder to control his impulses. He picked up a towel, meticulously dried each finger, and resumed his seat. "I informed the great king Esarhaddon of our depleted stores as you suggested, Adaiah." Nasseh nodded to Belit, who read Esar's short missive aloud:

> *From Esarhaddon, mighty ruler and great king of the earth, who rides under the power of Enki's stars, the Goat-Fish, to conquer the king of Sidon.*
>
> *To Manasseh, vassal King of Judah.*
>
> *When I send the rebellious king of Sidon to the bottom of the sea, I will engrave the names of my loyal vassals on a monument to commemorate my great victory. Yours is a simple choice. You will either be included with other loyal vassals who aided in my great victory, or you will be included in another monument—one in which I describe the destruction of Jerusalem, the city my father could never conquer.*

Nasseh grabbed the scroll from Belit and flung it at Adaiah. "Perhaps you'd like to personally refuse my friend Esar the blankets and grain for his soldiers."

"I see the conundrum, my king, but I—"

"Conundrum?" His nerves too raw to sit, Nasseh descended the dais and aimed his venom at the full council. "Without Esar's protection, Egypt breaches our southern boundaries!" Closing his eyes, he breathed deeply and reminded himself not to shout. When his voice grew louder than the noise in his head, he knew he'd lost control. *I refuse to lose control of anything.* When he opened his eyes, Adaiah stood beside him, another scroll outstretched. "What's this?" Nasseh looked at it as if it were a viper.

"It's a report on Judah's treasuries in all three fortified cities. I thought you'd want to see—"

"I don't." Nasseh slapped it away. Why add more noise to the details already hammering inside his head? Royal offerings were made three times a day at every Judean high place to every major deity of every nation. When offerings to the four-headed temple image fell short, Nasseh contributed from the royal treasury to ensure Abba's peace. Failure chased him like an assassin, robbing his sleep and crushing his confidence. Nasseh combed a hand through his hair, heaved a sigh, and returned to his throne.

Belit leaned over and whispered, "Shall I divine for you later as a haruspex—under the stars—or gain the answer immediately with *extispicy*?"

"Now. Use the lungs."

She hurried off the dais to consult her bevy of priests and priestesses, who waited behind a partition. Nasseh stroked Ra'ah's head. His guardian, now ten years old, rested beside him as always but had slowed too much to climb stairs to the harem. Eight concubines and four royal wives now visited the king's chamber, but Shulle would always be his queen. He smiled at the thought of her and looked down at Ra'ah. "Why can't you be nice to her cats?"

"My lord king." Shebna interrupted the silence, approaching the dais without an invitation. "If I might make a suggestion?"

"No. You may not," Nasseh said, leaning forward. "I choose to hear directly from the gods, Shebna, not my bickering advisors."

Belit left her priests, carrying a bowl filled with blood and the entrails of a lamb. Bumping Shebna on her way up the six steps, she sloshed a portion of the blood on his robe without apology. Nasseh had watched their war rage for years without any sign of a truce.

"Here is your answer, my king," she said, setting the bowl at his feet. "As you can see, the lungs that were taken from this morning's sacrifice are quite telling. One is half the size of the other, giving you the gods' clear instruction to send half the provisions requested by King Esarhaddon."

Shebna, lingering at the dais bowed. "As was to be my suggestion, my king. Write a second scroll to your friend, King Esarhaddon, and send half the supplies. He'll see your efforts as confirmation of continued loyalty."

Dohd Matti stood, swaying. "Send a scroll written in your own hand, Nasseh, and the Assyrian king has proof you approved the paltry shipment. Send the shipment and a scroll written by a scribe *without* your seal, and you can deny knowledge of it." He wagged his finger and slurred his final counsel. "Plausible deniability—if King Esarhaddon is angered by the slight."

Nasseh groaned and massaged his temples. Had he really once admired Dohd Matti? His character was deplorable, but he was still alive because he was family and he'd proved himself cunning when it came to trade agreements.

When Nasseh raised his head, Kenaz stood beside Shebna. "You've built a strong friendship with King Esar," his cousin said. "The king knows your loyalty and that you would never put his troops or Judah in danger. Explain our dire situation."

"Dire situation?" Matti laughed too loud. "No king admits a *dire situation* and keeps his throne."

"I will write a message to my friend," Nasseh said, bristling at the dohd he despised and the cousin he respected. "But Judah cannot be in a dire situation." Kenaz was too honest for his own good, which made him an excellent husband to Shulle's friend Adnah but a naive advisor.

The courtroom doors slammed open, and Nasseh bolted from his throne. "This is a closed session!"

"I come in the name of your sovereign, King Esarhaddon." An Assyrian messenger ran up the center aisle and, dispensing with a bow, placed a scroll in Nasseh's hand. "I've been commanded to place this in your hand and await your decision."

Tamping down his annoyance, Nasseh broke the seal and read the tiny scroll aloud.

Sidonian king fleeing south. Assyrian troops in pursuit. Send Judah's troops to meet Assyrian army with requisitioned supplies immediately.

Nasseh focused on the missive, hands shaking. The gods said send half. Esar, his friend and sovereign, commanded more. Judah had no more to give.

"Judah will provide half the provisions," he said, avoiding the messenger's bold stare. "I'll send the rest after spring harvest is complete."

Nasseh caught glimpses of the messenger's slow grin. "I'll need a scroll—written by your own hand—to explain why I've returned with less than the requisitioned amount."

Rising from his throne, Nasseh towered over the cocky Assyrian. "I'll send an explanation written in your blood."

The man sobered. "I'll relay your message to King Esarhaddon."

43

That night the angel of the LORD went out
and put to death a hundred and eighty-five
thousand in the Assyrian camp. When the
people got up the next morning—there were
all the dead bodies! So Sennacherib king
of Assyria broke camp and withdrew. He
returned to Nineveh and stayed there.

2 KINGS 19:35–36

675 BC, Ten Months Later

After their midday meal, Zibah reclined on a couch beside Shulle while Penina and Jericho giggled as they primped and polished them for tonight's banquet. Zibah reached for Shulle's hand. "Let's skip the banquet and go to bed early. The Assyrians won't miss us, will they?"

Shulle chuckled and looked her direction. "Are you very nervous?"

"Yes, but the distractions are helping." Yaira had sent word earlier that she wasn't feeling well and couldn't join Zibah for their daily weaving. Adnah went to tend her, so Shulle brought Penina and Jericho, whose constant chatter had been great entertainment. Their current topic turned to the two cats prowling the chamber, leftover kittens from Cat's last litter.

"It seems every Yahwist in Jerusalem already has plenty of our cats," Shulle was saying. "I'm not sure how we'll slow down production."

Zibah laughed and gave Shulle a sidelong glance. "You've been married a long time, my dear. I suspect you know how to keep a cat from conceiving."

"What do you mean?" Shulle bolted upright, clutching the linen sheet to her chest. "I wouldn't use my herbs on a cat."

"I meant keep her away from male cats," Zibah said, startled at her terseness.

Retraining her features, Shulle forced a chuckle and resumed her place on the couch. "Though it's her second birth, I think Adnah's still nervous." She turned away, her voice wobbly. "Adnah dreamt she rolled over and crushed Kenaz. When she woke, he was sleeping on the floor. She asked why, and he confessed that she'd rolled over and shoved him off the bed!"

Little-girl giggles soothed the tension in the room. Shulle teased them, and Zibah grew more convinced her daughter-of-the-heart ached for a child of her own. Shulle and Nasseh had lived as husband and wife for nearly six years now, and to her knowledge, Shulle had never conceived. But what could have caused such a strange reaction? *I wouldn't use my herbs on a cat.*

It felt like she was hiding something. *My herbs.* Had she returned to āšipūtu activities with Belit? She'd vowed after Jashub's execution that she would stop. Zibah wanted to believe she'd kept her word. If not āšipūtu activity, then what? *My herbs.* A treasonous thought occurred. Surely, she wouldn't use herbs to prevent conception. It was a queen's duty to provide an heir—even if she feared he might be like Nasseh's other sons.

"How are my grandsons progressing with their lessons?" Zibah asked, searching for the truth discreetly.

"Very well," Shulle said. "I'm using the simple smile and frown parchments to help them recognize emotions, but I think their greatest advantage is that they have each other. They don't feel as isolated as Nasseh did." She sobered, and the chamber fell silent. "I wish he would spend more time with his sons. I don't think he's seen them in weeks."

Before Zibah could probe further, she felt subtle vibrations that stole her attention. Memories of an army's approach, Sennacherib's siege, his general's demands, Hezi's illness.

"Zibah, you're pale. Are you all ri—" Shulle sat up, looking toward the open balcony. She must have felt it too.

"I need some fresh air," Zibah said, not wishing to frighten their girls. "Come with me to the balcony, Queen Shulle. Girls, prepare our best robes for this evening and choose the jewels for our hair." They squealed with delight and ran to the wardrobe, oblivious to the intensifying vibration beneath their feet.

Shulle's eyes widened as they approached the balcony. "So many," she breathed.

The Assyrian army spread like a wasting disease over the countryside as the royal procession entered Jerusalem's Horse Gate. Zibah covered a sob, crouching behind the balcony railing at the sight.

Shulle wrapped her in protective arms. "I'll send a messenger to Nasseh. You will *not* sit at a banquet with Esar, tortured by fear."

Zibah shook her head. "These are angry tears, Shulle. The moment my son allowed Assyria's army into Jerusalem, he scorned every miracle Yahweh worked to keep them out. May Yahweh forgive me, but I don't know how to forgive him."

The shock on Shulle's face was convicting. What had she told Shulle all these years? *"Anger is a necessary destination on our journey, but if we live there, it becomes our grave."* Zibah wiped her tears and balled her hands at her side. The grave must not claim her. Nor would she allow it to claim any of those she loved—including her foolish, wicked son. She closed her eyes to fight the inner battle before she could face what entered the palace below. *Yahweh, You promised to capture Nasseh's heart. Find a way to break his anger at You—and my anger at him.*

"Nasseh had no choice." Shulle released Zibah but still cradled her hand gently. "My girls heard rumors in the market that Esar finally captured the king of Sidon with eight other Arabian kings who had given him sanctuary. All nine rulers were beheaded, and Esar hung their heads around captives' necks to show what happened to kings who defied him. Nasseh could hardly refuse when Esar demanded shelter in Jerusalem on their way back to Nineveh."

Zibah recognized the terror in Shulle's eyes—the same she'd felt at Sennacherib's threats. How would Nasseh cope when Belit's trickery failed or Assyria betrayed him? The ice around her heart began to thaw. "I never met Sennacherib face to face, but with Yahweh's courage and for my son's sake, I will look into Esarhaddon's eyes tonight."

Shulle followed her back into the chamber, and the girls finished dressing them in an atmosphere more somber than before. Feeling a prompting in her spirit, Zibah paused in their preparations and took Shulle's hand. "Yahweh will bless you with children of your own when the time is right, love."

She blinked furiously, tears threatening her newly applied makeup. "I'm grateful we don't have children yet."

"Yet?" If Shulle held out hope for a child, perhaps she wasn't purposely preventing conception.

"I could never sacrifice my child in the fire as Gemeti was forced to do." Shulle's eyes communicated more than words. "The gods will punish me with barrenness, no doubt."

Zibah felt both indignation and relief that Shulle would refuse to participate in child sacrifice—but refusing to conceive? Fighting tears, she laid her hand against Shulle's cheek. "Perhaps someday my son will realize his great error and you'll both experience Yahweh's freedom to have a child of your own."

Her chamber door opened, and Nasseh appeared. "My two favorite women," he said, crossing the room with arms wide open. "You both look stunning."

Zibah swiped away tears and stood to greet him. "To what do we owe this pleasure, my son?"

Now taller than Hezi, he bent to kiss her first and then his queen. "I've come to escort you both to the banquet." Nasseh offered one arm to her and the other to Shulle. "Esar places great value on the way a man treats his family. I want him to see I've placed the queen and queen mother at the pinnacle of my kingdom." A hundred barbs came to mind, but Zibah covered each one with a sheath of grace.

Zibah and Shulle descended the harem stairway on King Manasseh's arm and entered the courtroom that had once again been transformed into a grand hall. The air was festive, the way it was at Shulle and Nasseh's wedding celebration. The difference being several hundred Assyrians in attendance. Zibah glimpsed three in shiny armor at the head table on the dais but avoided their faces. The thought of seeing Sennacherib's son, hearing his voice, knowing he was raised by the man who'd unleashed terror on her life—

He is my instrument too.

The words, though not audible, were unmistakable—and true. Assyria and Sennacherib had been God's instrument, not only bringing hardship but also the most magnificent blessings in Zibah's life. Taken captive as a child because of Judah's stand *with* Assyria, she was miraculously freed and adopted by Abba Isaiah. After Hezi's illness and Jerusalem's siege, they witnessed 185,000 Assyrians die without a single wound, and Hezi lived to father a son he adored. Perhaps King Esarhaddon thought he was using Nasseh, but *he* was the instrument in Yahweh's hand that would somehow bless her son.

By the time Zibah lifted her eyes to the front of the hall, she saw an amazingly ordinary-looking Assyrian on the elevated dais, sitting between his captains. Esarhaddon wore the typical squared-off beard, oiled and curled, but he was middle-aged and graying at his temples. Both eyes sagged with puffy, dark skin beneath and darted in every direction, as if waiting for an attack. At least twenty years Nasseh's senior, Esar likely replaced Hezi's role in Nasseh's life during the tour of nations, and her son had admired him to the point of deity since.

Shebna, Matti, Kenaz, and Adaiah looked extremely uncomfortable sitting at the head table with the Assyrians. Belit stood behind Nasseh's empty cushion, waiting as his personal guardian and advisor. The second table on the dais was filled with the other members of Nasseh's royal council. Assyrian guards lined the elevated stage, while Judean warriors were placed at the edges of the room and doorways.

"Try to enjoy the evening," Nasseh kissed Zibah's cheek and guided her and Shulle to the royal women's table where Gemeti and the others were already seated. Each woman offered Zibah a kind greeting but welcomed Shulle with the warmth of stones.

Royal musicians played lively tunes. Priestesses replaced the usual dancers, as they were better trained to manage the raucous Assyrians returning from a two-year campaign. Zibah averted her eyes, maintaining focus on Shulle in an attempt at casual conversation. Occasionally, Zibah caught a glimpse of Assyria's king, angry and brooding. He ignored the entertainment and Nasseh's chatter, preferring to stare at Zibah. If he hoped to unnerve her, he succeeded. With her last bite of quail, her eyes betrayed her and again wandered to Esarhaddon, who nodded and raised his goblet.

Flustered, Zibah dropped her spoon and pushed her plate away. "Why can't he leave me alone?" she muttered under her breath.

"Who?" Shulle asked.

"That monster just raised his goblet to me."

Shulle looked his direction and smiled—actually *smiled*—at the beast. "I believe he raised his goblet at me." Before Zibah accused her, Shulle shook her head and clarified. "He's not flirting; he's taunting me. He's always hated me and likes to provoke. I think it's because his mother, Queen Naqia, befriended me on our last night in Nineveh." She lowered her voice and continued, "It was the night I discovered Nasseh had taken Gemeti as his wife. When I returned to my chamber, Adnah was my gift from the queen. Since then, Naqia and I have corresponded regularly."

The news felt like a dagger in Zibah's chest. Had Shulle betrayed her again?

"I know it may sound as if I'm playing political games," she said. "But Naqia has become a true friend. In the beginning, she wrote to ensure Adnah's well-being because"—Shulle hesitated, her cheeks pink—"I've never told anyone, but Naqia is part Hebrew. Her abba was a priest of Bethel, exiled by Tiglath-Pileser."

"Her father was an Israelite?"

Shulle grinned. "I had a similar reaction, but I've grown to love her, Zibah, and for some reason she values me too. I have no hidden motives, I assure you, but befriending the king of Assyria's adored mother isn't a bad thing. Is it?"

"I suppose it couldn't hurt." Zibah hugged the sweet girl. *Oh, Yahweh, what are You up to?*

The clanging of goblets quieted the hall, and the two kings stepped to the edge of the dais. Holding his wine aloft, Nasseh said, "I'm honored this evening to welcome—"

"Perhaps I should make the announcements tonight." Esarhaddon nudged him aside, casting a net of tension over the room. "It is with great pride that I honor the men in this room who fought side by side to end rebellion in Sidon and Arabia!" Hoisting his goblet in the air, the hall resonated with Assyrian bass voices and shook with beating fists on tables. Had Esarhaddon not quieted them, the lamp stands might have toppled. "And I offer my sincerest gratitude to the kings who provided troops and supplies for Assyria's unstoppable army that overcomes all enemies." A cheer rose again, but he again cut it short. "And I vow tonight, before these witnesses, that the names of those loyal kings will be etched into a stone monument that stands forever before the palace in Nineveh. You, Manasseh, King of Judah . . ." He paused, and the whole room seemed to lean in. "You will be one of those names."

Zibah hugged Shulle, squeezing her eyes shut. *Thank You, Yahweh!* Even Gemeti pressed her hand over her heart, smiling with relief. Shulle released Zibah and turned to Nasseh's Babylonian wife. "Good news for our husband."

The woman's smile evaporated, and she leaned close. "I wish Esar would throw *our husband* into the fiery furnace that killed my son." She sat back and kept her voice low. "Tomorrow, I beg to return to Nineveh."

Esarhaddon lifted his arms to regain control. "Celebrate your king, people of Judah, for though Manasseh is young, he has a quick mind and a lion's heart. Tonight, however, I must teach everyone a hard lesson. You see, I received only *half* the Judean troops and supplies I requisitioned from your good king." A terrifying mix of confusion and glee rippled through the crowd. Judean nobles hoped for mercy, and Assyrian soldiers cheered for blood.

"Since King Manasseh's seal was missing from the treasonous list of woeful provisions, I must assume one of his council members is responsible." He turned to Nasseh, coaxing with a murderous glint. "Simply point out the advisor who sent the supplies, King Manasseh, and you'll be forgiven. Your advisor will be added to my captives, marched to Nineveh, and executed. The perfect solution to both eliminate a traitor and affirm your loyalty."

Nasseh stared into his wine goblet, seemingly paralyzed. Zibah watched his inner war rage as he began rocking from right to left.

"Trouble remembering which advisor you assigned to that duty?" Esarhaddon mocked. "Perhaps the council members should stand."

His soldiers advanced from the back of the dais, weapons drawn, until every counselor at both tables struggled to his feet. Shebna leaned on a cane, his back now bent with age. Matti swayed as usual, requiring the aid of an Assyrian captain to remain upright. Zibah's beloved nephew Kenaz and Adaiah, the royal treasurer, moved their lips—as did the other loyal Yahwists at the second table.

"Your decision, King Manasseh," Esar hissed through clenched teeth, loud enough for Zibah to hear.

"It was Lord Shebna." Nasseh never raised his head. Nor did Shebna. Shulle muffled a cry, and Zibah grabbed her hand under the table. Shocked. Relieved. Saddened. Horrified at Belit's smile.

Shebna, stooped by years of bowing to his king, placed a hand on Nasseh's shoulder. "You've chosen wisely, my king." Esarhaddon's guards grabbed his hand and wrenched his arm behind his back. He winced but didn't struggle. Shulle buried her sobs against Zibah's shoulder as they led him past their table.

Esarhaddon lifted his goblet. "All is forgiven. Resume the celebration!"

Nasseh scanned the crowd, and Zibah glimpsed a fleeting shadow of sorrow before he drained the remainder of his goblet and returned to the table with Assyria's king and his advisors.

Too nauseous to remain, Zibah whispered to Shulle, "Come, my dear. I'll take you back to your chamber." Motioning for Onan, her Hebrew guard, they fled the insanity.

Shulle's chamber guards opened her door, and the girls waited anxiously to hear the evening's details. "Your mistress needs rest," Zibah said. "Tonight, you may sleep in my chamber while I attend Queen Shulle." To their credit, they obeyed, and Zibah helped the grieving young queen remove her crown, her jewels, and the combs from her hair. Shulle crawled into bed without removing her robe or the paints from her face, still having said nothing. Zibah climbed in beside her, resting her back against the headboard and drawing Shulle's head into her lap. Stroking her hair, Zibah began humming a psalm until the warmth of their friendship lulled them to sleep.

44

They sacrificed to demons that were no gods,
to gods they had never known,
to new gods that had come recently,
whom your fathers had never dreaded.

DEUTERONOMY 32:17

I feigned sleep until Zibah's snoring began and then carefully extricated myself from her grasp. Tortured by the image of Dohd Shebna in shackles, guilt compelled me toward the door. How long had it been since I'd visited Dohd? I'd been too busy with my little girls and evening visits with Nasseh. Dohd and I hadn't quarreled; we'd simply grown distant. He was family, as he often reminded me, and I was grateful for so many things he'd made possible in my life.

But he was an evil man.

Still, I couldn't let Dohd go to Nineveh without saying goodbye. I opened my door wide enough to squeeze out of my chamber, but Onan blocked me with a chastising look. "Onan, please." My voice faltered. "You must take me to see him."

His chest deflated. "My queen, I cannot." The hard lines around his eyes softened. "The palace prison is no place for a queen."

"But it's a place for a niece to say goodbye." I laid my hand on his forearm. "Please."

He closed his eyes, expelling a long sigh and turned to his partner. "Guard the queen mother while I'm gone." We walked quickly through palace halls and into the night, the moon and stars my familiar friends. But our descent down stone steps into a foul-smelling netherworld almost made me regret my decision. Halting midway down a narrow hall, we stopped beside a heavy cedar door. Onan lifted a torch from its harness on the wall and stepped into a cell no larger than a horse's stall. Dohd was shivering in the corner and shaded his eyes from the torchlight.

I covered a sob and stood rooted to the bedrock.

He saw me before I could speak. "Get her out of here, Onan!"

Dohd turned away, but I raced toward the old curmudgeon and knelt at his side. "I'm sorry I haven't been more attentive. I've been too caught up in my own world, and I was afraid to take sides in your war with Belit. I should have—"

"I killed him." He lifted his eyes, a familiar dark evil in the rheumy depths. "Haruz. I didn't send him back to Jotbah. I had him killed and his body dumped in the wilderness."

I choked on a sob and stumbled back. Onan caught me. "You . . . You . . ." Emotions battled reason in the presence of Zibah's guard. One word escaped on a sob. "Why?"

"You are a fool, Meshullemeth, and all I've taught you is worthless."

Blinding hate sent me kicking and flailing at the man who had tortured me since I was eight years old. Only Onan saved him from my rage. Wrapped in the guard's restraint, I huffed my verdict-panted fury. "Your Assyrian torture will feel like a tickle compared to the demons' torment my incantations will inflict once you reach the Khuber River. I'll make sure your hideous life beyond erases any successes in your piteous earthly existence."

A slow grin softened his features, and then his low chuckle turned to a laugh.

Confused, I turned to Onan, and he, too, looked puzzled. By the time I looked again at Dohd, he shook his head—playing the teacher again. "You really are quite a disappointment, little Shulle. I thought after all this time with the queen mother you'd realize . . ."

He was baiting me. I wanted to walk away. Leave him to die in Assyria. "What did you think I'd realize?"

He leaned into the torchlight, all humor gone. "I've known since childhood Yahweh is the only true God. But unlike the starry hosts, Yahweh does what He wants. The gods you serve don't always obey, but they're far more cooperative. They aren't really gods though, are they?" The evil in his eyes sent a shiver through me. "They're demons you only imagined as gods who wait at the Khuber River."

"We're leaving, my queen." Onan gripped my arm and fairly dragged me from the cell.

"Oh, your gods are powerful!" Dohd shouted as the heavy door slammed shut. "They manipulate you by letting you taste their power."

His voice faded, but his words were etched forever into my mind. *Demons. They don't obey you. They manipulate you.* When Onan and I emerged from the prison into dawn's early glow, I was trembling violently.

He stood awkwardly beside me. "I know Lord Shebna is your dohd, my queen, but he has always been an evil man. His death was sealed years ago through the prophet Isaiah when Yahweh condemned him to be cast into a large country and die there."

"So, you believe Yahweh is the only god, Onan?"

A shadow of fear washed his face white. He looked right and left to be sure we were alone before answering. "Yes, my queen, I'm a devout Yahwist. But I don't shout it from the palace rooftop because I promised King Hezekiah I'd stay alive to protect Queen Zibah."

Nodding, I lowered my head, letting my curtain of curls hide tears. Ever since Dohd had taken me from my home in Jotbah, I'd been taught Yahweh's people were wicked. I helped deceive and manipulate them to gain power for those who abused it. At what cost? Abba was dead. Nasseh was Esar's toy. And I was more confused about the gods than ever. If Yahweh was the one God and only paradise or Sheol awaited, I needed to pursue Him with more intention. But His temple was full of idols, and I'd been conversing with *demons* for years. How could I enter His presence? The answer was simple.

I couldn't.

Sniffing back tears, I wiped my face and looped my arm in Onan's to begin our return to my chamber. "You and I will tell no one about this night."

He squeezed my arm to his side in a tender gesture. "As you wish, my queen."

~

For a week, I'd sequestered myself in my empty chamber, truly an orphan. Though it had been true for fourteen years, it meant nothing until Dohd's terrible revelation. If the starry hosts reigned in the life beyond, my abba wandered an empty netherworld, tortured without provision for eternity. If Dohd's final gibe at me was true—and Yahweh was the only God—my abba rested secure in paradise with Nasseh's abba and so many other faithful. But where did that leave me? An āšipūtu who hadn't spoken to the starry hosts in six years. A blasphemer and idolater Yahweh's Law sentenced to death. The eternal suffering with which I threatened Dohd would surely fall on me.

"Please, my queen, you must eat something." Adnah sat on my bed with a bowl of bone broth. "I know you're grieving Lord Shebna, but the king has ordered me to stay with you until you finish this soup." My friend held the bowl in one hand and rubbed her large belly with the other, looking as though her second child might arrive any moment.

"Pour it in the waste pot, Adnah, and go care for your little girl and Kenaz." I sat up and took the bowl from her hands. "There. You can tell Nasseh you saw me eating it." She shook her head to protest, and my tears sprung up like the ceaseless Gihon spring. Adnah would never tell a half truth—even one so small that came easily to me. Groaning, I set the bowl on my bedside table, flopped onto my stomach, and buried my face in my pillow again. "Just go, Adnah. I want to be alone."

She rubbed my back and ignored my plea. "Shulle, I—" The rubbing stopped. I heard shuffling sandals and whispers at my door.

Please, whatever powers might be listening, make them leave me alone. I'd told no one about my journey to the prison or Dohd's revelations, and Onan must have kept my confidence because everyone believed my grief was for my wicked dohd's certain death.

But I'd lost so much more in that cell.

The shuffling sandals stopped next to my bed. "Shulle, my love." Nasseh laid his hand on my back and sat beside me. "I know you're angry with me, but you must listen to my reasons for sending Shebna away and then forgive me."

If it were only that simple. "I'm not angry with you," I said. "Please, just go."

"Shebna is likely already dead, Shulle. He was the only one I could be certain would die before the Assyrians had a chance to torture him. It was the most merciful decision I could make."

I wanted to laugh at his reasoning, but it was true. "He didn't deserve your mercy, Nasseh. He was a cruel man."

Nasseh curled his body around me and snuggled his face close to mine. "Look at me, my love. Please." I obeyed because he was my king, and I found the tender boy I loved looking back. "I want you to come back to me." He moved a tendril off my face. "The concubines say my sons are out of control without your influence over them. I sent the boys' incompetent tutor away. I found someone else to teach them who understands their special—challenges—the way you understood me."

I covered my face, unable to stop more tears. "You've replaced me? I've been in my chamber a week, and you've found someone else to teach your precious boys?"

"Get out of that bed, Meshullemeth," said a man's deep voice. "'A little sleep, a little slumber, a little folding of the hands to rest—and poverty will come on you like a thief.'"

"Abba?" I bolted upright. The man I'd longed for and grieved fourteen long years stood beside my bed.

"Yes, my Shulle." He opened his arms, and I flew into the embrace that sheltered me like a fortress. I could do nothing but sob.

"Shebna lied to us, Shulle," Nasseh said, standing beside us. "He said Haruz longed to resume his farming, but it turns out your abba would have rather been in Jerusalem with you. It was Shebna who denied him."

His hand rested on my shoulder, and I grudgingly released Abba to thank my husband. "I can't believe you found him and brought him back to me."

"I'm forgiven then? No more seclusion and crying in your chamber?"

I wrapped his neck in a fierce embrace. "I think we both need forgiveness, my love. Perhaps there's hope."

45

While still growing and uncut,
    they wither more quickly than grass.
Such is the destiny of all who forget God;
    so perishes the hope of the godless.

JOB 8:12–13

671 BC, Four Years Later

Nasseh waited with Shulle and the queen mother on the platform outside the palace entrance, all eyes focused on the seemingly endless Assyrian procession. "Since when is the king *last* in a royal march?" he asked Shulle.

"Since the king of Assyria loves to play games."

"But Esar hates games," Nasseh said. "I've asked him to play Hounds and Jackals and—"

"Not those kinds of games, my love." Shulle laid her hand on his cheek, drawing his eyes up. "The kind of games people play with unspoken words and emotions that are hard for other people to understand."

He brushed her hand off his face. "You mean hard for *me* to understand." He'd been sole ruler for fifteen years and still didn't understand hidden meanings or word play. Gemeti had ceased her lessons on royal manners years ago—after he'd sacrificed their son—but the sacrifice was worth it. Molek had given Esar Assyria's throne. But now Esar demanded more than Molek ever did. Why must he wage war in the worst possible weather? Why march his army through Judah and across the Sinai in midsummer to fight Tirhakah—a third time?

Shulle leaned over and whispered, "You're fidgeting again."

"I smell like a pig. My lotions ran down my back at dawn." They'd been standing in the sun since midday. "My sympathy for Esar is dwindling, Shulle. I know after two failed campaigns and his son's death he's not himself, but—"

"Nasseh, we can't talk about his failures or the crown prince's dea—"

"I know!" he said, louder than intended. Ima raised an eyebrow, so he pressed his lips against Shulle's ear. "He didn't even reply when I sent another letter of condolence."

She pressed a kiss against his cheek. "You must be patient, my love. Queen Naqia said in her letters that last year's death of the crown prince changed King Esar."

"There he is." Zibah pointed to the crest of the hill across the Kidron, where the Assyrian banner and royal contingent paused for the trumpet's announcement.

"Yes," Nasseh whispered. "There he is." Dread filled his belly. Esar hadn't responded to his condolence letter, but in the message announcing this visit, he repeated the ultimatum he'd given upon his departure from that awful banquet four years ago. *"If your queen can't produce a son, you'll dethrone her and give Gemeti the crown."* What would Esar do when he discovered Shulle had no son and still wore the crown? Nasseh couldn't blame an advisor this time.

Shulle turned his chin with a single finger. "What's troubling you? Didn't Esar's message say he would only stay two days?"

"Yes, but—"

"It's only two days," she said, grinning. "We keep him well fed and drunk, and then he leaves us alone."

He hadn't told Shulle about the ultimatum. Why upset her when she couldn't make a child grow in her womb? He'd asked Belit to try every spell and incantation. Nothing had worked. Truth be told, Nasseh cared little about a child when he held Shulle in his arms. Belit was Nasseh's connection to the gods, but Shulle knew his heart. Like his finely tuned guards, his queen anticipated his need before he spoke it. And when Ra'ah's breath left him, she slept in Nasseh's chamber to quell the unbearable loneliness. How could he tell her Esar might take away her crown? It was the only deception between them, but it felt like a boulder.

"Who could be in the carriage?" Shulle's question drew Nasseh's attention to the procession that now crossed the valley. "Did Esar mention . . ." She shook her head. "No, it couldn't be."

"Did he mention what? He offered only the date of arrival and the demand for a banquet tonight."

"I haven't received a letter from Naqia in two months," Shulle said. "You don't suppose he brought her to meet Zibah?"

Or had Esar brought his mother to inaugurate a new queen? Assyrian guards flanked Esar's white stallion as they entered the city's Horse Gate, while three more guards followed the gilded carriage behind him.

Nasseh offered an arm to both Shulle and Ima. Ima's hand trembled. "The hills and valleys are covered with soldiers," she whispered. "Just like when they besieged the city."

"They're our protectors now, Ima." Esar remained on his horse, and Nasseh's confidence dwindled. "Judah welcomes you, mighty king and sovereign of our great empire. May I present Queen Mother Hephzibah and Queen Meshullemeth?"

Ignoring Nasseh, he addressed Shulle. "My mother tells me you are still barren."

Nasseh stepped in front of his wife. "You will address your concerns to me, King Esarhaddon."

The carriage door popped open and out tumbled two rambunctious puppies in a ball of tan fur, large paws, and playful growls. Assyria's queen mother followed, her growl less playful. "My son's manners have failed him today," Naqia said, taking the hand of a guard while descending two carriage steps.

"Naqia!" Shulle ran into an embrace warmer than political maneuvering. Nasseh knew they corresponded but hadn't realized the affection between them.

Assyria's king dismounted and everyone on the tiled street bowed—

all but Nasseh. Inclining his head in respect, Judah's king waited for his long-time mentor to approach—and the judgment that would most certainly come.

"My mother brought male and female hounds as a gift to your wife. She hopes their eventual offspring will *draw down the power of the stars* upon your wife's womb." He spoke loud enough for all to hear and then leaned close to whisper. "Because of my great respect for her and her āšipūtu powers, I've allowed this attempt on your queen's behalf. Don't imagine you can defy me again and live, King of Judah. I told you from the beginning your obsession with this woman would be your death."

Lifting his hands like a victor, he quickly turned and shouted to Jerusalem's citizens. "I look forward to sampling the finest fruit of your gardens, trees, and vines. Your generous provision will expand Assyria's reach into Egypt's golden pyramids so I might spread more wealth across the empire. Tonight, we celebrate the victory that will most certainly be ours!"

He left the crowd to their compulsory applause and retrieved Naqia, escorting her away from Shulle and halting before Nasseh's ima. "Queen Mother Hephzibah, let me present to you Naqia, Assyria's queen mother, the jewel of my crown, and the wind beneath Nisrok's great wings."

With one hand, Naqia drew Esar's face down to kiss his cheek. "You're a good king." She then bowed to Ima. "I've waited a long time to show you the respect you deserve, Zibah. May I call you Zibah?"

"I, well . . . of course. May I call you Naqia?" She returned the bow. "And I wish to thank you for loving my Shulle so deeply."

"She's easy to love."

"I've prayed for this moment." Shulle stood between them, hugging their waists. "Both my imas with me."

The puppies nipped at Naqia's robe. She lifted the male into Shulle's arms and held the female up to let it lick her cheek. "You will tend these precious animals with training and herbs and incantations, becoming so connected that when this little girl pups"—she nuzzled the female's sweet face—"the gods will open your womb as well."

"Surely, Nasseh can help me train them," Shulle said.

Naqia turned an angry frown on Nasseh. "What have the royal midwife and physician determined as the reason Shulle remains childless?"

"Shulle hasn't requested an examination."

"She shouldn't have to request it," the old crone huffed. "*You* are the king—for now."

46

Surely he took up our pain
    and bore our suffering . . . .
The punishment that brought us peace was on him,
    and by his wounds we are healed.

ISAIAH 53:4–5

Naqia's grip on Zibah's hand felt like an iron shackle. "Come along. You and Shulle can show me to my chamber. We'll discuss why our girl loves children but never mentions the sorrow of barrenness in her letters."

Zibah glanced at Shulle, who offered her an apologetic shrug. So this was Sennacherib's favored wife? An interesting choice for the man who had terrorized Hezi most of his reign. Now, it seemed, she and her son would terrorize Manasseh. A sudden wave of nausea swept over her. She pulled her hand from Naqia's and stopped midway up the harem stairs.

"Please, Shulle, show Naqia to a guest chamber. I'll find you in a few moments."

"Are you all right?" Shulle whispered.

Zibah pressed her hand against her stomach. "I'm sure it's just the heat."

"At least let me help you to your chamber."

"No, please. You go ahead." By this time, thankfully, a guard noticed them on the stairs and came to Zibah's aid, freeing Shulle to continue with Naqia.

Zibah hoped Shulle would show her to one of the plentiful empty chambers in the harem of Solomon's palace—far away from theirs. She pressed a hand over her eyes, attempting to right herself. *Yahweh, Naqia is flesh and blood, and half of that blood flows from a child of Israel. Show me how to not hate her.*

Inhaling a sustaining breath, she offered the guard an appreciative nod. "I think I'm ready now. Thank you." She leaned heavily on his arm, taking the remaining stairs slowly. As they approached Zibah's chamber, she thanked her escort again and reached for her chamber guard to steady her. "I'm looking forward to a little quiet, Onan."

"I'm sorry, Queen Mother," he whispered while opening the door. "I tried to stop them."

"Mistress Zibah, we were about to come looking for you!" Naqia sat beside Shulle on Zibah's favorite couch, and one of the puppies welcomed her with a small puddle on her carpet.

"Oh no!" Shulle shot off the couch. "Onan, could you have one of the guards take the puppies to the garden for a little exercise while the queen mothers and I visit?" She grabbed both balls of fur and shoved them into his arms before he could protest.

"Perhaps I'll go check on Yaira." Zibah tried to leave with Onan, but Sennacherib's widow was relentless.

"Nonsense!" she said, patting the couch. "We've called for the midwife and physician, and we have much to discuss before I return to Nineveh."

Zibah would have rather sat beside a viper. From Shulle's reports, she'd truly loved the monster, Sennacherib. The man whose threats caused Hezi to strip the gold from Yahweh's temple. The man who besieged Jerusalem for weeks, impaling innocent Judeans for sport. The man whose boasting offended Yahweh so greatly that Abba Isaiah prophesied his assassination years before his own sons killed him.

She sat beside Naqia, stared deeply into her eyes, and tried to see the woman behind the bluster. *Sennacherib's own sons killed him.* Regret crashed into the walls around Zibah's heart and words failed her. Naqia seemed affected by her silence and turned away, looking out the balcony.

"Your God killed my husband." Her words were matter of fact. No venom. Simply a statement of truth she'd come to accept.

"Yes," Zibah said. "Because your husband mocked my God."

Eyebrows lifted, Naqia grinned slightly. "Senn tended toward arrogance." Sobering, she sniffed and lifted her chin. "I loved him for it."

The admission left Zibah breathless. Before her sat a woman—like Zibah—who had adored her husband, no matter his political decisions and battle savagery. Naqia loved the man, *Senn,* who set aside his weapons and removed his armor to hold her tenderly in arms—arms washed clean of his enemies' blood.

"Tell me what else you loved about him," Zibah said, surprising even herself. She hated Sennacherib, but knowing his widow suddenly felt important. Shulle poured three goblets of watered wine, served them, and sat on the carpet at their feet, while Naqia recounted her fondest memories of a man who had brutalized most of the known world.

"And he was deathly afraid of spiders." Naqia laughed through tears. "If he saw one in my chamber, he squealed like a woman for me to kill it."

"Hezi was fascinated with dung beetles," Zibah said, shaking her head. "I'd catch him watching them, and he'd invite me to join him!"

Naqia's laughter wound down. "Didn't he use the image of a dung beetle as his royal seal?"

Yahweh, give me courage. It was Zibah's open door to share more about Yahweh. Did she dare? Images of Abba Isaiah and her brother Jashub flashed through her mind. Nasseh allowed his closest remaining family to live while maintaining their faith in Yahweh, but they hadn't made public confessions of faith in years. Heat crept up her neck as the words stuck in her throat.

"King Hezekiah chose the dung beetle," Shulle said, "because he trusted in Yahweh alone and equated the idolatry of his abba's reign with dung. He focused on destroying pagan religions, as dung beetles destroy dung." She glanced at Zibah. "Is that correct?"

Zibah's heart soared at the fearless explanation. "It is indeed, my girl."

"If your husband was so committed to his god," Naqia's brow furrowed, "why did Yahweh kill him?"

Zibah blanched at the hurtful accusation. "Yahweh didn't *kill* Hezi, but I've heard Nasseh make the accusation. For someone who doesn't trust

Yahweh's love, it's difficult to differentiate the subtle difference between murder and sacrifice."

"Your husband is as dead as mine," Naqia said bluntly. "Does it matter what we call it?"

Her candor fueled Zibah's courage. "Shulle tells me your abba was a priest from Bethel."

Naqia sat back with a wry grin. "And my *mother* was a Babylonian āšipūtu who taught me the truth of the starry hosts."

"It's my understanding that to enjoy a peaceful eternity in the netherworld," Zibah pressed, "one must accrue wealth and descendants, but the character of a person is of no consequence."

Naqia shrugged. "It's an abbreviated summary, but yes."

"As an only child, Nasseh has discovered the difficulty of meeting the required provision for Hezi's peaceful eternity. You would face a similar issue in that Esar is your only son. When considering your eternity, you must hope Esar's lineage is an endless dynasty—or your rest is in jeopardy." The woman shifted uncomfortably, and Zibah continued before she could cut her off. "But for all those who serve Yahweh, provisions for the afterlife are made here on earth through faithful sacrifices to Yahweh. Regardless of wealth or lineage, anyone who offers sacrifices with the faith of Abraham can live in paradise after death."

Naqia's warmth turned cool, but it was too late to turn back now. "Your abba would have been taught the sacrifices from the law of Moses, based on substitutionary sacrifices for sin, that allowed a penitent heart to fellowship with the one true God. The substitutionary sacrifices are most often unblemished bulls or lambs or goat—"

"I remember," Naqia said. "My abba told stories of butchering goats during your Feast of Passover." She sniffed and picked at her cuticles. "But my mother's skills as an āšipūtu proved more powerful."

Zibah's heart ached at the woman's deeply rooted deception. *Yahweh, only You can show her the truth.* "You asked me if Yahweh killed Hezi, and my answer is *no,* but to understand that his death was a sacrifice, you must understand that substitutionary sacrifice is necessary to wipe away sin so God's people can restore fellowship with Him. Remember Hezi's dung beetle? Though he was committed to wiping out sin in our nation, some held on to their idolatry and sin. Hezi was stricken with the same plague that wiped out 185,000 of your husband's soldiers."

"Senn said it was Jerusalem's āšipūtu that killed his soldiers." A spark of fear flashed in her eyes. "Your magicians' dark arts were stronger than those of Senn's sorcerer."

"Hezi tolerated no dark arts during his reign, Naqia. *Yahweh* struck down the Assyrians. No one except Hezi got sick in Jerusalem—*he* was the substitutionary sacrifice for our sin." Zibah let her words settle into the woman's heart before adding water to the seeds she'd planted. "My Hezi wasn't sinless, nor did he die like the sacrificial lambs on the temple altar. I believe his *near* death halted Yahweh's judgment on the nation of Judah's idolatry—much like an eternal King will reign in paradise after He has taken away all sin."

"I've never heard it all explained like that." Shulle's face was aglow, her cheeks wet with tears.

"Don't believe a word of it," Naqia said, glowering. "Tell me, Zibah, since you're the conjurer of Hebrew legends, is it Yahweh that makes Shulle barren?" She shifted her focus to Shulle. "Or has your daughter-in-law used her āšipūtu skills to deny your son an heir?"

47

Whether you turn to the right or to the left,
your ears will hear a voice behind you, saying,
"This is the way; walk in it."

ISAIAH 30:21

Naqia's question hung in the air like Leviathan, ready to crush me in its jaws. The laws of every nation demanded the execution of a queen who denied her husband an heir to his throne. I had no doubt Naqia loved me. But she wouldn't risk losing her son's favor by helping me commit treason.

A knock on the door broke the silence. The midwife and physician rushed inside.

"Leave," I said.

"But King Manasseh said we were to examine you and—"

"Now!" I shouted, jumping to my feet. Onan's imposing presence encouraged their quick retreat.

I turned toward the balcony. A confession would seal my death. Zibah might understand after living with the pain of King Hezekiah witnessing his brother's death in Molek's fire. But how could Naqia forgive me when her own son sacrificed to gods from all the nations? *Please, Yahweh. Abba and Zibah say You'll hear anyone who believes. Please don't let me die without a substitutionary sacrifice.*

"You're different with Nasseh now than in Nineveh." Naqia's voice was tender. Close. "You're protective. You feared for him when he spoke harshly to Esar."

I couldn't even look at her, let alone speak. Focused on the white clouds and blue sky, I nodded.

"The night we first met, you were too frightened to bear a child. Is that why—"

"No, no!" I said. "I wanted to give Nasseh a son until . . ." I squeezed my eyes shut, realizing I'd just confessed.

"Tell her why, Shulle." Zibah stepped in front of me. "Tell Naqia what my son does to the children of Judah."

I stared at the two women I loved and respected most. What could I say except the truth? "I refuse to love a child only to have it thrown into Molek's belly."

"Wha—" Naqia gasped.

I lifted my chin, surprised how freeing the truth felt. "Could you do it, Naqia? Could either of you lie with the man you loved, terrified you'd bear his child and have it snatched away?"

Zibah's eyes glistened, her empathy palpable, but Naqia's rage grew into a living thing. "How many innocent children has your imbecile husband thrown into a fire?"

Startled by her ire, I answered, "One, but he only did it because Esar sacrificed his sons."

"Esar would never!" Naqia looked as if I'd slapped her.

"But when he gathered troops to seize the throne from his brothers, his letter said he made sacrifices to *every* nation's gods—including Baal. Nasseh was certain he'd included Molek and Chemosh—"

She'd already begun shaking her head. "Assyria and Babylon would never engage in such a primitive practice. Esar abhors it." Lifting her hand to cup my cheek, her eyes softened. "But your crime is equal to your husband's, my girl, and I must disclose both to my son for his judgment."

Her words landed like a nest of snakes in my belly. I covered a shriek of panic and nodded my understanding. I looked at the balcony, considered leaping from it, but Zibah pulled me into her arms.

"Yahweh will make a way," she whispered. Kind words but little help. So far, the only way I'd seen Yahweh provide involved a sharp sword and saw.

Naqia separated us. "I must place you both under Assyrian guards so you won't warn Nasseh about his coming judgment. Shulle, you can show me to a chamber and then rest until tonight's banquet." She turned her attention to Zibah. "Pray your god will move Esar's heart to be gracious, but don't expect it."

Abruptly, Naqia laced her arm through mine and pulled me toward the door.

"Naqia." Zibah's voice was calm but firm. "You have great influence over the king of Assyria, and you know the truth of your Hebrew heritage. I hope you spend your afternoon on something more important than breeding puppies. Our children's eternity is at stake."

I held my breath, watching two strong queen mothers battle with their eyes.

Without a reply, Naqia fairly dragged me from the chamber and barked at Onan, "Your mistress is confined to her chamber. I'll send my guards to ensure it."

"My mistress won't leave but send your guards if you like." He bowed politely, his composure seeming to disarm her further.

"Find me a chamber," she said, tugging me down the hall.

I entered the room next to Yaira's and pulled her into a tight embrace. "Calm yourself, Naqia." Was she the one trembling? Or was I? Silence answered, and only then did I notice my shoulder wet with her tears. We wept together in the bond of friends too long apart and divided by life.

"Zibah is a fine woman," she said, when we released each other and wiped our faces dry. "I know why you've honored her so in your letters. This god you both serve will reward you for your faithfulness, I'm sure of it." Determination blazed in her eyes. "I'll make sure of it."

Relief swept over me. "Thank you, Naqia." Feeling more hope about my own fate, I was curious about my friend's. "If you believe in Yahweh's power to reward, why not serve Him yourself?"

"I could never return to the narrow ways of a righteous god. Me and my kind . . ." She raised her chin, her emotional armor restored. "I deserve every evil that comes to me, Shulle, but you deserve happiness. I'll find Esar and be back shortly to prepare you for the banquet."

She reached for the door, but I stopped her. "Naqia, you can't just wander around the palace."

"Of course I can," she said, grinning. "I'm the Queen Mother of Assyria."

The door clicked shut behind her, and I was left alone to wonder. Was Naqia the answer to Ima Zibah's prayer, the way Yahweh would use to deliver me?

48

Do not give any of your children to be
sacrificed to Molek, for you must not profane
the name of your God. I am the LORD.

LEVITICUS 18:21

S ince Shulle was entertaining the queen mothers and King Esar preferred sword drills with his men to an audience with Judah's king,
Nasseh relegated himself to dog duty. He'd walked Shulle's new
puppies in his garden, watched them attack butterflies, and offered them
dried fish for a snack. He returned with them to his chamber, where they
now barked and pounced, tumbling across his red carpet. Their antics
were a distraction but couldn't salve his wounded pride.

He abandoned his chamber for the balcony, and his new friends followed. "She's nothing like Ima," he said to the duo. Both tilted their heads,
confused. "We must work on your Hebrew."

Peering over the balcony railing, he watched his bustling capital city.
Harvest season filled the market with every kind of fruit, vegetable, and
grain, but the Assyrians were like a swarm of locusts. They'd swindled the
merchants, paid with threats instead of shekels, and left the city bare. Spot-
ting Naqia's carriage beside his stables, his anger flared again. From the
moment she stepped out of that coach, she'd commandeered his kingdom.
She was a spoiled, emotional old woman, ten times more troublesome than
Saba or Shebna had been.

"By the gods, where are you, King Manasseh?" Naqia's shrill voice
invaded his chamber. The traitorous puppies ran to greet her.

Furious, he marched in, ready to confront her, but Esar stood beside her with six of his guards. "You burned Gemeti's son in the fire?" The veins on his neck pulsed with rage.

"Of course. Right after you sacrificed to Chemosh and Molek."

Naqia turned to her son. "You see? I told you he was an imbecile."

"I'm not an imbecile!" Nasseh shouted.

Before his last word, Esar's dagger was at his throat. "Never disrespect my mother."

The blade bit Nasseh's neck. "Yet you let her disrespect your friend?"

Esar shoved him toward the couches. "I've told you a thousand times, Nasseh. Kings don't have friends. We form alliances." He waved his guards out of the chamber.

"But you're *my* dearest friend," Nasseh said, wiping a trickle of blood from his neck.

The old hag glared at him, while Esar paced and massaged his neck.

"What have I done wrong? When I sent my condolences, you said you'd sacrificed to *all* the gods of your empire. I did the sa—"

Esar roared and scrubbed his face before sitting on the couch across from him. "Human sacrifice is an abomination, Nasseh. You have a brilliant mind, but you do stupid things, and I don't have time to coddle you."

"King Baal of Tyre sacrificed three children last year," Nasseh pointed out. "Excessive, I agree."

Esar rolled his eyes. "I've turned a blind eye when King Baal offers a child, but he never kills his own son, Nasseh. Not a *prince*. How do you expect to have an heir if you kill your sons?"

"Gemeti's son wasn't my heir," Nasseh said. "Only Shulle's son will rule Judah. I have two sons and ten daughters and more children on the way. I can add more concubines anytime—"

Esar laid back on the couch, now massaging his temples. "You're going to wish you had that son back, Nasseh, when I tell you what Mother discovered this afternoon."

"Ask Esar how quickly an heir can be taken from you," the old witch interrupted.

"Quiet, Mother," he said, still massaging his neck.

But Naqia stood over him like a ruffled hen. "My son named his two eldest sons heirs to the kingdom. His firstborn would rule the empire from Nineveh; the second born would rule Babylon alone. Within a week of his proclamation, the gods claimed the firstborn with lung sickness." She leaned toward Nasseh, seething. "You're a fool to squander royal lives."

Nasseh bit back his anger and shot off the couch, pacing to quell his inner chaos. "I heard of your son's death, Esar, and sent another condolence letter. I didn't receive a reply."

"He doesn't want your sympathy," Naqia said. "He wants you to rule like a man."

Esar stood, halting Nasseh's pacing. "Did you kill Gemeti's child because she begged to return to Babylon when I came here four years ago?"

The revelation lifted Nasseh's eyes to meet Esar's. "I didn't know Gemeti betrayed me, but no. I told you. I offered my only prince, the only son of my two wives—my greatest treasure—given to the gods so they'd secure Assyria's throne for my dearest friend. And he did, Esar." The gravity of his mistake made his stomach roll. "I thought I knew your mind without your command being spoken—like you'd trained me. If I was wrong—" He drew his dagger and placed it at his own throat. "Speak, and I'll obey without hesitation."

Esar stared into his eyes. "Lower the dagger," he said. "Queen Shulle has meted out a greater punishment that I'll announce publicly at tonight's banquet."

Relief fought dread. "I don't understand." Nasseh sheathed his dagger while Esar picked up a puppy and retreated to the balcony.

The old crone spit on Nasseh's bare foot. "Esar sees something valuable in you. It's the only reason you're alive. I see something unique and lovely in your queen, which is the reason Esar pardoned her for the crime she's committed against you."

Nasseh finished wiping off his foot, refusing to look at her. "What are you talking about?"

"Shulle used the āšipūtu skills Belit taught her to prevent your seed from growing in her womb."

"What?" He shouted. "No, she . . . she wouldn't—" The colors in the room were suddenly too bright. He squeezed his eyes closed and clutched at his hair. The sounds of trumpets and cymbals erupted inside his mind. The air was too close. He stumbled toward his bedchamber, tearing down the dividing curtain. The home of their passion. The site of her betrayal.

"Denied you an heir." Naqia's lips still moved, but only snippets penetrated the clatter in his head. "Afraid you'd sacrifice her child to Molek . . . you must punish her . . . crime of marital deception."

Nasseh doubled over, gasping for breath. Panic gripped him. Escape his only thought. Where could he run? Who would help him? Shebna was gone. Shulle a betrayer. Belit her teacher. *Ima.* Ima could soothe the chaos. Ease the pain.

Fleeing his chamber, Nasseh heard shouting. He passed guards and Assyrians. Nobles and envoys. Shocked. Startled. "Get out of my way!" Ascending the harem steps two at a time, he rushed to the end of the hall. Past Onan, he burst into Ima's chamber. Breathless.

"Nasseh?" She'd been crying.

"Shulle deceived me."

More tears. "Yes, my love, I know."

"She called me an imbecile!"

"Shulle?"

"No, Naqia!"

"Nasseh, please." She opened her arms. "Please, may I hold you?"

The chamber felt like a cage. The air too thick to breath. "Ima . . ." He stepped closer. So did she.

"I won't trap you," she whispered. "I just want to calm you."

His fists clenched wildly, but something more powerful than chaos sent him hurtling into her arms. She stumbled back at the impact but left her arms loose around him as promised. Not suffocating. Not confining or restricting. His spasming frame towered over her, but somehow her smallness radiated peace. Slowly, almost painfully, he felt his tension release. He remained. Abided. And when she released him from her embrace, cold shuddered through him. The radiance on her face said she would hold him again if he wished.

"What will you do?" she asked. "About Shulle, I mean."

Sorting through the madness, he recalled Naqia's words. "Esar pardoned her," he said. "I can't kill her. Perhaps I'll send her with Esar's captive train to Nineveh after the Egyptian campaign."

"You know what happens to captives as beautiful as Shulle."

His Shulle. Beautiful Shulle. Treacherous Shulle.

A loud knock. An Assyrian guard entered without invitation. "King Esar to see King Manasseh and the queen mother."

Esar strolled in as if Jerusalem and the palace were his. "Good, Nasseh. You've recovered from your tantrum." He nodded respectfully to Ima. "My mother is high spirited, and though she means well, she can at times be—"

"A jackal?" Nasseh suggested.

Esar raised a single brow. "I was thinking *overbearing*. In the spirit of cooperation, I give you the satisfaction of publicly announcing Queen Shulle's dethroning and the consequences of her deception. After which you will finally, rightfully, announce Gemeti as your queen." With another nod at Ima, he turned and left the chamber, leaving Nasseh to consider the consequences Shulle should suffer for his pain.

49

As you do not know the path of the wind,
    or how the body is formed in a mother's womb,
so you cannot understand the work of God,
    the Maker of all things.

I waited for Naqia in the guest chamber for what felt like days. When the shadows grew long and my belly growled, hope of a way out dwindled. I peeked out the door and found an unfamiliar guard. "Excuse me, but have you seen the queen mother?"

"Which one?" His smirk was typical of Assyrian arrogance. Why had I hoped to get any information from him?

When I tried to leave the chamber, he snagged my arm and shoved me roughly inside. "You will remain in the guest chamber until I escort you to the banquet."

"Am I to go to the banquet looking like this?"

"It won't matter how you look." His smirk turned to a sneer, and my hope turned to ash.

Closing the door behind me, I leaned against it and slid to the floor in disbelief. I'd been so sure Naqia would save me. So certain Yahweh had heard Zibah's prayers on my behalf. What a fool.

The sun had long set when the hateful guard opened the door without knocking. "It's time." His fingers bit into my arm, hurrying me down the harem steps toward the courtroom.

When the double cedar doors opened, I experienced a royal banquet from the view of the accused. All attention was on me as usual, but I didn't lay my hand on Nasseh's arm to begin our march. Instead, the guard shoved me up the center aisle, and my knees turned to bread dough, failing to hold me. He circled my waist and carried me too quickly toward judgment.

I focused on my husband who stood at the edge of the dais. I saw others in the periphery. King Esar standing beside him. Nobles and soldiers seated at tables on the dais and banquet floor. Nameless, faceless someones who held no sway over my life—or my death. The guard planted me like a tree at the edge of the crimson carpet. Shaking violently, I kept my eyes on Nasseh, transfixed by his loathing.

"I present to you, Queen Meshullemeth," he said to his guests, still looking at me. "A woman guilty of both treason and marital deception." Whispered awe fluttered through the gathering but he continued, "She denied me an heir using the skills taught by this woman." He pointed to the rear entrance.

I turned and saw Belit approaching, shackled between two guards. She spit in my face when she arrived, her eyes black as the night—without a single spark of demon power. "At least you'll roam the netherworld with me."

"It's Sheol, Belit," I said with the certainty of the condemned. "And we will join Dohd in the eternal torture of those who deny the one true God."

The shock on her face gave way to panic when Nasseh levied his judgment. "Belit, chief āšipūtu and advisor to the king, you will be executed at dawn for your part in my wife's treachery."

"I had nothing to do with—" The guards thrust the blunt end of his spear into her belly, and she fell to her knees.

"I acted alone," I said. "Belit knew nothing—"

Nasseh descended the dais and towered over me. "We never act alone, Shulle. Our actions affect many people." He nodded to the guards at the rear entry, who opened the doors. My knees gave way at the sight of Abba, Penina, and Jericho shackled to guards. The girls' hysterical cries made Abba's resignation equally horrific.

"Please, Nasseh." I wet his feet with tears. "Please, don't hurt them.

Kill me. Torture me. Anything!" I gripped his legs, but he pushed me away and stepped out of my reach.

King Esar's voice rang out. "Because the great Naqia, Queen Mother of Assyria, witnessed Queen Meshullemeth's kindness to a handmaid in Nineveh, I've pardoned her from death, and King Manasseh will impose his merciful judgment."

Nasseh lifted me by one arm to face the nobility of Judah. "This woman is Meshullemeth bat Haruz, a maidservant in Jerusalem's palace for all her days, and the girls she exploited as personal slaves will be returned to their parents." He pressed his lips against my ear to whisper his final judgment. "Your abba will continue as my sons' tutor—until I discard him in the streets to beg." I covered a low moan, and he shoved me back at my guard. "Take her to the prison while I decide where she'll serve."

He returned to the dais, and King Esarhaddon raised his goblet. "Now that we've dispensed with the unpleasantness, let's celebrate the crowning of Judah's Queen Gemeti!"

I staggered through the cheering crowd, head bowed, as my guard led me from the courtroom. The cries of my girls still rang in my ears, and Abba's sorrow would forever be burned in my mind—but they would be allowed to live. As would I. Esar pardoned me because of the kindness I'd shown to Adnah a lifetime ago—but it was Yahweh who had saved me. My world was shattered, but Yahweh made a way. The God who hated me had made a way.

50

The LORD is good,
   a refuge in times of trouble.
He cares for those who trust in him.

NAHUM 1:7

669 BC, Eighteen Months Later

ibah listened as Shulle read one of Abba's scrolls, the words pouring over her soul like warm oil.

Therefore this is what the LORD, who redeemed Abraham,
   says to the descendants of Jacob:
   "No longer will Jacob be ashamed;
   no longer will their faces grow pale.
When they see among them their children,
   the work of my hands,
   they will keep my name holy."

The day Nasseh came to Zibah's chamber for comfort had marked a turning in their relationship. He'd asked her opinion on Shulle's punishment, and she suggested he consider both justice and mercy—and then requested Shulle as her personal maid. He'd agreed on the condition that his ex-queen be absent whenever he visited Zibah's chamber, which he did daily. Shortly after their agreement was struck, four large baskets of scrolls had been delivered to her door—the scrolls of Yahweh's prophets.

Shulle set aside this morning's reading. "What should I bring from the kitchen for our midday meal?"

"Would you mind checking on Yaira first?" It was the third day in a row she and Adnah hadn't joined them for the readings.

"Of course, I'll—"

A mournful wail erupted from Yaira's chamber, and Shulle jumped to her feet. "Stay here!"

"No! Help me stand." Zibah stretched out a hand from beneath the blanket tucked around her. The blanket dropped as Shulle took her hand. Together they hurried to the door and flung it open.

Yaira's chamber door was open. Her maid wailed. Kenaz and Adnah knelt over her body, weeping.

The floor beneath Zibah felt like it was tilting. Shulle steadied her.

"Yesterday Yaira asked for the saffron-colored thread for her weaving," Zibah muttered absently.

Shulle pulled her into a hug, shaking with sobs. "Yaira is seeing all manner of colors around the great throne, Ima Zibah."

"She's not your ima." Nasseh's voice wrenched them apart.

Shulle bowed, keeping her face shielded with her veil of loose curls. "Forgive me, my king. I didn't realize you were coming."

"She was my doda." His voice cracked, and he pulled Zibah under his arm. "Return to Ima's chamber, Meshullemeth."

"No!" Zibah grabbed Shulle's arm. "I need you both while I tell Yaira goodbye."

He turned away, sniffing and swallowing great gulps. "All right," he whispered to Shulle. "You may accompany Ima, but don't speak." Her son, even more stubborn than his abba, refused to admit his continuing love for Shulle. But they were together to say goodbye to Yaira. She would like that.

Someone placed Zibah's woolen blanket over her shoulders. She turned and saw Onan's eyes full of tears. "You mustn't catch a chill, Queen Mother."

What precious people Yahweh had placed in her life.

Steadied between her children's strong arms, she entered Yaira's chamber. Tears streamed down Kenaz's cheeks while the palace physician gave his report.

"The gods simply took her," the man said.

Kenaz offered him a few pieces of silver for his worthless comment and escorted him to the door. Then he drew Zibah into his arms. She leaned into him. Kenaz, the only son of Yaira's womb, and the first child of Zibah's heart.

"Did you hear the physician, Doda?" Kenaz asked over the top of her head. "Yahweh took her gently."

"Yahweh?" Nasseh's mocking held warning.

"Nasseh, please," Kenaz whispered. "The physician said 'the gods,' but your ima and I know there is only One."

Zibah had no stomach for debate tonight. Nudging aside her nephew, she crossed the chamber and saw Yaira's empty eyes for the first time. No—it wasn't Yaira—but the earthly shell that once housed her dearest friend. The finality of it overwhelmed her, but the certainty that she was with Jashub brought comfort. *Yahweh, I praise You for her gentle end.*

"Go fetch the mourners, dear," Zibah told the wailing maid. The girl ran out, leaving blessed silence in her wake. Shulle helped Zibah kneel beside Adnah, the precious girl who had seemed like family even before Kenaz married her. The children of their union had become the light of day to Zibah and Shulle after Penina and Jericho were taken away.

"We'll heal together," Zibah said, holding tightly to Shulle's and Adnah's hands.

Kenaz knelt on the other side of Yaira's body.

Nasseh paced behind Kenaz, agitation growing. "Aren't you angry that Yahweh killed her? He's taken both your parents now."

Zibah wanted to rail at his childish bitterness but dared not crack their fragile relationship.

"Everyone dies, Nasseh." Kenaz stood to face him. "Shouldn't I instead be grateful Yahweh took her without suffering?"

"And if her death had been slow and torturous, Kenaz? Would you admit Yahweh is capricious and uncaring?"

Anger shadowed Kenaz's features.

Zibah held her breath. *Please, Nephew, don't retaliate and add your life to our loss tonight.*

Their silent impasse lasted for what seemed an eternity, but Kenaz finally placed a hand on his cousin's shoulder. "If Ima had suffered, Nasseh, I might have been angry. I might have even questioned Yahweh's plan. But I would praise Him now because Ima will never feel pain again." He squeezed Nasseh's shoulder gently. "I don't believe Yahweh is angered by sincere questions or even when we express anger, but He commands our trust, my king. I hope someday you can trust Him."

Nasseh shrugged off his hand and pointed to Yaira's lifeless form. "That's what happens when you trust Yahweh."

He stormed out of the room, leaving Zibah's heart even heavier. "I'm sorry, Kenaz. He doesn't know how to—"

Her nephew helped her stand and tilted her chin up to face him. "Doda, you never need apologize for Nasseh. I love him, and since he appointed me to his council, I see the pressures he faces. Ima told me about your vision—that someday Yahweh will capture and rebuild his heart. Until then, we pray and remain faithful." He kissed her forehead, and she hugged him fiercely. After a deep sigh, he held her at arm's length. "Would you and Shulle help Adnah prepare Ima's body while I make the arrangements for her funeral procession?"

"It would be a privilege."

The bittersweet task was the last time Zibah would serve her friend. She and the others tenderly washed and wrapped Yaira's body with bandages and herbs. Weeping while massaging myrrh-scented oil into Yaira's wrinkled hands, Zibah led them in singing David's Shepherd psalm until the professional mourners arrived. Their wails accompanied the small funeral processional to the tombs in the Garden of Uzza where both Abba and Jashub were buried.

All three would have been proud of Kenaz. In spite of Nasseh's sulking, Kenaz boldly proclaimed Yahweh's faithfulness at his ima's burial, ignoring armed guards and idolatrous priests. No arrests were made. No pagan rites were spoken. And Kenaz's tribute to the one true God stood unchallenged and sparkling, like Solomon's temple before Yahweh's presence left it.

Zibah found a bench in the garden after the others had gone, sat down, closed her eyes, and lingered in the holy moment. Startled by a hand on her shoulder, she turned to find a little boy with dirty cheeks and wide eyes holding out a hand-sized gift wrapped in sackcloth.

"What's this?" she asked, receiving the small bundle.

"It's a gift from my—" He looked around like a conspirator and then whispered, "From my *family*. My name is Nahum, and I'm going to be Yahweh's prophet someday."

Fear for the boy shot through her, and she looked behind her, hoping none of the palace guards had heard. When she turned back to warn him—he was gone. She covered a grin at Yahweh's protection and the introduction of a new friend. Making sure again that she wasn't being watched, she unwrapped the small treasure and found one of Abba Isaiah's gold rings.

She rewrapped it quickly, her mind spinning with possibilities. Jashub had never worn this ring, and their other brothers—Kadmiel and Maher—had been killed in military service years ago. Who would Abba have entrusted with such a treasure? *"From my family,"* the boy had said. *"I'm going to be Yahweh's prophet someday."* With a certainty born of faith, she knew. Yahweh had saved a remnant of prophets somewhere in Judah, and He was preparing them to rise again.

PART 4

But Manasseh led Judah and the people of Jerusalem astray, so that they did more evil than the nations the Lord had destroyed before the Israelites.

The Lord spoke to Manasseh and his people, but they paid no attention. So the Lord brought against them the army commanders of the king of Assyria.

2 CHRONICLES 33:9–11

51

Then the LORD said, "Just as my servant Isaiah
has gone stripped and barefoot for three years . . .
so the king of Assyria will lead away stripped
and barefoot the Egyptian captives and Cushite
exiles, young and old, with buttocks bared—to
Egypt's shame."

ISAIAH 20:3–4

668 BC, Seven Months Later

Shulle rode behind Nasseh on his white stallion through a lush field
in Nineveh, her chin resting on his shoulder, while her hands explored him. He turned his head to kiss her, but her eyes wept blood,
her face the color of death. "Wake, my king," she cried. "You must wake."

"My king." Rough hands shook him. "You must wake." Nasseh bolted
upright on his couch. Baka stepped aside, nodding permission for a messenger to hand over his scroll.

"A message from the governor of Lachish, my king." The messenger
was just a boy. His hands shook violently, while his eyes flitted between the
growling dogs at Nasseh's side.

Nasseh shooed the boy away and swiped a hand down his face, wishing he could wipe the nightmare from his mind. He reached down to pet
Perez and Zerah, the twin hounds. He'd named them after the patriarch
Judah's offspring. Judah's daughter-in-law had been impossible to be rid
of—much like Naqia—but she'd blessed Judah with twins. Naqia's gifted

twins were now perfectly trained to Nasseh's hand signals and ready to breed. Their puppies would make fine additions to Judah's weaponry.

Breaking the scroll's seal, he read the governor's hastily scrawled message:

Assyria installation of new vassal kings in Egypt disastrous.
Assyrian frustrations meted out in raids on southern Judean
villages. Send troops quickly to defend.

"Orders, my king?" Baka waited.

Nasseh was at a loss. If he sent Judean troops to defend against Assyrian aggressors in Lachish, Esar would perceive it as an act of war. Though Nasseh had cooperated completely during the Egyptian campaign two years ago, Nasseh's sacrifice of Gemeti's son had deeply scarred their friendship. A grave miscalculation. He dared not make another.

"Summon Kenaz and Gemeti immediately," he said.

Two years ago, when Esar conquered Memphis and sent Tirhakah fleeing to Upper Egypt, the Assyrians marched twenty-one Cushite princes in a captive train through Jerusalem—barefoot and naked—just as Saba Isaiah had prophesied. Though he'd never admit it, Nasseh was haunted by the twenty-one dark-skinned princes marching toward Jericho with the same regal pride he'd admired in Tirhakah.

The event revived Yahwist sympathizers and spawned a new breed of Yahweh prophets who, instead of shouting in the streets, left scrolls of Saba's prophecy in unavoidable places—palace, temple, and city markets—so all Jerusalem knew the shackled, naked, and barefoot captives fulfilled the words written during Abba's reign.

Esar cared nothing about quelling a minor rebellion in Judah. He concentrated on training the Cushite princes to become vassals like Nasseh but selected roguish commanders to install them in Egypt instead of completing the task himself. No wonder his new vassals rebelled.

"Baka," Nasseh said, realizing he required one more advisor. "Summon Ima also."

"As you wish, my king."

Nasseh could recite most of Saba Isaiah's prophecies, but Ima knew their meaning.

Kenaz rushed into Nasseh's chamber, bleary-eyed, beard askew. "Yes, my king?"

"We'll wait until Gemeti and Ima arrive," Nasseh said. "Perez and Zerah are happy to see you."

The dogs had already tackled Kenaz, rolling and playing with him on the carpet, their mouths large enough to clamp down on his head. But Kenaz won slobbery kisses with pieces of dried fish from his pocket. A plentiful treat with which he spoiled them regularly.

Nasseh watched his cousin and considered his closest advisors. Kenaz, besides a welcome toy for his hounds, was always prompt but too candid with his wisdom. Gemeti was always late, lingering too long at a mirror before appearing. Her role, however, was important since she was the only āšipūtu he trusted—though she wasn't as accurate as Belit had been. Ima was steady. Predictable. Always loving. Even when she disagreed.

The familiar twinge of regret sent him to the balcony for some air. Shulle still filled his thoughts day and night. His dreams of her had been consistently foreboding of late. He couldn't ask Gemeti to interpret. Much was forbidden between them. Gemeti was useful, beautiful, and Esar's favored queen, but who would bear Nasseh's heir since she now refused his bed?

The sound of women's voices drew him back inside. Ima and Gemeti had arrived together, amiable if not friends.

Without preamble, Nasseh began. "Assyrian troops returning from Egypt have raided some of our southern villages. Gemeti, since the starry host of the Scales is most powerful now, have the priests make offerings to Shamash to see which way the scales tip. Retaliation or diplomacy. Kenaz, poll the council members to see how the people would react to closing Jerusalem's gates if the Assyrians come demanding more supplies."

He turned to Ima and saw tears slipping down her cheeks. "What's wrong?"

"Nasseh," she said, voice quaking, "have you considered that these Assyrian attacks could be Yahweh's judgment?"

He shook his head. "Have we not already been judged in years past? Yahweh's power is spent, Ima."

"Please, my king, listen." She laid a trembling hand on his arm. "Haven't you included me in this morning's meeting because you believe I know Yahweh's ways and prophecies?" She paused, gracious enough to await his nod. "I've seen prophecy and judgment fulfilled more than once in my lifetime, Nasseh—in nuanced ways. Many prophets have predicted Judah's continued judgment. What if the raids on our southern villages are a continuation of Yahweh's judgment? I'm too old to become a captive like I was as a child." Her tears returned, and she squeezed his arm, "Nor do I wish to see Abba's prophecy fulfilled and have my *descendants* taken away in chains."

Nasseh removed his arm from her touch and addressed all three counselors. "Thank you all for your input. Kenaz, Gemeti, report your findings to me, and I'll call a council meeting midmorning. Ima, you need not attend." He extended his arm toward the door. Stoic until they were gone, he then released the compulsions that drove him.

Fists clenching wildly, he went to his washbasin, submerged his hands in the myrtle-scented water, and thought of Shulle. Why had he invited Ima? Did she have contact with this new wave of prophets? Was she conspiring to protect and strengthen their cause like Dohd Jashub had been?

Another knock on his door snapped his nerves like a bowstring. "What?"

Baka again. "Another messenger, my king."

"Where is he?"

"Dead, my king." Baka held up a blood-stained scroll. "He made it to the Horse Gate with this in his hand—and an arrow in his belly."

Nasseh grabbed the unsealed message. It read simply. "Assyrians riding toward Jerusalem."

The morning turned out differently than Nasseh planned. Instead of a midmorning council meeting, he reclined at a table in his chamber across from Assyria's high commander. The dead messenger had given Nasseh enough time to refresh himself before the Assyrians arrived to break their fast.

"I'm angry that your troops raided my southern villages, Commander." Nasseh offered his guest a plate of goat cheese. "Try this. It's best smeared on bread with a few candied dates."

Shulle loves candied dates.

The man took the plate and smiled. "Thank you, King Manasseh." He ate like a beggar and ignored Nasseh's concern. "Since the vassal kings rebelled, King Esarhaddon will likely march on Egypt with a larger force to completely destroy the Nubian dynasty. You can expect a draft of more Judean soldiers, but it will likely take a year to gather reports from all our spies and draw up battle plans."

"Men from the villages you plundered won't help unless you make restoration, Commander. King Esarhaddon will hear about it if you don't."

With a warrior's quickness, he twisted Nasseh's hand behind him and drove his face into the floor. "My men are tired and hungry," he said. "We'll leave tomorrow with enough supplies to get us to Nineveh, where *I'll* inform King Esarhaddon our mission was successful." He released Nasseh and stomped toward the door but paused before opening it. "You should never agree to remove your dogs from a meeting, King Manasseh—no matter what sad story your guest tells."

He laughed as he opened the door, and Nasseh's war dogs raced inside. The commander quickly shut the door behind him, and Nasseh threw a vase at the wall. "Ah!" *You're an imbecile.* Naqia had called him that, and she was right. He'd believed the commander's ruse that dogs gave him a rash. Lying back on his rug, he stared at the ceiling while Perez and Zerah pressed their heavy bulk against him. They seemed to sense the calm that physical pressure gave him.

As his chaos eased, his thinking cleared. The task he'd given Kenaz was moot. There'd be no closing the gates against the Assyrians now. Perhaps Gemeti had caught a glimpse of the Scales before sunrise. If not, she could divine with a sheep's liver whether he should contact Esar or if contact would further damage their friendship.

He shot to his feet. "Come!" The dogs followed him out of his chamber. Baka offered to attend, but he'd been awake all night. "Get some rest, my friend. I have the dogs."

"Gemeti hates the dogs." Baka grinned.

"That's why I'm taking them."

His guard chuckled, and Nasseh's mood lightened. He didn't often make people laugh. Ruffling the dogs' ears, he jogged up the harem stairs. After meeting with Gemeti, he'd train with the dogs again. They'd keep his mind off Shulle.

Gemeti inhabited Nasseh's childhood chamber, the largest in the harem, at the top of the stairs. Her guards nodded as he entered, and he found her seated on a couch, facing her balcony. "What did you discover from the starry hosts this morning?" he asked on his approach.

"The sky was already too bright when you summoned me, Nasseh. I couldn't make an accurate prediction." She continued her embroidery without even greeting him.

Having been ignored by Assyria's commander, he was determined to have her attention. Wrenching the embroidery from her hands, he tossed it over the balcony railing. The hounds went wild, barking and dashing to the balcony, thinking he'd started one of their games.

Gemeti wasn't as playful. "I want my embroidery." She rose from her couch. "Send someone to fetch it at once."

She was red-cheeked and fuming, her breath smelled like bird droppings, and her hair was unkempt. Nasseh stormed toward the purple curtains partitioning her bedchamber, he yanked them open and his suspicions were confirmed. Maids were making the bed and emptying the waste pot.

Gemeti hurried to her defense. "I was so tired this morning, Nasseh. I harvested roots last night to treat one of your children's illnesses."

Nasseh turned slowly, stalking her like prey. "You went back to sleep after this morning's meeting in my chamber."

She backed away. "The power of the Scales gives success to new beginnings, Nasseh. Any decision for a new beginning, my king, will be blessed by the starry hosts."

Were she not Esar's favorite, he would kill her where she stood. For the moment, he'd find a more subtle way to punish her. "You will—"

A woman's scream rent the air. *Shulle!* Then Ima's reedy voice. "No! No, stop!"

Nasseh ran toward the sounds. "Dogs, come!" Hebrew guards huddled at Ima's door. "What?" he asked, shoving them aside.

"No, my king. Wait!" Onan, stopped him, blood streaming from a gash in his arm.

The dogs growled and lunged, but Nasseh splayed his hand. "Friend!"

Onan stepped back, a wary eye on the hounds. "My king, the Assyrian commander saw Shulle in the hallway and grabbed her. She screamed, and when your ima shouted at him, he took both women into the chamber and locked it." His jaw clenched. "I'm sorry, my king. I tried to free them."

Another scream pushed Nasseh through the guards to the locked door. Panic turned to rage. "Break it down!" Two guards kicked the panel, splintering the heavy cedar. Nasseh and his dogs hesitated at the threshold.

The commander stood at the couches, a dagger poised at Ima's throat. "Send those dogs at me, King, and I'll kill her and the hounds too."

"I wouldn't dream of sending the dogs," Nasseh said. "You might get a rash, right?" Shulle whimpered in a corner, and he took a slow step toward her.

"Leave the maid!" The knife grazed Ima's neck, starting a trickle of blood. "She's the one I want anyway. After our meeting, I saw the maid and assumed she was part of my accommodations. The queen mother tried to stop me. Your guards got a little ambitious." He nodded toward the guards behind Nasseh. "Command them to back away; I'll take your mother and the maid to my chamber, where my men will ensure my safety. I will release the queen mother unharmed and share the maid with my men." He smiled and shrugged. "See? Everyone's happy."

"Queen Naqia will be decidedly unhappy, my friend." The commander's confusion urged Nasseh on. "That *maid*, as you call her, is like a daughter to Assyria's Queen Mother, and the woman you've wounded is her dear friend." The man's face lost its arrogant smirk, and Nasseh scratched Perez behind his ears. "Would you like the *maid* to retrieve Naqia's personal letters to prove it? Or will you lower your blade and move to the servant's quarters with your troops?"

He sheathed his dagger and shoved Ima at Nasseh. "Will you always let Assyria's king and queen mother fight your battles, *Vassal* King?"

Nasseh passed Ima to Onan's waiting arms and beckoned Shulle with a wave. "Not always," he said to the commander. "Sometimes I let my dogs fight for me." With a decisive hand command, he launched the twins like stones from a sling.

"Nooo!" Both women screamed, and Shulle buried her face against his chest.

"Take Ima to Adnah's chamber," he commanded Onan. "Then tend to your wound."

"Shh, now. It's over," he said to Shulle, guiding her down the hall. "You're safe."

Kenaz met them at the top of the harem stairs, breathless. "I heard Doda was—" Perez and Zerah lumbered toward him, muzzles stained with evidence of their training.

"Clean them up," Nasseh said, "and have the cooks prepare a lamb for their evening meal. These dogs have earned a feast."

Gemeti stood in her open doorway. "The *new beginnings* have begun," Nasseh said, "just as you divined. You'll be moved to a smaller chamber. Ima will take your large suite since she'll be assigned new maids. And Shulle will live in *my* chamber—as my wife."

Nasseh cradled Shulle against his chest, pressing his lips against her head. "I love you, my treasure, and you'll never fear anything again."

52

I will maintain my love to him forever,
and my covenant with him will never fail.

PSALM 89:28

Nasseh lifted me into his arms and carried me down the stairs. I curled into his chest, unable to stop myself from shaking. Never fear anything again? I wanted to scream, *I fear you!* He was stealing me away from the happiest two years of my life. I had spent my days teaching Nasseh's sons with my abba and was surrounded by Ima Zibah, Adnah, Kenaz, and their children in the evenings.

"Please, Nasseh," I whispered. "Put me down. I can walk."

He pulled me tighter and whispered, "I almost lost you. I need you in my arms." He kissed my forehead again and looked down at me. His eyes sparkled, and I knew he still loved me. In his way. "Never deceive me again, Shulle." A spark of anger dimmed his affection.

I rested my head against his chest, adding a few more bricks to the wall around my heart. Should I fight or keep silent? Resist or cow to this ruthless king? *"Yahweh will make a way."* The words I'd seen fulfilled for the past two years.

"I want to give you a child, Nasseh, but I won't lose him to Chemosh or Molek." My declaration hung in silence as his chamber guards opened the doors without a command.

Nasseh carried me directly to his bed, laid me down gently, and sat beside me. Hands folded in his lap, he looked at them, not me. "I am your king, Shulle, and you will do as I say." He looked up then, his eyes softened by love. "But I would never intentionally do anything to make you or Esar angry with me."

It was as close as I'd get to a promise. I stared into the windows of his soul to find the boy I'd once loved. *Yahweh, protect me, and show me how to love a man more terrifying than death.*

～

One Year Later

I brushed away a tickle on my cheek, still lost in the blissful haze of half sleep. A cool breeze wafted over me, and another tickle. This one on my nose. I rolled onto my back and groaned, body begging mind for more sleep. A breeze blew over my face, this one rife with the sweet and spicy scent of candied dates. I opened my eyes to my husband's taunting smile.

"I thought you might sleep all day." He brushed curls from my face.

Trapping his hand on my cheek, I turned and kissed his palm. "How long have you been awake?"

Nasseh fed me a candied date before answering. "I didn't sleep much. You're beautiful when you sleep. Did you know it?" His eyes roved my body without subtlety or discretion, his fingers gently stroking my arm. "Do you love me, Shulle?"

He asked every day. Sometimes more than once. I held his face in my hands. "Look at me, Manasseh ben Hezekiah." His eyes met me like a dove, ready to fly. "I love you more now than ever before." It was true, and I could hardly believe it myself.

"But you seem so different."

I wanted to say, *Because for two years I learned to love as Yahweh loves,* but I dared not. Instead, I kissed him tenderly, sharing the sweetness of my date. "A woman changes when she becomes an ima, my love."

"Our son will be a great king." He hovered over me, his hands beginning to roam. I submitted to his passion, realizing the first month of our reunion that Nasseh's love for me wasn't love, but obsession.

During the first months I'd returned to his chamber, Zibah visited daily. We talked of true love that came through Yahweh, the endless Source without condition. Her relentless care and indestructible faith modeled a love that forgave betrayals—the way she'd forgiven me. The way she loved Nasseh despite his wickedness.

"Yahweh will capture his heart," she said one day, "and rebuild him as a righteous king."

"Impossible," I'd scoffed. "Nasseh is unreachable."

"I thought the same of you," she'd said, and I realized—no one was beyond Yahweh's grasp.

I combed my fingers through Nasseh's hair, determined to love the man though I hated his deeds. *Yahweh, protect the baby I carry.*

Nasseh forced another date into my mouth. "Even though we no longer sacrifice to Ishtar, being with you is still better than Gemeti."

I chuckled at the awkward compliment. "Gemeti is nice sometimes, Nasseh."

He kissed away the date syrup on my chin. "She's a leviathan."

"She's still your queen, and you should be kind to her."

"She hates you." He propped himself on one elbow. "Why are you defending her?"

I wanted to say, *Because I want to be blameless when Yahweh judges me at the end of my days.* "I just want to live at peace, Nasseh." I searched for any sign that he might want what I'd found. "Shouldn't we seek peace if we're bringing a baby into the world?"

"There is no peace for a king, Shulle." He laid his head on my belly. "Our children will provide for our peace in the netherworld. I think my concubines and other wives will have borne more than twenty when our child is born. Since you'll always be with me, you'll be provided for as well."

I ached that he didn't know the exact number of his children, but Nasseh's neglect had allowed Zibah reign over the harem. She and Abba taught Nasseh's children and their imas that Yahweh was unlike other gods. Patient, not forcing His will, Yahweh allowed us to choose—even to reject Him if we chose other gods.

"I'm honored that you're concerned for my eternity." It was a safe response. Though I wanted to shout the truth at him, I wouldn't change his mind in a single morning. A lighter topic was in order. "What will we name our little girl?"

"A girl?" He bolted upright. "Did Gemeti divine it was a girl?"

I chose to ignore his obvious disappointment. "Nasseh, do you see me smiling?"

"Yes."

"Would I *ever* go to Gemeti to divine anything?"

A slow grin curved his lips. "You're teasing me!" Scooping me into his arms, he twirled me in circles all the way to the balcony. The dogs followed, barking and ears perked. Nasseh set my feet on the cool tiles and looked east, shading his eyes from the springtime sun.

I felt the vibration under my feet. "The Assyrians are coming."

Fear stripped joy from his handsome face, and Baka rushed into our chamber. "The Assyrians—"

"Get the watchmen on the walls and ready the troops." Nasseh donned his purple robe and called for his steward.

"Is it reprisal for killing their commander?" I asked. "I wrote to Naqia months ago, explaining what happened." She hadn't answered, but I wouldn't tell Nasseh. "Perhaps these are troops sent to quash Egypt's rebellion and dethrone the new vassals. Maybe it has nothing to do with the dead commander."

His steward completed his work, and Nasseh rushed toward the door, Perez and Zerah with him. The tremors grew stronger beneath my feet, and panic overtook me. "My king! Please!"

He halted and looked at me as if waking from a dream. "What, Shulle?"

"I'm afraid, Nasseh. I don't want to wait alone."

He rushed back. "The dogs will stay with you. Bring them to the Throne Hall after you've dressed. I'll protect you and your child, Shulle." He signaled to the dogs to stay and left.

The dogs looked at me and whined. "*My* child?" I asked them.

Quickly choosing a robe, I applied only a touch of color to my lips and cheeks then heard the trumpet's call for the emergency council meeting. My chambermaid worked my curls into a loose braid. I didn't even glimpse in a mirror before rushing out the door and across the hall and through the private entrance of the king's court. Kenaz and Gemeti had arrived before the other counselors and waited beside the dais.

Kenaz offered a quick wink, but Gemeti glared. "Why is she here? She's not Judah's queen."

Nasseh rose from his throne, towering over her. "But I am Judah's king."

Gemeti inclined her head, submissive but barely.

A dozen Assyrian soldiers marched into the courtroom, and Nasseh met them at the front of the dais.

"The great sovereign of Assyria marches against Egypt." Their leader threw a parchment at Nasseh's feet. "I, Manno, new commander of the imperial Assyrian guard, am sent in advance to requisition every soldier in Judah."

Nasseh bent grudgingly to retrieve and scan the message. Stumbling backward, he fell onto his throne.

"Nasseh?" I knelt beside him. "What is it?"

He swallowed with effort and whispered, "Esar died on the march to Egypt. Two weeks ago. In Ashkelon. It's his son, King *Ashurbanipal,* who demands all Judah's soldiers." His features hardened. "Why wasn't I notified immediately of Esar's death, Commander?"

Manno scoffed. "Would an eagle tell an ant it lost a feather?"

Nasseh shot to his feet. "Esarhaddon was my best friend."

Manno choked on a derisive laugh but sobered quickly. "You are a vassal of the Assyrian empire and will submit to King Esarhaddon's chosen heir, who assumed command of the army and empire on this campaign against Egypt. You *will* supply troops, grain, and supplies. To show any resistance becomes a negotiation of how many in Judah die."

Nasseh held his gaze, never flinching. "Tell King Ashurbanipal I will send my fighting men, all the grain he's requested, and all requested supplies. I will, however, keep the watchmen on Judah's walls to maintain order in one of his empire's most lucrative trading posts. He can check his father's records and know I speak truth."

Waiting for the commander's response was excruciating. "Very well," he said. "We march with the required provisions at first light." The Assyrians left without bowing. But at least they left.

Nasseh stared at the doors that swallowed them. "Assyria is no longer our friend and protector. Gemeti, we begin sacrifices to *all* gods tomorrow, demanding Tirhakah's victory over Ashurbanipal."

"All the gods?" I whimpered.

Eyes fixed on his queen, he ignored my question. "I give you the honor of choosing the first child from my harem. Sacrifice another at each new moon until Egypt is victorious."

Kenaz climbed the first step of the dais. "Please don't do this."

Perez and Zerah stood between him and Nasseh, hackles raised and growling. "It's done." The king retreated with his dogs, and his advisors left too. Alone, I laid my hand on my belly and felt my baby move. Tears streamed down my cheeks as fear overwhelmed me. Fear for my child. Fear for Judah. But most of all, fear for myself because—*Yahweh, forgive me*—I wanted Nasseh dead.

It was my child's only hope.

53

Do not put your trust in princes,
in human beings, who cannot save.

PSALM 146:3

664 BC, Four Years Later, Heshvan (November)

asseh leapt out of bed, taking a warrior's stance and panting before realizing the horrible slaughter was a dream—his second nightmare tonight. Perez and Zerah perked their ears but relaxed when only stillness reigned. Donning his robe and leather slippers to protect from winter's chill, Nasseh crept silently to his son's cradle. Shulle had refused a wet nurse, as she'd done with their daughter three years ago, so the babe slept in their chamber. Insanity. How was a new ima to get any rest when constantly awakened by a newborn?

He watched the rise and fall of his son's chest and laid his hand there to feel his beating heart. "You are a strong boy, Amon." Emotion cut off his whisper, but he clenched his teeth, fighting for resolve. "You will please the gods and keep Judah safe."

Four years ago, he'd watched three of his children sacrificed to Molek before reports of Assyria's overwhelming victory over Egypt reached Judah. He knew why the gods had denied his requests and spurned his offerings as he begged for Egypt's defeat of the Assyrians. The concubines' children were no real sacrifice because they meant nothing to Nasseh. He saw them on the day of their births and lined them up in rows at royal functions.

"But you're *my* son," he said, curling Amon's tiny hand around his finger. Shulle's children—both Amon and Bekira—were the jewels of his heart. He'd watched them draw nourishment from Shulle's breast and witnessed their first smiles. He'd celebrated the first time they rolled over. Even the dogs had grown protective of them without being trained.

I must leave Perez and Zerah in the palace during the ceremony. They'd never allow Gemeti to offer Amon in the fire.

"Are you all right?" Shulle's sleepy voice cut him like a knife. "I didn't hear him cry."

"He didn't." Nasseh pulled her into his arms. "Our son sleeps soundly because he's loved."

She rubbed his back, quiet in his embrace. "Are you upset about last night's treaty signing? Do you fear King Baal or the Egyptian princes will betray us?"

"No. Tyre's vengeance for Esar's attack seven years ago will keep them loyal, and Egypt will be the last to suffer if Assyria retaliates against our coalition's demands."

"What's wrong then? I hear something in your voice."

He hugged her tighter. Could he tell her? Would she forgive him? "I've had troubling dreams." *Coward.*

"I still think you regret signing the treaty," she whispered.

He held her at arm's length, memorizing her beauty in the lamplight. "The coalition is Judah's only hope of survival, Shulle. We can't meet Ashurbanipal's tribute demands, and he's nothing like Esar. He doesn't build. He only destroys."

"Then we'll pray he leaves us alone. Aren't the Elamites and Persians keeping him busy in the east?"

He'd noticed her using the word *pray* a lot—like Ima. But he didn't want to challenge her, not with the news he needed to tell her. "The Assyrians are coming, Shulle."

She held her breath. "You received reports?"

"No, but the gods have revealed it in my dreams. Look at me, Shulle." Her eyes glistened in the low glow of warming braziers. She must understand the gods would only give them success if they offered their greatest treasure. "We'll seal the coalition at today's celebration with offerings to the gods of our visiting kings."

He watched the realization dawn. "Tyre worships Baal-*Melqart*," she said.

"Yes, my love, and we will offer—"

She lunged toward Amon, but Nasseh grabbed her, pinning her arms at her sides. "No!" she screamed. "No! You can't kill him!" Shrieking and kicking, she tossed her head like a madwoman.

"Shulle, listen to me!"

The dogs grew agitated and confused, barking and prowling around them. He didn't dare release Shulle to give them a hand signal.

"Friend, friend!" Their growling stopped, but four guards rushed into the chamber.

Two secured her legs. The others lifted her from his arms. She bit one man's arm, and he struck her. Nasseh drew his dagger and drove it into the man's jugular.

Instantly covered in blood, Shulle stilled—as did the remaining guards.

Panting, Nasseh held his dagger at the ready. "You will treat my wife with care." The men nodded, and he wiped the dagger clean before sheathing it. "Take her to the queen mother's chamber. Today, she makes the greatest sacrifice in Judah. The gods and *we* will honor her for it." The men carried her to the door, and Nasseh called out after them. "Make sure neither my wife nor Ima attends the treaty celebration."

54

He sacrificed his children in the fire in the
Valley of Ben Hinnom.

2 CHRONICLES 33:6

Get your hands off me!" I screeched as soon as Nasseh's chamber
door closed behind me. The guards placed my feet on the mosaic tile, and I broke into a sprint toward the harem staircase.
Would Nasseh sacrifice our three-year-old daughter too? The guards
chased me up the stairs and followed me to Bekira's room.

The maid bolted to her feet, blocking Bekira's bed the moment she
saw the guards. "I'm taking Bekira to Ima Zibah's chamber," I said, scooping up my sleeping three-year-old and charging past Nasseh's men.

"Open the door!" I shouted at Onan. Obeying without question, he
let me pass. I stopped on the threshold, whirling on my pursuers. "Leave!
You've done as the king asked. The queen mother's guards will tend us
now." I slammed the door with my foot and pressed my back against it,
listening to the men outside.

"By order of King Manasseh, the queen mother and Mistress Shulle
are forbidden to attend today's treaty celebration and sacrifices."

"Ima?" Bekira lifted her head and rubbed sleep from her eyes.

"Shulle?" Zibah held a lamp aloft and stood at the curtained partition
separating her sleeping chamber from the sitting area. Her eyes widened.
"Is that blood on your robe, love?" She started toward me, and her show of
concern threatened my thinly veiled hysteria.

"It's not my blood. Please, Ima. May I lay her in your bed while we
speak privately?" I walked toward the chamber while asking. I had to remain calm for my daughter. Hysteria would only frighten her more.

She started to whine. "I want to play with *Savta*." But Bekira's eyes were closing when I laid her down.

"You may play with Savta when the sun rises, my love. Sleep now so Yahweh can help you grow big and strong." My throat tightened around the words. *Yahweh, please keep her alive to grow big and strong.* I turned away quickly. Zibah tucked the blankets snuggly around Bekira while I changed into a clean robe the dear woman had already laid out for me.

"Your savta loves you." She kissed my daughter's cheek and left the lamp in a high niche on the wall. Her expression filled with concern, she laced her arm through mine and led me to our favorite couch.

I was shaking violently by the time we sat down. "He's going to kill our son!" I covered my uncontrolled wail with both hands, trying to protect my sleeping daughter from a truth she couldn't yet grasp.

"He wouldn't." Zibah grabbed me, and we rocked together. "He loves Amon."

I leapt off the couch. "You said we should trust Yahweh. You said He would build Nasseh into a man I could love."

Head bowed, long gray hair hanging in stringy tendrils, she looked small, powerless. Like Yahweh. Why had I trusted any god?

"How can you sit there and do nothing while my son is murdered?" My hysteria vanished as seething rage replaced fear. "Will Yahweh do nothing too? Sit idle and watch while my son is offered to a demon they call Baal-Melqart?"

She lifted weepy eyes, shaking her head. "I don't know."

Stunned. Appalled. I groped for a response. "That's it?" I screamed. Bekira whimpered, and I ran to quiet her. "Shh, my love. Ima's sorry. I'll talk quieter." I hummed the fish song, and she was asleep before the second verse.

I returned and Zibah had retrieved her spindle and a basket of wool. She sat on the edge of the couch, letting the spindle whirl while her hands spun the wool into perfectly even thread.

"How can you spin when your grandson is about to be sacrificed?"

She kept spinning.

"If He ordained Sennacherib's murder by his own sons, why can't someone kill Nasseh before he murders *my* son?"

Her head shot up, eyes lit with fire. "Do you think Yahweh stops a beating heart without care? How would He differ from earthly kings if He acted on impulse, disregarding eternity?"

I thought of the guard I'd bitten a few moments ago and Nasseh's quick dagger. Is that the action I demanded of Yahweh now? *Yes, Yahweh, if it saves my son.*

But the realization that Nasseh would be damned to Sheol for eternity buckled my knees and bowed my head. "So, we can do nothing to save Amon? It's hopeless?"

Zibah tipped up my chin. "We're *helpless* in this moment, Shulle, but we're never *hopeless*. Not as long as we serve El Shaddai, the Almighty One."

She'd been just as grieved as I when she heard the news, panicked even. "How?" I asked, more in desperation than in wonder. "How can you so quickly overcome your fear and speak with such certainty? And why do you still trust a God who promised twenty-two years ago to save your son but—" Tears choked my words. *Save her son. Not mine.* I pressed the balls of my hands against my eyes. Anger, fear, confusion, and faith roiled inside me. "How can I trust a God who is silent and invisible and feels so far away when I need comfort *now? Here!*" I pounded my chest and melted into a puddle.

Gentle arms enfolded me. "I don't understand why Yahweh allows evil to win or why Hezi had to die or why Nasseh has destroyed everything his abba believed in." She laid her cheek on my head and sighed. "My fear still rages, my precious Shulle, but of this I'm absolutely certain." She swallowed several times, and I knew she, too, was fighting for control. "My God is good. He has a plan. And His victory will somehow be bigger than our sorrow."

She gripped my shoulders and looked into my eyes. "And that's why I keep my hands busy, spinning my prayers into thread and weaving my praise into patterned cloth. If you keep busy with me, we'll make a garment for Manasseh that covers him with Yahweh." Releasing me, she held out her hand. "Now, give me a little help to get back on that couch."

I blindly obeyed, letting her faith command us both. While the lamps burned dimly, we used the spindles in silence, and I begged the God of Abraham, Isaac, Jacob, *and* Zibah to save my son.

Bekira was up with the sunrise and added the joy of a child's presence to our dark mood. Her spiraled curls bounced as we danced to Savta Zibah's lively singing. When the sounds of celebration rose outside, I fought back a new wave of panic and set Bekira on the floor with her blocks, while Zibah and I began our praying—and spinning—in earnest. The beating of drums signaled the beginning of sacrifices, and my hands shook so violently, I could no longer draw wool from the basket. I pressed my hands into my lap and waited for the sudden cease of percussion—the moment all sound would still at Melqart's fiery swallow.

I felt a subtle vibration beneath my feet. Had I imagined it? Was it the drums? The sensation swelled. Undeniable tremors. Distant screams halted the drums. Festive music changed to disorganized panic. Only an army's approach shook the ground with that kind of violence; only an attack created those sounds of chaos.

Zibah and I ran to the balcony, peering toward the city's southern boundary—the Valley of Ben Hinnom. Burning day and night with the downhill flow of Jerusalem's refuse, it was also the site of today's celebration. Assyrians on horseback now filled the area, plowing through the celebration as if through a fallow field, cutting down everyone in their path. Zibah slid behind the balcony railing, shaking, eyes glazed, her greatest nightmare playing out before us.

"Ima?"

Nothing.

I shook her shoulders. "Ima, talk to me."

Still no response.

I scooped Bekira into my arms and ran out of Zibah's chamber to my daughter's, praying her nursemaid was there. The woman was standing on Bekira's balcony, witnessing a similar sight in the city market below. I shoved my daughter into her arms. "Take Bekira into the servants' quarters. Dress her in sackcloth. The Assyrians kill royalty first, and I won't have two children die today."

"Yes, mistress. I'll protect her with my life."

With a plan to keep my girl safe, I returned to Ima Zibah's chamber and coaxed her from the balcony to her bedchamber, where we could hold each other and pray. "El Shaddai, Creator of the heavens and earth, protect Your children—" A memory interrupted my prayer and sparked hope. "The drums were still beating when we felt the vibration."

Dawning brightened Ima's features. "You think the Assyrians came before they sacrificed Amon?"

"I don't know, but . . ." The sounds of mayhem drew nearer the palace. "I have to see what's happening." I watched the battle between fear and faith rage on her features.

"No, please!" She clutched at me. "Don't leave."

"We'll go together," I said.

She followed me but sat with her back to the railing. I searched for my husband, praying he carried our child, but I saw only corpses in the Valley of Ben Hinnom. Such a horde gorged the city's southern gates that our guards couldn't close them. Assyrians, now on foot, marched among them with swords, cutting down citizens, bringing their reign of terror to a city complicit in rebellion against Ashurbanipal's empire. I searched the chaos for any sign of my child. Any of our family. Surely, the watchmen had seen the invaders coming and alerted Nasseh's guards to get all royalty to safety.

Finally, I spotted Kenaz rushing through the gate that separated Upper and Lower Jerusalem. "Ima, Kenaz is running toward the palace with something in his arms!"

Zibah covered a gasp, cautious hope on her features.

The Assyrian invaders slashed their way through the throng. "Ima, I see Nasseh too!" I screamed.

He was among those at the Upper City gate, but he was limping, bleeding from wounds on his head and arm. A horseman approached, cutting down all those around him, clearing a path for the gate to be closed. The horseman circled, singling out my husband.

"No!" I screamed when the horseman whirled a long chain in a circle over his head and released it. The links wrapped around Nasseh's neck like a rope. With a single yank, he fell, and the soldier dismounted, joined quickly by three more Assyrians. Surrounding him, they blocked my view.

Frantic, I hugged Ima Zibah tight, hiding her eyes against my chest. "What can we do?"

"We wait," she said, shaking violently.

I turned my eye toward heaven. "Please, Yahweh! You said you'd save him!" Overcome by racking sobs, we held each other tight—and then heard Nasseh's bone-splitting shriek.

I jumped to my feet and searched the street below. The soldiers had hauled Nasseh to his feet. Blood dripped down his beard. The chain from his neck was now laced through a shiny bronze ring in his nose and down to encircle his wrists—making even the slightest movement a blinding burst of pain. And where was Kenaz? Assyrian soldiers continued the slaughter, but I saw neither Kenaz nor my child.

"Shulle!"

I spun around to see Kenaz at Zibah's door with Amon in his arms—and an Assyrian commander at his side.

My legs nearly buckled. Zibah grabbed my arm and stood. We leaned on each other, walking into the chamber. We stopped less than a cubit from Kenaz, and I reached for my baby.

The Assyrian pushed me away. "Are you Meshullemeth?"

I bristled. "Yes. Give me my son."

The commander nodded permission to Kenaz. I pressed him against my chest and nestled my face into the perfect bend of his neck, trying to calm his terrified cries.

"And are you Hephzibah, Queen Mother of Manasseh?"

"I am," Zibah answered, voice quaking.

The man shouted over his shoulder, "Bring them in."

Two guards escorted a beaten and bloodied Mattaniah into the chamber. Gemeti walked in unscathed.

The commander pushed Matti toward Zibah. "This old man says he's Mattaniah, your son's uncle and advisor."

"Yes." Zibah's brows knit together, voice stronger. "Why have you beaten him?"

"He said he should replace your son on Judah's throne, and I gave him a lesson in loyalty." Amusement laced his tone as he offered his hand to Gemeti. "The priestess needed no such correction. She will train the boy as he grows."

"She isn't fit to train a dog," I spat.

Zibah stepped in front of me. "Forgive my daughter-in-law, Commander." Her tone remained calm though I knew she was as terrified as I. "Surely you agree that an infant is best nurtured by his own *mother* and *grandmother*." She used the Akkadian terms as a further display of diplomacy.

The man pointed at Kenaz. "I've assigned him to be the child's guardian." He then nudged aside Zibah and reached for my son's tiny hand, gently admiring him. As I drew a breath to thank him, he grabbed my throat. "You owe me an apology *and* undying gratitude for saving your son's life."

"Forgive me." I squeaked out, as black spots appeared in my vision. "Thank you."

He released me with a shove, and I gave my son to the man I respected most.

"Lord Kenaz and Priestess Gemeti will raise the prince in harmony," the commander said. "My troops will leave most of Jerusalem's walls standing, and a contingent of Ashurbanipal's army will remain to ensure order is preserved." He turned to leave.

"Wait!" I called out. "What will happen to my husband?"

He faced me, emotionless. "King Manasseh is being sent to Babylon. In deference to Queen Mother Naqia's edict to keep peace between her grandsons, King Ashurbanipal transfers custody of all royal prisoners to his brother, King Shamash-shum-ukin. He will decide your husband's fate." The commander ordered Gemeti and Matti out of the chamber, and I kissed Amon's downy-soft head before Kenaz took him away.

The door clicked shut.

"Nasseh is going to Babylon," Zibah whispered and then recited, "'Some of your descendants will be taken away and become eunuchs in the palace of the king of Babylon.'"

I sat beside her, my stomach knotting with anger and confusion. "Which is true, Ima? Isaiah's prophecy? Or your vision that God would capture Nasseh's heart and rebuild him? Yahweh can't fulfill both."

She looked at me and raised a defiant brow. "Never begin a sentence with *'Yahweh can't.'* Our minds are too small to imagine what He can do."

55

So the LORD brought against them the army
commanders of the king of Assyria, who took
Manasseh prisoner, put a hook in his nose, bound
him with bronze shackles and took him to Babylon.

2 CHRONICLES 33:11

Babylon
664 BC, Chislev (December) to 662 BC, Nisan (April)

Nasseh barely remembered the first month of his captivity. Infection burned through his body, and the blinding pain of the bronze ring made the netherworld a living reality. The day he was loaded onto a quffa and sailed south on the Euphrates, his mind cleared. He wasn't going to Nineveh.

"Where are you taking me?" he shouted at the nearest guard. The man ignored him, but Nasseh recognized Sippar and a line of quffas bound for Babylon. Saba's prophecy pounded him to his knees. He retched and let darkness swallow him.

When he revived, he searched the quffas behind him but couldn't see King Baal or the Egyptian princes from the coalition. "I demand to speak to King Shamash-shum-ukin," he croaked through dry, cracked lips. If the other kings were among the captives, Nasseh must be first to beg for clemency. Desperation surpassing fear, he shouted at the guard beside him. "I said I *demand*—" A crashing blow brought sweet oblivion.

When his reed boat docked, he barely noticed Esar's magnificently restored city while being dragged toward a large building between two guards. They descended a narrow staircase lit with torches. Smells of blood and waste mingled with sounds of despair. Dampness clung to the walls, and rats scurried across the steps. He groaned at the memory of Dohd Jashub's execution and knew he was a prisoner in Babylon's palace. Regret battled with anguish. Would he be executed quickly or tortured first?

Barely able to focus, he noted doors on both sides of a hall. From underneath each door, men's hands reached through a hole as they passed. Grabbing. Begging to touch humanity.

Reaching the end of the maze of halls, his captors dropped him in a cavernous room. Nasseh looked up at two empty-eyed men beside a table lined with weapons of torture. He barely staved off the urge to be sick.

A third man, dressed in royal robes, arrived and turned in a slow circle to showcase the noxious room. "Welcome to your new home, King Manasseh. My grandmother Naqia says I can't kill you. My brother Ashurbanipal says I can't release you. So, you'll be my guards' entertainment for as long as you survive Babylon's prison." He patted Nasseh's shoulder on his way out. "You'll receive one meal a day and one blanket a year."

Nasseh lunged from his knees to grasp the king's cloak but missed and landed on his face. Guards dragged him a few paces to a tiny cell where fresh straw waited with a single blanket and a bucket.

"No, please! No!" Terror revived Nasseh's strength. "I can't! Please!" He flailed but couldn't free himself. "Nooo!" He clawed at the heavy cedar panels. Frantic. Insane. Pressing his face to the small opening at the bottom, he shrieked. "The walls will crush me! I'll die!"

"That would be a mercy for you," a low voice chuckled in reply, and the small opening was covered.

Nasseh screamed till he had no voice. Cried till he had no tears. Exhausted beyond death, he curled on his side and waited to stop breathing.

The scraping of a bowl shoved through the opening marked the passing of each day. Only when the bucket was full of excrement did the door open for a replacement. The guards ignored his cries. His demands. His pleading. No one listened. Not even the gods. Time was nothing. Manasseh was nothing.

29th Tebet (January)
A new night guard, Assoros, gave me five things to torment me: today's date, a candle, flint stones, blank parchment, and kohl to write with. If the date is correct, I've been in this living Sheol barely two weeks.

Oh, one more torment. A corner of the parchment is smeared with brown, sticky paste. I smelled it. Licked it. Syrup—from candied dates. I dreamt of Shulle. The gods are playing tricks.

12th Adar (March)—Six Weeks Later
Can't live like this. Haven't eaten for a week. Assoros left a candied date with my bread and gruel. I let the rats eat it. Perhaps they'll feast on me next.

14th Adar (March)—Two Days Later
Assoros woke me. Fed me gruel. Too weak to refuse. Too delirious to die. He left another date. This one, I ate.

14th Nisan (April)—One Month Later
Assoros opened my cell so I could see his monthly shipment of dates. The box was wrapped in cloth—Ima's uniquely patterned weave. All the packages of dates had been from home and were meant for me! I lunged for the package in his hands as he slammed the door. I shouted murderous threats, vows I could never keep from a prison cell. How cruel the irony of today's date. Passover. Twenty-three years after Yahweh—and I—killed Abba. I deserved far worse than Assoros's torment.

22nd Nisan (April)—Eight Days Later
Assoros brought the first piece of edible bread in seven nights. The other nights the gruel came with moldy, maggot-infested bread. Was he forcing me to give up yeast like a Yahwist? I hadn't celebrated the Feast of Unleavened Bread since I was eleven. I picked off the maggots and ate the bread just to spite him.

14th Iyar (May)—Three Weeks Later

Assoros's whistle has become as familiar as his packages. Though both were annoying at first, the familiarity has become one of my few comforts. Today, is the fourteenth—the day the package arrives. I waited to hear him un-wrap it outside my door, but his key turned the iron lock instead. He stood at my threshold and offered me the box. I reached for it, expecting him to pull it away. He didn't. I grabbed it like a lifeline. He closed the door and relocked it. I haven't opened the package. I'm saving it—for a bad day.

20th Iyar (May)—Six Days Later

Today was bad. The noise in my head swirled into a single tune—the song Assoros whistles. I finally remembered where I'd heard it. King David's Shepherd psalm. How could he know a Hebrew psalm? I opened the pack-age. Ate the dates. I vomited them into my bucket. Assoros can have them back.

663 BC, Fifty Days After Passover

Manasseh was sleeping when he heard the key trip the lock. "Assoros?" He pushed himself up, straw sticking to his sweaty body. He shielded his eyes from the guard's torchlight.

"Come, Manasseh. I have something to show you." Assoros motioned toward the hallway with his torch, but Nasseh hesitated.

Was it a trick?

Nasseh stood at the threshold, where Assoros affixed shackles to his wrists and ankles. The other guards slept in the cavernous outer room, and Assoros pressed his finger against his lips.

Nasseh nodded. He had no desire to wake them either. Holding his chains so they didn't clank, he followed Assoros up an alternate set of stairs, amazed there were two entrances to Sheol. Assoros opened a small door and led Nasseh into a grassy clearing near a canal. Overwhelmed by the glorious sights and smells of partial freedom, Nasseh fell to his knees and brushed his hands over the soft grass.

Pure joy rumbled from his belly into a laugh, and for the first time in seven months, he looked to the moon god Sin and his starry hosts. "To you, great Sin, and the Twins rising in your wake, who illuminate the heavens and survey the whole earth—"

Assoros's low chuckle stole the glory. "King Manasseh, what a fool you are."

Nasseh scurried to rise, but the guard stomped on his ankle shackles and sent him crashing to the ground face first.

"Will you pray to that grass in your teeth? Or dig up a worm to worship?" Assoros hauled him to his feet. "Why would a man, created in Yahweh's image, worship anything less than the Creator?"

Nasseh pulled from his grasp, a derisive laugh escaping his own lips. "Yet again the Hebrew god proves his disdain for me by giving me a Yahwist guard to torture me. Why *wouldn't* I turn away from one so cruel to more powerful gods?"

"If your gods are more powerful, why are you in chains and Yahweh's guard is—as you say—tormenting you?" Assoros's lopsided grin faded. "*Marvel* at the moon and stars, Manasseh, but *worship* the God who hung them in the sky."

Nasseh stared at the inky black heavens, the winking stars pale in light of his brutal reality. Perhaps all gods were cruel. Perhaps the moon god Sin had conspired *with* Yahweh to imprison him. Had Belit cast a spell before her execution? Or Gemeti cursed him after her son was sacrificed? Nasseh examined each god in the night sky like a gem cutter preparing a crown. The Twins were the brightest this month, promising light and revelation. Belit had always planned the whole year's celebrations in Sivan, claiming she could predict weather patterns all the way through winter. Saba taught that Yahweh revealed the Law to Moses in the month of Sivan. The twin stars represented the twin tablets on which the finger of God wrote those laws from a dense cloud full of thunder and lightning with a great trumpet blast.

Where was Yahweh's power now?

Belit healed and cursed with incantations. Gemeti divined the gods' will through sheep livers. Yet Yahweh remained silent while his followers were killed. "Your god is a dried-up wineskin." Nasseh sneered. "He may have hung the stars, Assoros, but starry hosts now rule him."

The guard never flinched, his eyes fixed on the sky. "No one rules the Almighty," he whispered, sending a shiver through Nasseh. "Yahweh's sovereign power is driven by His love."

"Love?" Nasseh choked on the word. "Ask the dead Yahwists in Judah how much their god loved them."

Assoros turned from the stars and looked into Nasseh's soul. "Earthly suffering and death don't disprove God's love. From Yahweh's perspective, if the suffering of His faithful brings light to those in the darkness, how much more glorious is eternity for all?"

"How does suffering bring light to darkness?" Nasseh scoffed. "And how can Yahweh's provision—slitting a lamb's throat—surpass a nether-world stocked by future generations?"

"I've heard you're a brilliant man. Surely, you don't believe gold, oil, and grain transport to a spirit world." Before Nasseh could defend his beliefs, Assoros added, "Tell me, King Manasseh, how did you *feel* watching your grandfather, your uncle, and dozens of Yahweh prophets die?"

Blood drained from Nasseh's face. "How do you know who I've executed?"

"Your reign of terror is celebrated among Assyrian royalty. But your haunted face proves *you* don't celebrate it. The false gods you worship shackle you with guilt and shame." The guard bent to one knee. "The Yahwists' suffering can bring light into your darkness, Manasseh. You have much for which to atone, but Yahweh hasn't forgotten you. Let Him capture your heart."

Nasseh searched his guard's face. Was he tormentor or savior? "How did you learn of Yahweh?"

"Do you think you're the first Hebrew prisoner I've talked to?" He pulled Nasseh to his feet. "We must return before the other guards wake."

Thoughts tangling with the chaos in his mind, Nasseh pondered the scant odds of a God-fearing guard in Babylon's prison. And the even scarcer chances of that guard being assigned to him.

When they arrived at his cell, Assoros removed the shackles and said, "No place on earth is beyond Yahweh's reach—including a man's heart." Nasseh stepped inside. The door slammed shut. Assoros's whistle faded.

Nasseh stood alone in a darkness more crushing than his cell walls. Were the moon and stars truly just lights in the sky, hung by the One God he'd fought all his life? *It can't be.* He'd seen the other gods' power. But what about Saba's painless execution? The strange glow of his tree.

Yet, if Judah worshipped Yahweh alone, was every other nation wrong? *Melchizedek—king of Salem.*

The thought betrayed his assumption. Melchizedek, a foreign king, had worshipped Yahweh, historic proof that any man from any nation could worship him.

Like Assoros.

Nasseh's hands began to shake. Memories, like a swarm of hornets, assaulted him. Dropping a dagger to save a lamb. Drawing a sword and Abba died. Innocent blood to atone for the guilty. Passover abolished. Eliakim's pale face flashing in the darkness. Reaching for his wife's hand in the temple. The Shema chanted as the massacre in the temple began. *"Hear, O Israel: The LORD our God, the LORD is one . . ."*

Nasseh had thought he knew a better way. Thought Matti's and Shebna's voices wiser than Saba Isaiah's or Ima's. If āšipūtus' potions and divinings were mere manipulation, then Nasseh had killed hundreds—thousands—because he'd believed lies. *I almost killed mine and Shulle's son. Oh, Amon!*

Nasseh screamed and emptied his stomach in the bucket. On his knees now, he replayed Saba Isaiah's prophetic words from the tree that no one else had heard. *"You're a builder, Grandson, but Yahweh will build you—after He captures your heart like He's captured mine."* Foolishly, Nasseh thought he could silence Yahweh with a saw.

Groaning, he fell on his side, weeping, while Dohd Jashub's last words joined the shouts of mercy in his mind. *"Yahweh doesn't hate you. No matter how many Yahweh followers you kill, we'll scream forgiveness from our graves . . . May Yahweh deal with you as gently as you'll allow, while He draws your heart back to Him."*

Was his heart turning? It felt more like a rending of his chest.

14th Nisan (April)—Passover (Eight Months Later)

Yahweh, God of my abba and ima, Assoros brought me lamb and bitter herbs instead of gruel and bread. He placed a thumbprint of lamb's blood above my door and said I need only believe and eat to be forgiven. I want to, but why would You show mercy? Can there be atonement for one as wicked as me?

Rats try to nibble my sacred meal, and I wonder—are doubts doing the same to my soul? How can I shoo away atrocities too many to count and memories too grievous to bear?

22nd Nisan (April)—Eight Days Later

I ate the atoning meal and refused bread until tonight—truly celebrating with Assoros the meaning of Passover and Unleavened Bread for the first time in my life. Almighty God and Creator, merciful and immeasurable, who has ever sinned more than I? Yet not even my wickedness reaches beyond Your ability to save. Forgive my sins, Yahweh, too vast to count. You stripped my royal robes to prove You wait in paradise. You sent me to a dungeon to set me in Your presence. I will worship You until I draw my last breath.

A tear fell on the parchment, threatening to blur the words Nasseh had just written. Hands shaking, he dropped the piece of kohl and extinguished his candle. The lilting tune of David's shepherd song washed over Judah's exiled king, and he fell into the first peaceful sleep of his life.

56

Amon worshiped and offered sacrifices to
all the idols Manasseh had made.

2 CHRONICLES 33:22

Jerusalem, Judah
653 BC, Eleven Years Later

Ima Zibah dropped her spindle again, and the thunderous snoring she so vehemently denied echoed in her chamber. Abba glanced up from the prophet's scroll he was reading and winked at me. He'd become our guardian for our afternoon women's activities since Perez and Zerah died five years ago. The dogs were my constant shadow after Nasseh was taken captive. Zerah never had puppies, so they became family pets, and when they stumbled deaf and blind into walls, we became their protectors as they'd been ours.

I left my loom to retrieve Zibah's spindle. Abba chuckled. "How many times have you done that today?"

"Fifteen." I placed the spindle in Zibah's lap and detoured to the couch to kiss his forehead. "And I'll do it fifteen more if needed."

"You've taught my granddaughter your kindness." He captured my hand as I turned toward my loom. "Where is Bekira? I miss her."

"She's practicing needlework with the noblemen's daughters. She needs to spend some time with girls her own age. It's not good for a girl to be around old people all the time."

He waved me away with a disapproving frown. "She gets wisdom from her eighty-five-year-old savta and lessons on the law of Yahweh from me." He went back to reading his scroll. "Gossip is all she'll get from spoiled noblemen's daughters."

I hid my grin, believing he might be right, but a girl must learn to filter truth from gossip. My heart ached a little, missing Adnah. She and her daughters hadn't joined us for an afternoon of savta's *wisdom* in over a week.

My heart did a flip in my chest. *I could have had a grandchild by now.* Bekira was fifteen years old, at least two years beyond betrothal age. Many of her friends married last year. She'd been patient while we planned her brother's coronation. Tomorrow, my Amon would be twelve and officially rise to Judah's throne. As he became more and more often surrounded by Assyrian-appointed guardians and counselors, I saw him less each year of his life—and ached for him more.

"No. No!" Ima Zibah's head tossed side to side. "No!" She woke with a start.

I rushed over to kneel beside her. "Another nightmare?"

She waved away my concern and grinned down at the spindle in her lap. "I used to laugh at old women who dropped their spindles while taking impromptu naps." She patted my cheek and lifted the spindle. "I dreamt about when I was a girl in Abba's household. We fed the prophets while they hid in caves."

She'd told me the story a hundred times. "You've been dreaming about that a lot lately."

"Maybe old people even repeat themselves in their dreams." She chuckled at her wit, but I wondered if Yahweh was speaking to her. He'd revived a remnant of prophets, who were wreaking havoc among Jerusalem's pagan leaders.

"Have you heard from Nahum recently?" I asked. He'd come to visit yesterday, but I hoped the mention of a prophet's name would both jog her memory and stir Yahweh's Word within her.

Zibah removed Isaiah's gold ring from her pocket, the one Nahum had given her years ago. "I wish he would visit. I'd like to know if the prophets are safe in Tyre."

I laid my head in her lap. "The prophets are safe, Ima." Disappointment warred with relief. Perhaps it was Yahweh's mercy that her memory waned. Under Gemeti's and Matti's influence, Amon had followed his abba's pagan practices, ignoring Kenaz's teaching and my prodding.

Lifting my head, I smiled to reassure her. "Nahum came to see you yesterday, dressed as a traveling merchant, remember? Kenaz brought him to your chamber selling spices. Nahum kissed your cheek and said he'd leave a prophet's scroll in the Garden of Uzza. Then Bekira told us last night that the whole palace was in an uproar about a mysterious scroll found in the royal garden."

Zibah clapped, as delighted to hear it today as she had been last night.

Bekira barged into the chamber. "Ima, I won't marry an Egyptian prince!" I stood and gathered her into my arms. "I won't," she said, sobbing.

"What Egyptian prince?"

Mattaniah rushed in, huffing from his stairway climb. "She'll marry the man I've chosen." He leaned on a cane, his health far worse than Zibah's though he was younger. His mind, however, was as sharp as a spear's tip. "I'm still the royal patriarch."

"But I'm her nearest male relative," Abba stood to face him. "And I forbid her to marry a pagan."

"A Hebrew maiden must approve her betrothed." Zibah remained seated, her tone calm yet firm enough to overpower both men's bluster.

"She is the king's daughter, Zibah." Matti stepped around Abba, towering over her. "Bekira must marry royalty."

"Royalty?" I fumed. "My daughter will marry a man *she* deems acceptable."

Kenaz rushed into the room. "Shulle, don't let Beki marry the Egyptian."

Matti's face grew three shades redder. "If she doesn't marry the prince I've chosen, I'll persuade the council to refuse any other match."

Bekira had dried her eyes and stood facing her Dohd Matti, the man who held her future hostage. "I'd rather remain single than marry a man who worships false gods."

Narrowing his eyes, Matti stepped to within a handbreadth of my daughter. "Then you'll spend your life playing nursemaid to your brother's children."

I shoved my way between them. "Perhaps Amon should find a wife before you hire a nursemaid for his children."

Matti turned a slow wicked grin on Kenaz. "I believe the council decided on a wife for your son."

I stared in disbelief. "Kenaz, what have you done?"

"It was just decided . . . we, um . . . I mean, the council . . ." He scrubbed his face as if wiping away his tentative reply. When he turned to Shulle again, this time she was startled by his sadness. "We've ensured King David's lineage remains unbroken—and faithful to Yahweh."

"Yes," Matti blurted, "that's exactly how he auctioned off your son to the highest bidder."

"I didn't *auction* him," Kenaz shouted. "I'm Amon's guardian. I secured a match that's both fiscally beneficial and—"

"Who gave you the right?" My whisper stilled the room.

Kenaz turned to me again, and the sadness I'd seen was overshadowed by the flexing muscles in his jaw. "The royal council gave me the right, Shulle. Tomorrow, when Amon turns twelve, he'll sit on Judah's throne and sign a betrothal contract, legally binding him in marriage to Jedidah, the daughter of our royal treasurer, Adaiah. The council approved it unanimously."

I began trembling. "Get out. Both of you. Leave. Now."

Kenaz reached for my hand. "Shulle, please let me explain."

Pulling away, I stepped toward the door and shouted, "Guards! Get these men out of the harem. The Queen Mother needs to rest immediately!"

Our faithful guards stood by the open door. Matti grinned on his way out, having successfully placed a wedge between Kenaz and me. I knew he and Gemeti tried to divide the Yahwists with bitterness and fighting. But I was too angry, at the moment, to consider the damage this might cause to the foundation we'd built in Nasseh's absence.

Kenaz ignored the guards, remaining in my chamber after Matti's footsteps faded. "Adaiah and his daughter are faithful Yahwists, Shulle. Providing Amon with a faithful wife is the best long-term plan for a faithful king on Judah's throne." He took a step toward me, and I retreated. Hurt rounded his shoulders. "Please, trust me."

The waiting guard cleared his throat. "Councilman. Please."

I turned my back and heard the door close. Bekira fell into my arms. "I'm proud of you," I said. "Your strength is a testimony to the legacy of those who gave their lives for their faith."

"I would die for Yahweh, Ima. If He asked it of me." She squeezed me in a fierce embrace, and I looked over her shoulder at Ima Zibah.

Ima had placed Isaiah's gold ring on her finger and was twirling it. "Everyone dies, precious Bekira, and we all leave a legacy. The question is, Does our legacy speak Yahweh's truth to those who follow?"

Yahweh's truth. As Bekira joined her savta with a spindle in hand, I pondered the niggling question that had haunted me since Nasseh's capture. What was Yahweh's truth? I'd renounced all pagan gods and idolatry years ago. I trusted Yahweh though I couldn't see His form and prayed though my ears couldn't hear His voice. I was a Yahwist. Committed. Devoted.

But how could I know which of His promises to believe? Egyptian captives had marched naked and barefoot. True to Yahweh's word through Isaiah. Nasseh was taken captive to Babylon. Again, true to Isaiah's prophecy. But what of Zibah's vision? Was Yahweh's word to her untrue? Less reliable because she wasn't a prophet? *Yahweh, show me the truth of my husband's legacy.*

I went back to my loom, giving Zibah time to sow her incomparable wisdom in my daughter's fertile heart. I listened to Zibah's stories— familiar and well loved. Gentle whispers blew over my spirit, and I knew Yahweh was at work beyond what I could see. Shadows grew long, and I set aside the loom's shuttle as shofars blew from our city walls. Bekira ran to the balcony. "Assyrians, Ima. The man leading them has a different kind of armor, perhaps a high official."

I hurried past Zibah, who had wakened to our fright, and met my daughter on the balcony. At least fifty Assyrians were entering the Horse Gate, the lead horseman wearing the same armor I'd seen on Esar's personal guard.

"I'm going to the throne room," I said.

I turned toward the door and bumped into Abba's mountainous form. "I'm coming with you," he said, placing a cloak around my shoulders. "You'll not face Assyrians alone."

Bekira stood beside us. "May I come?"

"No!" Abba and I said in unison. I forced calm into my voice and walked into the chamber. Abba and Bekira trailed behind me. "I need you both to remain here and help Ima Zibah with her evening meal." I knelt beside her and offered an explanation I hoped was true. "I haven't heard from Naqia in months. Perhaps she left instructions that I be informed of her passing, and they've sent the king's guard. If King Ashurbanipal intended Judah harm, he would have sent a whole army."

Ima stroked my hair. "Assyria always means harm, my girl. But Yahweh will make a way."

I pressed the back of her hand to my lips, absorbing her peace. "He always does." I fairly ran out of the chamber, down the stairs, and through the main hallway and entered the courtroom. Gemeti saw me first. "This is a closed council meeting. You must leave."

Another blast of the shofars interrupted her tirade as more councilmen streamed in before the Assyrians' arrival. I continued my march to the dais, where Amon sat on a cushion at the feet of his three guides. Judah's throne remained empty—as it had for eleven years.

"I assume you're aware that the Assyrian contingent is led by one of Ashurbanipal's personal guards," I said to the queen.

"How do you know that?" Gemeti asked.

Before I could answer, the courtroom doors opened, and a dozen

Assyrians entered. I stood aside, near the dais but not on it, hoping to be invisible.

Gemeti stood when they entered, so the captain addressed her first. "Are you Prince Amon's mother?"

She hesitated. "No, I . . ."

I stepped forward, emboldened by her games. "I'm Meshullemeth, wife of King Manasseh. I'm Prince Amon's ima."

The captain appraised me and turned his attention to Kenaz. "I require a private room to speak with Queen Meshullemeth and her son."

"She's *not* the queen!" Gemeti stomped her foot.

The captain ascended the dais's six steps, overshadowing Gemeti in both stature and tact. "According to the sovereign will and power of the mighty King Ashurbanipal, Meshullemeth bat Haruz is queen of Judah. You will be silent or die." She slid onto her stool without another word, while the commander returned his attention to Kenaz. "The room?"

"Yes, follow me." Kenaz showed us through the hidden door behind the dais. We crossed the private hall and entered the king's chamber, now used for my son's private instruction. The surprised chamber guards stepped aside for the Assyrian captain.

Kenaz tried to follow us, but the captain grabbed his collar and hauled him backward. "I will speak with them alone." Kenaz drew breath to argue, but the captain stepped into the chamber and slammed the door.

Amon hugged my waist, trembling. I wrapped him tightly in my arms, reveling in his willingness to be held. Though I sent my boy loving messages every day, we often went weeks with no contact at all. Kenaz said Gemeti and Matti began ridiculing him two years ago for his attachment to me, and the need to prove his manhood had driven a wedge between us. A wedge displaced by today's Assyrian captain.

"How old are you, Prince Amon?" the captain asked.

"Eleven," he mumbled.

The captain looked down his long, slender nose. "Speak clearly and with confidence, young prince. As if your life depended on the tone and volume."

Amon cleared his throat. "I am twelve tomorrow, Captain."

"Much better." He clapped and even smiled. "I saw evidence of festival preparations. Is it for your birthday celebration?"

"For my coronation." Amon released me and stepped toward the captain. "I'm to be married tomorrow too." A smile bloomed on his face and melted my heart. Perhaps he really did like this girl, Jedidah.

But the captain's expression clouded my hope. "Your son will not be crowned king tomorrow," he said.

Amon's mouth fell open. He looked first at me and back at the captain. "I'm the rightful heir in the line of King David. I *will* be king of Judah tomorrow!"

The Assyrian inclined his head in a mocking bow. "And finally, the arrogance of a king is revealed." He looked up with a grin. "I'm sorry, young prince, but you can't sit on your father's throne while your father is in it." My son's face reddened, gathering steam for a childish reply, while the captain's eyes locked on me. "King Manasseh has been held in Babylon's palace prison since his capture over eleven years ago. While in captivity, he helped uncover a coup in which Shamash-shum-ukin planned to overthrow his brother and my lord, King Ashurbanipal. Your husband will be rewarded with his freedom—as soon as the siege on Babylon ends, and we rescue him from the palace prison."

Panic ripped through me. "He's still in the city with the king he betrayed?"

"I assure you, Queen Meshullemeth, no one is more anxious to break through Babylon's wall than my lord, Ashurbanipal. When he does, your husband will be promptly returned to rule Judah." He offered a slight bow and left Amon and me standing in a swirl of conflicting emotion.

At least mine were conflicting. I saw only anger roiling on my son's features. Laying my hands on his shoulders, I spoke to him as I would to the man he'd become in less than a day. "Amon, you are still the crown prince of Judah, and you may still sign your betrothal to Jedidah tomorrow if you wish. But we've been given a great gift today. Your abba is alive."

"And coming back to steal what is mine." He looked into my eyes, and

I saw one more emotion—fear. "I will double my guards since the only thing that saved my life eleven years ago was Abba's capture."

I tried to embrace him, but he shoved me away and stormed toward the door. "Amon!" But he was gone, and I was left with the truth. Nasseh's capture was the only thing that saved our son's life. I had despised my husband that day. Wished for his death. I turned in a circle, taking in the furnishings and trappings of the king's chamber. Gemeti's touches graced every wall, but the memories of my life with Nasseh still lingered here. The years had dulled my hate, but I couldn't bear the thought of returning to my husband's chamber of fear and restrictions after worshiping Yahweh freely for so long now.

Nasseh had been a prisoner in Babylon for eleven years, but I'd been a prisoner to Dohd's deception since I was eight. I'd known freedom since Nasseh's capture. Freedom to worship the one God I could fully trust. Would I become a prisoner again to fear and circumstance when over half my life was spent?

Bekira's courage came to mind. *"I would die for Yahweh, Ima. If He asked it of me."* My fifteen-year-old daughter lived free. Unchained. Matti's threats had no power over her. Married or not, she served Yahweh. Alive or dead, she was with Yahweh. Her certainty freed her from every bondage.

I remembered the question that haunted me. *Lord, which of Your promises are true?* I'd believed too many lies over too many years. Been deceived too many times. If *all* Yahweh's promises didn't prove true, then He was a liar. But I *knew* Yahweh didn't lie. Still, I wrestled with the proof that Isaiah's prophecy was true—and Zibah's vision a lie. *Yahweh, help me understand.*

Will you remain chained to your limited understanding?

I gasped at the question, realizing it wasn't my own. I'd thought all my chains gone, but silken tethers of my control still bound me. Frantic for wisdom, hungry for knowledge, I tried to arrange the pieces of my broken world into a semblance of peace.

Can you trust My love when you don't know My plan?

The gentle cords of His kindness wrapped around me, drawing me to my knees. *Trust Your love?* Yahweh was to me everything that men in my life hadn't been. The Father who never went away, the Teacher who didn't lead me astray, and the Bridegroom who would never betray. "Yes, yes!" I cried, lifting my hands in rapturous surrender. "I trust Your love for Manasseh ben Hezekiah; Your promise for him, though, I don't understand." I pressed my hands against my heart, so gloriously alive that my chest throbbed, and I anointed the king's chamber with the most holy moment of my life. No matter what happened when my husband returned, I would never be chained again.

57

And when [Manasseh] prayed to him, the
LORD was moved by his entreaty and listened
to his plea; so he brought him back to Jerusalem and to his kingdom.

2 CHRONICLES 33:13

Babylon
651 BC, Two Years Later

ounds of the Babylon prison hummed in the periphery of Nasseh's
awareness while the clear trilling of David's shepherd psalm grew
closer. Assoros's key jingled in the lock, and as had become their
nightly custom, they busied themselves emptying the waste pots in every
cell while the other guards and prisoners slept.

When they'd finished their rounds, Assoros paused outside Nasseh's
cell, seeming troubled. "We must say goodbye, Nasseh."

"Are you going on a journey?" The thought of a single night without
his guardian sent Nasseh's heart into an erratic rhythm.

"No," he said. "You are."

"What journey?" he asked, panic rising. "I don't want to leave you."

The guard retrieved a box he'd hidden a few steps away. Like the packages Nasseh had received each month, it was wrapped in Ima's patterned
weave. "Take them with you when you leave here."

Confused, Nasseh held the familiar package. "This isn't the fourteenth."

Assoros chuckled. "You should present this gift to Ashurbanipal when you meet him."

Nasseh studied his friend. "Assoros, why would I meet—"

"Take care, King Manasseh of Judah. May Yahweh bless you all the days of your life." He walked away, taking his torch with him.

"Assoros!" One of the sleeping guards stirred, and Nasseh hid in the shadows of his cell. What was Assoros thinking? He'd left Nasseh's cell unlocked, his wrists and ankles unshackled. Glancing out his door, he found the guards still sleeping and looked longingly at the stairway. But where would he go once outside the palace? Babylon was a thriving city now. He could be lost for weeks. He had no silver to travel, no clothes. He went back into his cell and closed the door. Lying on his straw, he clutched the box of candied dates and fell asleep.

Nasseh woke to odd sounds. Men talking, not the guards grumbling. Cell doors opening. Prisoners crying. Not screaming from torture but crying as if—happy. "King Manasseh!" someone shouted. "King Manasseh of Judah, are you here?"

Was it a trick? Should he answer?

"Maybe he's not here." Another voice. "Maybe Shamash-shum-ukin killed him before we could rescue him."

"I'm here," Nasseh said quietly, unsure if he wanted to be heard.

His cell door swung open. He huddled in the corner while two Assyrian soldiers stared. "You're King Manasseh?" One took a step into the cell with his torch held high. He grimaced and covered his nose. Nasseh had forgotten he likely stunk.

"I'm Manasseh."

Those two words unlocked a future beyond his dreams. Still clutching the box of dates, he was taken up the prison stairs and past dead bodies in palace hallways. Pandemonium raged in the streets, but he was delivered to a quiet palace chamber, where he was washed, lotioned, and perfumed. Maids cut and styled his beard, dressed him, and placed a crown of gold on his head. Finally, six guards escorted him to a courtroom.

Shamash-shum-ukin—the king he'd met thirteen years ago—sat bloodied and chained beside a king on his throne. Though he'd never seen King
Ashurbanipal, the man had the same arrogant grin as his abba, Esar. The
escort halted at the foot of the dais, and Nasseh looked around the expansive hall, hoping to see Assoros. He was alone with guards and kings, having no idea why he'd been summoned.

"King Manasseh," Ashurbanipal snapped his fingers to gain his attention. "Are you well?"

Assessing his new clothes and jewelry, Nasseh could only marvel. "I've
improved considerably since yesterday."

Ashurbanipal's laughter echoed in the near-empty hall. "I wish to
honor the man who saved my life. Were it not for the messages sent
through your guard to the prefect of Ur and his superior, the prefect of
Uruk, my empire might have been lost—or at least severely weakened by
my brother's treachery." The king left his throne, descended the dais, and
offered him a scroll bearing the royal seal. "Your resourcefulness and loyalty have secured your freedom."

Nasseh blinked several times, thinking perhaps he'd become dehy-
drated again and was hallucinating.

The king of Assyria tilted his head. "King Manasseh, I ask again. Are
you well? It is my intention to restore you to Judah's throne, but I cannot
let a madman reign in a thriving trade city." The guards laughed with their
king, and Manasseh chuckled with them. The whole thing was absurd.
He'd sent no guard with messages. Just as he was about to confess to the
error, Ashurbanipal placed a hand on his shoulder. "I'm alive today because you dealt shrewdly with the traitorous guards and sent faithful Assoros to Ur repeatedly with news of my brother's scheming. You have
earned back your throne, King Manasseh, and my debt."

Confused. Dumbfounded. Searching for the right words, Nasseh
bowed to one knee. What could he say that wouldn't ring false or reveal his
total ignorance of the events the king had described? "I'm grateful for your
mercy, King Ashurbanipal. I'm sure your father would be proud of you."

"And what's this?" Ashurbanipal tapped on the box of dates in Nasseh's arms.

"For you," he said. "A gift."

The king's brows rose, and he grinned at his guards. "A prisoner who can smuggle gifts into Shamash-shum-ukin's prison. I like this man more every moment." Again, the guards laughed, and Ashurbanipal untied the hemp cord on the simply wrapped package.

When Ashurbanipal began lifting out pieces of parchment, Nasseh was more surprised than he was. But the king's features grew stormier after reading each one. "Where did you—" Pausing a moment, his eyes narrowed. "I don't want to know." He returned to the dais and emptied the whole box of parchment pieces over his brother's head. The chained man watched hundreds of missives fall to the floor, and he squeezed his eyes shut in recognition.

"It would appear," Ashurbanipal said to his brother, "King Manasseh has given me the traitorous correspondence proving your conspiracy."

Stunned and confused, Nasseh wasn't even frightened when Ashurbanipal stormed toward him—until he saw the blood lust in his eyes. "You have justified a torturous, public death for my conniving brother, and I'll reward you with an escort to Jerusalem befitting a *friend* of the empire."

There was a day when those words would have thrilled Nasseh. Now they sent a chill through his veins.

At dawn the king's best soldiers introduced Nasseh to the empire's finest caravan master, who promised to prove his reputation by making the forty-day journey in twenty-five. Nasseh's guards hung two large baskets, connected by two sturdy leather straps, over his one-humped dromedary. Nasseh rode in one basket, while supplies of equal weight filled the other. The caravan refueled with food and new camels in major trade cities along the way, and by the time they reached Damascus, Nasseh felt strong enough to venture into the world-famous market.

He hadn't realized, however, how suffocating the press of bodies would feel after so many years of solitude. "Keep them back!" he shouted at his six-guard escort. The Assyrians cleared a path, and he finally spotted the booth he needed. Running, hands fisting wildly, he arrived breathless and gasping. "Measure . . . one-half mina . . . true weight . . . candied dates . . . package them . . . wooden box."

The man gawked at the six Assyrians, stiff as a statue. "I sell my dates in jars. Or baskets—if you buy a large quantity." He swallowed audibly, hesitant to haggle further.

Nasseh had intentionally left his gold crown at the inn, but he was still a king. "Look at me," he said soft but firm. The man glanced at him but kept a cautious eye on the guards. "I said, look at me!" Nasseh's shout captured the man's attention, but Nasseh was determined to remain calm. "I'm Manasseh ben Hezekiah, returning King of Judah, and I'm return-ing home to tell my wife I can no longer provide for her eternity in the netherworld because it doesn't exist. Only Yahweh is true and only His paradise exists, which I think she knows, but I can't be sure until I see her. I'm hoping to return to her the exact gift she sent me each month of my imprisonment—candied dates in a *wooden* box." Nasseh motioned to a curtained compartment under the mounds of dates, assuming it was where the man kept his best products and true weights. "Use your finest box and bronze lions to weigh my purchase. I'll pay a fair price, and all will be well."

The merchant glanced at the guards once more before removing the small bronze lion already on the right plate of his scale. Reaching below his counter, he replaced it with another bronze lion that looked identical but was undoubtedly the true-weighted one-half mina. After rummaging to find an ornately carved wooden box, he grumped before hearing Nasseh's offer.

"You know, since the drought started, I've been getting twice the price for my dates." He shrugged while filling the box. "Not that I would de-mand it, of course, but since you said you've been away, you might not realize—"

"How long was the drought?" Nasseh had noticed the smaller fruit on trees as they'd traveled.

The merchant wiped syrupy hands on his filthy robe and closed the box. "You've been away a long time." He handed the box to Nasseh and leaned close so the guards couldn't hear. "Five years. Some say it's the reason Ashurbanipal waited so long to attack Babylon—though he knew of his brother's treachery two years before."

"Thank you for the insight, my friend." Nasseh motioned to one of his guards. "Pay the man double what his dates are worth."

"Yes, Lord King."

Nasseh watched to be sure his order was obeyed and thought back to the years of drought when Assoros faithfully delivered Shulle's candied dates. Not once had he kept a box for himself. Not a single time had he mentioned his need for food or grain. Every night, he'd filled Nasseh's water cup and delivered his bread and gruel as if all of Babylon and Assyria had untold storehouses to spare. Of all the men he'd met—kings, priests, merchants, and slaves—he'd never known anyone like Assoros.

When the eastern sky glowed with the promise of dawn, Nasseh woke his six guards and ordered his dromedary fitted with a saddle for the day's journey. He'd considered purchasing a stallion, sending messengers ahead to Jerusalem, giving his family and advisors two days to prepare a welcome. But riding his stallion would feed his pride. Reaching Jerusalem *tonight*—on a camel—would strengthen his resolve. He was determined to honor Yahweh with every step of his redemption, and he'd need Yahweh's strength to face the wife and son he'd betrayed.

58

Then Manasseh knew that the LORD is God.

2 CHRONICLES 33:13

Jerusalem, Judah
The Day of Nasseh's Return, Ab (August)

I placed a cool cloth on Ima Zibah's head, hoping to make her more comfortable in the summer's punishing heat. Two maids used ostrich-feather fans to stir the hot air, but perspiration still dripped down my back and soaked my robe. Abba knelt beside me, his lips moving in silent prayer. Like Hannah in days of old, we'd become bolder in approaching Yahweh since pagan altars defiled His temple and priests no longer atoned to the one true God. His presence dwelt in our hearts and was even more powerful when we gathered together.

Kenaz and Adnah knelt across the wool-stuffed mattress where our greatest treasure lay. Ima had suffered what the palace physician called "falling sickness" three days ago. She'd awakened confused, the right side of her face drooping.

"There has to be something more we can do," I said, knowing there wasn't. "Perhaps the physician—"

"She hates the physician." Kenaz chuckled, lightening the mood.

Adnah leaned into her husband and reached over Zibah's sleeping form to take my hand. "When should we call the children to say their goodbyes?"

Even the question felt like a betrayal, and tears gathered in my throat, choking off a reply. Dreading her death was completely selfish. I no longer feared eternity, knowing she'd step from this world into paradise very soon. Neither did I grapple with disappointment that her vision hadn't been fulfilled. Was I omniscient? Could I know what transpired in Nasseh's heart in a Babylonian prison? Human reason no longer held me captive. I'd chosen faith that need not fully understand. But my heart remained. And I would grieve the only ima I'd ever known.

Shofars sounded from the perimeter of Jerusalem's wall. Kenaz's eyes met mine. "It's Nasseh," he said. "It has to be." We hadn't heard the shofars since the Assyrians reported his forthcoming release—two years ago.

Abba struggled to his feet, towering over me. "I hope he brought another dog with him because my daughter won't be sharing his chamber."

I stood and nestled into his arms. "I know you want to protect me, but you can't talk that way to Judah's king, Abba."

He held me tighter and pressed a kiss to the top of my head. "I won't watch him torment you, Meshullemeth."

His shoulders shook, and we wept together—two parents afraid for their children. Amon was fifteen with the temper of a wounded lion; Bekira, a pure and faithful Yahwist. The Nasseh I knew would have them executed by tomorrow at dawn.

"Is it him, Kenaz?" Abba released me when Kenaz returned from the balcony.

He nodded, his pale face reflecting the churning inside me. "I'm going to the Throne Hall," he said. "Each of you should pack a bag for travel. When darkness falls, I can send word to a prophet here in the city who can get many Yahwists out before Nasseh can mount an organized offensive."

I covered a gasp as he rushed out the door. Seeing the fear on Abba and Adnah's faces, I remembered my vow. *No matter what happens when my husband returns, I will never be chained again.* I wiped my tears and returned to my knees, trusting Yahweh would do more with my prayers than Kenaz could do with a messenger. I reached across the bed to take Adnah's hand. Abba knelt beside me, and together we offered our fear to the One who gave back calm. Bowing my head, I fought the old chains—fear, approval seeking, and yearning for false love—praying to the only Master who would ever rule me.

"Ima?" A small voice drew my eyes to the window where dusk had faded to darkness. The maids were gone, but they'd left a few lamps flickering in Ima's chamber. "Ima?" Bekira's voice again, stronger this time, came from behind the bedchamber's dividing curtain.

I held my hand up to Ima Zibah's face to check her breathing. *Thank You, Yahweh.* I pushed to my feet while answering, "Bekira, love, we were just getting ready to call for the grandchildren." I ran headlong into a man standing between my two children. "Who are—" His hands fisted wildly, and he rocked from left foot to right. The dawning sent me to my knees.

"Yahweh brought Abba home to see Savta," Bekira said.

"Welcome home, my king," Adnah said.

Bekira crouched beside me when Nasseh walked over to greet his mother. "Abba hugged Amon when he saw him and begged his forgiveness," she whispered. "Amon shoved him away, Ima. It was awful. But Abba didn't get angry. He said he'd talk with Amon later—privately."

My heart lurched. Would Nasseh have Amon executed quietly for rebellion? Or would he really talk with our son?

"I'm sure you wish to spend time alone with your family," Adnah was saying.

"Yes, but I'd like to enjoy a meal with you and Kenaz tomorrow evening." My husband's voice was thready and weak. "Haruz, it's nice to see you here. Kenaz tells me you've been a faithful guardian over my two favorite women."

"Ima, get up." Amon pulled me to my feet. "You're a queen, not a servant."

"A queen?" Nasseh turned.

Amon stepped in front of me, suddenly my protector. "Ashurbanipal restored ima's crown—though Gemeti is my advisor." So much for his protection.

"I will speak with Queen Shulle alone," Nasseh said, his tone firm but not unkind.

"Much has changed since you've been away," Abba said. "I won't allow—"

"I won't harm her, Haruz."

My stomach tightened. Our children left without contest, but Abba paused to whisper in my ear on his way to the door. "I'll be right outside this chamber. If I hear you cry out, not a guard in this palace can keep me from you." He kissed my cheek and was gone.

I kept my eyes on the floor, but shuffling footsteps drew my attention. Nasseh stood at the side of Zibah's bed. "How long has Ima been this way?"

"Three days." I returned to my place, opposite him, and tried not to stare. Manasseh ben Hezekiah was gaunt and balding with blotchy skin that made him look twice my age. He clutched a small wooden box as if he'd never let it go. "The physician said—"

"Kenaz told me," he said. "Falling sickness."

"Yes. She woke once. Yesterday. She recognized Kenaz and me but no one else."

"Not Matti?"

I looked down at my hands. "Matti died last year, Nasseh."

"I see." He kissed Zibah's forehead before kneeling. "I've come home, Ima. I hope you can hear me because I have much to tell you." He laid the box on the bed beside her.

Feeling like an intruder, I turned to go.

"Wait," he said with a desperation that pierced me. "Please, don't go. I'd like you to hear how I intend to rule Judah."

He was a king in the line of David, and Yahweh had placed him in authority over me. Until Nasseh required something my true Master forbade, I was under the same obligation as every other Judean to honor him.

"All right," I said, returning to kneel opposite him but keeping my head lowered.

"Thank you," he whispered. Startled by his consideration, I peered up at him—as he offered me the box. "This is for you."

I held it for several heartbeats. Without moving. Without speaking. The Nasseh I knew would never buy someone else a gift. In all the nations we visited during our yearlong travels, he only ever purchased treasures for himself.

"I'm sorry I didn't wrap it like your packages." Lines appeared at the corners of his eyes when he smiled, softening his features. "I don't know if they'll taste as good as the ones you sent me."

What was he talking about? Curiosity got the better of me, and I opened the box. "Ooh." The sight and smell of my favorite sweets stirred me. "Nasseh," I whispered. "I haven't had a candied date since . . ." My words died amid the memories of the awful day he was captured.

"Did the drought affect Judah as well?"

I looked at him again, his eyes so clear and guileless. I'd forgotten how to walk with him through each step to the conclusion. "When the Assyrians attacked Judah that day, Nasseh, they took away the person who doted on me with candied dates. The sweet treats became a reminder of the husband I'd lost, so I asked the palace cooks to keep them off my menu."

He looked as if I'd stolen his last shekel. I braced for his anger, not knowing how I'd offended.

"It had to be you," he said. "Who else would have sent them?"

"Sent what? Nasseh, I don't understand."

"Someone sent me a box of candied dates every month for thirteen years, Shulle!" Frantic now, he shot to his feet and drew back the dividing curtain, marching straight toward Zibah's loom. "The package was always wrapped in this cloth. The exact pattern! A guard named Assoros came to my cell each night. He brought candles, parchment, and kohl to write with. He took me outside sometimes and showed me the stars."

He charged back to the bed and pulled me to my feet. "Assoros laughed at my prayers to the stars and showed me Yahweh." He boldly searched my eyes. "I can't provide for your eternity, Shulle. There is only one God, Yahweh, and somehow—like Saba and Dohd Jashub said—He will forgive me when I make atonement according to His laws. But you must atone for your sins too. I want you to be in paradise with me."

"Yes, Nasseh! I will be!"

I wrapped his neck in a strangling hug, and at first, his hands rested lightly on my hips. Slowly, he pulled me tightly against him, burying his face against my neck and releasing great sobs that shook us both. When he finally quieted, I kissed the tears from his cheeks, and we knelt side by side at Zibah's bed.

Her hand lay in the box of dates, fingers sticky with syrup, and with eyes still closed she spoke in a whisper. "Yahweh . . . captured . . . your heart."

Nasseh laughed through his tears and brushed her cheek. "Yes, Ima. He did." His expression grew thoughtful, and he turned to me. "Saba Isaiah said those exact words before he was executed. Assoros said the same phrase. I think my prison guard was more than a Yahweh follower, Shulle."

"You think he was a prophet?"

"I think he was an angel."

The words hung between us. I was skeptical but didn't want to damage Nasseh's faith. "What makes you think so?"

With a wide smile, he recounted the evidence. "Assoros seemed harsh at first but was never cruel. Each night we served prisoners and guards while they slept. He taught me humility without humiliation, the need for rest, and the joy of true friendship. I was released because I *supposedly* sent Assoros to other provinces with information about Shamash-shum-ukin's coup—but Assoros could never have made trips to Ur or Uruk and still returned to my cell each night."

He sat on the bed, leaning over his ima with a face alight with joy. "Do you know what this means?" he asked, not waiting for her response. "It means Yahweh had to capture me to free me. He tore me down to build me up—so I could lead His people in truth."

I covered a knowing grin, hoping Ima Zibah had heard his words. Surely, she would miraculously wake and tell him of her vision fulfilled.

But she had slipped away in those moments of her son's revelation of his redemption, her celebration far greater than any here on earth.

Nasseh buried her beside Yaira, in the tomb with Isaiah and Jashub. Judah mourned Hephzibah bat Isaiah for thirty days, the period designated for kings. The day after mourning ended, my husband's righteous reign began when both our children were married under a wedding chuppah.

Bekira walked seven circles around the prophet Nahum, much to everyone's delight. The leader of Yahweh's prophets admired our daughter's faith, and Bekira loved the man and his God. Our wounded lion was less anxious to wed, but I saw respect in Amon's eyes for his bride, Jedidah. She'd proven kind and patient during their three-year betrothal, and her abba's Yahwist faith was rooted deeply in her soul. Though Amon remained sullen and disrespectful even after Nasseh shared Yahweh's miraculous intervention in the prison, we held out hope that Jedidah's influence would soften our son's heart.

After depositing both couples in their wedding chambers for their first week of marriage, Nasseh and I returned to the Throne Hall to host the monthlong feast and celebration. Nasseh, still at odds with tradition, placed a single table on the dais where both the men and women of the royal family celebrated together. Nasseh had barely finished his roast lamb when he leaned over to whisper, "I'm tired of people."

I chuckled nervously. "Then this will be a long thirty days." We'd snatched only an occasional meal together since his return. He'd been busy reinstating Yahweh's prophets, forming his Yahwist-only council, and restoring the temple to its sacred state. Or had he avoided me because *every* part of Isaiah's prophecy had been fulfilled? Had Shamash-shum-ukin made my husband a eunuch? I loved him too much to ask.

"I miss you, Shulle." He slipped his hand under the feast table and laced his fingers with mine. "I have a gift in my chamber for you."

"Now?"

He stood and pulled me to my feet. Nasseh hurried us through the private exit and across the hall. Then we were at his chamber door, and my nerves were frayed. I turned to face him. "Perhaps we shouldn't leave our guests."

A wry grin reminded me of the boy I'd first loved. He brushed his lips across mine, drawing me to the tender man he'd become. "They can wait until morning."

"Morning?"

"Until you've had time to enjoy your gift." His hands settled on my waist and turned me toward the door, which his guards now opened. "Thank you, men," he said, nudging me inside.

All four guards saluted, pounding fists to hearts. I'd never seen them respond like that—nor heard my husband thank them.

"Meet Assoros!" Nasseh announced.

I searched the expansive chamber for an angelic being but instead found a ball of golden fur bounding toward us, his silky black muzzle the signature of our beloved Assyrian Shepherds. I dropped to my knees and gathered the rascal into my arms, defending against his sharp puppy teeth. "Where did you find him?"

"He arrived today as a gift from Ashurbanipal." Nasseh sat on the floor beside me, a sad smile on his face. "Yahweh showed me a different kind of guardian when He sent me Assoros. We'll train *this* Assoros to be a new kind of guardian for our family."

Family. I liked that word. Releasing the puppy, I scooted closer to my husband, remembering Naqia's counsel of so many years ago. *Love him with your best, but first you must discover your best.* I'd discovered my best by surrendering my chains to Yahweh. I was free to love him now—no matter what had happened to him in Babylon. "Thank you for making me a part of your family's legacy."

He slipped his fingers into my hair and whispered, "Yahweh is the legacy." He kissed me tenderly, and finally—when we were old enough to be grandparents—I experienced the wedding week of my dreams. Babylon had taken away my husband angry and broken. Yahweh returned him whole and healed. Now we'd face our future together and some sweet day see those waiting for us in paradise.

Epilogue

Afterward he rebuilt the outer wall of the City of David, west of the Gihon spring in the valley, as far as the entrance of the Fish Gate and encircling the hill of Ophel; he also made it much higher. He stationed military commanders in all the fortified cities in Judah.

He got rid of the foreign gods and removed the image from the temple of the Lord, as well as all the altars he had built on the temple hill and in Jerusalem; and he threw them out of the city. Then he restored the altar of the Lord and sacrificed fellowship offerings and thank offerings on it, and told Judah to serve the Lord, the God of Israel. The people, however, continued to sacrifice at the high places, but only to the Lord their God.

2 Chronicles 33:14–17

Author's Note

I'm often asked which parts of the story are fact and which parts are fiction. I hope you'll read 2 Kings 21 and 2 Chronicles 33 to find out. To help you further, in the character list at the beginning of the book, I've listed biblical characters in bold and placed an * beside historical names in the character list.

Here are some more fun facts . . .

Queen Naqia, favored wife of Sennacherib and mother of Esarhaddon, was one of those truth-is-stranger-than-fiction historical characters. According to *The Role of Naqia / Zakutu in Sargonid Politics* (Assyrian State Archives, Book 9), she may have had Hebrew origins. She ruled the empire while Esarhaddon was on military campaign. And when her son died, she imposed a "loyalty oath" on the whole empire, requiring those living in it to declare allegiance to her grandson, King Ashurbanipal. Though she was definitely a spitfire, her relationship with Judah's queens was completely fictional.

Assyrian (Kangal) Shepherds were historically used as war dogs in ancient Assyria though not necessarily trained to the level portrayed in the book. I'm an animal lover, so the violence wasn't intended to offend, but rather to show the depravity of this ancient culture.

The Bible affirms King Manasseh's wickedness surpassed the sins of the pagan nations Yahweh had driven out of the Promised Land (2 Kings 21:19). To make this barbaric king someone you'd want to spend four hundred pages with, I attached a twenty-first-century concern to a seventh-century BC story. Why? Because I believe examining a current-day challenge under the lens of ancient culture might help us look deeper into the issue—and ourselves.

Jewish history revealed Manasseh possessed a profound knowledge of the Torah and could interpret Leviticus in fifty-five ways (Sanh. 103b).

This was the first piece of a puzzle that led me to portray this twelve-year-old king as a gifted high-functioning autistic adolescent who was embittered by his abba's death. Though I portrayed both Manasseh and Haruz with the need to self-soothe, difficulties discerning social cues, and often misunderstanding and being misunderstood, their cognitive abilities and values varied because they—like everyone on the spectrum—were unique and deserved to be known and treated as individuals.

While interviewing health professionals and parents of high-functioning autistic (HFA) adolescents, I heard the same phrase spoken—unprompted—by *every* person: "If you've met one person with autism, you've met one person with autism." If you know someone who's "on the spectrum," he or she likely responds differently than Manasseh or Haruz to people and places, but—like my fictional characters—his or her triggers might be similar. There is, however, an important distinction I'd like to emphasize. ***My research uncovered no evidence linking autism to violence.*** King Manasseh's violent choices were related to the universal condition of *sin* and were largely due to his youth and the wicked, unscrupulous people around him.

His downward spiral began with his rejection of Yahweh and his rabid pursuit for power and human wisdom. "You will be like God," the serpent said to tempt Eve in the garden (Genesis 3:5), prompting her to seek the same knowledge and power that cast Satan from God's presence. Sin is our declaration of independence from the Creator.

Was Nasseh's sin so different from ours?

The same God who captured Nasseh's heart has led you here to capture yours. God knit Nasseh together in his mother's womb. God allowed Nasseh to reject Him and then guided Nasseh home. The same God who captured Nasseh captured me and can capture you—along with all the Manassehs in your life.

READERS GUIDE

1. As Shebna revealed his life's path in the prologue, in what ways did you identify with him? Was he an underdog you hoped would overcome his faults, or did you know from the start that he was "bad to the bone"?

2. In chapter 4, Shulle asked King Hezi why Yahweh extended his life by only fifteen years. It was a child's curiosity, but the book's common thread is similar: Why do bad things happen to good people? How did some of the characters answer this difficult question? How would you answer it today?

3. While still very young, Shulle and Nasseh were taught distorted ideas about sexuality, and their marriage reflected those aberrations. Considering the climate of our culture and human sexuality, what counsel would you give today's youth?

4. In chapter 34, when Zibah asked why God allowed injustice, Yaira suggested that instead of asking *Why* questions, she should ask *Who* questions, such as, *Who* is sovereign over the kingdoms of earth? Is it wrong to ask God why? When asking Him questions, how do you hear the answers?

5. While enjoying a leisurely morning—before his death that evening—Hezi comforted Zibah with these words: "The blacker the darkness, the brighter God's spark." Jashub encouraged Kenaz after their friends were killed by saying, "We learn the Truth in daylight so we can walk in darkness." What practical steps can we take during the good times to prepare for the hard things in life?

6. Freedom versus bondage is a recurring theme. In your opinion, which character's journey demonstrated the greatest transformation of bondage to freedom? Please explain.

7. In chapter 56, Shulle experienced freedom from her chains of fear when Yahweh asked, *Will you remain chained to your limited understanding?* In what ways have you allowed your understanding to hold you captive? What does an *unchained* life look like for you?

ACKNOWLEDGMENTS

Through every stage of writing and editing this book—and especially through the education of the autistic community—I've been reminded how uniquely and purposefully we are formed in our mother's wombs. Thanks to all my first readers from the VERY rough first draft: Tracy Joy Jones, Meg Wilson, and Emily King. I'm deeply grateful to my sensitivity readers, including family members of high-functioning autistic (HFA) adolescents and health care professionals: Pepper Basham, Juli Foreman, Katie Donovan, Kathy Capehart, Julie Beebe, and Brenda Drexler. Your wisdom and experience were invaluable in forming both Manasseh and Haruz, and any misrepresentations of HFA are errors on my part.

Thanks to my prayer warriors: BFF team, my family, author Carol Ashby, and my faithful newsletter subscribers! And to my assistants Jill Flood and Amanda Geaney . . . I couldn't do what I do without you!

As always, the team at WaterBrook is beyond amazing. Special thanks to Beth Adams and Lissa Halls Johnson for their superior editing skills.

Finally, to my husband, you're the one who handles all of life alone when I'm on deadline and cheers me on when I doubt myself. Thanks for being my friend, my breath, my life. I adore you.

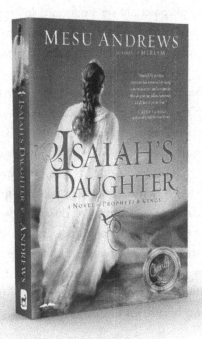